To Catch a Knight

Michelle Morrison

Kindle Direct Publishing

One thousand candles lit the great hall of Middleham Castle for the King was in residence and shadows had no place in his court.

Servants stumbled over each other in their haste to bring heavy trays of food to the thick wood tables. Nobles from England, Wales, and even Scotland gathered 'round those tables and they could not want for so much as a morsel of venison or a joint of goose. The wine flowed ceaselessly, and the rich aroma of fresh-baked pies and thick stews competed with the smoke from the great fireplace and the sweat of men who had ridden hard hours to break bread with their sovereign.

At the head table, King Richard III's closest advisors and most powerful allies jested with each other and drank to his health.

Richard surveyed the assembly with pleasure. A well-run court and a sumptuous feast would do much to assure those gathered that he held the throne securely; that no man, least of all some Welsh bastard who had been in exile for a decade, could challenge him. Still, would that he could be sure of support from the man sitting next to him. The smile on his face quickly faded and Richard turned to the man seated at his right, Edmund, Earl of Brackley.

"Know you not that I reward my supporters well?" the king asked, his voice tight. He sought the earl's unqualified pledge of support should the Earl of Richmond, Henry Tudor, try to take his throne.

Brackley laid down the bone upon which he had been gnawing but did not bother to wipe the grease from his florid face or thick hands. Stout as well as heavily muscled, the earl's dark, hooded eyes peered from a harshly sculpted face. The earl was once handsome, but cruelty was stamped in his features, leaving them coarse and unappealing. That and the mutton grease glowing wetly on his chin contrived to squelch any comeliness the earl might have had. "What need have you to reward me?"

Richard's right hand fumbled with the hilt of his jeweled dagger, sliding it halfway out of its sheath before shoving it back in its golden casing. Deliberately, he grasped his right hand with his left under the table to still its nervous movements. "That hell-spawned Richmond will surely try to invade England again and I would have your pledge of troops to crush him. It is but what you owe me as my vassal."

Wiping his mouth on the back of his hand, Brackley leaned forward and grasped his goblet, taking a deep draught before turning back to Richard. "Of course it is. But my men wish to be home, working their fields. It will take much to pull them from their families. Should I manage to persuade them, how would I be compensated?"

Richard knew Brackley employed a force of mercenary troops who had never touched a plow, but he was not in a position to argue. He had received word just this day of another defection from one of his marsh lords to the west. He thought frantically for a title or property he could bequeath the earl, but his resources were heavily tapped, having given away many crown lands to ensure the cooperation of other powerful lords. He tugged on the high velvet collar of his fitted cotehardie and smoothed the fur lining of his cloak--for all outward appearances, a calm, powerful sovereign.

"Tis said you are seeking a young wealthy wife as your last was a sickly woman."

Brackley laughed heartily, holding his goblet out to be refilled by a passing serving maid. "Nay, she lasted barely two years and her fortune even less. But I've seen naught at this gathering to catch my eye. A wealthy wife is important, but that she be comely is just as important."

And strong, thought Richard, considering the rumors he'd heard of the earl's physical abuse of his two past wives, both of whom died a few short years after wedding the man.

Glancing back at the earl, Richard saw the man's goblet pause halfway to his mouth as he stared across the great hall. Turning, Richard spotted Elena de Vignon, one of his ladies-in-waiting standing at the top of the staircase leading into the hall. She was a beautiful and amusing woman and Richard had decided to keep her with his retinue after his wife had died some months back. She had a sharp wit, which she cleverly hid behind her comely face and delightful figure. She now served his niece, the Princess Elizabeth, who was visiting Middleham.

"Now she might be enough to keep a man loyal to Satan himself," Brackley murmured.

Richard quickly calculated the benefits of offering Elena to Brackley. She was one of his favorite court ladies and he had been prepared this very night to betroth her to Lord Edgeford, a handsome young fop who would inherit a fortune as soon as his sickly father passed away. Richard knew that the girl had been eyeing the young nobleman for months, carefully enticing him. Richard was amused and slightly impressed with the determination and shrewdness with which she pursued the insipid lordling.

With a flick of his nervous fingers, the king batted away the young woman's wishes. Clever favorite or no, the safety of his crown was of greater importance than the marital whims of one young woman. Richard turned back to Brackley with a careful smile, his fingers alternately ruffling and smoothing the fur at his cuffs.

"Yes, but would she keep you loyal to the King of England?" he asked in a low, harsh voice.

The earl glanced sharply at Richard and then slowly leaned back to consider Richard's hasty offer, his bulk causing the dried wood of the chair to creak in protest.

"She's got ties to the Lancasters, but she has a tidy dowry set aside which I would be willing to pad." Richard warned himself not to appear too desperate, but he was not a man to underestimate his enemies and he wanted to guarantee that the Earl of Richmond had a force to reckon with should he have the nerve to invade England.

Richmond was a distant relative of the Lancasters, the rival branch of Edward III's descendants who had been battling with the York household for England's throne for generations. Richard stood confident in his claim to the throne, but Henry Tudor's popularity continued to grow, especially in that troublesome region of Wales. For the earl was Welsh and that infernal tribe clung to its own. No, he would not underestimate his enemy. Richard glanced to the young woman on the landing and then looked back to the earl.

Brackley watched the girl descend the staircase, and the king knew what he was thinking as if the earl had spoken the words aloud. *What a rash fool you are, Richard,* the king read. The earl no doubt realized that the girl had family who would be more than happy to have connections to an earl—he didn't need Richard's permission to wed her, not really. Richard bit the inside of his lip and prayed Brackley would overlook that fact. Richmond's claims were ludicrous and his chances of actually winning the crown from Richard were next to nil. The earl really had nothing to lose.

"I accept, Your Grace."

Richard ran his hand along his forehead, grimacing when he discovered the cold sweat there, but as he watched Brackley, relief filled him, and his confidence returned. He *would* be victorious, regardless of the cost! Rising to seek out the other men whose loyalty—and troops—he would need to keep the throne should Richmond invade; Richard scanned the room. Spotting a man he had not expected to attend the hunting and feasting activities, he stepped off the dais and made his way to the fireplace.

***

Across the huge room, a man Richard did not count among the important and powerful, Sir Gareth ap Morgan, stared moodily into his mug. His grey eyes cloudy, he ignored the drunken laughter of his childhood friends, Cynan and Bryant. A scowl marred his forehead but was partially covered by the dark brown hair that fell in an unruly wave across his brow. His full mouth pursed in a grimace and his strong, square jaw was hidden behind the hand in which it dejectedly sat.

What was he doing with his life? he thought disgustedly. Since he had become a knight nearly a year before, he had milled about Richard's court, hoping for a noble assignment which would put his courage and skill to the test. But the most important task he had as yet received was to deliver a missive to the dead Queen's cousin. Gareth rode to Bedford, carefully protecting the document thinking it to be a matter of state only to discover it contained an invitation to join the King here at Middleham to enjoy the hunting. Taking a deep pull from the strong ale, he did not pay attention to the jest Cynan made regarding his dark visage.

"He keeps scowling as such and 'twill soon be me fetching the maids to him instead of the other way around!"

Bryant, slight of build and fair of skin but with inky black hair, burst out laughing at the image his friend evoked: that of the craggy faced Cynan wooing young women. Though the same coloring as Gareth, Cynan's face showed the evidence of too many boyhood brawls. On more than one occasion in their youth, Gareth had wooed a serving wench with his good looks into a dark corner where Cynan had taken over with whispered flattery, the woman never the wiser.

"If that be the case, he'd best be joining the monastery at Dolwyddelan!" said Bryant with a laugh as he nudged Gareth.

Jostled out of his reverie, Gareth shook his head in mock reproach at the ale-sodden wits of his friends. The three had been close since they were but young striplings in the mountains of Gwynedd in northern Wales. Their fathers were herdsmen and both Cynan and Bryant had been content to follow in their fathers' footsteps. But Gareth had always thirsted for adventure and grew up convinced that his destiny lay elsewhere. After much badgering, his father agreed to call upon an old family friend with some influence among England's nobility who had placed him in the service of a lord for knightly training."Don't you even think of chasing a skirt while you're here, Cynan, or I'll be telling Enid and you'll have no peace!" he said, forcing a teasing tone to his voice.

"It's not peace I'm worried about losing should my wife think I was straying," said Cynan with a comic glance at his lap.

Laughing hard, Bryant gasped out, "The folk would definitely have a hard time believing you're as stalwart as you boast if they saw you running from your wife with your tail between your legs!"

Gareth chuckled at the thought as he raised his mug to his lips, but his hand froze in mid-air as his eyes swept over the crowd to the top of the broad stone staircase. Cynan followed his line of sight and let out a low whistle. "Now there's a woman who might even change the mind of such a determined bachelor as you, Gareth."

Bryant craned his neck to see at who they were looking. "I could definitely change my mind about red hair on a woman."

"It's not red, you oaf," Cynan argued. It's more to copper, or--"

"Chestnut," Gareth broke in.

"Exactly," Cynan said expansively as he filled his mug from a large pitcher on the table. "Chestnut. The exact color of the horse I wanted when I was ten years old. Do you remember that?"

Bryant made a joking remark, but Gareth did not hear it. Never before had he been struck by a woman as he was by this one who looked around the room from her high vantage point. Perhaps the troubadours knew something after all when they sang of love at a glance. As the woman slowly made her way down the steps, Gareth took in her creamy complexion and slender figure, both of which were complemented by the dark green gown she wore.

Velvet, he thought. She's a lady of great standing to wear velvet. With a sigh, he watched her make her graceful descent. No lady of great standing would give a second glance at a mere knight from Wales. Still, he would give much for the chance to at least talk to her. Perhaps she was interested in more than a title and a position in court.

***

From the top of the flight of stairs leading into the great hall, Elena de Vignon surveyed the noisy gathering, her cinnamon-brown eyes searching for Lord Edgeford, sparkling with determination when they alighted on his tall figure. Pinching her cheeks to make sure they were enchantingly pink (had not Lord Edgeford used those very words himself?), Elena slowly descended the staircase, grateful, as the pungent smell of the hall reached her nose, that she had elected to eat in the privacy of her room.

Carefully lifting the embroidered hem of her forest-green cotehardie from the soiled rushes that covered the floor, she joined the group of young women who sat at the table to the right of the king's seat. Not once did she allow her gaze to stray again to the table where she knew Edgeford sat.

Selecting a seat where she was sure he would have a clear view of her, she carefully arranged her heavy velvet skirts before turning her attention to the conversation at the table.

"...the fact remains that marrying Anne brought him a great deal of wealth, Catherine, and the sooner you realize that is all your husband will care about--"

Catherine, short, slender, and incurably romantic turned and wailed, "Elena, please tell Margaret to stop her tiresome lectures. I came to court to escape such lectures from my mother and nurse!"

"Liar," Elena laughed. "You came to court to find a wealthy husband!"

"Is that not all you are here for?" asked Margaret scathingly.

Elena turned to face the dark-haired girl who, even seated, was tall. "I shall not settle for a husband who is merely wealthy."

"What other requisites must he possess," Margaret asked, her blue eyes narrowing with cynicism.

Elena stared across the table. "What matter is it to you? I thought you do not even wish to wed. Are you not planning on devoting your life to God?"

"'Tis the only occupation where a woman has any say in her future."

"As long as that future obeys the dictates of the pope and every bishop and priest from here to Rome," Elena retorted.

"And I suppose Lord Edgeford will give you free reign to do whatever you desire."

Elena smiled. "Within reason, I am sure."

"And he probably will not even mind that your father is a Lancastrian earl or that your discretion where men are concerned is less than immaculate."

"I believe King Richard favors me well enough," Elena said tightly, abruptly turning her back on Margaret. Elena had always believed that sheer determination could make any dream a reality. Her father, upon realizing she was to be his only child, had lavished upon her the knowledge and schooling usually reserved for sons. She was determined to use both her intelligence and her wits to make Edgeford her husband. She had overcome her father's ties to the Lancasters, now she had only to overcome the gossip that had plagued her for the past year.

Casually glancing in her lord's direction, she discovered him still seated in the middle of the great hall, but now his hair was tousled, his cheeks were flushed, and he seemed engrossed in a very private discussion with a shapely brunette, their heads nearly touching as they spoke. Something the woman said must have amused him because he threw back his head with laughter before grabbing the woman's hand and pressing a fervent kiss to her knuckles.

Elena scowled in anger. Men were so simple, she thought. Out of sight, out of mind, wasn't that what her cousin Sarah always said? Just this morning when Elena had walked with him in the orchard, he told her that hers was the most beautiful laugh he had ever heard, and all other women's laughter would forever fall discordantly on his ears. Fortunately, she was not naive enough to believe everything men told her.

Upon first coming to court, she had quickly fallen in love with one of the king's advisors, Lord Marchon. He was polished and worldly, handsome and dashing. They spent hours in the king's private gardens, talking about books and kingdom politics, music and poetry. He sent her crystal bottles of perfume, posies of flowers, handkerchiefs of silk.

Elena had believed his devotions of love and his promise for a beautiful life together. So fervently had she believed that she did not cry out when he woke her in her bed. The court was in York and Elena's bed was but a hard pallet in a curtained alcove off the main hall. It scarcely offered privacy, but Marchon's kisses were persuasive and if they could be married immediately, there would be no real harm in consummating their love, could there?

"Married?" he asked, a confused frown marring his handsome brow. "But I thought you understood, my sweet." And in cold hard terms, he spelled out his idea for their "future together." She would become his mistress and live in a rented house in London, available to him at his every whim, forbidden, unfortunately, from being seen with him in public, much less at court.

Elena was so angry, she shrieked and struck at him, raking his face with her nails. When she reared back to throw her fists at him again, she succeeded only in throwing herself out of the bed, out into the main hall where men were drinking, serving wenches on their laps. The uproar her arrival started only intensified when Lord Marchon stepped out of the alcove, adjusted his clothing, and left. For the rumors that flew through the court over the next fortnight, she may as well have given her virtue over. And just when she thought her shame could grow no heavier, Margaret told her about his wife.

"His wife?" Elena asked, her hopes crumbling about her hem. Margaret nodded sympathetically.

"She's related to the Duke of York's wife. She will be arriving in the next day or two." Not only was she related to the Duke of York, she was beautiful and wealthy, and Elena was assigned to wait on her while she was at court. Humiliation had burned through Elena's veins, pulsing her hurt and her anger through every fiber of her being.

Since that time, Elena had vowed she would not be fooled again. She perfected the art of flirtation, never taking seriously a word uttered by a courtier, making sure she would not appear the fool for any man. But the damage to her reputations was done. She was never sure if there was a knowing leer behind the flattering smiles of her fellow courtiers.

Lord Edgeford was the first man who seemed to believe the best about her. Whether or not he'd heard the gossip, Elena felt sure he did not believe it. When they were married, she would finally be free of the malicious rumors--free to be the gracious, powerful noble lady she was born to be.

Lord Edgeford was different and her flirtations were no game: she meant to marry him. But she would not permit herself to care too deeply for him.

Elena realized that she was still staring at Edgeford and the dark-haired woman. Quickly turning her head, her gaze collided with the gray eyes of a man several tables over. Brushing a lock of thick brown hair out of his eyes, the man smiled and bowed his head at her. Elena was just about to glare her disapproval over such familiar behavior when the king's booming voice called to her.

"Lady Elena, my dear child. Come bid your sovereign good even!"

Smoothing her skirts, Elena approached the raised dais that held the king's table, and curtsied.

"No, no. Come around here and let me introduce you to someone."

Elena ascended the steps and approached the king, nodding to those lords who glanced at her and curtsying deeply to Richard.

"Your Grace," she murmured, hoping Lord Edgeford would see her up here and on such close terms with the king. Despite her assurances to Margaret, Elena was still not sure that the king of the York household would totally dismiss her father's distant relationship with the Lancastrians. Her grandfather had, after all, been granted his land in northern England from that formidable Lancaster, Henry V.

"Here is our fair child." Richard addressed an older man on his right. Elena pulled her attention to the man Richard was addressing and cringed inwardly as the heavy-set man eyed her speculatively from beneath bushy black brows.

"Indeed, Your Grace," the man said in a gravelly voice.

Taking Elena's hand, Richard squeezed it reassuringly as he introduced her. "Edmund, this is Elena de Vignon, daughter of Jean Paul de Vignon who owns quite a sizable estate up near Doncaster. Elena, this is the Earl of Brackley, a true and loyal friend."

The earl pushed himself to his feet and Elena took a small step backwards; not only was the man of heavy build, he was well over six feet tall. The earl issued a curt bow and Elena could not help but wonder why the king was introducing her to Brackley. The earl immediately sat back down and took his knife to the meat on his trencher.

As Richard turned to address his page, Elena curtsied to their backs and quickly descended the stairs. Still bewildered as to why the king had called her up in the first place, she looked about for Edgeford and saw him watching the group of dancers at the end of the great hall.

As she approached the edge of the circle of onlookers, the dance ended, and several young men began calling for the Gavotte—a scandalous dance involving kissing between partners. Elena sought out Edgeford, only to find him being dragged onto the dance floor by the brunette he had been laughing with earlier. In a fury, she stamped her foot on the hard stone floor and was silently cursing the woman when she felt someone touch her arm. Elena whirled around.

In front of her, a man straightened his jerkin and brushed his hair out of his eyes. "Would you care to dance?" he asked.

She surveyed her would-be partner. While a distant part of her brain registered the man's clear-cut features, warm gray eyes and well-developed shoulders, the practical part of her brain was offended by the man's worn woolen hose, his scuffed brown boots, and his plainly cut jerkin. She was about to refuse when she remembered that midway through the Gavotte, the dancers changed partners. Quickly counting off couples from Edgeford to determine where she should position herself to become his partner, she turned back to the man. "Very well. Shall we start over here?" she asked.

Her partner gingerly took her hand and led her to the line of dancers. As the steps progressed, Elena scarce paid him any attention, intent as she was on watching Edgeford. During a complicated step, she glanced briefly at her plainly dressed partner and knew he was irritated by her preoccupation. When it came time for him to kiss her, she artfully turned her head at the last moment, so his lips merely grazed her cheek. By the time he had to relinquish her as his partner, he seemed very put out, but then the dark-haired woman was his partner and Elena wished them both good riddance.

Turning her attention to her new partner, Elena felt quite pleased her scheme had worked. As she and Lord Edgeford danced, she concentrated on smiling her prettiest and laughing her softest. Edgeford obligingly responded.

"Ah, at last I am given the honor of a dance with the fair maid Elena."

"Not such an honor, my lord, as I am nearly an old maid," Elena said, lowering her eyes modestly. How she wished she could blush when she wanted as cousin Sarah was able to do!

The man laughed. "My dear Elena, not for one moment do I believe that you are worried about becoming an old maid. Nevertheless, I have it on the greatest authority that you will be betrothed before the night is out."

Elena smiled her most dazzling smile, fully aware of the catch in her partner's breath as he looked into her sparkling eyes. As the dance ended, a page touched Edgeford's arm.

"My lord, the King has instructed me to inform you that he has time now to hear your petition."

Turning back to Elena, Edgeford bowed low over her hand. "Pray forgive me for abandoning you, my lady. I only hope we will share many more such enjoyable dances in the future."

Elena watched the tall man as he made his way gracefully through the drunken revelers to meet with the King. She clasped her hands in front of her to keep from clapping in delight. She had only been hoping the earl would approach the king by month's end. Indeed, it now seemed she would be Lady Edgeford by that time. So absorbed was she in her thoughts, she did not notice the man standing at her side.

"My lady?"

Elena turned to find her original dance partner. She stared at him blankly.

The man cleared his throat. "I fear we were not partners long enough to discover each other's names." He bowed low over her hand. "I am Sir Gareth ap Morgan."

A Welshman, Elena thought, closing her eyes with a grimace. Why did every lowborn man in Christendom think she was eager to make his acquaintance? No doubt he had heard of her questionable virtue and sought to make the most of it. Opening her eyes, she saw the man staring at her expectantly.

"And you are..?" he urged.

"And I am on my way to becoming the lady of a wealthy estate, so please think not to woo me to bed with tales of your battlefield glories or proud stories of your herd of sheep back home."

The knight flushed to the roots of his hair, his brows drawing together sharply. He seemed at a complete loss for a response. The King's herald calling everyone to attention saved Elena from having to speak further with him.

She turned expectantly, all thoughts of the Welshman at her side disappearing. The herald made several announcements concerning the next day's hunting activities before Richard himself stood and addressed the room.

"'Tis been a long while since we have had the celebration of a wedding, has it not?" Cheers and bawdy comments answered the king. "Well 'twill be a long while still till we have another!" The king laughed at the response he received. "'Twill be a long while because this wedding must be done properly as the groom is a friend of Ours, and the lady a gentle maid. You must wait until Michaelmas to revel at the nuptial of this good couple." Elena smoothed her gown and smothered a knowing smile as Richard turned and gestured for her to join him.

So pleased was she as she approached the king's dais that she didn't even hear Gareth's muttered curse as he walked away.

"The Lady Elena de Vignon has been a beautiful and graceful addition to Our retinue, would you not agree?" More cheers greeted this comment. "For that reason, I kept her with Us even after Our beloved Queen's death.

"Though We are loathe to part with her, My dear niece, Princess Elizabeth has convinced Us that to deny one of Our loyal subjects the joy of having such a woman to wed is unjust."

Elena surreptitiously looked around for Lord Edgeford.

"We have thought much on the subject of Lady Elena's husband and it is with great pleasure that We call forth the lucky man, Edmund, Earl of Brackley."

Elena looked around in confusion. Who? Then she remembered. As the earl stood and walked around the table to take her hand, Elena felt dizzy as the blood rushing from her head dimmed the noisy sounds of the great hall. This must be a terrible mistake, she thought. I'm supposed to marry Edgeford, not this old—the clammy hand of her fiancée as it grasped hers stopped her frantic train of thought. Across the room, she spotted Edgeford who raised his goblet to her in a silent toast. In a daze, she heard the king finish saluting their happiness and before she could stop him, the earl was pressing a hard, bruising kiss to her lips. She smelled the ale and sour wine on his breath and felt the stiff bristles of his beard as they scraped her skin. She jerked her head back, but the earl had already turned away to down the goblet of wine Richard had handed him. She stiffly accepted the embraces of the Elizabeth and the other ladies-in-waiting.

"Be of good cheer," Margaret said, not unkindly, upon seeing Elena's face. "He is, after all an earl. Would you not rather be a countess than a mere Lady?" At that, the confused look on Elena's face slowly disappeared to be replaced by the haughty expression Margaret was used to.

"I know not what you are talking about," Elena said in a voice that sounded tight and brittle to her own ears.

"Be not coy, Elena. We all know that you have been planning to marry Lord Edgeford."

Elena ground her teeth. How dare these women speculate on her plans? "Perhaps you had best return to your tea leaves, Margaret. I care not a bit for Edgeford. We are merely acquaintances."

"Elena, few women are ever pleased by political marriages. They are almost always to doddering old men we know nothing about. Can you not admit you are frightened?" Margaret asked. "Think of Princess Elizabeth. Rumor says His Majesty is considering wedding her and he is her uncle! Think what worries she must be faced with being the most important political pawn in the country."

"She would be queen; how worrisome can that be? You are just trying to frighten me. 'Tis just what you would like to see, is it not? Me sobbing into my cups over some man. Well, I shall not give you the satisfaction," Elena said sharply.

With a shake of her head, Margaret turned away and curtsied as Princess Elizabeth approached.

Elena cast a speculative glance at the king's niece. If the rumor Margaret mentioned was true, the princess might be sympathetic to Elena's wanting to avoid a distasteful marriage and could be persuaded to argue her case before the king. Smiling her warmest smile, Elena offered Elizabeth her seat and a glass of wine.

Chapter 2

Gareth watched the King's niece draw the Lady Elena down beside her, speaking with great animation as Elena stared into space. He could not help but laugh. There was justice in the world. He had no doubt that she had set her cap for the tall fop she had maneuvered to dance with. 'Tis what she deserves, he thought, as he doubted that cold woman could have loved such a foolish man—or any man for that matter.

Still, if her only interest was a title, she should look a sight happier at catching an earl. With a shrug, he looked around for Cynan and Bryant and saw them standing with a small group of men who gathered at the back of the great hall, talking quietly amongst themselves.

As he started across the room, a serving maid stumbled in front of him, falling on the ground and dropping a pile of empty trays. Gareth quickly helped the young woman up, brushing off her worn skirt before he knelt to retrieve the trays.

"Thank you, milord," the maid said timidly, a shy smile touching her mouth.

"Be careful. God only knows the last time these rushes were changed," Gareth said, nodding to the floor. "Were you to fall again, we may not be so lucky as to find you," he teased.

The young woman nodded, obviously amazed that the knight had not cursed or yelled or simply stepped right over her. When Gareth chucked her gently under the chin, she blushed bright pink and stared after him with adoration as he continued on his way.

"Tis not a rumor, I tell you," a short man of sturdy build was saying as Gareth joined his friends at the back of the hall. "And Henry Tudor has just as much claim to the throne as Richard does."

"More so, I say, since Henry has not killed innocent boys for it!" answered a broad-shouldered man with iron-grey hair. The men stopped talking when they noticed Gareth, but Cynan spoke up.

"'Tis all right. Gareth is Welsh and bears no great love for Richard."

Gareth frowned and glanced around at the men gathered in the shadows. Several of them he knew as knights, men at arms. A couple he'd not seen before but could tell by the cut of their cloth they were noblemen, landholders.

"Aye, and it's Welsh blood that will put Henry Tudor on the throne," said a man whose accent clearly bespoke his lineage, though Gareth did not recognize him.

"But 'tis not his Welsh blood that grants him the right to the throne," hissed one of the noblemen.

Though Gareth's knowledge of Henry Tudor's ancestry was sketchy at best, he knew the man to be a direct descendant of John of Gaunt, the first Duke of Lancaster. The houses of Lancaster and York—both children of the great Edward III—had been warring for the crown since before Gareth was born. King Richard's brother, Edward IV, had claimed the throne for York after killing the Lancastrian king, Henry VI.

Though the fighting had largely involved small, scattered battles between the noble families, should Henry Tudor successfully return to England, the war could escalate to encompass the entire country.

"King Charles of France has promised Henry money and ships. And with he and Oxford planning the battles, all we need do is raise troops for them to lead," said the grey-haired man.

"When will he land?"

"'Tis not been determined yet. Just stay at the ready, for when the call comes, we will have to move quickly."

Gareth turned to whisper in Cynan's ear. "'Tis treason these men speak. Why did you include me?"

"Because I've known you since we were babes and you're no man of Richard's."

Gareth would have argued further but Cynan stepped closer into the circle of men.

Some logistical talk ensued about chains of communication, but Gareth paid it no heed. He chewed on his lower lip, mulling over Cynan's comment. He'd not spoken to his friend of his frustrations since joining Richard's court, had made no mention of his disenchantment with his sovereign, not to mention the persistent belief that Richard had murdered his own nephews to secure the crown for himself. Nonetheless, Cynan seemed to cut right to the heart of Gareth's inner turmoil.

The group broke up as Viscount Lovell, one of Richard's council members walked by.

Gareth pulled Cynan aside. "You should be more careful. What are you thinking meeting like this in Richard's own keep? You're going to get yourself drawn and quartered."

"We're hiding in plain sight. And where better to recruit embittered subjects than in the viper's own nest?" Though Gareth had made sure to speak quietly, Cynan spoke in a normal tone of voice.

"Will you hush! This is the king's own residence. Do you think you can speak ill of him and not be heard?" Grabbing Cynan's tunic, he pulled him outside where the cool air was refreshing after the enveloping heat of the great hall. Bryant put his mug down and followed them. "You never did have any sense as to when to keep your mouth shut, Cynan."

"His wife tells him that all the time," added Bryant as he shut the rough door behind him.

"Do not tell me you're mixed up in this, too."

"If you mean do I want Henry Tudor on the throne, then yes, I'm mixed up in it, too."

Gareth sighed. "You are going to get yourselves executed as traitors."

"If I am a traitor because I would see a good and noble Welshman on the throne over a scheming murderer, then so be it, I am a traitor," said Cynan fiercely.

"There has not been any proof that Richard had his nephews killed," Gareth protested, though he knew there could be no other explanation for the boys' untimely disappearance.

Bryant spoke up. "Gareth, do you mean to say Richard holds your loyalty and honor?"

"He is the king and I a knight. He must have my loyalty by all the vows I took when I first put on these spurs."

"And your honor?" Cynan asked. "Do you believe in your heart that he is best for England and Wales? Do you believe that his claim to the throne is more just than his Lancastrian rival?"

Gareth paused, loathe to betray his oath as a knight but unable to admit he was Richard's man at heart.

"Come back to Gwynedd with us."

"What?"

"You can hear the arguments for Henry Tudor from much more level-headed men than I. Besides, your father has not seen you in over two years."

"Do not tell me my father is involved in this nonsense?"

"Of course he is. You do not think he would give up the chance to put Wales ahead of England, do you?" Cynan asked

"I thought he had enough sense to live to see a grandson someday."

"You are talking like a coward," Cynan spit out.

"Cynan!" Bryant said sharply.

Cynan took a deep breath and visibly relaxed. "I am sorry, Gareth. No one could ever accuse you of cowardice. 'Tis just that if you could only distance yourself from this court, you would see who the true ruler should be. Please, come back home with us."

"And I suppose if I do not, you two will stay here, constantly nipping at my heels, eh?"

"Aye, and Enid will surely give you no end of trouble for that!" laughed Bryant, referring to Cynan's wife.

Gareth chuckled as he shook his head at his friend. "I can only promise to think about it now."

"You do that," said Cynan, winking at Bryant. "For you never can tell when Richard will send you on another important mission of state." Gareth held open the doors to the hall for his friends. "Perhaps this time, he will send you to Scotland to borrow a sack of flour from James!" Gareth laughed good naturedly as he shoved his friend through the doorway but remained outside in the cool evening air.

He took a deep breath and tried to settle the jumble of information muddling his brain. His father caught up in a plot to unseat the king? His countrymen rallying to Richmond's banner? His best friends taking part in secret meetings? He must be losing his head.

Gareth took another calming breath and prepared to face his king as if he knew nothing. Treason was definitely an easy way to lose your head.

Chapter 3

Elena crawled into the soft down bed she shared with Catherine. As she lay there shivering, waiting for the linen to warm, she repeated to herself like a litany, "'Tis better this way. The king has favored me. 'Tis better this way."

While she had mildly cared for Edgeford she felt nothing but fear for the earl. Lord Edgeford was handsome and devoted to her--had she not convinced him to follow her here to Middleham? The earl was another matter. Before she entered the bedroom, she had heard Margaret and Catherine talking about him.

"I never saw his first two wives—they may have been sickly women. But 'tis been a long-standing rumor that he's hard on women." In the darkened doorway, Elena shivered, remembering the earl's thick hands and meaty forearms.

"Do you think Elena will be happy with him?"

Elena heard a sigh she assumed was from Margaret. "I do not know, Catherine. He is a powerful earl. Elena always made it clear that a title was what she sought, so I hope being a countess will make up for whatever else she may have to bear."

Despite her litany, Elena could not keep Margaret's words from her mind: "He is hard on women." Surely the king could not know this and still betroth her to him? Elena sat up in bed with a start, causing Catherine to mumble in her sleep and grope for the covers. Perhaps he did not know! Perhaps he believed the earl to be kind and gentle. Flopping back against her pillows in relief, Elena vowed to seek out the king at the first opportunity and tell him what she had heard. Perchance she could still be married to Lord Edgeford by midsummer, after all.

Awakening early the next morning, she dressed with extra care, choosing a demure high-waisted gown of soft pink and covering her hair with a fine veil. She hurried downstairs, hoping to catch Richard while he broke his fast. All she found at the great table, however, were crusts of bread and rinds of cheese.

"Has His Majesty risen yet?" she asked a sleepy-eyed serving girl.

"Aye, my lady. Risen, eaten, and left for a fine day's hunting, I'll wager."

Stomping her booted foot against the soiled rushes, Elena cursed her luck. Her luck over the next two days was just as bad. No, Elena thought, worse, since she had to spend those days with the Lady Elizabeth, listening to her plan Elena's wedding as if she were a simple child with no say on the event--even had she wanted it to occur. By the third day, Elena had given up hope of talking to Richard any time soon as his entire entourage was preparing to remove to Nottingham Castle.

"Do not tell me," Elena grumbled to herself. "The grouse hunting is better there."

Margaret paused in the midst of packing one of Princess Elizabeth's trunks. "You really have no idea of what is going on, do you?"

Elena rolled her eyes before turning to face Margaret. "What does it matter the reason. The king could decide he wants to stand on his head, and we would be trussed out in the middle of the night to witness it."

Margaret quickly covered the distance between them and put her hand over Elena's mouth. "Have you no thought for your life? Royal favorite or no, if the wrong people heard you speaking as you do, they could make your life miserable."

Before Elena could jerk Margaret's hand away from her mouth, Margaret continued. "The reason we are going to Nottingham is because that is to be King Richard's stronghold for the war which will surely arise should the Earl of Richmond invade England." Margaret quickly pulled her hand away from Elena's face and glanced at the other ladies in the room. They were all gathered around Princess Elizabeth, staring out the narrow window at the knights in the bailey below.

"We are removing to Nottingham because Richard must have heard news that Henry means to invade soon!" Margaret hissed.

When Elena still stared blankly at her, Margaret threw her hands into the air. "This means nothing to you, does it?"

"This means sleeping in tents or roadside inns for nothing. King Richard cut Buckingham's rebellion short, he can certainly prevent the taking of his crown by a Welshman who has spent most of his life out of England."

Margaret looked surprised by Elena's grasp of the world outside of the women's solar. Buckingham had helped Richard attain the throne, then turned around and helped the Earl of Richmond in his first bid for the crown.

No matter how petty other's thought her, Elena made it a point to always be aware how matters stood in the world of political intrigue that had ruled England for years. Glancing at the chattering, giggling group of ladies, Elena knew she was an oddity. No doubt her unconventional education had given her a glimpse into the world of politics that few other court ladies had been granted. Margaret seemed the only other lady who was aware of the world outside of fashion and courtships, but the two rarely got along. Elena found Margaret too strident and knew the other woman viewed her as nothing more than a social climber.

Within an hour, Elena was mounted on her grey palfrey, carefully arranging the dark blue skirts of her kirtle about her. As she tucked the edge of her veil over her nose and mouth, a large hand landed firmly on her leg. Stifling a scream, she looked down into the hooded gaze of her fiancée.

"I trust I will find you well when next we meet in London, my lady," he said, his loud voice coming from deep within his barrel chest.

"You are not riding with us?" Elena hoped the earl couldn't hear the relief in her voice.

"I have business for the king which will take me along a different route. Rest assured I will be in London by Michaelmas."

Elena forced herself to nod but could not force a smile. Gathering her reins, she kicked her small horse into a gallop. There must be a way out of this sour predicament, she thought. Perhaps if she wrote her father...But her father had expressed no joy when his daughter left to become a lady-in-waiting to Richard's queen.

He had not sent so much as a word since she had been at court, and her mother's few letters had been disappointingly brief. Catching up to Margaret and Catherine, she slowed her horse to a walk. The summer sun beat down unmercifully and Elena readjusted her veil over her face to filter out as much of the road dust as possible. This was going to be a miserable trip, she decided.

Chapter 4

Several rows back, Gareth spat out the mouthful of grit he had inhaled as a small gray horse galloped past, stirring up clouds of dust. He reached up to pat Isrid's neck. "You can believe I never thought to see you as a pack horse either," he whispered to his steed. Because neither Cynan nor Bryant owned a horse, Gareth had loaded all of their belongings on Isrid and walked with his friends. He adjusted his thick leather hauberk as a rivulet of sweat ran down his back and cursed as he felt a rock rolling around in his boot. Taking off his helm, he hung it on Isrid's saddle. *I may only look like a man-at-arms now,* he thought, *but at least I will not pass out from the heat.* "I will admit it to you if no one else," he confessed to the horse, "I have grown accustomed to riding. I do not think I am going to be able stand more than three or four miles of this torture."

"Are you whining again, Gareth?" Cynan asked good-naturedly.

"Just bemoaning your lack of foresight in not borrowing a horse when you came to visit. We could be riding this dusty road instead of eating it if you had but thought ahead!"

"I never thought I should live to see the day when Gareth ap Morgan would be too puny to walk a few miles on a beautiful summer day, did you Bryant?"

Visibly trying to keep from smiling, Bryant looked at Gareth in mock pity. "Well, Cynan, you must admit that broadsword does look awfully heavy. And those shiny silver spurs are none too light either!"

"But I wager that the heaviest thing our friend carries is the title of *Sir Gareth,* wouldn't you say?" Both men burst out laughing while Gareth leveled an exasperated glare at them. In truth, Gareth had missed their constant teasing. Now smiling at his friends, he thought how little they each had changed since they were youths. He had always loved the tales of chivalry and honor of King Arthur's court, thinking out elaborate games for the three of them to play: games in which he always got to save the fair maidens and vanquish the evil sorcerers. Cynan had played along willingly but took even greater delight in teasing Gareth about his "lofty ideals." Bryant was the quiet follower, playing whatever games his friends dreamed up, content to let them be the heroes.

The three followed the troops in front of them as they made their way through the dusty countryside. There had been no rainfall for a fortnight and the tall grass on either side of the road was coated in dust. The flowers hung their heads limply and even the thick copse of trees further back from the road seemed to be gasping from the dry heat.

Six hours later, even Cynan and Bryant were too tired to tease Gareth. The walk had not been particularly strenuous as the roads were good, but the sun had beat down unmercifully all day and the dust raised by thirty horses and twice as many men was chokingly thick. By the time they stopped at sunset to camp outside a small town, they were all exhausted.

"I do not know how you have lived without the cool mountains of Gwynedd, Gareth," said Cynan as he flopped down onto his blanket. "I could have sworn we were marching in the Holy Land to meet Saracens, it was so hot today."

"'Tis days like today that make me wish I was home again," Gareth agreed.

"Then why do you not come back?" Bryant asked, unfolding his small pack.

Cynan propped himself up on his elbows. "Yes, why not? It has been at least two years since you last visited your father and," Cynan glanced around to make sure no one was within hearing distance. "You could learn more about our plans to aid Henry Tudor."

Gareth stared at the flames of their small campfire as he stirred what he hoped would taste like stew. "Soon. I will come visit soon," he said answering Cynan's first proposal and ignoring mention of the exiled earl who had already attempted one landing in England to overthrow King Richard.

Cynan scoffed disgustedly. "Can you not see, man, nothing noble is going to happen to you while you are in the service of this butcher! If you remain in Richard's service, you are going to find yourself fighting honest Welshmen--one of whom seeks the crown so he can rule Wales and England fairly."

"Enough, Cynan! I am bound in fealty to the crown, despite who wears it and I cannot abandon my post just because you like not who wears it."

Cynan started to argue but Bryant broke in. "That stew looks like 'tis ready to eat, Gareth and if we're not careful, the aroma is going to attract a crowd." With a meaningful glance at the men scattered around, Cynan and Gareth nodded in understanding and turned their attention to eating.

Travel the third day proved no more comfortable than the first two. The late afternoon sun beat down on the entourage as it made its dusty way down the hard-packed road. The ladies drooped in their saddles, unmindful of their bedraggled state. One old man nearly tumbled off his horse as he dozed. The foot soldiers trudged wearily along, too hot and tired to even choke on the ever-present dust. Even the horses lagged, their heads bobbing wearily in time to their slow steps.

Gareth's first sense of danger was a cold prickling on his sweaty neck. Looking up sharply, he stared into the thick forest that began twenty or thirty paces off to the left. Glancing to the other side of the road, he saw no threat: the road fell away to the sharp bank of the river.

Turning back to the forest he squinted his eyes, trying to see into the near-total darkness. Nothing. He looked at the soldiers around him. They plodded steadily along, but he noticed that the group had spread out in a long, broken chain. The nearest group of men, which included the king, was far ahead. The procession's lead horses were so far ahead as to be completely out of sight. Turning to Bryant, he whispered, "Do you feel anything strange about this place?"

"What do you mean?"

"I know not. I just have this feeling that this is an ideal spot for an ambush."

"Who would ambush us?" Cynan broke in.

"Your friend Henry," Gareth replied.

Cynan looked as if he was about to say something and then paused. Slowly shaking his head, he said, "No, I don't think the timing is right. Besides, we would have heard something first. Both Bryant and I have sworn to follow your father into battle."

"My father in battle? Sweet Christ!" Looking around, Gareth quickly lowered his voice again. "Since when has he cared about wars more than the ruttings of his flock?" Before either man could answer, he continued. "Never mind that now. How would you even know if these were Tudor's men? You two have been with me the past month. An entire war could have been planned and you two would know nothing about it."

"He's right, Cynan, we'd have no way of knowing if we should fight for or against them."

"Just a minute," Cynan interrupted. "For or against who? We are working ourselves up over another of Gareth's 'eerie feelings,' are we not? Now here is the plan: if there are just ghosts in these woods, we'll fight 'em off. But if there are goblins too, I say we run for it." Before he could laugh at his own joke, a blood curdling war cry pierced the quiet air.

"By Saint Dafydd, Gareth was finally right!" Cynan gasped.

Confusion spread through the dazed ranks as men scrambled to position themselves in front of Richard and his retinue. When Gareth moved to mount Isrid, Cynan grabbed his arm. "You must wait, Gareth, until we can determine who is attacking."

"No, 'tis you who must wait. I have work to do." Gareth grabbed the reins but paused to look at his friends before spurring Isrid on. Something he saw in their eyes made him grit his teeth and say, "Alright! You two try to take cover. See if you can retreat back down the road and duck into the forest. Who ever this is should not expect to find you there."

Cynan grinned at Gareth as Bryant tugged on his sleeve, urging him back down the dusty road.

His heart racing as adrenaline pulsed through his veins, Gareth swung Isrid towards the thick of the fighting, which was centered around the king and women. Richard cursed the attackers and tried to swing his sword at them but was hampered by his own soldiers who sought to protect him.

Gareth swore as he saw one lady's horse cut down; to his relief, she was quickly snatched up by the knight nearest her. Digging his spurs into Isrid,

Gareth plunged into the fight. Henry Tudor's men or roadside bandits, no lady deserved to die in a man's battle.

As Gareth moved into the thick of the fighting, Richard pushed his great steed out from behind his men, trying to force his way up the road.

Some of the attackers followed him and his knights, leaving the group of women. They're trying to draw the enemy away, to protect the women, Gareth thought. But not all of the attackers were following the king. Forcing his way through the brigands with his horse, Gareth drew his sword with his right hand as he fumbled for his helmet with his left.

When he could not undo the buckle that secured it to the saddle, he abandoned it and concentrated on attacking as many of the enemy as he could.

Gareth had been in few actual battles in his short career as a knight, but that did not deter him from hacking his blade into sinew and bone at every opportunity. He took out his frustration with his life on the attackers, swinging his sword with such speed that it sang through the air like a Viking scald from days of old.

When his sword handle grew slippery with sweat and blood, he only managed to slap one man across the face with the flat of his sword. Isrid, however, trained as a warhorse, quickly trampled the dazed man and moved forward.

As his mount surged ahead, Gareth had a moment to look up and assess their position. There were just a few attackers to the number of Richard's men who remained in the road, but these were mostly squires and green knights like him.

Seeing Richard's squire, Gareth yelled as loudly as he could. "We're not but a few miles from Haddon Hall. Take the women and as many mounted men as you can and ride on." The young squire, pale with fear, nodded and yelled to the other squires. Within moments, nearly all of the women were fleeing. Gareth started after them to make sure none of the attackers would follow, but the men seemed intent on getting to Richard and were abandoning the women. Turning back, Gareth saw two women heading north, back up the road the company had just come down. "God's wounds! They're going to get themselves killed!"

***

"Your Highness I really think we should have gone the other way with the rest of the women," Elena gasped as she clung to the mane of her horse. "We shall become lost or be set upon by more attackers!"

"Worry not Elena. Neither will happen," Princess Elizabeth called back.

"But--"

Slowing her horse until Elena's smaller palfrey caught up, Elizabeth said, "These are the men of my cousin, Charles Woodville. They are here to escort me home."

"But why are they attacking?"

"Do hurry Elena. We must get further down the road. Richard meant to marry me to solidify his hold on the throne. I cannot and will not marry him."

"Do they mean to kill the king?"

Elizabeth looked over her shoulder at the fight. "I do not think they would be too concerned if that happened."

"What?" Elena asked, unsure she heard Elizabeth aright over the noise of the battle behind them. "Your Highness, do you know what you are saying?"

Glancing sharply at Elena, Elizabeth said, "He killed my brothers, Elena. Furthermore, I will not enter into an incestuous marriage with my uncle."

"But Your Highness--"

"Elena, please be quiet and just ride. I swear no harm will come to you. You may even return to Richard's party once I am safely away."

Elena would have argued more, but the look in Elizabeth's eyes made her close her mouth.

***

Back at the battle, Gareth whirled his horse to follow the two stray women. Suddenly, three more well-armed men tried to pull him from his horse, one grasping his sword arm at the wrist, another trying to grab Isrid's reins, while the third picked a sword from a fallen comrade's grasp and approached Gareth from the opposite side. Isrid effectively dislodged the man trying to pull at his reins. When his head was free, the horse bit into the man's shoulder, sending blood pouring down his arm.

Meanwhile, a battle rage Gareth had never before felt seemed to seep into his eyes along with the sweat and blood from a cut on his brow. Possessed of strength he didn't think he had left, he pulled his sword arm free at the same time he swung Isrid around to confront the armed man. His opponent was momentarily frozen with surprise at the unexpected move, but Gareth didn't pause as he brought his sword around to stab at his opponent.

In a disconnected part of his brain, Gareth marveled at the feel of his sword in his hand--it felt as light as a feather, as supple as a whip. Wheeling Isrid around again, he did not even feel the blade that sliced along his leg, but instead used the injured limb to kick the blade's wielder in the face. Gareth's final opponent stood immobile, staring past Gareth's shoulder and Gareth thought he was going to have an easy kill when he heard a whirring sound and turned in time to see a large stone leave a leather sling. As if in a dream, Gareth saw the missile coming toward him, but--as in a dream--he felt he was moving through water. Suddenly, time sped up as the rock raced towards his face and cracked him soundly on the side of the head. All he saw after that was the hard-packed dirt of the road as it rushed up to meet him.

***

The last rays of sunlight were fading from the sky when Gareth slowly regained consciousness. When he was able to pry his eyes open, he saw the fuzzy features of Cynan and Bryant. Slowly sitting up, he rubbed the lump under the blood-clotted hair on the side of his head. He was still in the middle of the road and his mouth was coated with dust. Spitting vociferously, he pushed himself to his feet, grabbing onto Bryant when he wobbled.

"Where's--" he spat another mouthful of dirt and his voice sounded like a bullfrog's to his own ears. "Where's Isrid."

"Somewhere in these accursed woods," said Cynan. "He stayed near you after you fell off in the fray--"

"I did not fall off!" he said too loudly. His head threatened to split like a frostbitten cabbage.

"--and only bolted when some bastard tried to mount him."

"I did not fall off. And if you had taken a blow like that one, you'd not be troubling me so."

Before Cynan could respond, they heard someone approaching through the forest. Trying to see in the rapidly fading light, the three men drew their swords.

"Thank God!" said Bryant when Gareth's horse stuck his nose out of the thick clump of trees.

Gareth stumbled over to Isrid and leaned heavily on his horse's neck. "Where is everyone else?"

"You mean those who lived? They are no doubt at Haddon Hall by now. Of course, a few men were not as lucky as you and they will not be rising from this God-forsaken road," said Cynan.

Gareth tried to scan the scene of the fight, but the moon had not risen, and it was so dark he could barely discern the outlines of his friends much less the carnage in the road. "And the attackers?"

"They went up the road," Bryant said, gesturing in the direction Richard's troops had come from.

"We'd best be joining the living in Haddon Hall, then," Gareth said, still feeling as if he were about to lose his balance at any moment.

Neither Cynan nor Bryant spoke for a moment. "We are not continuing with Richard's court," said Cynan.

"What? Why not?"

"We are returning to Wales," said Bryant. "We want you to come with us. We--"

Cynan interrupted, "Those men who attacked were Woodvilles."

"How do you know?"

"Because we were hiding in the woods, if you'll remember. We heard them talking after Richard got away."

"Meant they to kill the king?" Gareth asked incredulously. He had not thought Richard's sister-in-law, mother to Lady Elizabeth and the missing princes, would have dared try regicide.

"No," Bryant said before Cynan could speak. "They only sought to win Lady Elizabeth free. I would wager one of the women who fled north on this road was Elizabeth herself."

"But why? She was in no danger."

"Only in danger of being wed to Richard," Cynan said.

"That is ridiculous!" Gareth broke out. "That would be incestuous!" Although it was pitch black, in the silence following his cry, Gareth could easily picture each man's expression. Cynan's eyebrows were no doubt raised mockingly, arms crossed over his chest as he stared unblinking in Gareth's general direction. Bryant was most likely biting his lower lip and staring at his toe scuffing the ground. He hated when Cynan and Gareth argued, even though nothing had ever come between their friendship.

Gareth finally broke the silence. "King Richard would not do such a thing." But even to his own ears he did not sound very convinced.

"Did that bump on your head loosen you of all sense or does your 'knightly duty' prevent you from doing what is right?"

Before Gareth could respond to Cynan's taunt, Bryant said, "At least come back to Wales and see your father. He's been awfully lonely since you left."

Gareth took a deep breath and slowly exhaled. No doubt the crack in his head had allowed what common sense he had to leak onto the parched dirt of the road. "All right. I will go with you." He started to add that he wouldn't hear anymore arguments or accusations against Richard, but something stopped him. He was suddenly curious as to what his father would say about Henry Tudor.

Cynan and Bryant broke into relieved laughter. "What an adventure we shall have!" Cynan yelled as he picked his friend up in a bear hug which made Gareth's sore head pound.

"Put me down you oaf, or you will be carrying me over the Cambrian Mountains yourself!" When he had both feet on the ground he asked, "So where do we camp, oh fearless rebel?"

"'Tis too dark to travel far. Think you it will be safe if we just move into the forest?"

Gareth chewed his upper lip. "'Tis the best we can do, at least until the moon rises."

The three men made their way into the dense forest. By the time they reached a small clearing, the moon had risen, illuminating the landscape. Gareth allowed his friends to administer rudimentary medical care to his injured head and leg, gritting his teeth as their clumsy fingers cleaned and bandaged his wounds. Afterwards, they set about setting up a makeshift camp. They spread out their bedrolls and were about eat a meager supper of dried beef when they heard a woman's piercing scream. Grabbing up their weapons, they dashed back to the road. Bursting out of the thick copse of trees they stared in amazement. They had expected to find a woman beset by highway bandits or wolves. What they saw was a woman sitting on her horse in the middle of the empty road. Well, not quite empty, Gareth thought. Now that the moon was up, he could clearly see the ten or twelve dead bodies that were the result of the earlier melee.

"My lady, what ails you?" Gareth called as he approached her.

The woman turned, startled by the approach of three unknown men. She was about to scream again when Gareth held up his hand. "Fear not, my lady. I am Sir Gareth of King Richard's contingent. You are quite safe from harm."

"Where is the king? I am part of his retinue," she said in what Gareth thought was, despite its quaver, a surprisingly haughty tone of voice.

"We suspect he is in Haddon Hall, my lady."

"Then you must take me to him."

Gareth looked at Cynan and Bryant before turning back to the lady. "I am afraid that is not possible my lady. But we will get you to safety come first light. For now, we are encamped not far from here."

Approaching her horse, he offered her a hand down. She ignored it and asked, "Why can you not escort me to the king now?"

"Because it is too dark to travel and the roads are dangerous this time of night," Gareth said.

The woman considered his reply before allowing him to help her down. She was no doubt bone weary and frightened.

As Gareth lifted her down, he tried to determine if he knew her, but her veil covered most of her face. She hadn't indicated she knew him when he introduced himself, so he could only speculate at which lady-in-waiting the three of them would play nursemaid to until they were able to leave her at an abbey, or perhaps one of the border lord's keeps.

"How came you to be back here, my lady? Did you not escape with the other women?"

The woman hesitated and Gareth wondered if she, too, had been hit on the head. Finally, she answered, "I was with the others, but my horse bolted, and I became separated from the group." For some reason Gareth had the impression she was not telling the truth but shrugged. What espionage could one lady-in-waiting engage in?

When they reached the clearing where the men had spread out their blankets, Elena said, "Where is the camp? Where are the others?"

"Others, my lady?" Bryant asked politely.

"Where are the tents? Where are the other ladies?"

"My lady, they are all with King Richard, as Sir Gareth told you."

Seemingly recovered from her earlier shock, she sputtered in fury. "After all I have been through today, you expect me to make do with no inn? No camp? Where, precisely, am I supposed to sleep?"

Bryant hurried over to his bedroll and picked it up. "You may gladly take my blanket, my lady."

"A blanket? Have you no cots, no tents? This is ridiculous! I cannot be expected to sleep rolled up in a blanket with three servants. I am Lady Elena de Vignon!" Gareth's head snapped up and he grimaced at the pain the sudden movement caused his tender skull. "I am part of the king's court. I cannot--"

"You are more than welcome to climb back on your horse and continue down the road if you do not like our accommodations," Gareth snapped. "But should you choose to stay, pray remember that we are not servants and will not be treated as such."

In the bleaching moonlight, Elena stared in mute outrage at him. Before she could respond, the three men silently stretched out on the ground. Elena slowly wrapped the rough blanket around her shoulders and carefully sat down.

"If you have any measure of sense, you'll unsaddle your horse before you sleep."

"Gareth, she's a gentle lady; they're not trained as a stable hand," Cynan argued.

"Then she shouldn't be riding."

"You are the rudest man I have ever had the displeasure to meet," said Elena as she sat up abruptly.

"Just ignore him my lady, I'll see to your horse for you," volunteered Bryant.

With a sigh of relief, Elena laid back down.

"You will at least have the courtesy to thank Bryant for tending your horse, lest I be provoked to call you the rudest woman I have ever had the displeasure to meet," said Gareth.

Though the moon's light washed her face of color, Gareth could read her indignant thoughts easily for her outrage was laughably evident. She could not believe his gall, would tell the king of his arrogance as soon as she reached him. And yet, she realized—for Gareth saw the dawning realization lift her brows in surprise--she must first reach Richard and he and his friends were her only way there. "My thanks, Bryant, for both your blanket and your assistance," Elena said sweetly before cursing Bryant's companion under her breath.

"Know you this lady that you are so unchivalrous, *Sir Knight*?" Cynan asked quietly as he and Gareth settled down to sleep.

"Aye. She's a conceited lady of Richard's court who has no manners to those without a title."

"Do I know her?"

"I've no doubt you'll recognize her come morn," Gareth said and then turned his back on Cynan and went to sleep.

***

"You're right, Gareth, I do remember this beauty," said Cynan as he peeked at the still-sleeping Elena the next morning. "But I do not remember having any occasion to know whether she's conceited or not."

"Trust me, she is." Gareth flushed as he remembered her saying, "Do not think to woo me with proud stories of your herd back home." He rubbed his sword arm with his left hand. It was stiff and sore from its exertions of the day before and Gareth was reminded of his first month of training with a sword. Then, as now, he had scarce been able to lift his sword arm above his head, but that ache was nothing to the throb in his head and the soreness of his leg.

The men washed down their breakfast of dried meat with wine and rolled up their blankets, but still Elena slept. As Gareth and Cynan saddled the horses, Bryant walked over to Elena. "My lady?" he called softly. "My lady, 'tis morn and we must be going." Elena did not respond.

Gareth finished saddling Isrid and walked over to Bryant. Nudging Elena with the toe of his boot he said loudly, "If you mean to sleep all day, kindly return Bryant's blanket so we may continue our journey."

Elena opened her eyes at the harsh voice. Her evident confusion gave her face a softly innocent look before she realized where she was, and the haughty mask slipped back over her features. When she remained on the ground, Gareth said sharply, "Are you coming or not?"

With an exasperated sigh, Elena stood, her obviously stiff and cramped muscles slowing the effort. Bryant smiled shyly at her and bent to retrieve the blanket.

"Shall I help you onto your horse, my lady?" Cynan asked, trying hard to keep from laughing at Gareth. Never had he seen his friend treat a woman so. And never before had he met a woman quite as imperious as Elena.

"Not before breakfast, I think."

"You slept through breakfast," Gareth said. "Now get on your horse."

"How dare you address me in such a manner!"

Gareth ignored her as he climbed onto Isrid. Cynan helped Elena mount and then handed her some dried meat. "I'm afraid you will have to eat while we ride, my lady." Turning to Bryant he said, "You go ahead and ride the first leg. I'm so glad to be going home, I'll probably fly instead of walk."

Bryant laughed as he climbed up behind Gareth. "You will be flying until your feet hurt. Then you'll be hollering for me to give you your rightful seat."

"Where's that?"

"On the horse's ass, no doubt," Gareth broke in and the three men laughed good-naturedly.

Chapter 5

Elena stared at the men, appalled that they would use such vulgar language in front of her. She shifted her gaze to the hard brown thing in her hand. Was she supposed to eat this? She took a tentative bite, or rather, she tried to take a bite, but could not tear off so much as a morsel. Glancing up to make sure none of the men were looking in her direction, she tried again, pulling on the meat with both hands. She succeeded in tearing off a large chunk, which she proceeded to chew, or rather tried to chew. What am I to do now? she thought. This was like trying to gnaw on boot leather. Elena was wondering if she could discreetly spit out the meat when Bryant leaned over and held out a wineskin.

"If you take a swallow and let it sit in your mouth a bit, 'twill be easier to chew, my lady."

Elena took the skin and poured some wine in her mouth. As she sat there with her large mouthful, trying to ignore the wretched taste, she saw the amused look in the grey eyes of the man in front of Bryant. Tears of anger and humiliation pricked behind her eyes and she pointedly turned her head away from his mocking look. The insolent knave! Elena finally managed to chew the now-soft beef and took another swallow of wine.

They rode through the forest over what looked like no road or trail Elena had ever seen. She couldn't understand why they weren't traveling on the main road. Surely that would have been the fastest route to Haddon Hall.

"Is this not prettier to look at than some old dusty road?" was Cynan's response when Elena questioned him.

Elena glanced around the heavily wooded surroundings. The trees were lush and green, and pink flowering vines crept up many of the trunks. The sun scarcely made its way through the thick leaves, and instead cast a soft green light over them as well as the forest floor. Beneath the horses' feet, the ground was soft with moss and years of accumulated mulch. Elena shrugged. "I would prefer to be back with King Richard's party than enjoy the scenery. Why can we not travel the road?"

The three men exchanged glances. Finally, Bryant spoke up. "My lady, we fear for your safety. The villains who attacked us yesterday may still be around. We would not jeopardize your safety."

Elena opened her mouth to tell them that the Woodvilles were by now long gone. She snapped it shut again when she realized she would be revealing more than she had claimed to know. As they rode, she tried to decide what, exactly, she would tell the king. If she told him of Elizabeth's escape, he may thank her for the information. If he realized that Elena was aware of *why* the princess escaped, he may very well want to silence Elena, for were he to marry his niece, the public outcry would be immense. She could offer her silence in return for the groom of her choice. Elena smiled at the thought and did not notice the tree branch just ahead.

"Ooof!" she said as the hanging leaves whacked her in the face. She sputtered angrily and glared over her shoulder at the offending tree. A sudden thought replaced her annoyance with fear.

King Richard was not a man to endure her threat with good grace. Yes, he would silence her, but not by paying her price. Though she knew the king favored her, she also knew that the position of lady-in-waiting carried no weight in matters of state. It was entirely possible that the king would use other, more permanent means to silence her. The image of Richard's two young nephews—long since silenced--floated before her eyes, causing her to smack into yet another branch.

"God's nightgown!" she cursed.

"Need you help, my lady?" the shy man—Bryant, she thought—asked.

"No!" Elena said sharply and then more calmly, "No...thank you."

Though the day was warm, Elena felt a sudden chill run down her spine. Trying to think of anything else, she turned her attention to what she would tell Margaret and Catherine.

"I am cursed!" she muttered as she realized that spending even one night away from the other women, in the company of three men, no less, would destroy her already fragile reputation. Frustrated that she had no answer to either of her plaguing questions, Elena distracted herself with complaining about the journey, delighting when the horrid man glared his displeasure at her.

Several hours later, Elena was too tired to complain anymore. She wearily dismounted with Bryant's help and made her way into the nearby bushes. When she returned minutes later, she found the men already mounted again and waiting to leave.

"You can not mean that is all the rest we get!"

"We have much distance to cover before nightfall. We can ill afford to waste the daylight while you idle the time away," said Gareth.

Elena glared at the man who had not said one polite word to her since she'd laid eyes on him. When they met up with Richard again...

"Perhaps we could at least let her stretch her legs, Gareth," Bryant ventured.

Gareth, Elena thought. She would remember that name to tell Richard.

"No. She's holding us up as it is. We continue until dusk."

Bryant looked at Elena apologetically as he helped her back on her horse, but Elena was too furious to notice. She clenched her teeth so hard her jaws began to hurt, and she slapped the reins on her delicate palfrey.

***

"What be the reason the normally chivalrous Sir Gareth is treating the Lady Elena so?" Cynan asked Gareth as they made their way through the forest. "Is she not the one whose looks you were so taken with the other night in the great hall?"

"That was until she opened her mouth. That woman makes an adder seem a pleasant conversationalist."

"I don't know. She seems merely high spirited to me."

Gareth laughed harshly. Cynan studied the back of his friend's head while a thought began to take shape in his head.

"She'd make a winsome wife. But not for a blundering Englishman. She needs a Welshman to appreciate her spirit."

Gareth looked over his shoulder. "Lest my memory fails me, you already have a wife, Cynan. I'm sure Enid would not be particularly amused by such talk."

"I was not thinking for myself, you fool."

"I'd not have her if she were the last woman in all of Wales, England, or Scotland. Or Ireland, for that matter."

Cynan chomped down on his lower lip to keep from laughing. Baiting Gareth had always been his favorite pastime. "Aren't you the conceited ass today," he remarked. "I was not thinking of you, either. I think Bryant has taken a fancy to her."

Gareth glared at Bryant who was walking several paces ahead of them, leading Elena's horse. Cynan saw Gareth's eyes narrow and his hands clench convulsively on the reins.

"Don't you dare put such thoughts into his head, Cynan. That woman would make his life miserable and I'd sooner see him dead than married to her."

Cynan shook his head and smiled. Enid would be proud of him, he thought. She was a master at reading people's hidden emotions, and he looked forward to telling her of Gareth's reaction to the haughty English lady.

***

By the time they did stop in the shadow of a monolithic boulder, it was dusk, and Elena was weaving in the saddle from exhaustion. As Cynan and Bryant immediately began gathering wood for a fire and pulled out food for dinner, Gareth helped Elena down from her horse. As soon as her feet touched the ground, she felt her knees buckle. Gareth caught her by the waist and held her until she steadied herself, trying to ignore the way her body felt pressed against him, concentrating instead on the texture of the fine linen of her dress under his fingers. He could not keep the fresh, sun-warmed scent of her hair out of his nose, however, nor could he ignore the way her breath tickled his left ear.

He could tell when her head stopped spinning, when she realized she was pressed against him, his hands on her waist, her head on his shoulder.

She quickly raised her head and her weary eyes glared imperatively at him.

"Take your hands off of me," she said as she pushed him away. Gareth immediately let her go and she had to clutch at her horse's mane to keep from falling.

As he stalked to his horse and began unsaddling it, he was disgusted with himself for his body's reaction to Elena's nearness. His hands still tingled from holding her, his chest could still feel her soft form pressed against it. He pulled Isrid's saddle off and began rubbing the powerful horse down. Glancing over his shoulder, he saw Elena still standing, clinging to her horse's mane.

More sharply than he intended, he said, "Unbuckle that saddle and groom your horse."

Elena jumped and opened her eyes. She glared at him before turning and fumbling with the straps which held the saddle on. Several minutes later, she had only managed to undo one buckle and was leaning wearily against her patient horse when Gareth approached.

"Watch carefully. Next time you do this yourself."

Elena clenched her teeth in anger, but said nothing, watching as he deftly undid the straps and slid the saddle off the horse. He walked back to his horse and picked up the rag he had used. Returning, he handed it to Elena. "Rub her down well so she'll not catch a chill."

When Elena just stared at the rag, he took her hand roughly and showed her what to do. She rubbed her horse until her arms ached and Gareth said, "Now wipe your saddle down and then you may go wash up at the stream. 'Tis through those trees over there."

As Elena stumbled to the stream, Bryant and Cynan exchanged surprised glances. Never had Gareth treated a lady so. He took every part of his knight's oath seriously and chivalry towards the fairer sex he had, until this lady, meticulously obeyed.

When Elena returned, Gareth handed her a bowl of watery soup. Elena stared at the contents of the bowl and said, "Might it be too much to ask what this substance is floating in the gruel?"

"Say, there's nothing floating in mine," Cynan complained.

Ignoring Cynan's attempts to lighten the mood, Gareth started to answer Elena, but Bryant broke in, "'Tis the meat you ate earlier today, my lady. When we boil it up with some barley, it gets a little more palatable."

Elena took a sip. "There is nothing on this earth that could make this 'meat' taste better. Could not one of you hunt a rabbit or some venison? 'Tis not as if we hadn't been in the forest all day, and since it's clear I'll be sleeping on the ground again tonight, is it too much to ask for a decent meal?" she finished imperiously.

Taking one look at the wrathful expression on Gareth's face, Cynan and Bryant hastily swallowed the last of their soup and quickly escaped to the stream.

"You are lucky to have a blanket to lay on the ground. Is it too much to ask that you might be grateful to have anything to eat at all?"

"Perhaps the serving wenches you are used to are content with your miserable hospitality, but ladies of rank expect more consideration from those who serve them."

"Serve them? If you think we are your servants, you are sadly mistaken. Tell me, is it customary for future countesses to belittle everyone and everything? Would you be more gracious if you were wedding Edgeford rather than Brackley come Michaelmas? On second thought, I met Edgeford. He seemed entirely too pleasant to meet your demanding expectations. 'Tis just as well you're marrying Earl Brackley. However, I must warn you to watch your temper around him. I understand his treatment of his wives makes them grateful for the smallest scrap of warmth and comfort. Why--" Gareth stopped at the look of terror on Elena's face. She stared at him, her warm brown eyes open wide with fright, something Gareth never expected to see in the gaze of someone as dictatorial as Lady Elena. The bowl of soup tumbled from her grasp unnoticed.

Despite her earlier whining and complaining, Gareth was instantly contrite. No woman who knew of Brackley's treatment of his wives-and what woman in England did not?--could possibly look forward to marriage to him, despite his immense wealth and power.

"My lady, you must not pay attention to me when I get angry. I say foolish, meaningless things. I--"

"How did you know of Lord Edgeford?" she asked in a much-subdued voice.

Gareth was caught off guard by her question. "What?"

"None but a few of my friends knew I wished to wed Edgeford."

"We danced the night your betrothal was announced. I saw how you chose our places in line so that when we traded partners, you would be with him."

"We danced?"

"Aye, my lady. The Gavotte."

Elena nodded. She remembered the dance, but not her partner.

Rising, Gareth handed her his bowl of soup. "I am accustomed to not eating. You'd best take this. You will need your strength tomorrow as the woods will be thicker. There are no trails for horses, and we may be walking most of the day."

Recognizing her expression as one of a battle-shocked novice soldier, Gareth knew that Elena did not even taste the bland broth, but she finished every drop and obediently curled up on her blanket when he said, "Get as much sleep as you can. We'll be leaving at sunup."

He watched her for a long while, long after Cynan and Bryant fell asleep. Although the summer evening was warm, he knew when Elena started shivering, knew its cause, and knew he could do nothing to alleviate it.

He couldn't help but feel sorry for her. No woman deserved the treatment she would receive at the hands of Brackley. His own cousin had suffered beatings for three years before her husband died of a fever. Gareth remembered at the man's funeral, when he found out about the beatings. Gwenllian had not shed a single tear for her husband and when Gareth called her to task for not mourning, she flew into a rage, describing the times he had hit her for no reason at all.

Gareth felt the anger growing inside him as he thought of his cousin's husband, but he now transferred that anger to Brackley. Though he was tired, he lay awake for several hours after Cynan and Bryant dozed off, planning a horrible and fitting death for the vicious earl.

Chapter 6

The hideous knight, Gareth, awoke late the next morning. Elena was up and trying to warm her cold muscles by hopping from foot to foot. He stretched before rising and gave her a smile. But if Gareth seemed friendlier to her after their talk of the night before, she was angrier. Mad at herself for letting this boor know that she was frightened of her impending marriage, she stared at him coldly and turned away. She attempted to smooth her hair into some semblance of order, though she didn't know why she should worry how she looked in front of these three, especially Sir Gareth.

Gareth's smile faded as he observed Elena's glare and she felt a moment of satisfaction as he rose and helped Cynan and Bryant pack up their few things. She would teach him to speculate on her personal life. For the next two days, she complained about the heat, the dust, the bugs, the quality of the food (still dried beef), the shortness of their breaks, and finally, Gareth's horse.

"Would you kindly get your horse out of my face?" she asked when they were stopped for lunch the next day beside a stream. Isrid had taken a fondness to Elena and was nuzzling her neck as she sat on a fallen log. Cynan who had been drinking water from the stream choked on what was either a laugh or a swallowed rock.

"Are you suddenly unable to walk?" Gareth asked.

When she stared, uncomprehending, he snapped, "If you like it not you can move."

Elena shot her meanest look at Gareth before leveling it on his horse. Isrid proved as oblivious to it as his master and began nibbling on her long braid. "Stop that!" she shouted.

"Here my lady, I'll get rid of him for you," said Bryant as he grabbed Isrid's halter. "Come on, you."

"My thanks," said Elena. She was not about to have Gareth lecture her again on manners.

Cynan leaned toward her. "You will be happy to know, my lady, that you shall sleep under a roof tonight. We'll be staying with distant kin of Bryant. Although," he leaned forward in a conspiratorial manner, but spoke loudly enough for Bryant to hear him, "although I hear they're hoping he won't be too distant much longer. Seems they've a lass who has set her cap for Bryant. The fool just won't settle down."

Elena stared at Cynan. What did she care of the marrying tendencies of the Welsh? But glancing at Bryant, who was turning five shades of red, she forbore from saying so. Bryant had at least treated her with some measure of

35

respect and consideration for her station.

"Are you married?" she asked Cynan, amazed that she was reduced to making small talk with a man-at-arms.

"Is he ever!" Bryant burst out, clearly thankful that Elena had nipped Cynan's gossiping in the bud. "I believe he's anxious to get me married so he won't be the only one who has to answer for his whereabouts."

"Enid worries a might too much," Cynan explained.

"Either that or she knows you well enough not to trust you!" Gareth said with a laugh. "How many skirts did you chase in your first year of marriage?"

"Leave it to you to forget that 'tis not the chasing, 'tis the catching and I haven't caught a single skirt since Enid and I were wed."

Elena was amazed at the men's crudity. Truly, few men she knew were bound by oaths of fidelity to their wives. In fact, the higher a man's rank, the more permissible it was for him to have mistresses. Still, Elena had never had to listen to discussions of such behavior.

Turning back to Elena, Cynan said, "Bryant and I have a wager as to when Gareth will wed. Bryant says 'twill be within two years, but I have high hopes that he'll hold out for at least ten." When Elena turned to glance at Gareth, Cynan asked, "Would you care to place a wager, Lady Elena?"

Elena sniffed. "I wager he never marries."

"The bachelor life for you, she's declaring, Gareth. Be he too handsome to stay with one women you think?"

"No, I simply don't think any woman would be able to put up with him for more than a fortnight."

Cynan and Bryant laughed and slapped their friend on the back.

"Seems she's just met you and she already knows you better than both of us," Cynan said.

"More like she's well versed in being difficult, herself," Gareth said, stung as he stalked off into the woods.

In spite of herself, Elena joined in Cynan and Bryant's laughter.

***

As they traveled that afternoon, Elena noticed that they were steadily climbing a gentle incline. The trees soared overhead, meeting in a canopy of pine needles overhead, filtering the light to a cool green. The layers of pine needles on the forest floor muffled the horses' hooves and absorbed any quiet comments the men made. Elena found herself actively listening to the chatter of squirrels, and the song of birds for the first time in her life. She felt an odd sense of peace that had nothing to do with fine clothes or good food or hot, scented baths. The anger she had forced herself to maintain over the past two days slowly dissipated and Elena actually found herself enjoying her strange adventure.

They arrived at the small village that was their destination just as the sun dipped below the horizon in a brilliant splash of gold and orange. Although Elena was tired, the beauty of the sunset and the warm glow it cast over the small village only added to her sense of peace. She found herself looking forward to a real bed with an appreciation she had never before felt.

To call the village small was being generous. Elena glanced at the four stone houses that were gilded by the setting sun, becoming for a fleeting moment, as grand looking as a stone fortress or royal palace. Small children scampered in and out of the open doors, startling wandering chickens. Two women returned from the stream, carrying a heavy basket full of wet clothes between them.

Smoke drifted lazily up from two of the houses' chimneys, carrying the smell of roasting meat to the weary travelers. Elena's mouth watered at the scent and her stomach rumbled appreciatively. Taking a deep breath, she felt the peaceful quiet of the evening soak into her very bones.

"I never knew England could be so beautiful," she murmured, not intending for anyone to hear her.

"That's because you're not in England. You're in Wales," said Gareth who was walking, leading her horse.

"What? Wales? But I though you were going to take me back to King Richard?" she cried.

"I never said that. I said I would get you to safety. We did not come within a day's traveling distance of one of the border lord's keeps, so I will have to leave you at the first abbey we come across until word can be sent to Richard and he can send someone to fetch you."

"That is simply not acceptable! I can't just sit in some Welsh abbey braiding my hair while I wait for an escort to Nottingham."

"Then perhaps you should assist the sisters in their charitable works to make the time pass more quickly."

"Why can't you escort me to Nottingham?"

"Because I go to see my father in Gwynedd," Gareth said tightly.

"You mean you're deserting the king?"

"I have no set duties with Richard. My father I have not seen in two years."

They stopped in front of the farthest of the small houses. As Cynan and Bryant dismounted, the door burst open and a short burly man came out, quickly followed by what looked to Elena like at least a dozen children. The burly man gave Bryant a quick hug before releasing him to the children who climbed all over Bryant, laughing and shouting. While his arms were burdened with three toddlers, a dark-haired young woman who looked to be about sixteen took advantage of his position and bestowed a wet kiss on the corner of his mouth.

"The would-be fiancée," Cynan explained in Elena's ear as he helped her down from her horse.

"Ah," said Elena, trying unsuccessfully to smother a smile.

They were ushered inside by the man, who introduced himself as Gruffydd, and his wife Catrin, a short plump woman with crinkly laugh lines around her eyes and mouth. Upon Catrin's instruction, Bryant's love-struck cousin Marared took Elena into the other room of the small house where she was finally able to take off her travel-stained gown and bathe.

"I swear I never thought I'd live to appreciate warm water again," Elena said as she stepped into the bucket of water the girl brought in and bent down to splash water onto her bare arms and chest.

The girl grinned and held up a plain gown. "You can wear this this evening if you like so we can wash your chemise."

"It's over there on the chest," Elena gestured. "I suppose 'tis too much to hope you might have some soft soap?" she asked with a grimace as she rubbed the rough lye soap over her legs.

"No. That is all we have. I did put some mint in your water though so you'd smell good. My mother says it's alright to smell like a fresh mint tart as long as you don't act like one!" Laughing loudly, the girl did not notice the grimace on Elena's face.

"Lovely," Elena muttered. "I've always wanted to smell like a nauseating desert. By the way, how is it that your family speaks English? Aren't you Welsh?"

"Yes. But we live so close to the English and sell and buy things back and forth so often that one of us must speak the other's language and I can't imagine them English ever trying to learn Welsh." Belatedly realizing that Elena must be English, the young girl lowered her head in embarrassment and turned to straighten Elena's clothes.

The girl gasped when she picked up Elena's chemise. "I've never felt such fine cloth." Turning to the dark blue kirtle, she delicately traced the embroidered and beaded neckline. "Is this one of your court dresses?"

"No, it's one of my older travel gowns." Despite her antagonism she had earlier felt over having to stay with Welsh peasants, the girl's admiration and naivete relaxed Elena's enmity and she surprised herself by saying, "You may try it on if you wish."

The girl looked at her in amazement but in a flash removed her rough gown and slipped the blue linen over her head. "I feel like a queen," she said, swishing the full skirt around the small room. Surveying the cloud of dust that followed the whirling hem, she said, "I'll wager we could brush the dust out of this till it looks like new." She ducked out of the room before Elena could say a word. She quickly returned with a horsehair brush and another bucket of water.

"I brought some fresh water if you'd like me to help you wash your hair."

If bathing had felt good, washing her hair in the cool mint-scented water was heavenly, Elena thought a few minutes later. Marared scrubbed her scalp and worked the tangles out of Elena's long hair.

"Such an unusual color your hair is," the girl said as she combed it out. "I usually hate combing my sisters' hair, but yours is so pretty to look at, I don't mind."

Elena looked over her shoulder in surprise. Another woman had never complimented her. Men had written poems about the color of her hair, but the women at court had only criticized it, commenting on its brassiness or the way it made her skin look sallow. Elena knew they were only being spiteful, but it still caused her to be surprised at Marared's honest compliment.

Once she was clean from head to toe, Elena dried herself with a small cloth as her self-appointed maid vigorously brushed the dusty gown.

"How's that?"

"It will do." Elena hesitated, then said, "Thank you." Marared beamed.

When Marared was finished, she took Elena's chemise to wash while Elena slipped on the borrowed gown. It was coarser than her own clothes, but loose fitting and considerably lighter and cooler. Plaiting her hair in a long braid over one shoulder, she dumped the rocks and dirt out of her boots and put them back on. She stepped into the larger room, surprised to find it empty. Marared was scrubbing her chemise in a pail on the large rough-hewn table.

"They're all outside," explained Marared. "It gets too hot in here with eleven people eating dinner. Fifteen would make it unbearable. There," she said as she rang the water out of the chemise. "I'll just hang it outside and 'twill be dry before you leave tomorrow."

Elena followed the girl outside and saw everyone gathered around a long table under a huge tree. There were two spots open on the benches that flanked the table. Marared scurried into the one next to Bryant, leaving Elena to sit next to Gareth.

As she sat, Gareth glanced at her and away and then turned back to her. She ignored him until he continued to stare. "Are you staring because I sprouted wings and a halo?" she asked sarcastically.

Gareth laughed and the sound blended with the noisy chatter and giggling of the children surrounding them. "No. I would die of shock if you did that. Now hooves and a forked tail would not surprise me..." Elena pointedly turned her attention to the wooden plate in front of her.

"We've the first berries of the season as a special treat this eve," said Catrin when they had devoured the simple meal of mutton, carrots, leeks, and barley.

"I'll fetch them, Mama," said Marared. "Elena can help me prepare them."

Elena stared at the girl in disbelief.

"Go on," said Gareth. "It won't kill you, I promise." Elena turned her stare to Gareth. She was about to utter a brusque retort when she was suddenly distracted by the color of his eyes. In the fading twilight, they were a smoky gray, full of warmth and a curious sparkle. His gaze roved over her face and to Elena, it felt like a caress, lightly touching her eyebrows, skimming along her cheekbones, and settling on her lips, light as a feather's kiss. Her heart pounded within her breast. Her cheeks warmed and an unfamiliar warmth spread through the rest of her body as well. Without quite knowing why, she rose and without so much as a sarcastic comment, followed Marared into the cottage.

"If you'll take this bowl out, I'll clean up our mess," Marared said, indicating the pile of stems and inedible berries on the table when they were done.

Next they'll be having me empty their chamber pots, Elena thought. Except, of course, that they don't have any! As she approached the table outside, she noticed that the younger children had dispersed, but Gareth, Cynan, and Bryant were still talking with the village adults. They had lit several torches and Elena paused to study Gareth's face by the soft glow. She knew that she was invisible to them as she stood outside of the ring of light and she could observe her brusque escort unnoticed.

He was utterly handsome, she realized with a start. She had not noticed the squareness of his jaw before or the straightness of his nose, the full curve of his lips. Her gaze lingered on that full curve and she suddenly wondered what it would be like to kiss those lips. He raked his dark hair off his forehead with a hand that was strong, but not coarse. Elena fancied that such a hand could grasp her tightly to him even as it gently caressed her hair and neck.

It was several moments before Elena realized that the people around the table were speaking in a strange mixture of English and Welsh. It had been years since she'd spoken Welsh, taught as she was by her Welsh grandmother. In Richard's court, she'd hidden her Welsh background as it was even less desirable than her family's Lancastrian ties. The garbled words slowly began to unfurl in her mind. As she concentrated, she was able to decipher many of the words.

"'Twill be before Michaelmas, I can assure you. He'll land in South Wales but will travel north to gather soldiers. I would have us ready to greet him when he lands. *Parod ac awyddus.*" Elena did not recognize the speaker's voice--it must be Gruffydd, she thought.

"*Cymreig ar y gorsedd,*" said Bryant. A <u>Cymreig</u> is a Welsh person, Elena thought. Something about a Welshman on the throne?

"But what of his claim to the crown? Does it meet the laws of inheritance?" asked Gareth.

"Had he no ties to the royal family, I would support him over one who murders children."

"That cannot be used to justify what you plan. There has never been a shred of proof that Richard harmed his nephews in any way," Gareth argued.

"*Crist trugaredd!* I suppose they've just disappeared off the face of the earth, eh Gareth?" Elena had never heard Cynan speak so harshly. He had seemed a man who saw a joke in every situation. "Surely you don't believe--"

"Regardless of that," Gruffydd interrupted, "his right is as strong as Richard's. He's a descendant of John of Gaunt."

"Through his grandmother. That is not—"

"*Digon!*" exclaimed Cynan. "Is the fact that he's Welsh not enough to want him on the throne?"

In the silence following Cynan's outburst, Elena was sure they would hear her heart beating as it raced in her chest.

"As a matter of fact," said Gareth quietly after several moments, "it is."

Elena gasped. They were planning to help the Earl of Richmond overthrow the king! It was treason! Hearing Marared behind her, Elena quickly composed her features and carried the bowl of berries to the table, forcing her expression to careful neutrality.

Gareth studied her face as she sat down. She knew he was wondering how much she heard and whether she'd understood any of it. Elena absorbed herself in eating and did not pay attention to the noisy jests of Cynan as he teased Bryant and Marared. Scarcely tasting the ripe fruit, Elena wondered what she should do. That she must warn the king of the impending attack was obvious, although she knew he was preparing for its possibility. Perhaps if she could discover more of the Welsh plans, her information could thwart the rebellion. And a grateful Richard would no doubt be willing to reward her with the groom of her choice, would he not?

***

"Elena?" Marared whispered in the dark room. Elena was bedded down with girl and her youngest sister in the only bed in the house. Outside a fine mist of rain had started to fall and the breeze entering the small room was pungent with the smell of wet hay and wildflowers.

Elena sighed and rolled onto her back. "Hmm?"

"Do you think Bryant and I make a handsome pair?"

Silently, Elena thought that Marared would talk poor Bryant's ear off in a matter of days if they were wed, but she said, "I suppose so."

"I think so too. I dream all the time that he'll ask me to marry him before I turn seventeen. My cousin over in Newtown is already expecting her first babe and she is only ten days older." Marared was silent for several minutes and Elena was just about to drop off to sleep when the girl said, "You know what else I think?"

If I pretend I'm asleep, perhaps she'll leave me alone, Elena thought. "What?" she said.

"I think that you and Gareth make a handsome couple as well."

Elena's eyes flew open. "What?"

"You're both so attractive, you'd have beautiful children. And I think you'd look sweet with a wreath of flowers in your hair as a bride."

This is ridiculous, Elena thought. "I'm betrothed," she said flatly.

"To who?"

"To a very powerful earl."

"Oh."

Elena rolled back on her side. "What a pity," Marared continued. "From the way he looks at you, I'd say Gareth is quite taken with you." She then proceeded to fall asleep. Elena stared into the darkness for a long time, unable to sleep when minutes before she had been utterly exhausted.

Chapter 7

The rain-washed morning air was crisply cool. A light breeze helped dispel the pre-dawn mists and the ale-induced fog in Gareth's head as he took deep, restorative breaths. Cynan and Bryant were mounted on a huge gray workhorse and Gareth moved to tighten the straps on Isrid's saddle.

He glanced up when Elena came out of the small house and felt his loins tighten. Shrew though she may be, she was a beauty. Her cinnamon-colored hair glowed richly in the shafts of sunlight that pierced the dispersing clouds. She had plaited it in one long, fat braid that hung over her shoulder. Her creamy skin now had a healthy glow from her days spent in the saddle and thick lashes fringed her nutmeg-colored eyes. Gareth laughed under his breath. Cinnamon, cream and nutmeg? He was no doubt hungry for food, not a woman. Still…did she not have the tongue of an adder, the spice of her looks and intelligence would make her a woman to be treasured.

He watched her look around and knew when she realized her small gray palfrey was nowhere to be found.

"Where is my horse?" she asked.

Gareth continued loading Isrid as he said, "It would never make it over the mountains we'll soon be crossing. Besides, we'll travel faster if we're all mounted."

"That still doesn't explain where my horse is."

"I traded her for this one," he jerked his chin toward the large horse on which Cynan and Bryant were mounted.

"How dare you! That animal was given to me by Queen Anne just before she died, you oaf. King Richard will hear of this, I can assure you!"

Gareth swung around. In an instant he had Elena by the arm. "I care not for the precious symbol of how prized you are by the King of England. 'Twill be a symbol of a meaningless reign before the year is out."

"Gareth!" Cynan said sharply.

Gareth glanced at his friend and flushed.

"You do mean to commit treason! You! A knight sworn to serve King Richard!"

"I am sworn to serve the crown which rules Wales and England, not the man who wears the crown."

"What is the difference?" Elena demanded.

Gareth paused. He had been struggling with the same question all night. Though he had no great fondness for Richard and abhorred the thought of how he had obtained the crown, he had, in truth, done no harm to England. In fact, he had lifted many taxes and devised a fair and successful

Council, which met once a quarter in York to keep the peace, disperse punishment, and settle disputes. Glancing from Elena's furious face to Cynan's and Bryant's wary ones, Gareth sighed. He hoped his father would be able to offer him advice on determining his loyalties.

Gareth ran his fingers through his hair and turned back to Elena. "Get on the horse. We can argue as we ride, but we are losing daylight."

"I am not going anywhere with a traitor."

"Fine. Stay here with Gruffydd and Catrin. I'm sure they'll be able to drop you at the abbey the next time they go to Llangollen for the yearly fair in six or eight months. In the meantime, I'm sure they could use you to tend the herds and help with the younger children."

Elena strode furiously to Isrid and waited to be lifted up.

"I'm so glad you decided to join us," Gareth said amiably as he took the reins and quickly mounted. When Elena continued to stare at him expectantly, Gareth leaned down and lifted her unto the saddle in front of him.

The three men waved goodbye to Gruffydd's family who had gathered around to hear the English woman argue with Gareth. With little urging, the horses broke into a spirited gallop.

"Where will you leave me?" Elena asked several minutes later.

"Despite what you may think," Gareth said, "Wales is not a Godless country. There are many abbeys and monasteries scattered throughout."

"So, where will you leave me?"

"Unfortunately," Gareth continued as if Elena had not interrupted, "Since none of us ever thought to take up the life of a holy man, we have little or no idea where the nearest abbey is."

"Couldn't you have thought to ask before we left?"

"Catrin says there is one about two days' ride south, but we cannot afford the time to ride there and back. You will simply have to enjoy our beautiful Welsh scenery until we come across one that will not delay us overlong."

"Heaven forbid you should be inconvenienced," Elena said caustically.

***

The next five days were duplicates of the one following their departure from Gruffydd and Catrin's home: they rode hard all day, stopping at night at a small village or hut where one of the men was invariably related to at least one of the occupants. As they ate, they would discuss Richard's downfalls and the merits of Richmond--the greatest of which seemed to be the former's lack of Welsh blood and the latter's abundance of it. Although Elena knew a good deal of Welsh, she did not tell Gareth and was content to let him ramble on. For some reason she could not fathom, he seemed to feel compelled to translate a carefully edited version of what they had spoken about before they went to sleep. Although she never let the three men see it, she was growing more and more disturbed by what she was learning of her sovereign.

Elena had long prided herself on her knowledge of the political games that were played at court. She knew details of Buckingham's rebellion she doubted Richard even knew, and she could recite the line of the Woodvilles--Edward IV's in-laws and a constant burr to Richard--back for two generations. But despite her time spent in court, she never knew that a majority of the churchmen who served on his governing Council were from Richard's home in northern England and that these men had no knowledge of the workings of the rest of England. In truth, Richard placed such a greater value on the northern shires that he all but ignored the needs of the southern shires.

And, though Elena refused to mention it to Gareth or his friends, she knew that Richard had planned to marry his niece, King Edward IV's daughter, Lady Elizabeth. Elena remembered the frightened determination on Elizabeth's face that day less than a fortnight ago when Richard's entourage was attacked. A marriage between two so closely related would have been ruled incestuous by the Church, except that the clergy running the Church were undoubtedly Richard's men.

And no matter what evidence was lacking, there was always the question of Richard's two young nephews. They had not been seen since Richard's coronation and speculative rumors about their fates had been whispered even in Queen Anne's presence.

On the evening of the fifth day since leaving Gruffydd and Catrin's house a thick, wet fog set in, blanketing the forest in a swirling veil through which they could see no more than a few feet in front of them.

"Cynan!" Gareth called ahead. "Are you sure you can find the house in this fog?" he asked, referring to their day's destination.

Cynan reined his horse in until Isrid was even with it. "It can't be more than an hour away, even with this weather. I've no taste for sleeping in the fog and would have us push on."

Gareth grinned. "Still afraid Lucifer will sneak up on you?" When Cynan shot him a withering look, Gareth said, "Very well, continue, but let's hurry. I'm about to fall out of my saddle with exhaustion. It looks like Bryant's already out," gesturing at his sleeping friend whose head was resting on Cynan's back.

"Aye, he's been asleep for the past hour or so." Gareth looked down at Elena who, seated sideways in the saddle, was comfortably curled against his chest, asleep. The fog had spangled her hair with diamond droplets and Gareth resisted the temptation to touch them. Nudging Isrid on, he followed Cynan.

Cynan's estimate proved to be far short of true. Two hours later, Gareth's head kept nodding forward and he would jerk himself awake and urge the slowing Isrid on. Elena had not once awakened and even through his exhaustion, Gareth couldn't quell the tender feelings her form evoked as it pressed against him for warmth and comfort. Without realizing it, his head bent forward until it rested on the silky softness of her hair. Despite their days on the road, she still smelled fresh and clean. Like mint, he thought.

Gareth awoke with a start, realizing Isrid had finally slowed to a stop. Rubbing his eyes, he nudged his horse with his spurs. "Come on, boy. We've got to catch up to Cynan." He stared hard into the darkening fog but could see no movement indicating Cynan was in front of him. "Cynan!" he yelled and his voice was muted and swallowed by the swirling fog.

Elena started at Gareth's shout and straightened. "Are we there yet?"

"Damn!" Gareth muttered. Glancing down at Elena he said, "No, we're not there yet."

"How much further, then?"

Gareth hesitated. "I'm not sure."

Elena turned to ask Cynan but saw only thick white mist in all directions. "Where is Cynan?"

Again, Gareth hesitated. "I'm not sure."

Elena turned back to look at him, acutely conscious despite her worry, of how close their lips were, inanely noticing the plush stubble that covered his face. "What do you mean you're not sure?"

Gareth cleared his throat. "I think I fell asleep and Isrid stopped. Cynan must have kept riding thinking I was still behind him."

"How could you do something as stupid as that?" Elena demanded.

"Perhaps I was exhausted as I've had to guide the horse for five days since you're too frightened to do it!" he shot back.

"And I suppose if I hadn't been here you would be any less exhausted?"

"No, but--" Gareth closed his mouth abruptly and quickly jumped down from the horse.

"Where are you going? Don't you dare leave me stranded on this horse alone!"

Pulling the reins over Isrid's head, Gareth glared at Elena. "Not another word do I want to hear out of you, do you understand? Not a complaint, not a whine, not even a loud breath. In fact, why don't you go back to sleep? 'Tis the only time I can be sure you won't be hollering about your comfort."

Elena silently ran through the litany of foul names she had assigned to Gareth over the past week. When Gareth pulled Isrid forward sharply, Elena quickly grabbed the horse's mane to keep from falling off. Realizing she would have an easier time riding the horse astride rather than sideways, she threw her right leg over Isrid's neck and rearranged her skirts.

Gareth led Isrid through the thick fog, trying to stay true to the direction he hoped would lead him to Cynan's uncle's small keep. In the eerie silence of the fog-shrouded woods, Elena lost all track of time. She was just about to doze off when Isrid came to an abrupt halt.

"What is it?" she whispered.

"Straight ahead, do you see it? A fire. Cynan must have realized we'd fallen behind and lit a fire hoping I'd see it. 'Tis a wonder he was able to find wood dry enough to burn."

"How can you be sure it's Cynan and Bryant?"

Gareth laughed. "How many other travelers do you think would be out on a night like this in the middle of Wales?"

Elena shrugged and held on tightly to the saddle, eagerly anticipating the warmth of a fire on her chilled fingers. In a few minutes, they entered the small clearing.

"Damn," Gareth muttered under his breath. It was not Cynan and Bryant they had stumbled upon, but four large, vile looking men sprawled around the fire. Mercenaries, Gareth thought as he spotted the motley array of armor and weapons piled haphazardly about. And drunk too, no doubt, judging from the empty wine skins lying about.

"Hoohoo, laddies! Did I not tell you, "Ask and ye shall receive?' Now we were just wishing we had a woman and here one comes to us. Led by a servant, no less."

The other three men pushed themselves us. "And a comely wench, she is."

"I've not had one that clean since I was a boy," said a third as he stood. "Come'ere, lass. Come and enjoy our hospitality."

Turning, Gareth pushed hard against Isrid. "Back! Get back!" Isrid backed a few paces but stopped when he ran into a tree. "Come on you--" A large hand on Gareth's shoulder spun him about.

"You wouldn't be meanin' to keep her all to yourself, now would you, whelp?"

Gareth looked over his shoulder at Elena. "Run!" he yelled as he swung with all his might at the man in front of him, landing a cracking blow to the man's nose. "Go on!" he yelled again as Elena stayed where she was.

Spurred to action by the urgency in his voice, Elena reached for the reins that were dangling in the mud. She screamed as one of the men grabbed them first. Twining her hands in Isrid's mane, she kicked the horse as hard as she could. Isrid reared up, nearly throwing her. Holding on to him with all the strength in her legs, Elena pulled on his head to turn him around, but a second man was grabbing for her from the right. She kicked as hard as she could, aiming at the drunken man's face and then swung Isrid back toward Gareth. He was battling the other two men, who, despite their drunkenness were moving swiftly. Though Gareth was smaller than either brute, he landed blow after blow on chin, nose, and stomach. Elena stifled a scream as the men finally organized enough to circle Gareth. One of them grabbed Gareth from behind and the other moved to deliver a crippling blow, but in a flash of movement, Gareth twisted from his captor's embrace and, as if from nowhere, a knife flashed in his hand. The meaty fist that had been aimed at Gareth now glanced off the other man's shoulder. Before the man had a chance to recover from throwing the punch, Gareth brought the knife down to land between his attacker's shoulder blades.

The stabbed man fell onto his partner and the two landed on the ground. Spinning quickly, looking for other adversaries, his gaze met Elena's. Without urging, she moved Isrid around the fire. As the stunned mercenaries regained their senses and groped their way to their feet, Gareth swung up behind her. Applying his spurs harder than he ever had to Isrid's flanks, he sent the powerful horse into an immediate gallop. Elena squeezed her eyes shut as the horse easily cleared the fire and crashed through the brush on the other side.

Although he knew not which direction they were headed, Gareth kept Isrid at a full run until the horse began to tire. When he dismounted and began leading his horse, he realized that Isrid had been running up hill for the last half mile. Pausing to pat the gallant animal on the neck, Gareth looked around, noticing that the fog was almost gone at this higher elevation, replaced by bright moonlight. He continued leading Isrid, being careful to avoid rocky spots over which the tired horse might trip. Halfway up the mountain in front of them, Gareth spotted a huge cluster of rocks.

"You'll have to walk a bit," Gareth said quickly to Elena who, despite her weariness, could not close her eyes. "This mountain is very steep and I would have us get to those boulders lest your suitors decide to follow us."

Elena nodded and threw her leg over the saddle. Gareth grabbed her waist as she slid off the horse and held her up when her knees went out from under her. "I'm afraid we must hurry," he said apologetically. "Though they were drunk, those men were trained mercenaries and I fear they may still have wits enough for a chase. Do you have the strength?"

No, Elena almost said. But remembering the look on the man's face that had grabbed for her sent a burst of adrenaline coursing through her veins. "Let's go," she said.

They scrambled up the steep face of the mountain. Elena clenched her skirts above her knees with one hand as she sought for rocks to pull herself along with the other. The blood began to ring in her ears and she felt herself growing dizzy when Gareth finally stopped. He thrust Isrid into a shallow cave concealed behind several boulders and reached for Elena.

In the pale moonlight that leaked through the rocks, they clung to one another, thankful to be alive, thankful to find some small comfort after their harrowing escape. After several long moments, Elena's breathing slowed, but her heart kept racing. As the fear of danger faded, she became more aware of Gareth's strong arms around her, his hard chest warm under her cheek. A shiver that was not from cold and which she had never before felt ran through her body and she slowly raised her head.

Gareth rested his cheek on Elena's wind-strewn hair. He clutched her tightly to him as harrowing thoughts of her near fate flashed through his mind. When he felt her stir, he instinctively bent his head lower and when she raised her face toward his, his lips tentatively claimed hers. Elena offered no protest, merely a soft sigh which Gareth quickly swallowed as his mouth pressed more firmly against hers.

Elena's lips parted, as if of their own accord, seeking more of Gareth's kiss. When his tongue softly traced the sensitive skin just inside her lip, Elena leaned closer to him, a low moan escaping her throat. Gareth's sensual exploration of Elena's mouth grew bolder at that sound and his arms tightened around her, pulling her closer still until their bodies were touching from head to toe.

When the kiss finally ended, Elena experienced an entirely new sensation: shyness. Gareth, too, seemed not to know how to act, and clumsily turned away and began unbuckling Isrid's saddle.

"We'd best get some rest," he said after several moments of strained silence.

"Yes," Elena said shakily. Clearing her throat, she said, "Do you have any idea where we are."

Gareth grinned ruefully. In the dim light, Elena could only see the flash of his white teeth and unwillingly hungered for another kiss. "To tell the truth, I haven't the faintest idea where we might be. I'll have to take a look tomorrow morning."

As Gareth shook out his blanket, he said, "I'm sorry, we'll have to share. Cynan and Bryant have your blanket."

Elena tried to keep her voice steady as she said, "That's alright."

She did not know how she was going to sleep so close to Gareth. She silently said a prayer of thanks that it was too dark for him to see her shaking hands as she took an edge of the blanket and lowered herself onto the ground near him. As he drew close against her, trying to fit under the narrow strip of wool, all thoughts of comfort, of beautiful dresses, of his rudeness over the past weeks, of her anger at a lady of her station caught in such circumstances, all of those thoughts faded away as her lips tingled with remembrances of his kiss and recollections of his valiant fight to save her. Before she could follow those thoughts, Elena was asleep.

She awoke slowly the next morning, aware even before she opened her eyes of Gareth's arms around her, cushioning her from the hard ground and keeping her warm. When she did open her eyes, she found herself snuggled against him, her head nestled beneath his chin, her lips pressed against his skin. The musky smell of worn leather and warm skin clung to his neck and was oddly appealing. Gently lifting her head, she saw that he was still asleep, the lines of his face softened by slumber. Before she had a chance to study him, though, his eyes slowly opened and Elena stared, fascinated. She had never thought grey could be such a warm, interesting color.

"Good morning," he said, startling her out of her reverie. She quickly drew back and sat up.

"I don't suppose there's anything to eat but dried meat, again, is there?" she said, trying to sound annoyed.

Gareth smiled and rolled over to his saddlebag. "As a matter of fact, I was saving these just for such an occasion," he said as he pulled out a small package and handed it to Elena.

"What is it?"

"Open it and see."

Elena untied the string and gasped in delight. "Dried figs! " She quickly took a bite of one and closed her eyes in ecstasy. When she finished the fig and licked her fingers, she started laughing. Gareth looked at her askance as she fell back on the blanket laughing still harder. When Elena finally caught her breath, she wiped her eyes and said, "I don't even like figs!" Gareth shared her mirth for a moment until the urge to kiss her was too great. Leaning over, he silenced her laughter with a languid kiss.

She began to kiss him back, but in the light of day, she was suddenly reminded of her position, of the inappropriateness of how they had spent the night. "Don't!" she said as she pushed him away.

Embarrassed, Gareth rolled to his feet and stalked out of the small cave. What had he been thinking? he wondered as he looked into the sparse woods on the mountain, looking for any sign that they had been followed. She was still the same spoiled wretch who had tormented him for the past fortnight. Last night's kiss was simply born of relief to be alive and—

"I'll be damned," Gareth said, thoughts of Elena immediately evaporating as he looked around at the mountain range they were in. Quickly scurrying back to the cave, he said, "Gather everything up! We're not but a day's ride from my father's keep."

Elena finished her fig and slowly stood, smoothing the wrinkles from her gown. Although Gareth seemed to have forgotten what had transpired between them the night before and just moments ago, Elena could not help but remember and the memories made her feel embarrassed and awkward.

"Come on! Pack up the bag while I saddle Isrid."

Taking refuge from her embarrassment in haughtiness, Elena snapped, "I am not a stable hand and I refuse to be treated like one."

Gareth laughed. He was so glad he would be home by nightfall even Elena couldn't dampen his spirits. "Then pray, sit ye down, my lady whilst I, the noble and gallant Sir Gareth do attend your every need." With a cheerful, if tuneless, whistle, Gareth quickly packed their few belongings and saddled Isrid. Leading the horse outside he began to walk north, across the broad mountain. Elena followed several paces behind, scolding herself for being so flustered by a silly kiss. She'd been kissed before, had she not? And by far better men than lowly Sir Gareth ap-something or another. Of course, a small voice whispered in her head, not by a better kisser than Sir Gareth. The very skin behind her knees tingled when she remembered their passionate kiss of the night before. Elena watched Gareth's broad shoulders as he picked a careful path across the rocky mountainside.

He was unlike any of the men she had ever been attracted to. Whereas Lord Edgeford was tall and slender, Gareth was just a few inches taller than her, and compactly built, his arms and chest bound in hard muscles. Edgeford had golden blond hair that fell in carefully placed waves: Gareth's thick unruly dark brown hair forever seemed to be curling in the wrong direction. Edgeford's pale blue eyes gazed with tranquility on life while nothing escaped Gareth's multi-faceted grey eyes, taking in every detail of the world around him, sparkling with curiosity. In truth Elena was not sure if she liked or scorned Gareth for those very differences.

***

By nightfall, Gareth and Elena were riding into the quiet bailey of a small stone and wood keep. Despite her weariness, Elena noticed how immaculate everything seemed, even for a keep of this size. Firewood was stacked in neat rows against one wall; the hard packed dirt around the keep was swept clean of any clutter or debris; a trim hedge encircled what looked to be a well kept garden and arbor; and the pale stone of the keep gleamed warmly in the pearly light of dusk.

A guard approached them with a pine torch and cried, "Ho! Stand and be known!" Recognition dawned in his voice as he shouted over his shoulder, "'Tis Sir Gareth! He's home!" Within moments, the bailey was alive with activity. The door to the keep swung open with a loud creak and several men poured out, among them, Cynan and Bryant.

"Are we glad to see you!" said Cynan. "Did you take the scenic route?" he joked.

Helping Elena down, Bryant asked, "My lady, are you alright?"

"Yes, of course." Elena suddenly felt flustered and conspicuous with all of the people crowding around them.

"Gareth!" Gareth and Elena both turned at the booming voice behind them. An older version of Gareth was pushing his way through the small crowd. When he reached Gareth, he hugged him tightly and muttered what Elena could only guess was a Welsh prayer.

Gareth and his father spoke animatedly for several minutes before Gareth remembered Elena. Turning, he switched back to English and said, "Father, this is the Lady Elena de Vignon. I'm afraid she's our reluctant travel companion."

"Blessed St. Dafydd! You don't mean to tell me you've abducted her. I'll grant you, she's a beauty, but--"

Laughing at Elena's incredulous stare and his father's mistaken conclusions, Gareth interrupted. "You need not begin praying for my blackened soul, father. Lady Elena was traveling with King Richard when his party was attacked. She was separated from the group and we were going to escort her to an abbey or one of the border lords' keeps, but..."

"But you've forgotten every Welsh method of tracking and traveling you used to have to find them and here you are, where you least expected to be, eh?"

"In truth, this was my final destination, but I doubt the Lady Elena ever hoped to visit this far into Wales."

Turning to Elena, Gareth's father said, "Welcome, my lady, to Eyri Keep. I am Morgan ap Cyryth. I am honored to have such a fair lady in my humble home. Please come inside so you can bathe, rest and eat."

This was more like it Elena thought. She wondered why Gareth had no manners when his sire was so courtly, but she was not about to waste another moment on the son while thoughts of a bath and clean clothes were foremost on her mind. Placing her hand in Morgan's, she let him lead her into the main hall, a large room with polished wooden walls and freshly strewn rushes on the stone floors. The tables were grouped in a large U shape and each had a pitcher and several loaves of bread placed in the center. Large chairs, complete with embroidered cushions were gathered near the one large window that was open to the beauty of the summer day.

The entire hall bespoke hospitality and comfort and Elena was immediately at ease. There was more grace and warmth to this hall than in Middleham, or Nottingham, or even her parents own manor.

"Enid!" Morgan yelled. A small round woman hurried across the hall.

"You needn't shout, I'm not deaf. Although if you keep yelling as such, I may soon be so," she nagged good-naturedly.

"Enid would you help dear Lady Elena be as comfortable as possible in this drafty place? Lady Elena, this is Enid, Cynan's most tolerant wife." Enid was shorter and older than Elena, but energy and efficiency radiated from her. Her black hair was pulled back from her head with a blue kerchief and fell in a lavish cascade down her back. Although she was not beautiful in the conventional sense of the word—her face being too round and her complexion too ruddy—her sparkling dark eyes and smiling mouth, along with the extravagance of her long hair combined to make her very attractive nonetheless.

Elena smiled at the woman and followed her up the staircase. "Is this your first time in Wales?" Enid asked.

"I used to visit Newport with my parents when I was younger."

"Och, south Wales is like a whole different country. I'm sure you'll like it much more up here! But tell me, how did you come to be traveling with the boys?"

Elena hesitated. Morgan had spoken to Enid familiarly, yet he had asked her to wait on Elena. Was she a servant or wasn't she? She certainly wasn't going to gossip with a serving woman, and yet she was Cynan's wife...The Welsh were a most disconcerting people, Elena thought. Without quite knowing why, Elena found herself telling Enid the entire story of their journey since leaving Middleham, even about Lady Elizabeth's flight.

When the story was finished, the women chatted about English and Welsh beauty secrets as Elena bathed in a large wooden tub. Enid built a small fire for Elena to sit in front of while she dried and combed her long hair. When she was dressed in a clean kirtle, Enid made her sit while she wove her hair into an intricate knot. As Enid rambled on about everything from how she came to marry Cynan to Gareth's boyhood foibles, Elena wondered at the ease and enjoyment she felt at Enid's company. She never spoke so casually to the women in Richard's court--not even Catherine and Margaret. Remembering Marared, Bryant's cousin, Elena wondered what was so different about these Welsh women that made them so likable.

"That gown suits your coloring just so," said Enid when they were done. Elena rubbed her hands over the soft linen. It was a rich shade of cinnamon and as beautifully made as any she owned.

"My thanks for lending it to me," Elena said.

"Now, let's get you something to eat before you faint."

***

Gareth was sitting next to his father at the head table enjoying his second mug of honey mead when his eyes alighted on Elena as she descended the steps into the main hall. As she paused to glance around the crowded room, he was reminded of the first time he saw her, less than a month before. She'd been wearing velvet, he remembered, and he had been sure she wouldn't deign to speak to him. Taking a large gulp of mead, he mumbled to himself, "And she didn't!" In fact, she was rude and self absorbed. Well, she was still both of those, but perhaps tonight with no kings or earls about, she'd be more inclined to dance with him than she had that first night.

Enid guided Elena to a seat at the end of the head table, next to Bryant. Calling to one of the serving girls, she handed her Elena's empty plate and clapped her hands to make the girl hurry. Before long, Elena was stuffing herself on fish, lamb, and rough bread spread thick with butter and honey. As her hunger began to abate, Elena started listening to the conversation of the men at the table.

Her command of the Welsh language was still a little rusty, but the words she did grasp told her that they were speaking of King Richard and Henry Tudor. Not again, she silently moaned. Although she and Gareth had argued heatedly over the politics of Lancaster and York--Gareth was the first man who had ever condescended to discuss politics with her-- she was heartily sick of the whole subject. Tonight, she wanted to relax and enjoy the comforts of a lord's manor, even a small one such as this.

"Is something wrong, my lady?" Bryant asked politely.

"What?"

"You sighed rather mournfully. Is the food not to your liking?"

"It's quite good. Of course, sticks and mud would have tasted good after that horse hide you fed me this fortnight past," she said with a rueful smile. "Actually, I was hoping for some lighter entertainment than another discussion of political intrigue."

"Did I hear a call for lighter entertainment?" Cynan broke in. "Gareth! Show some manners for once and ask the Lady Elena to dance. She grows weary of this dull chatter." Turning to Morgan, he asked, "May I call for the musicians, sir?"

"Indeed," Morgan replied with an amused smile.

"Wake up you lazy beggars," he bellowed across the hall. "I've not seen my wife in months and I mean to dance with her right now."

Those who played instruments good-naturedly scurried to tune them while others broke down the trestle tables to make room for dancing. Cynan stalked down the reluctant Enid and dragged her to the newly created dance floor.

"A rousing tune, lads, with lots of spins and turns!"

As the musicians began playing, Gareth rose and approached Elena.

"Would you care to dance, my lady?" he asked politely.

Elena glanced up in surprise; she'd been watching the dancers. Though she had seen that he had bathed and changed when she entered the hall for dinner, she only now noticed how handsome he looked. His face was freshly shaven and the ornery lock of hair temporarily smoothed out of his face. His green wool jerkin flattered the width of his shoulders and the narrowness of his waist. Elena did not allow herself to scrutinize too closely his snug woolen hose that clung to his muscular legs. "I'm rather tired. I think I'll sit this one out."

Gareth raised an eyebrow, his hand still extended to accept hers. "This is no king's court, my lady. There are no earls or earls to impress. In fact, I'm the only knight among the lot of us. Wouldn't you just like to dance and have fun for once?"

Elena thought for less than a second. "Yes, I believe I would."

Dancing had heretofore been a means of flirting to Elena. She had used it to show off her grace and poise: to allow her suitor his fill of gazing at her. Now as Gareth whirled her effortlessly about the room, she laughed with delight, enjoying the quickening music, the swirling skirts, her partner's firm grip on her hands and waist.

When the dance ended and Gareth made to escort her back to her chair, she refused, making him dance again and again. When he finally begged off claiming his still-healing leg was sore, Elena forgot all manners of modesty and asked Bryant to dance. Bryant flushed beet red, but obligingly danced two more songs with her.

"Quite a spirited girl, there," Morgan noted to Gareth. "Are you sure you didn't bring her home for other reasons? There were, after all at least four abbeys between Nottingham and here."

"Would that I had known of them," Gareth said, his eyes never leaving Elena, who was with her fourth dance partner. "She was not so biddable on the road as she is on the dance floor."

Morgan glanced sideways at his son who was still watching the young woman. "And were you as biddable as you would have had her been?"

Gareth finally looked at his father. "Perhaps not," he said with a grin. Turning back to the dancers, he saw Elena making her way back to the table. Pouring her a goblet of wine, he handed it to her as she sat down.

"My thanks," she said breathlessly.

"I'm amazed you have energy enough for so much dancing after our long journey."

"But this is so much more fun than English court dancing! Bryant said they were country dances...."

Elena continued talking animatedly about the dancing, but Gareth was distracted by the high color in her cheeks and the tendrils of chestnut hair that had escaped her intricate coiffure. Her warm brown eyes and creamy complexion gave off a golden glow in the fire and torchlight. When Elena paused to take a draught of wine, the droplet left on her lip, which she dabbed away with her finger, mesmerized him. As he leaned closer to her, he caught the scent of cloves, his whole being caught in the web of her beauty and spirit.

"Don't you agree?" she asked, turning her wide eyes toward him.

"Of course," he murmured, suddenly catching himself and shaking his head to clear it of its delusions.

***

Elena sucked in a breath at the slumberous look in Gareth's eyes. She was well practiced at knowing when a man was staring at her and she knew Gareth had watched her dance the last quarter hour. She had been absurdly pleased by that fact. But now as she stared back at him, all thoughts of coquetry and flirtation, in which she was so well versed, evaporated and all she could remember was the way his lips felt as they had explored hers. When Gareth shook his head and leaned back, Elena felt as if someone had dumped a bucket of cold water on her head. Was he telling her that he would not deign to kiss her again? Telling her that, no, he did not find her as attractive as she seemed to find him? Angry with herself for romanticizing this crude Welshman and furious with him for stirring up these emotions, Elena stood and said coolly, "I believe I will retire now."

Chapter 8

Elena avoided Gareth as much as possible over the next few days and Elena passed much of her time with Cynan's wife, Enid, discussing everything from mundane matters to her dreaded fiancée. As she talked with Enid, she discovered that more and more of the Welsh she had learned as a child came back to her.

"I am amazed how quickly you've learned our language," Enid said ten days after Elena and Gareth had arrived at Eyri Keep.

Elena laughed and put down her embroidery. "I told you, I used to visit south Wales with my parents every summer when I was a child."

"I know, but 'twas a long time ago. Surely you could not remember all you learned. Most English--" Enid laughed--"and Normans and French, and everyone else, think that Welsh is a horribly complicated language to learn and complain most bitterly about it. They say they cannot keep straight our pronunciations or words."

"'Tis no different than keeping household lines straight, I think. For some reason I can keep straight the lineages of most royal families. I just see this neat order in my mind of who married whom and the children they had. 'Tis the same for me for languages. I just seem to see the language in my mind. It becomes quite easy after that."

"You can read, then, can you?"

"I can. As an only child I quickly found I could bend my father's will to nearly anything I wanted. I decided I wanted to learn to read when I was six and he was unable to refuse."

"'Tis amazing. I think Cynan would give me most anything I asked, but he would draw the line at teaching me things like reading or politics." Over Elena's shoulder, Enid saw Gareth enter the room.

"I suppose I am a bit spoiled as a result of my father's indulgence," Elena explained, unaware anyone but Enid was listening, "but what else have women to look forward to? I'll not accept being told what to do and where to go. If that makes me spoiled and spiteful, so be it," she finished with a shrug.

"Don't let Earl Brackley, hear you talking so," said Gareth with a laugh as he crossed the room and leaned against the empty fireplace. "He'll be calling off the wedding if he finds out you're not as sweet and biddable as you look. He'll--" Gareth froze at Elena's expression. It had been days since she'd thought of the crude earl...her fiancée. Caught off guard as she was, she was unable to school her features into careful nonchalance and she felt her eyes widen, physically felt the blood drain from her cheeks.

As she stared at Gareth, she saw him chew his upper lip, watched his brows draw together as he realized that his teasing comment had been a terrible reminder. He glanced to Enid for help, but she was glaring at him, undoubtedly cursing him for his stupidity. Despite the jolt his words had caused her, Elena felt a small smile curve her lips at Enid's scowl and Gareth's obvious worry. Clearly hoping to distract Elena from his faux pas, he said, "I've come to ask if you ladies would care to go for a ride. 'Tis a beautiful day and the mountains are full of wildflowers."

"I've got to finish this tunic before Morgan travels to Aberystwyth next week. But do take Elena. 'Tis not right that we work our guest so. Look at the beautiful stitching she has done on the cuffs."

Gareth complimented Elena's handiwork as he took her limp hand in his and pulled her to her feet. "You could definitely use some fresh air," he said.

Once they were outside on horses, Elena turned to Gareth and said, "I must get back to England as soon as possible. I cannot marry that man! I have to convince King Richard of that fact. But everyday I am away from court is one more day preparations will be made!"

"Perhaps you should stay away from Richard's court indefinitely. He's had no word from you since the attack on the journey to Nottingham. Perhaps he'll think you're dead and the fat earl will marry someone else."

"And what will I do instead? Live in an isolated Welsh keep wearing borrowed gowns? I think not."

"There are worse things that could happen," Gareth said tightly, refusing to meet her gaze.

"No, I must return to Richard's court."

"If there is a court to return to," Gareth said in Welsh.

"Why would there not be?" Elena asked, also in Welsh.

"Since when do you speak our language?"

"Since I was a child. Enid has been refreshing my memory."

"Did you not think it something you should mention before now?"

Gareth bit his lip and Elena knew he thought of all the conversations Elena had heard at dinner between he and his father concerning Henry Tudor.

"I only remembered a few words until Enid and I began talking. It didn't seem important," she lied, though she was not sure why.

Suddenly loathe to turn his thoughts to worrisome matters of state on such a beautiful day, she cast about for a topic that might distract him.

"What of your mother?" she asked.

"My mother?"

"Yes. Where is she?"

"She died giving birth to me."

Elena frowned. That news was given to expectant fathers near as much as "'Tis a healthy boy," or "You've a beautiful girl."

"I'm sorry," she said.

"'Twas quite a while ago. I've had a few years to get over it," he joked lamely.

They did not speak for several minutes as their horses climbed to a peak overlooking the shallow valley in which Eyri Keep lay. Sheep dotted the green fields around the keep and the air was filled with the sweet smell of evergreen trees and sun-warmed grass. Though it was high summer, the tallest peaks to the north were still capped with snow as white as the clouds which dotted the crisp, brilliant blue sky. The valley below was lush with hundreds of shades of green from the palest yellow green of the birch trees, to the blue green of spruce and the deepest emerald of the mosses and ferns. At the mouth of the valley, rippling fields of wheat rippled in the balmy breeze that came off the foothills.

Elena felt Gareth's gaze on her. She turned as he asked, "What are you thinking?"

"Wales is a strange place," she answered without thinking.

"What do you mean?" he asked his voice sharpening in defensiveness.

"It affects me strangely. I've never really cared about my surroundings but now I can't stand to be inside for more than a few hours. I have to come outside and just look. It's like..." Her voice faded and she shrugged. "I can't explain it."

"We call it *Cymrectod.*"

Elena searched her mind for that word. "I don't know what that means."

"It is the intense feeling all Welsh have for this land. Are you sure you have no Welsh relatives? Perhaps you are *Cymraes,* after all."

"A Welshwoman? No. I am English."

"English by birth, perhaps, but Welsh by spirit."

"How you do talk in riddles," she said with edginess in her voice. She did in fact have a grandmother who was Welsh--the reason she and her family had visited south Wales for five summers as a child. But being Welsh was not something to boast of in Richard's court and Elena had carefully forgotten her Welsh grandmother. Nudging her horse, she led the way up the narrow path that zig-zagged up the mountain. Nearly an hour later, they reached a wide plateau at the peak. Gareth dismounted and helped Elena down. He quickly removed the horses' saddles and let them graze freely.

"Shouldn't you tether them?" Elena asked.

"Isrid will not go anywhere and the other horse is too timid to go anywhere alone. She will stay with Isrid."

Elena nodded as she raised her arms over her head and stretched. The sun was warm on her face, but a cool breeze kept it from becoming hot. She closed her eyes and took several deep breaths of the invigorating air. This is heavenly, she thought. I wish I could just live on this mountain and sleep outside under the stars. Elena opened her eyes and dropped her arms abruptly. Where on earth had that thought come from, she wondered. What of her comfortable chamber at Eyri Keep? What of the glittering beauty of Richard's court with men and women alike bedecked in rich velvets and satins, jewels on every finger, entwined in ladies' hair? Music playing softly, candles glowing. Turning to watch Gareth as he climbed atop a huge boulder, she thought, perhaps my Welsh blood is awakening. The idea was vaguely disconcerting. She did not wish to examine the feeling too deeply.

Seeking to distract herself, she called him. "Gareth?"

Gareth smiled down at her from his perch on the boulder where he had been reveling in the peace of the day. She realized she had never called him by his given name, had, in fact, avoided calling him anything at all. "Hmm?"

"Why do you support the Earl of Richmond's claim to England?"

Gareth's smile faded. He jumped down from the rock and approached her.

"Have you ever heard of Llewelyn ab Iorweth or Owain Glyn Dwr?"

Elena frowned in concentration. "They were rebels, were they not?"

Gareth rolled his eyes and sighed. "That is the English version of history, I am sure. They were Welsh princes who both sought to free Wales from foreign rule. Llewelyn in the early thirteenth century, Owain in the fourteenth. Since the days of the Norman Conqueror, William the Bastard, there is scarce a Welshman alive who does not dream of a free Wales."

"What has this to do with Richmond? Surely you can't think he would give up Wales simply because you would help him gain the throne?"

"Of course not. I said we dream of a free Wales. But besides being dreamers, we Welsh are practical. We've not the arms or soldiers to fight off England again. But since we cannot be free of England, the next best thing is to have a Welsh king on the throne. Henry Tudor is Welsh and we would have him rule us rather than Richard of York."

Elena pictured the line of Edward III's descendants as she had described to Enid. Richmond was only distantly related to the Lancasters through a succession of marriages, his mother being great granddaughter to John of Gaunt, earl of Lancaster. "His claim to the throne is shaky."

"And Richard's is not?"

Elena ran through the English line again. "He can claim relation to Lionel, Edward III's second son, as well as the Yorks."

"Henry Tudor is still Welsh."

"And that's all that matters to you?"

"It is the most important quality of many. He is our *mab darogan*--our son of prophecy. And he has sent a letter to those who support him here in Wales assuring us that he will right the wrongs Richard has caused the Welsh. My father showed me this letter and it has decided me."

Elena opened her mouth to defend Richard, but quickly shut it again. There were too many arguments against King Richard, not the least of which was the suspicion of his part in his nephew's deaths. "Is that why you only refer to him by his Welsh last name instead of his English title, Earl of Richmond?"

"I suppose so," Gareth answered slowly. Changing the subject, he said, "I wasn't aware that Richard had begun tutoring the ladies of his court. I have met few English women who were so interested in politics. How came you to be familiar with the affairs surrounding the crown of England?"

"I'm actually not the least bit interested in any of it. I simply have this annoying ability to remember in detail little bits of history I've picked up since I was a child. I guess my father thought it amusing that his six-year-old daughter could rattle off the dates of every King of England's reign."

"And you're not the least bit interested, eh?"

Elena smiled in spite of herself. "Well perhaps, just a little interested. But only because it's such a forbidden topic for women to discuss."

Gareth laughed. "And is the forbidden fruit that much sweeter?"

"Not really. As I've discovered, politics can be dreadfully boring. Now planning a new dress, that is interesting."

Gareth laughed again. Suddenly he leaned over and kissed her. For a brief moment she leaned into the kiss and her lips opened softly. The next instant she pulled back abruptly.

"I told you once not to do that to me," she said forcefully.

"Ah yes, I forgot," he said, his voice brusque with anger. "A mere Welsh knight should not reach so above himself as to kiss the future wife of so threatening a man as the earl of Brackley. Heaven knows who he'd blame or what his punishment would be. Thank you for reminding me." Turning abruptly, he quickly gathered their horses. Elena remained rooted in the same spot, staring at an eagle as it circled the sky. After a few moments, he fetched their horses and lifted her to the saddle.

While the ride up had been accompanied by a comfortable, friendly silence, the trip back down the mountain might have been that of a condemned man's march to his execution.

Elena sat limply in the saddle, once again thinking of her fiancée, though in truth, her fear of her betrothed's fists occupied her thoughts for a short time only. The majority of the return trip, her mind was plagued with thoughts of Gareth. Though she'd pushed him away two times, her lips had burned for his kisses. But how could this be? she asked herself.

He was the exact opposite of everything she looked for in a man. She doubted he had not a sheep to his name, much less property or a title. Years before when she had accompanied her mother to Edward IV's court, she had been amazed at the beauty of a formal court.

The elegant men and women, the beautiful clothes, the courtly manners. In particular, she was taken with a beautiful woman with rich brown hair and sparkling jewels. Elena never learned who she was, but for two days, she watched as the woman enchanted every man in Edward's court. Elena saw her receive a ruby ring, a handkerchief of fine Venetian linen, a precious crystal bottle of cologne, and more attention than anyone else.

Still a child, Elena had decided that she would someday lead that very life. She wanted the prestige, the glamour. An only child, she had never lacked for attention, but doting parents could hardly compare to gallant lords.

Now she was dreadfully confused. Gareth was none of these things, could give her none of these things. Why, then, did her mind constantly replay their kiss of the night they had escaped the mercenaries? Why did she wake up in the morning with her face pressed to a pillow, disappointed that it was not Gareth's warm throat, disappointed that the covers smelled like linen and not leather and sweat, disappointed that a rough blanket had kept her warm instead of his arms? Nothing could come of it. Nothing should come of it, she told herself sharply, but Elena could still not get him out of her mind.

When they returned, the small bailey of the keep was full of people. Women were chattering, children were running about screaming and laughing while a motley assortment of hounds chased them, and men were talking animatedly.

"What's going on?" Elena asked, breaking their strained silence for the first time since the mountaintop.

Gareth stood up in his stirrups to get a better view. "'Tis my kinsmen Owain and Rhys! They live on Anglesey. Seems they've come for a visit and brought three large deer with them. There will be fresh venison tonight," he said with a laugh. Quickly dismounting, he waded through the throng of people. Elena leaned sideways to see him heartily embracing his cousins. She was about to try to slide off her horse when she heard Gareth cry "Elen!" She sought him out, only to see him enthusiastically kissing a woman with the blackest hair Elena had ever seen. Seething jealousy poured unexpectedly through Elena's veins. Had he called for her so she could see this vulgar display? Twisting in the saddle, she lowered herself ungracefully to the ground and stalked toward the main door.

She had just reached the lower step when someone touched her elbow. Turning Elena looked up into deep blue eyes heavily fringed with thick black lashes that matched the shock of silky hair and trim beard of one of the handsomest men she had ever seen.

"Hello. What have we here, Gareth?" the man said in a deep voice tinged with humor.

Gareth's good humor seemed to evaporate as he stiffly obliged with introductions. "Rhys, may I present the Lady Elena de Vignon a visitor from England. Lady Elena, my cousin, Rhys Thomas, and his brother, Owain."

Elena smiled beguilingly when Rhys bent low over her hand and murmured, "I am enchanted, my lady. May I say how fortunate Wales is to have you in its borders." Rhys's older brother, Owain, simply nodded a brief greeting before turning back to his conversation with Morgan. Gareth was aware that Rhys had not relinquished her hand as he turned and pulled the dark-haired woman forward. "Lady Elena, this is my sister Elen. Amazing is it not that two such beautifully different women should share such a similar name?"

The black hair and blue eyes which were so striking on Rhys were equally attractive on his sister who was looking at her brother with a look of mock disgust. Turning to Elena she smiled. "Please forgive my brother, Lady Elena, I fear the sun has been too much for him and his brain is a bit addled." Elena appeared to be translating the rapid Welsh in her head. As soon as she did, she realized that Elen was joking.

With a laugh, she said, "Would that more Englishmen were as addled!"

Everyone but Gareth laughed. Taking Elen's arm, he said, "You're not married yet, are you Elen? You've not forgotten you vowed to wed me should I remain single by my twenty-fifth year. As I recall, that should be coming up in a few months, is that not right, father?" Laughing, he and Elen entered the main hall behind Morgan.

***

The feast was a merry one, rivaling that of the night of Gareth's return. Musicians played rollicking dances, wine and ale flowed freely, and Elena was reveling in the attention paid by the handsome Rhys. In spite of herself, she also found she truly like Rhys's sister Elen. Though they had spent little time talking, Elena felt a kinship for the Welshwoman she had scarce felt for any of her friends in Richard's court.

As she waited for Rhys to bring her a goblet of spiced wine, Elena let her eyes roam around the crowded hall. When she spotted Gareth whispering in Elen's ear she frowned. The man was making a fool of himself, she thought. In their few minutes of conversation, Elen had told her that she was hoping to wed a man from Beaumaris in Anglesey. Now Gareth was undoubtedly annoying the poor woman and acting, Elena felt, most unchivalrously toward a nearly betrothed woman. That she could think of nothing but the "unchivalrous" way he had acted towards her, a legally betrothed woman did not strike her as odd. When Rhys returned and presented the goblet with a flourish, Elena could not help but asking, "Should we rescue your sister? She looks to be tediously bored with Sir Gareth's attention." At Rhys's enigmatic smile, she hurriedly added, "Having been subjected to conversation with him, I can well sympathize."

"Then by all means," he said, and Elena could not but wonder if he weren't silently laughing at her, "let us go and save my dear sister. Although I must warn you, she may not wish to be saved. She's near an accomplished flirt as I am." Taking Elena's arm, he led her towards Gareth and Elen.

Elena immediately felt foolish. "Oh. Then perhaps we'd best leave them be. Shall we dance?"

"No, no. It will be most entertaining, I assure you, to further annoy Gareth."

Elena was prevented from arguing as they approached the couple and Rhys said, "You're not saying anything that would force me to defend my sister's honor, are you good cousin?"

Gareth's eyes strayed to Elena who quickly lowered her eyes and feigned absorption in pushing back the cuticle of her left thumb. "Not that you're half man enough to take me on," he said with a laugh, "but no, I'm merely trying to convince your sister she'd be miserable married to old Dylan ap Gruffydd. Don't you think she should stay here and marry me?"

"Now wait a moment," Elen protested in mock indignation. "Dylan is not old, he's mature. Perhaps if you weren't such a whelp yourself, I'd be inclined to consider your offer. As it is, I'm afraid you're just no match for Dylan." Elen shook her head and put on a sickeningly sweet dreamy face. Elena could not help joining in the men's laughter at Elen's theatrics.

When he caught his breath, Rhys said to Gareth, "Perhaps I'll have more luck convincing the same of Lady Elena." He cocked an eyebrow at Elena and said, "What say you, my lady? Care for a life of adventure?"

Elena laughed and was about to respond with an equally flirtations answer when Gareth cut her off.

"Sorry, Rhys, you've neither wealth nor a title to woo her with. The Lady Elena is already engaged to a rich English earl."

While Rhys pretended to be crushed, staggering about clutching his heart, Elena glared at Gareth and prayed more fervently than she ever had that he would drop dead on the spot. Gareth returned her scowl

Elen watched Elena and Gareth speculatively. "Rhys!" she called trying to distract him from his antics. "Why don't you console your breaking heart by dancing with Elena."

"Very well. If that is the most I can--" at the pointed look from his sister, he shut up and gently took Elena's arm.

Chapter 9

When they were gone, Elen stared at Gareth, awaiting an explanation. When none was forthcoming, she prodded, "Well, aren't you going to explain that little display of temper?"

Although he and Elen had been friends since they were children, the one trait Elen had that never ceased to annoy Gareth was her ability to sound like a nosy mother hen. She was doing that exact impression now.

"What display of temper?" Gareth asked, feigning ignorance.

"You're quite taken with her. It's written all over your face."

"What? Don't be ridiculous, Elen," Gareth started to turn away but Elen caught his shoulder.

"You are! You're in love with her, admit it."

Gareth ground his teeth in anger. Lowering his voice, he said crudely, "The only thing I'm taken with is her body. I find it quite irresistible. But since I'm sure she would like to go to her marriage bed with her maidenhead intact, I guess I'll just have to--" Elen's slap prevented any further words.

Her blue eyes flashing with anger, Elen said, "I can still thrash you, Gareth ap Morgan. Don't think I can't. And after what you just said, you soundly deserve it." Elen took a deep breath and stared at Gareth's flushed face. "But since I also know that in your heart you didn't mean it, I'll pretend you didn't say it." She turned to leave but paused. "Just don't treat her so again, Gareth. It does you no honor."

Gareth watched Elen approach Elena and speak with her for a few moments. The two women then turned and went up the stairs. Gareth took a big swallow of ale.

Where had Elen come up with the insane notion that he was in love with Elena? He could barely tolerate her presence; she was always whining about her clothes, the quality of the food, the hardness of her saddle...Gareth paused. Now that he thought of it, he could not recall Elena complaining once since they reached Eyri Keep. And if he was truthful with himself, he had enjoyed her company today until he had tried to kiss her. Gareth cringed inwardly as he relived Elena's outraged rebuffs. Would he never learn? he thought.

Taken by her angelic looks and occasional good humor, could he never remember that she was a spiteful, self-centered woman who considered him nothing more than a lackey? That she haunted his dreams nightly; that he could not get her scent out of his mind; that his lips were forever remembering the softness of hers simply meant that he had been too long without a woman--a situation he could and would easily rectify.

And when his father left for Aberystwyth the following week to meet with Henry's supporters, he would take a short detour to drop Elena at the abbey at Dinas Mawddwy and then rejoin his father at the meeting of Welsh lords. She would be safe there and he would be able to get her out of his mind once and for all!

As he reviewed his plan with a self-satisfied smirk, a small voice niggled the back of his brain. Though he tried to ignore it, he could not help but hear its cry that though Elena might not always act a lady, his own actions were not above reproach. Gareth shook his head in confusion as he remembered cruel taunts and boorish behavior. Never had he acted so towards a lady of rank. Towards any lady, for that matter. He had always extended his knightly vows of chivalry and courtesy to all women, servant and noble alike. Why now was he treating Elena so rudely? Could his cousin Elen be right? Was he in love with the Englishwoman? If so, how could that be?

"Now that is a face of a man with an empty ale pot!"

Gareth looked up and smiled as his father joined him at the table. Glancing in his mug, he realized it was indeed empty. Thankful for the excuse, he waggled the mug at his father. "Two years I've been gone and I can't get another pint?"

"Well if we're celebrating your being home, we shouldn't drink this swill," Morgan said, pushing his own mug away. Gesturing for a servant, he asked for something Gareth couldn't quite hear before turning back to his son.

"What think you of the new fields we've plowed? I'm thinking the drainage will be better for the barley."

Gareth grinned. There was nothing more important to his father than the land and even with a possible war on the horizon, his crops would always take precedence in Morgan's life. "They look well thought out. I'd wager you can't wait for colder weather to plant."

Morgan chuckled. "All in good time, all in good time."

The servant arrived with a bottle of golden liquid and two clean mugs.

"Don't say you're going to share your mead with me. You only ever save that important guests."

"And who's more important than my prodigal son, I say?" his father asked as he carefully peeled the wax from the cork and opened the bottle. The fragrant scent of honey reached Gareth's nose as his father poured a generous mugful. He had only ever had his father's rather famous mead twice before—and those on momentous occasions such as funerals or grand assemblies. He let the fumes fill his nose before taking a sip. The mead was smooth and rich, slipping past his tongue sensuously. The bite of liquor came after he swallowed, letting him know that if he drank more than a cup or two, he might find himself waking up under a table or in some maid's bed. He took another sip and considered the second option would not be so bad, especially as it would help distract his mind from Elena.

His father spent several minutes inspecting the color of his wine, assessing its bouquet and rolling it about on his tongue before declaring, "Not a bad batch, if I do say so myself."

Morgan went on to bring Gareth up to date on the changes he'd make to the breeding stock, the walls he'd had repaired around the fields and any number of other groundskeeping details he could remember (and he remembered them all). Gareth knew it was pointless to remind his father that he had chosen his path as a knight, not a land steward.

Morgan believed that once Gareth had exorcised his obsession with "swordplay and jousts," he would return to his birthright as a minor Welsh lord. In truth, Gareth knew he could not spend all of his days as another man's knight—the body could only withstand so many years of that abuse. He just anticipated that his permanent return to Eyri Keep would be much further off than Morgan was counting on.

By the time Gareth reached the bottom of his mug, his head was pleasantly fuzzy and his father was just finishing his description of the last quarter's Rent Day.

"How did you and Mother meet?" Gareth had no idea where the question had come from. The last sip of mead, he suspected.

Morgan stopped speaking abruptly, glancing at his son in surprise. "Where on God's earth did that question come from?"

Gareth felt his neck warm. He affected a nonchalant shrug. "Just curious. I don't think I ever heard you say."

Morgan took a deep pull of his mead and stared off into the distance, a wry grin on his face. "We knew each other since we were young. She lived just the other side of yon hill," he said with a jerk of his chin to the north.

Gareth nodded his head. Of course, they'd known each other for years. Probably grew up loving each other and knowing what their future held.

"Hated me on first sight, she did."

"What?" Gareth asked.

Morgan smiled and refilled both their mugs. "Yes. Found me insufferable, I don't doubt. I was very full of myself, especially as I became a young man. I was convinced I was the best thing to happen to Eyri Keep and the lucky ladies of Wales. She, of course, would have nothing to do with such a conceited ass. At first, it didn't bother me for there were so many other accommodating lasses about, you know?"

Gareth smiled and shook his head in mock reproach.

"But after a while, it irked me that she didn't think I was as wonderful as I thought I was. I decided to change her mind."

"Won her over, did you?"

"Tcha! No. She hated me even worse then. Told me she wouldn't have aught to do with me were I the last man in Wales. Two years her abuse went on. Why, she even went and betrothed herself to another man!"

"Truly?" Gareth was amazed. He'd never heard the story and was a little ashamed that it never occurred to him to ask.

"As true as I'm sitting here. Of course, by that time, I was head over heels for her. And it wasn't just because she wouldn't have me. She was a fine young woman. Beautiful, of course, but smart as a whip, too. She could manage people sweet as you please. She had the skills of a healer from her grandmother, and the cunning of a general. Why this one time—ah, but that's a story for another time."

Gareth was about to protest that he wanted to hear it, but curiosity at how his father turned his mother from enemy to ally was all-consuming.

"So how did you sway her?"

"Humbled myself. Took a sack of grain and half a dozen sheep over the hill to her house. Told her they were an early wedding present. She thanked me but I could see suspicion in her eyes. So, then I told her how I'd been a right stupid ass for most of my life and that she was no doubt smart to marry another man, but that I'd loved her for nigh on two years and suspected I would for another two hundred. I didn't expect her to do anything about it. Well, perhaps I did, but I pretended I was noble, at least. I finished by telling her I wished only for her complete happiness in life and that if she ever had need of me, she only needs send word and I would cross a continent to aid her."

Gareth whistled low between his teeth. "And then what happened?"

Morgan's smile turned wily and he drained his mug of mead before answering. "I heard the next week that she had ended her betrothal. When I ran into her a few months later at the Michaelmas feast, we talked as if we'd been best friends from the cradle. We were wed by St. Catherine's Day."

Gareth frowned. "So, a sack of grain and some livestock changed her mind?"

Morgan slapped him on the back of his head. "A son of mine should be better able to hold his liquor. No, a few gifts did not buy your mother's affection, ye fool. But hatred and passion are both strong emotions, you see. Two sides of the same coin, if you will. In fact, sometimes they can be confused for one another. And if that's the case, it may only take one person to flip that coin, even just the once, for the passion to take over."

Gareth shook his head when his father made to refill his mug. He wanted what wits he had left to mull over his father's words.

Morgan, evidently unaffected by the potent wine, eyed his son closely. "So, be there a lass whose hatred need be flipped to passion?"

"What? No! Why would you even ask that?"

"Twenty-five years you've been my son and this is the first time you think to ask how your mother and I fell in love. Surely something has prompted such a question."

"No!" Gareth repeated defensively. "I—that is, I've thought about it before, but I haven't been home in a few years and before that…"

"Mmhmm," Morgan said, and promptly buried his nose in his mug. "Well, if you convince yourself of that long enough, you may find yourself years down the road wondering if you passed a grand passion by for fear that it was just hostility." With that, Gareth's father stood and walked a perfectly straight line to the stairs.

Gareth rested his wobbly head in his hands and told himself that his situation was nothing like his father's had been. He and Elena were from two different worlds, had completely different wants out of life. Why she—Gareth paused in mid-thought. An image of Elena, gazing at the mountains earlier today, a look of utter contentment on her face as she described how being in Wales made her feel filled his vision. He shook his head, reminding himself for the hundredth time of all the insults she had cast at him, the way she had care for only her own comfort, the plans she had for advancing herself at court.

A young serving woman walked by and smiled at him coyly. No, Gareth decided. There was a simple explanation for his malaise. And he was going to remedy the problem tonight. Setting down his mug of ale, he followed the swishing skirts of the serving woman.

Chapter 10

As Elena entered the bailey from the dim hall she squinted. This could have been the bailey of Middleham just a month ago. People were milling about, loading supplies onto packhorses and bidding farewell to family members. The only difference was that she had not cared that she was leaving Middleham and she found she was dreadfully sorry to be leaving Eyri Keep. She had felt more at home and at ease here than any other place she could remember. Spotting Enid, she started to walk towards her until Cynan grabbed his wife and kissed her passionately in front of everyone. Elena turned away, embarrassed to witness such an intimate scene--a scene that was being looked on with understanding and amused glances from everyone else. Enid had announced the night before that she was with child.

"Your horse is over here with us, my lady," Bryant said as he touched her elbow. Turning, Elena saw him staring at Cynan and Enid. When he realized she had caught him staring, he flushed. She was just about to turn in the direction he had indicated when Enid called her name.

"Here, I've packed you a few little goodies to make your travel and stay at Dinas Mawddwy more comfortable."

"Thank you, Enid. That's very kind of you." Elena could not remember ever saying that to another woman before.

"Are we ready to go?" Gareth asked.

"We were just waiting for you, you slugabed," said Cynan.

"I'll have you know I was up before the dawn this morning taking care of all the things you didn't finish yesterday," Gareth exclaimed with mock indignation.

Enid pulled Elena close and whispered in her ear, "They always tease each other the worst right before a journey. Like little boys, they are."

Elena smiled but her eyes never left Gareth. She had not seen him since the night of Rhys and Elen's arrival and she refused to believe that she had missed him, told herself she was simply curious as to where he had kept himself through meals, games of charades, dancing, and picnics Elena had enjoyed with the others.

Gareth turned to help Elena mount her horse when a blond woman dressed in servant's garb threw herself into his arms.

"You didn't say goodbye when you left me this morning," the woman said huskily.

Gareth looked extremely uncomfortable. "Yes, well, goodbye Senena," he said as he patted her back, trying to avoid Elena's stare.

"Here's something to remember me by on your travels." Grabbing his jaw, Senena tilted Gareth's head and kissed him soundly.

Amazed by the woman's audacity, Elena turned to look at Cynan and Bryant's reactions. Cynan was laughing with Enid in between kisses of his own. Bryant took one look at Elena, blushed, and began intently studying the toe of his boot as it scuffed at the dirt of the bailey. Gareth struggled out of Senena's goodbye kiss as Rhys strode up and bowed low to Elena.

"It grieves me to be unable to escort you to your journey's end, my lady. I hope it will not be long ere you visit Wales again."

Gareth had turned to Elena and was gesturing impatiently for her to mount her horse. Pointedly ignoring him, Elena leaned up on tiptoe and said, "Here is something for you to remember me by until we do meet again," and kissed him full on the mouth. When Rhys moved to embrace her further, she quickly turned and climbed upon her horse unaided, despite the fact that her hands were shaking and her knees felt wobbly. Never had she been so bold with a man. And in public, no less! But the greatest emotion she felt was disappointment. Though brief, Rhys's kiss had left her cold, left her wanting...

"Gareth!" Morgan shouted. "We will meet you at Aberystwyth in one week's time. Agreed?"

Gareth tore his eyes from Elena's flushed face and looked across the bailey to where his father was already mounted. "Agreed. Godspeed!"

"And to you, my son."

"Take care of this English jewel, Gareth. I would be sore disappointed if she came to harm," Rhys said.

Gareth bestowed a sour smile on his cousin's retreating back before mounting his own horse. Bryant quickly followed suit, but Cynan and Enid were laughing so hard they had to hold each other up.

"Perhaps you had best stay here, Cynan. You seem to have caught some disease which renders you incapable of controlling your mirth," Gareth said acidly. Cynan paid no attention to him but kissed his wife once more and sprang onto his own horse.

Enid approached Elena and wiping tears of mirth from her face said, "You are a jewel indeed, Elena. Please come and visit us again. I feel sure you could teach us a trick or two."

Elena forgot her mortification enough to smile at the Welshwoman. "I would enjoy that," she said, and meant it.

"Godspeed, my lady."

"Goodbye Enid." Nudging her horse, Elena followed Bryant who sought to keep up with Gareth's galloping steed.

***

They kept up the grueling pace for three quarters of an hour until Cynan, his mirth long since dissipated, caught up to Gareth and yelled, "The horses cannot keep up this pace! We must let them rest!"

Gareth nodded grimly, angry with himself for not slowing earlier. They finally stopped near a stream and let the horses drink.

"Be there any demons chasing us Bryant and I don't know about?" Cynan asked Gareth who was standing upstream of the horses staring into the thick forest that surrounded them.

Turning to his friend with an apologetic smile Gareth said, "I'm just anxious to get this task over and done with so we can get to Aberystwyth quickly."

"Are you that committed to Henry Tudor's cause then?"

"You aren't?"

"I'm not speaking of my conviction. I've known for two years that I would support the Welshman's claim to the English throne over Richard of York's. You only decided two weeks ago to join us."

Gareth knew his friend was trying to help, but the last thing Gareth needed to be reminded of was that he was breaking his knightly vows less than a year after taking them.

"I'm committed to it. Two weeks or two years, Henry Tudor is the better man to wear the crown."

Cynan studied his friend and then looked over his shoulder to where Elena was seated with Bryant on a large rock. She was plaiting her hair, which the sun had turned to a glittering tumble of copper and Bryant was shyly watching her from beneath his lashes. Turning back to Gareth, he lowered his voice. "Perhaps you're not so anxious to give her up as you would have us think."

Gareth frowned. "What? Who--oh, her I don't know what you are talking about. I can't wait to get her out of our hair. She's a self-absorbed, whining--"

Cynan broke in. "Beautiful woman who--"

"Enough, Cynan. If this is what being married has done to you, turned you into a gossipy meddling old woman, then the day will come when I'll fall on my own sword before vowing 'I will.'"

Since they were children, Cynan had taken no greater joy than in teasing Gareth. But the true strength of their friendship rested in the fact that Cynan knew when to quit. Abruptly changing subjects, he said, "If this good weather holds, we should be able to reach Dinas Mawddwy in what? Four days?"

Gareth silently thanked his friend. "Yes," he said nodding.

"Perhaps we'd better get moving again before the horses drink so much they slosh when they walk!"

Gareth grinned at his friend, feeling much less tense than he had since Elena had kissed Rhys in the bailey. Tightening Isrid's girth strap, Gareth mounted and swung his horse back onto the road. They kept up a brisk pace until dusk when they stopped in an empty cottage.

"What is this place?" Elena asked as Bryant helped her down from her saddle.

"It's called a *hafod.* Herdsmen usually stay here during the summer while their sheep or cattle are grazing in the fields over that hill there," Bryant answered, gesturing west. "But this summer has been unusually dry and a few weeks ago a fire swept through the paddock. The men who were staying here barely got their cattle out in time and they've not been back since. It's rather crude," he said apologetically as he ushered Elena inside. "But at least you won't have to sleep on the ground tonight."

Gareth bought his saddle bags into the small shelter and glanced at the bed Bryant indicated. Thick ropes were laced back and forth across the rough frame which itself was only six or seven inches off the ground. Sitting on the low bed, Elena flopped back onto the ropes. It was surprisingly comfortable for being so crude, she thought as she stretched her arms above her head. With a chuckle, Bryant ducked out the door.

"The least you could do is help Bryant unload the horses," Gareth said curtly.

Elena turned her head until she could see Gareth standing in the doorway. When she remained silent, he said, "He's out there unloading the things from your horse. The least you could do is help him before you lounge about and wait for somebody to serve you."

"You have the sourest disposition of any man I've ever known," she said as she pushed herself up. Since Gareth was still standing in the doorway, she could not help but brush against him as she went outside.

"If that's so, it's because you are the most exasperating woman I've ever known," he replied wearily.

Elena turned back around. "Now how can you say that? I've been a model of uncomplaining sweetness for weeks now." She turned and disappeared into the hazy twilight. Gareth heard her laughing at something Bryant must have said. He rubbed the tense muscles in his neck and mentally cursed his quick temper with Elena; she truly had been a model traveling companion today. Simply because he had been unable to keep her and their one kiss out of his mind while she obviously felt nothing in return was no reason for him to treat her so unchivalrously. She clearly preferred men like his cousin Rhys.

Gareth flung his pack down and stomped outside. He clenched his teeth as he thought of Elena kissing his cousin. What had transpired between them during the past week? Rhys was nothing more than a flirt, could Elena not see that? Gareth turned to start a fire in front of the hut and paused. Perhaps Elena was fully aware that his cousin had no serious intentions. Perhaps she was only seeking what respite she could before marriage to the cruel Brackley. If that was the case, Gareth could not blame her if she kissed every man from here to London. And yet, why was she so put off when he tried to kiss her a second time?

That first kiss they had shared after escaping the mercenaries had literally stolen his breath with its intensity, its passion, its sheer *rightness.* Had Elena not felt the same? He shook his head in confusion. The day he understood Elena de Vignon would be the day he was made King of England.

***

The two-day trip passed uneventfully, if too quickly for Elena. Though her muscles were already screaming for relief from the constant jarring of riding, her mind dreaded the conclusion of the trip. The abbey was one step closer to England, one step closer to the Earl of Brackley. Though she should be anxious to return to Richard's court so she could perhaps talk him out of the betrothal, she felt only dread. As they rode into the walled-in yard surrounding the abbey at Dinas Mawddwy in the late afternoon of the third day from Eyri Keep, Elena reined in her horse to take one last look at the soaring peaks of the Cambrian mountains. Though she would see them again, it would be as an Englishwoman going to meet her fiancée, not as a temporary Welshwoman who danced to bawdy country tunes.

"Elena?" Gareth asked from inside the bailey.

With a sigh, Elena turned her mount and nudged hit toward the gate. As she passed under, the wall's imposing shadow fell across her and, Elena thought, across her future.

Gareth saw Elena shudder and asked, "What is it?"

The eyes she turned on him were wide with fear and Gareth's hand fell to his sword hilt as he stood in his stirrups to look behind her. There was nothing on the empty dirt road they had just traveled and Gareth sat back down. "Are you alright?" he asked with more gentleness than he had shown her for days.

Elena nodded and started to dismount. Gareth quickly jumped down from Isrid and hurried over to help her. She could feel the concern in his gaze and resisted the urge to turn her face into his shoulder and weep out her fears and confusion. His shoulders were well muscled and looked as though they could easily bear her concerns.

"My thanks," Elena was all she allowed herself to say.

"Had I known you would be so subdued around an abbey, I would have brought you by one weeks ago," Gareth responded with a laugh.

Reminded that he was eager to be rid of her, Elena forced her desire for him to a distant corner of her heart and took refuge in anger. "Has the sun addled your brain? I was merely enjoying the pleasant quietness of the evening until you began talking."

The smile on Gareth's face faded at her sharp tone of voice. "Pray forgive me," he said sarcastically. "I attributed your paleness to discomfort. I stupidly forgot that you have been a month without the rouging powders you Englishwomen are forced to resort to enhance the complexion."

Elena leveled her most withering glare at Gareth but he seemed immune to it as he turned and greeted the abbess who was making her way towards them.

"Your companions inform me that you have an Englishwoman seeking refuge?" The dour-faced woman said in Welsh.

"That is correct, Reverend Mother," Gareth said meekly. Elena would have laughed at his expression—that of a naughty lad trying to appear good—were she not still angry with him.

"From what is she seeking refuge?"

"She was separated from King Richard's retinue in an attack several weeks ago and she merely wishes to remain in your safe keeping until an escort can be arranged to return her to England."

"That could be months!" the abbess declared.

"Yes, Reverend Mother, I realize that. You see, it would be best if it took several months as Lady Elena is well aware of our plans to aid Henry Tudor gain the throne. If Richard found out what she knew, he may assume she was a willing conspirator."

"You seek the overthrow of our sovereign, then?"

Out of the corner of her eye, Elena watched Gareth and though he didn't show it, she felt sure he was panicked. She had heard his father assure him that this abbey was sympathetic to Henry's cause, but she was gaining the distinct impression that this abbess was as loyal to Richard as an English nun. "We seek only a Welsh ruler for Wales, madam."

The abbess stared at him through narrowed eyes before asking, "Does she have any luggage?" When Gareth shook his head, she continued, "She'll have to wear a habit. We cannot have her wandering about in unnecessary finery. Bring her in."

Elena stared at the woman's retreating back in amazement. Turning to Gareth, she raised her eyebrows.

"At least you'll be safe here," he said defensively. "And you can return to England as soon as she is able to arrange a safe escort."

"Yes, in several months! I can't stay in an abbey for months! Especially not with old Mother Doom."

"Elena, hush! There is no where else I can take you that can ensure any hope of seeing you home safely. Will you please try to behave?"

"I am not a child, Sir Gareth. I need not be told how to act," Elena said as coldly and regally as she could. But despite her carefully constructed haughty demeanor, she was loathe to have Gareth and his friends leave. Turning, she reluctantly followed the abbess into the dim stone building.

***

Within the hour, the men were ready to depart.

"I'm sure we can find lodging in the town if you require," the dour abbess said.

"That won't be necessary, Reverend Mother," said Gareth. "We would like to get a few more miles down the road before nightfall. We must reach Aberystwyth within three days and we dare not tarry."

The abbess pressed her lips into a thin line. "Very well."

Gareth waited for her blessing. When none was coming, he glanced at his friends and then cleared his throat. "May we have your blessing, Reverend

Mother?"

The abbess hesitated a brief moment. "Go with God."

Gareth nodded at her. Turning his horse in a tight circle, he spurred it into a gallop, Cynan's and Bryant's mounts close behind.

"She's an old dragon," Cyan remarked several miles down the road when Gareth finally slowed his horse.

"Though I may burn in hell for saying so, I agree with you," Gareth said wryly.

Bryant looked worriedly over his shoulder. "Are you sure we should have left Lady Elena there? They seem none too friendly."

"The Lady Elena can well handle even the sternest of nuns. She has the tongue of an adder and a backbone of steel."

When Bryant looked unconvinced, Cynan said, "Perhaps after Aberystwyth we could come back by here and check on her."

Bryant's frown eased. "Mayhap we should take her back to Eyri Keep as well. Surely she's as safe there as in an abbey."

Though Gareth refused to name the emotion that made his blood boil at Bryant's suggestion, jealousy made him say, "Need I remind you, Bryant, that Lady Elena is engaged to be married?" He was about to say more, but the crimson flush that crept up Bryant's face made him bite his tongue. Thank God that woman was out of his hair! he thought. Perhaps now he could concentrate on the importance of Henry Tudor's cause instead of forever wondering at Elena's relationship with his friends and family.

As he urged his horse back into a gallop, he missed Cynan's comforting pat on Bryant's shoulder that accompanied his knowing grin.

Chapter 11

"Captain, you must gather your men at once. The rebels are to gather at Aberystwyth in less than a week. You haven't a moment to spare," the abbess insisted.

Sitting on a hard stool by the fire, Elena started. Did the abbess not remember she was here? The abbess was speaking to a rough looking man who reminded Elena more of the mercenaries she and Gareth had encountered rather than a captain of the king. Trying to remain as still as possible, she concentrated on the rapid Welsh.

"They were here not two hours ago to drop this *ynfyd plentyn* off. They told me their plans and expected me to bless their journey."

Ynfyd plentyn, Elena racked her brain for a translation. The abbess had such a strange accent, quite unlike any of Gareth's friends or family. Stupid child? Elena sat up straight. She was just about to tell the abbess exactly what she thought of her hospitality when a realization struck her. The old crow must not realize I understand Welsh, Elena thought. Why else would she speak so boldly in front of me? Elena swallowed. Unless she means to kill me. Her pulse quickened and Elena thought frantically. No, that can't be it. If the abbess is turning in Gareth as a rebel, she must be for Richard and would want no harm done to one of Richard's favorites. And yet, I was traveling with those very rebels! The woman must think I don't know what she's saying. Elena willed her breathing to slow and concentrated on the captain's response.

"If I chased down every Welshman who wanted to kill the king, I'd need several thousand more men and the king's leave to slaughter every babe in it's cradle. Now if you'll excuse me, madame."

Elena dared a peek over her shoulder towards the captain's voice. Her heart froze and her breath rushed from her lungs as she recognized the face of one of the drunken men, she and Gareth had stumbled across in the fog not a week before! She turned back to the fire, willing herself into the smallest space possible that the captain might not notice her.

"You idiot. It is not three Welshmen you are chasing down. It is a meeting between Welsh leaders and Henry Tudor's closest advisors! They are meeting at Aberystwyth in three days." When the captain remained unconvinced, the abbess's eyes narrowed to mere slits as she said, "I'm sure King Richard would not be pleased to hear that one of his captains refused to prevent traitors from plotting against him. I send monthly reports to His Majesty's religious advisors and I would not hesitate to tell them of such shoddy soldiery."

The captain stared at the abbess for several seconds before saying "'Twill take me several hours to gather my men. They've been training throughout these mountains."

"Then you'd best not waste any more time here, had you?" the abbess said acidly. Without a further word, the captain stalked out of the small room.

"You must go and change. I can't have you wandering about in such clothes." So absorbed was Elena in thinking of a way to warn Gareth that she did not even realize the abbess was addressing her in English. "You there!" Elena jumped and quickly stood.

"Yes?"

"Take these clothes and change in the next room. Be sure to cover your hair with this veil."

"Is there a privy I may attend first?"

"Out back. Go and return quickly and disturb none of the sisters on your way."

"Of course not, madame," Elena said as meekly as her temper would allow. Once outside, she ducked around the main building of the abbey in the direction she had seen Bryant lead her horse. She said her own prayer of thanks that she came across no one as she crossed through the vegetable garden to the stable. As she made her way through the dimly lit stalls, a loud grunt stopped her in her tracks. She waited in agony for several seconds before continuing on. As she rounded a corner, she discovered the source of the grunt and cautiously edged her way around the sleeping stable hand who was clutching a large jug in one hand. Finally, at the far end of the stable, she found the horse she had ridden since her arrival at Eyri Keep.

The large mare raised her head at Elena's arrival but did not whinny or neigh; Welsh horses were trained for silence. "Greetings, Breila," Elena whispered as she untied the rope from the horse's bridle. "Now," she asked the horse, "dare I risk the time it would take to saddle you?" One look at Breila's back which came to Elena's nose and she knew she must have a saddle. Looking around the stall, she saw her saddle hanging on the wall. Cursing each clink and rattle of the trappings, Elena wrestled the saddle to Breila's broad back. She cinched the straps as tightly as she could and prayed she would not fall off when they reached a gallop. "If only there were another entrance to this barn," she muttered as she led Breila toward the open door.

As she was about to pass the sleeping stable hand, he snorted abruptly and sat up. When he saw Elena, he slurred, "Her grace said I wasn't to let you go anywhere."

Elena set her face into its most imperious expression and looked down her nose at the man who was trying to stand. Mustering her Welsh vocabulary, she said, "I am going for a ride. I suggest you keep your mouth shut lest I be tempted to tell the abbess what sort of drunken lout is maintaining her stables. I'm sure she would not be at all pleased with such conduct."

The man's eyes grew wide with fright and as he ducked his head he asked sheepishly, "Is there anything I can do for you while you're out riding, my lady?"

"Yes. You can try to sleep off your intoxication so you may be sober when I return." The servant obediently lay down and Elena marched resolutely to the great barn doors. Peering outside, she waited several minutes until the one nun in sight finished weeding a vegetable patch and went into one of the smaller buildings surrounding the main abbey.

Pulling Breila behind her, Elena ran for the cover of the nearby forest. Once inside the protective darkness of the trees, she struggled into the saddle and turned her mount west in the direction Gareth and his friends had taken. Keeping to the shelter of the forest, she followed the direction of the road until the encroaching darkness prevented her from seeing where she was going in the thick woods. Rather than stopping, she cautiously made her way to the road, which was faintly illumined by a sliver of the new moon.

As Breila plodded confidently on, Elena finally reflected on the consequences of her rash actions. By riding to warn Gareth that Richard's men were on his trail, she was, in effect, aligning herself with Henry Tudor, Earl of Richmond. But did she support the Welshman's claim to the throne? Never before had Elena been posed with such a question. As a woman she simply had to accept the mandates of those in power. Never before had she been given the opportunity to affect the outcome of a political gambit. It was at once a frightening and heady feeling.

Suddenly a bird screeched overhead, startling Elena and sending all thoughts of kings and causes from her mind. What had possessed her to venture unescorted into the depths of Wales? She would no doubt end up dead and deservedly so for acting so stupidly. If wild animals did not eat her, she had no doubt highway men would strike her down. Roads in England, let alone Wales, were no place for unescorted women.

If only Gareth were here, he'd--Elena stopped in mid-thought. She didn't need Gareth. Any man would do, she merely needed an escort to discourage any predators, be they man or beast, from attacking her. And yet, a small voice inside her said, she had never felt as secure and protected as she had the night she and Gareth stumbled upon the group of mercenaries. Gareth had told her to escape, giving no thought to his own safety. Elena doubted any men of her acquaintance in Richard's court would ever be so selfless. Certainly not the foppish Edgeford. He more likely to call for his guards and then run for safety. As for her fiancée, although she scarcely knew him, she would not be surprised if Brackley offered to share her with the ruffians.

The later it grew and the colder Elena became, the more she wished she were nestled against Gareth's warm chest, as she had been that night in the cave. She did not feel well, not at all. What in the world was she doing out here?

Elena awoke with a start as Breila stumbled over a rock. How long had she been asleep? She looked up at the sky. The moon had set, but she had no idea how to read the stars. Suppose she had missed an important turn off?

Elena reined in the huge mare.

"Now what do I do, Breila?" she asked her mount. The horse snorted softly in reply. "Well if you hadn't let me fall asleep, I might have a better idea of where we are!" When Breila remained quiet, Elena relented. "Of course, I had no idea where we were when we began this journey so I don't know how staying awake would have helped." Elena reached down and patted her mount's neck. "You're forgiven, Breila."

"Who's that?" a rough voice called out from the trees to her right. Elena froze, her heart lodged in her throat preventing a reply. "I say, who's been foolish enough to pass our lair in the middle of the night?" When the question was followed by thrashing about in the underbrush, Elena wrapped both hands in Breila's mane and dug her heels into the horse's sides as hard as she could.

"Run!" she screamed. The tired horse sprang into a gallop, quickly putting distance between them and the voice in the bushes. Elena dared a glance over her shoulder and saw three figures stumble onto the road.

"Get the horses!" one of them shouted. "There's only one!"

Elena turned her attention back to staying on her mount. As they ran, Elena realized she must have slept longer than she thought for the sky was lightening behind her. She reined in abruptly as Breila crested a peak. Below she could just make out the road which zig-zagged back and forth all the way down the mountain. Elena hesitated for a second before sending Breila off the road and straight down the mountain. The horse nearly sat on her haunches as she slid down the steep slope, creating a landslide of rocks and dirt. They reached the next level of road and again Elena urged Breila across the road and straight down the mountain. Her strategy worked three more times before the exhausted horse could not keep her feet under her any longer. Elena screamed as Breila's feet went out from under her and she and the horse tumbled down the mountain. Elena tried to protect her head and face as she slid, but she did not see Breila's hoof as it grazed the top of her head, knocking her unconscious.

***

Elena awoke to a blindingly bright sun. She squinted as she sat up, partly from the glare, partly from the tremendous throbbing in her skull. She was coated in dust and for the first time in her life she felt the urge to spit. Slowly easing herself to her feet she closed her eyes when the world began to tilt dizzily. After a few moments it seemed to level out and she opened her eyes cautiously. If this is the thanks I get for trying to be a heroine, Elena thought, Joan of Arc can have it.

"Breila?" she choked out. "Where is that damn--" Elena froze when she saw the huge horse sprawled several feet away from her. With staggering steps, she crept over to the horse and knelt down by its head. Breila whinnied softly but did not move.

"Oh, Breila, I'm so sorry," Elena whispered. Although she could see no obvious wounds, the horse's awkward position left no doubt in her mind that Breila's back was broken. To Elena's surprise, tears filled her eyes and began coursing down her cheeks. She stroked Breila's face and the horse made a valiant effort to rise. Elena sucked in a breath, hoping that she had been wrong about the horse's injuries, knowing she wasn't as soon as Breila whinnied in pain and fell back against the ground heavily. Tears streaked Elena's dusty face as the horse's breathing finally slowed and then stopped altogether. A sob escaped her and she pressed her face against Breila's neck.

All her life, horses had been like servants to her. They had served a purpose and she forgot their existence the moment that purpose was accomplished. Unlike her friends, she had never seen her horses as pets, never felt more than a passing interest in what was carrying her. Now she was suddenly overcome with heart-wrenching grief for the horse she had ridden but a few days. What a noble animal, Elena thought. She kept going when I pushed her, when she must have been exhausted. Elena sobbed harder, her breaths coming in great heaves. After several minutes, her innately sensible self began to reassert itself.

Pushing herself up, she told herself firmly, "I'm going to make myself sick if I carry on like this. And that is no thanks for Breila's sacrifice." She looked around, wondering where she was. Crouching down, she could just see the road below through the thick cluster of trees. She turned back to Breila and with one finally caress, left the horse and began making her way towards the road.

She had no idea what time it was, but the sun was high in the sky and the heat was pressing down on her oppressively, filling her nostrils with the smell of hot pine needles and scorched earth. Elena walked for hours, wishing she would come across a stream or a pond or even a hut where she might ask for water. Though her stomach had long since given up complaining at its emptiness, her throat was parched and her head felt light for lack of water.

Her head drooping, she kept walking down the winding road, back and forth as it descended the mountain. In some places it was no more defined than a worn place in the grass. In others, it was wide and smooth enough to allow a cart to pass. When she stumbled over a rock, she bent to inspect her foot. Though she wore boots, they were of thin, delicate leather, meant to peep out from under her gown as she rode, not to support her as she hiked through the Welsh mountains. As Elena straightened, she smoothed her kirtle, the same one she had put on that last morning at Middleham. It was no longer the deep rich blue that was so difficult to achieve in a dye. It was now faded and crumpled, full of dust. She pulled up the hem and frowned at what was once a cream-colored chemise of fine Italian cotton. It was now a dingy grey and not a little tattered.

Pushing her tangled hair off her face with a sigh, Elena continued down the road, stumbling more and more often. If only this heat would abate, she might be able to clear her mind. A rock found its way into her boot but she was too tired to stop and remove it so she continued to limp along. When the sky began to cloud over, Elena was so wrapped in her misery she did not even notice. It wasn't until the first drop hit her face that she glanced up hopefully.

"Thank God!" she said as loudly as her parched throat would allow.

The first drop was quickly followed by several more and Elena let them fall on her face with pleasure. This was no fine mist of rain, but huge cold raindrops that cooled her deliciously and did much to restore rational thought to her muddled brain. Picking up her pace, Elena walked as briskly as her sore feet would allow.

***

"It's no use Gareth! The river is too swollen," Cynan shouted over the roar of the Dovey river. The steady downpour of the last hour had filled the narrow stream until it was spilling over its banks and the shallow ford that the men had sought to cross was now impassable.

"We'll have to backtrack and try to cross higher upstream," yelled Bryant.

"Damn!" Gareth bit out. They had made slow progress all day because Bryant's horse had thrown a shoe. Now with this delay, they would be at least a day late reaching Aberystwyth. He wheeled Isrid in a tight circle and led the way back up the muddy road.

***

The rain was no longer refreshing. It was cold. Elena was soaked through and she could scarcely see a few feet in front of her as she waded through the bog that was the road. She pushed her wet hair out of her face. She was suddenly as hot as she had been when the sun had been beating down on her. Gasping for breath, she stopped and raised her face to the downpour. The next minute she was freezing again, shivering in an effort to warm herself. Without realizing it, she resumed her wobbly way along the road, oblivious to everything but the steady drumming of rain on her head as she vacillated between being hot and cold in the downpour. Suddenly, the way ahead of her was no longer dark grey--it was pitch black and her knees buckled as she slid to the ground, unconscious.

***

Isrid reared suddenly, nearly throwing Gareth who was caught unaware. "What the hell?" he yelled and was about to jerk Isrid back down when he saw what had startled the animal. Huddled in the middle of the road, not a hoof's stride away was a crumpled form. Bryant and Cynan reined in and Bryant yelled, "What is it?"

Gareth dismounted and pointed. He approached the still figure, saw that it was a woman, and crouched down to determine if she was still alive. When he rolled her over and wiped the mud from her face, he felt as if someone had kicked him sharply in the stomach. "Blessed Christ!"

"Gareth?" Cynan yelled.

"It's Elena!" he called back as he scooped her up and carried her back towards Isrid.

"What? How could it be?"

"I'll be damned if I know. Here, hold her!" Cynan jumped off his horse and took Elena's bedraggled form as Gareth quickly mounted. Settling her as gently as he could in front of him, he brushed her tangled hair back from her face, the back of his hand grazing her cheek.

"She's burning up with fever! We've got to get her inside somewhere!"

"There's not so much as a hut for miles, Gareth, much less a town that might boast a healer," Cynan said.

"Yes, there is. In Machynlleth."

"Machynlleth? Are you mad? In case you don't remember, we turned back from that ford because we couldn't cross it. Machynlleth is several miles on the other side. We'll never make it!"

"We'll have to make it," Gareth said implacably. Every moment they argued his stomach clenched into tighter knots. Elena had not made a sound since he had found her.

Bryant was staring at Elena's huddled form. Turning to Cynan he said, "Our horses are strong. They can swim the ford. We'll tie lines onto each other so we won't get swept away."

"Not you too, Bryant! I thought at least you'd have some sense. The best we can do is find shelter in the trees and try to build a fire."

"There isn't a dry stick to be had in all of Wales, right now, I'll wager," Bryant argued.

Gareth had had enough. Urging Isrid up against Cynan's mount he grasped his friend's wrist. "She'll die if we don't get her dry and warm soon. We must try to cross the river." When Cynan started to shake his head, Gareth continued more urgently, "What if this was Enid, Cynan?"

Cynan glanced at Elena's pale face and then back to Gareth's eyes, wide with fright and filled with desperation. "Enid will have your head if you get me killed, Gareth. Let's go."

Gareth had never felt such relief before. Spurring Isrid vigorously, he headed for the flooded river. At least the accursed rain is slowing, he thought frantically as they approached the swollen banks of the Dovey. The river had risen several inches since they had left and it was traveling as fast as a horse could run.

Cynan shook his head but said nothing. Bryant pulled a length of rope from his pack and quickly secured it round his waist. He tossed it to Gareth who wrapped it around himself and Elena before finally handing it to Cynan. Bryant urged his apprehensive horse into the quickly running water. As Gareth followed, Elena awoke and grabbed at his drenched shirt. Gareth glanced down quickly and in the grey light of the storm, her eyes were dark, sparkling with fevered intensity.

"They're after you," she whispered hoarsely.

Gareth had no idea what she was talking about but knew that he needed every bit of concentration for guiding his horse across the river. "'Tis alright, my lady. We're safe now," he soothed. "Just go back to sleep and I'll wake you when we're home."

"At Eyri Keep?" she asked as her lids drooped closed.

"Yes."

Wrapping his right arm more tightly around her, Gareth wiped the rain off his face and guided Isrid into the dark water with his left. The bank of the normally shallow ford dropped instantly into water that easily reached Isrid's chest. Gareth felt the swift pull of the water as is swirled around his feet and he wondered fleetingly if Cynan hadn't been right after all. The water quickly deepened and Isrid was soon swimming. Gareth prayed his horse would not tire before they reached the other side.

Gareth could hear Isrid's loud breathing over the roaring rush of the water. He looked behind him to see Cynan patting his horse's neck, shouting encouragement to the frightened beast. Looking down at Elena, Gareth prayed they would make it across. Branches and bits of debris pelted his legs and Isrid's sides with the force of arrows as the river shot them downstream.

Squinting through the steady downpour, he guessed Bryant's horse would reach the far bank in a few more strokes and for the first time, he began to believe they would make it. Bryant's horse was not ten feet from the bank and had just got its feet on the river bottom when a huge log slammed into it, throwing it off balance. The horse screamed and scrambled clumsily to regain its footing. As soon as it was on its feet it bolted for the shore. Bryant held a tight rein on him but the horse refused to be stayed. Gareth felt the rope lurch and nearly lost his balance in the saddle. Elena moaned as the wet cord cut into her waist.

"Bryant!" Gareth yelled. "Pull back! Pull back!" Isrid strained against the pull of Gareth on his back and Gareth and Elena were suddenly pulled off the horse. Though the rain was cold, the river was freezing. Gareth struggled to the surface, pulling Elena up with him. Her full skirts caught in the current, trying to pull her away from him and still unconscious, she was a dead weight, dragging Gareth under. Just as he got both their heads above water, he felt another abrupt lurch as the horse reached the opposite shore and tried to run. Bryant quickly jumped off and began hauling in on the rope. Gareth's feet had just touched bottom when Cynan splashed up and helped them to shore. Gareth collapsed in the mud until his gasps for breath slowed. He quickly reached for Elena, convinced she should be dead after such a trial. Her pulse still beat strongly but despite the dunk in the cold water, her skin still burned to the touch.

"We've got to get her to shelter," Gareth yelled over the roar of the water. Both Bryant and Cynan nodded grimly. Cynan untied the swollen rope from Gareth and Elena while Bryant chased down his still-jittery horse. Within minutes they were tearing along the muddy road to Machynlleth.

Two hours later they rode into the small town, exhausted and mud spattered. Gareth stopped at the first inn they came to. With Elena in his arms, he kicked the door open and strode across the small room.

"I need a room. Now," he gasped. "My wife is ill. Get a fire going immediately."

The innkeeper and his wife stared at him as if he were Lucifer himself until he bellowed, "Move!" Quickly jumping up, the woman ran upstairs while the man gathered an armload of wood from a box in the corner of the room. Gareth followed the man upstairs, willing his legs not to collapse until he reached the bed. As soon as the innkeeper had a fire going, Gareth said, "Get out. No not you," as the wife moved to follow her husband. "I need your help undressing her. She's soaked through and burning with fever.

Although the woman had first seemed as timid as a field mouse, she soon proved both competent and wise as she deftly pulled Elena's kirtle and chemise over her head. "There's a cloth on that washstand," she said, gesturing with her chin as she laid Elena gently on the bed and began pulling off her boots. When Gareth handed her the cloth, she briskly rubbed Elena dry and quickly pulled the covers up.

"I'll prepare a compress," the woman said as she spread Elena's clothes in front of the blaze. "You'll want to add a few more logs to that fire and get out of your wet clothes. You'll do your wife no good if you catch the fever yourself."

Gareth stared at the closed door for several moments before rousing himself enough to unlace the cuffs of his shirt. He paused with his hands on the waistband of his chausses and glanced at Elena. Perhaps he shouldn't even be in here. At the time, saying she was his wife had seemed like the best reason to have an unchaperoned young woman with him. Now he wondered what Elena's reaction would be should she wake the next morning to find him in the same room. He was about to grab up his shirt and join Cynan and Bryant when the innkeeper's wife returned.

"Here, you may borrow this shirt while yours dries. It belonged to my brother. He died last spring. Your friends are settled in the small room downstairs." She set a large wooden bowl on the floor beside the bed and began applying a wet cloth to Elena's face. The smell of chamomile filled the room as she dipped the cloth back into the bowl.

"Perhaps I should sleep with my friends downstairs and allow you to tend to her," Gareth said, easing towards the door. When the woman shook her head he said, "I'll pay you well. You obviously know much more of healing than I do and--"

"And should she wake up in the middle of the night how do you think she'll feel to have a stranger here instead of her husband. No, come here and I'll show you what to do."

Gareth pulled the borrowed shirt over his head and crossed the room apprehensively. The woman stood and motioned him to sit on the edge of the bed next to Elena who appeared deathly pale in the firelight.

"Just wring that cloth out and wipe her face and throat gently with it." When Gareth did as she instructed, she leaned over and pulled the rough blanket down. "She's got a bit of a rattle in her breath. You'll want to put the compress on her chest as well to ease her breathing."

Gareth swallowed and concentrated on keeping his hands steady as he drew the pungent cloth between Elena's silken breasts.

"No not like that. You won't do her any good to just sponge her off. Here," she took the cloth from Gareth and dipping it back into the bowl, took his hand in her and pressed it over the cloth to Elena's chest. "Just hold it there for a few minutes and then rewet it. I'll go and see if there's anything to feed you."

Gareth looked studiously at the wall above the bed while he held the cloth against Elena's chest. When he removed it, he carefully avoided looking at her and concentrated on meticulously dipping the cloth in the fragrant water and wringing it out. How long did he have to continue this, he wondered as he changed the cloth pressed to her forehead.

Elena inhaled suddenly and began tossing her head. Gareth froze, afraid to touch her. "Gareth!" she called. Gareth's eyes widened. What if she'd been conscious while he'd applied the cloth to her--

"Gareth," she called again. "They know, they..." Her words faded into an incoherent mumble.

"Shh," he whispered, awkwardly stroking her hair. "I'm right here."

Elena's eyes opened a little. "Gareth?"

"Yes. We're in an inn. Can you tell me how you came to be in the middle of the road? Elena? Why were you following us?"

Elena seemed not to understand what he was asking. "Promise," she mumbled.

"What? Promise what, Elena?"

"Don't...don't leave me again..."

"Don't worry," Gareth assured. "I'll be right here until you feel better."

"Promise," she whispered as her eyes closed again.

"I promise," he said, and since she seemed to be asleep, he leaned over and kissed her lightly on her fever-hot lips. Gareth leaned closer. Despite the fever, she was so pale he could make out a light sprinkling of freckles across her nose. He ran his finger over them lightly, smiling. He jerked his hand away quickly when a light tap on the door was followed by the innkeeper's wife carrying a tray.

"Since we've not had visitors for several days, I'm afraid there isn't much food ready, but I brought a bit of bread and some broth," she said apologetically. "You should try to get some liquid down her throat." When Gareth reached for one of the bowls to feed Elena, the woman shook her head. "If she's sleeping now let her be. Besides, you look exhausted. Why don't you eat while I change the compresses and then you can try to wake her."

Gareth nodded and took the steaming bowl of broth. He drained it in one long gulp and began gnawing on the thick dark bread. When he had finished eating, she took the empty bowl and said, "If she should take a turn for the worse, just pound on the floor. Ours is the room right below this one and I'll be right up. Now just keep changing those compresses until she starts to sweat. When that happens, keep her covered and warm. If the fever doesn't break by morning, I'll fetch the healer."

Gareth thanked the woman who closed the door softly behind her. Taking a deep breath, he moved back to Elena's side and took up the compress. Against his will, his eyes strayed to her bare breasts, which were the color of warm ivory in the light of the fire. Quickly turning his head, he busied himself wringing out the cloth. When he had replaced it on her chest, he drew the covers up and reached for the full bowl of broth.

"Elena?" he said softly. "You must try to get some of this down." With his free hand he shook her gently until her eyes opened. "Try and drink, Elena."

Gareth lifted her head and held the bowl to her lips. She only drank a few swallows, and he spilled just as much down her neck, but he felt a great sense of accomplishment. "Good girl. Go back to sleep now." But she was already out.

Chapter 12

Gareth awoke to dim sunlight filtering through the downpour. He sat up abruptly, his muscles sore from their awkward position in the hard chair in which he had fallen asleep. Moving as fast as his cramped muscles would allow, he crossed the room and felt Elena's face. It was still hot, but she was now drenched in sweat, the covers bunched around her waist. "Damn!" Gareth said. "I should have covered you hours ago." Cursing his stupidity, he drew the blankets up to her chin, tucking them around her shoulders. He then sat down on the edge of the bed and smoothed her damp hair off her face.

Despite her illness, Gareth thought, she's still the most beautiful woman I've seen. Her normally chestnut hair, now wet with sweat, was a dark red, her lashes russet fans against her cheeks, her eyebrows arching softly above. Without thinking, Gareth raised his hand and traced the curve of her cheek, the line of her mouth.

At his touch, Elena's eyes opened and she whispered, "Water." Gareth was instantly on his feet, searching for a bucket or pitcher. "Where could it-- Oh damn it all to hell!" Gareth bellowed as his foot kicked over the bucket of water near the foot of the bed. He quickly righted the bucket, but not before all the water drained out.

"I'll be right back," he told the dazed Elena, and jerking the door open, he bolted down the narrow staircase. Cynan and Bryant jumped up when he entered the main room.

"Where is fresh water?" he asked the startled innkeeper.

"I took a bucket up to your room last--"

"I spilled it. Where do I find more?" Gareth turned as the door opened, letting in a blast of rain and the innkeeper's wife who was lugging two buckets.

"Is that fresh water?" he demanded.

"Aye," said the woman as she handed him a bucket. "Is she worse?"

"I don't think so; her fever is starting to break." Without another word, he grabbed the handle and dashed back up the stairs. Cynan and Bryant stared after him in surprise for several seconds.

"An unlikelier nursemaid I've never seen," Cynan said sardonically.

Bryant glanced at their hosts before turning to Cynan and lowering his voice. "Do you think 'tis quite proper for Gareth to be in Lady Elena's room like that?"

Cynan looked at his friend with a suspicious smile tugging at his lips. "Since when are you so worried about propriety, especially with an English lass?"

Bryant flushed deeply and shrugged. "I just don't think Lady Elena will be pleased 'twas Gareth who spent the night with her."

"And who do you think she would have rather had with her last night?" Cynan asked, all pretense of a straight face vanishing as he laughed.

"That's not what I meant," Bryant denied hotly. "I meant I don't think Lady Elena would prefer to have any man tending her whilst she's ill."

"'Tis a common enough excuse, claiming to be ill," Cynan gibed. If there was one thing he enjoyed more than tormenting Gareth, it was making Bryant blush.

"Have you no decency, you clot? You'd best keep your mouth closed, lest I be tempted to repeat some of your remarks to dear Enid."

"Now you don't play fair, Bryant," Cynan said. "You go telling her such things and 'twill be she claiming illness every night for a month!" When Bryant looked unimpressed, Cynan relented. "All right, all right, I'll stop hounding you and our fair English visitor."

"She's Welsh," Bryant said.

"Who is? What are you talking about?"

"Lady Elena. She's not just English, she's Welsh, too. Her father's mother is from Glamorgan."

"And how do you know this? Gareth never made mention of it to me."

A smug look crossed Bryant's face. "She told me when we went for a walk a few weeks ago at Eyri Keep. Shortly after we arrived."

Cynan looked at his friend dubiously. Perhaps the Lady Elena would have preferred his company next to her sickbed instead of Gareth's after all.

***

The rain continued until midday when a dim sun broke through the clouds and began to coax steam from the sodden ground. The Abbess of Dinas Mawddwy had long since given up hope of finding her ward alive. The river Dovey was still a rushing torrent and the English captain and his men were encamped next to the flooded ford, unable to cross and bitterly cursing the abbess who had forced them from their dry quarters to march in the accursed bogs of Welsh roads.

***

Gareth stood and stretched, tightening and releasing his leg muscles, reaching his arms over his head. He walked over to the small window and pushed the shutter open. The cool evening air that wafted in was scented with the invigorating smell of wet pine needles and aromatic heather. Gareth breathed deeply before turning back to Elena. Her fever had broken but an hour ago and after a day of tossing about and mumbling, she was finally sleeping peacefully. He smoothed the tangle of curls that was spread across the lumpy pillow, wrapping the silken strands around his finger. In the tranquil silence of the evening, he wondered about the pulling emotions that had kept him tied to Elena's side since he had found her in the middle of the road. Since she had rudely insulted him at Middleham over a month before, they had been like cats and dogs, always at odds with one another. Now Gareth wondered how much of that was his wounded pride rebelling at her rejection. In all fairness, his pride demanded from the back of his mind, she had acted like a petulant child, complaining about every discomfort as if it were life threatening. Good lord he had never heard one person whine about the state of her clothes in all his life!

And yet, somewhere during the journey through Wales and the stay at Eyri Keep, she had matured. Or perhaps he had finally seen the real Elena. Gareth sighed and moved over to the hard chair he had inhabited when he hadn't been sitting on the edge of the bed tending his beautiful patient.

Whatever the cause behind it, she had managed to ingrain her very essence into his soul so that he could never fully forget her. Gareth thought of his father's serving girl he had spent an athletic night in bed with. Sweet Christ, he could not even remember her name. All he could remember was running his hands through hair that wasn't a coppery chestnut and kissing lips that weren't petal soft under the pressure of his kiss; a touch that did not stir his blood as Elena's did. Leaning back in the chair, he stretched his legs out, kicking over dishes from their supper.

No matter how he turned or positioned himself, there was simply no comfortable position and his body rebelled at having to spend one more minute in the uncomfortable contraption. Abruptly standing, he surveyed the empty half of the bed. Elena was sleeping soundly and peacefully. Surely, she would not even notice if he curled up in a small corner of the bed. Before his common sense could present any arguments, his weary body had collapsed on the straw pallet. Straw? he thought. It feels like feathers. He promptly closed his eyes.

But before he fell into a deep slumber, his heart inexplicably called to mind the intense emotion he had felt when he had found Elena in the road. Beneath the fear and worry had been another feeling: exhilaration. Exhilaration that he did not have to give her up so soon. That he would have a few more days, perhaps a week with her. Exhilaration and...love...

***

Elena frowned in her sleep.

They had just stumbled onto the band of mercenaries.

"Go Elena, run!" Gareth shouted, thrusting Isrid away. Elena whirled the horse around and kicked as hard as she could. Instantly, it seemed, she was on the far side of the clearing. Reining in as hard as she could, she turned to see a huge claymore begin its decent toward Gareth's unprotected head.

"Gareth!" she tried to scream, but no sound came out of her throat. She tried to make Isrid turn and go back toward his master but the animal would not budge. "Gareth," she whimpered as she pounded on the horse's shoulders. And suddenly Gareth was free. They had escaped and he held her in his warm embrace, chasing away her fears, running his hands comfortingly up and down her back. She nestled her face in the base of his throat, inhaling his warm masculine scent.

Elena opened her eyes. The languorous feeling her dream had wrapped her in stayed with her and she quickly closed her eyes, trying to recapture the feel of Gareth's lips on hers. It was no use. She opened her eyes again and stared at a stubbled chin. Trying to roll over she discovered a heavy arm pinning her against a firm chest. Following the chest to a broad shoulder, she was disturbingly pleased to discover Gareth asleep next to her, his face boyishly innocent in slumber, his breathing slow and even. Trying not to disturb him, not to awaken him, she inched closer to him, until her lips lightly pressed against his throat. Closing her eyes, she dozed.

***

Gareth buried his head deeper into the fragrant pillow. He couldn't remember the last time he had been this comfortable. Inhaling deeply, he flexed his arm muscles and felt them tighten around a soft form. He quickly opened his eyes and discovered Elena nestled against him, her chestnut hair spread underneath him like a silken blanket. Blessed Christ! What had he done? She would kill him if she thought he'd taken advantage of her in her weakened state. Gareth sat up as far as he was able. His right arm was pinned beneath Elena, his legs entangled with hers, the twisted blanket barely covering her from shoulder to thigh. How was he going to free himself without waking her?

Before he could so much as lift his free arm, Elena shifted, her head tilting up, her eyes slowly opening. Gareth's heart stopped. "My lady, I swear--" he began, but Elena silenced him with a warm and drowsy kiss. For several seconds, he froze, unable to believe that she was willingly kissing him. When she did not pull away and continued softly exploring his lips, he tentatively slid his left hand along her waist. Elena responded by pressing closer against him, a soft moan escaping her lips. At that, Gareth took control of the kiss, shaping her lips to his, tracing their soft outline with his tongue. Elena clutched at his shirt, twisting the fabric in her grasp as she pulled him even closer.

Gareth's only thoughts were to savor each moment. Feelings he had suppressed for weeks now surfaced and his heart thudded loudly in his chest as the kiss deepened. Without quite realizing what he was doing, Gareth eased Elena onto her back, covering half of her body with. He felt her hands as they tangled in his hair, pulling his lips back to hers when he would have broken the kiss. He could feel his heart pounding in his chest, his blood racing hotly through his veins as he tried to reign in his passion.

Elena had to be suffering effects of the fever, he thought. She simply wouldn't be accepting--no, responding to--his advances were she in her right mind. Gareth lifted his head and propped himself up on his right elbow. The last time he had seen her at the abbey in Dinas Mawddwy, she had made it abundantly clear that she held him in utter contempt. He gazed down at her closed eyes as he felt her cheek and forehead. They were cool and dry.

Perplexed, he watched as Elena's eyes opened slowly. Their slumberous depths were clear and rational and they told him in no uncertain terms that she wanted him to kiss her again. Gareth lowered his head but paused just shy of her lips to look into her eyes again, trying to assure himself that this was what she wanted. At his hesitation, Elena lifted her lips to his, continuing in the motion to push him onto his back so that she now lay sprawled across his chest. In their moving about, the blanket had become hopelessly entangled in their legs and when Gareth raised his hand to Elena's back, he found not rough wool but warm and silken skin beneath his fingertips which he traced upwards until his fingers encountered Elena's equally silken tangle of curls.

From there, as if they had a mind of their own. His hands slid back down her back and then around to her midriff. He felt the goose bumps rise on her skin when he lightly brushed the sides of her breasts, which were pressed to the rough fabric of his shirt. Elena's hands slid down his chest to tug at the hem of his shirt, pushing it up around his armpits before leaning on him again, never once breaking their kiss.

All of this proved too much for Gareth. He felt that at any moment he would go insane with wanting her. Amazed at himself that he had been content to let her do so much of the seducing, he smoothly rolled her onto her back and, tearing his mouth from hers, began trailing kisses down her throat, across her collarbone to her breasts. Elena's hands tangled in his hair again, running restlessly through his rumpled locks as her breathing came in quick and unsteady inhalations. She gasped and arched against him when he trailed his tongue along her navel. Gareth was just about to tug his breeches off when Cynan pounded on the door and shouted, "Gareth! Wake up! The rain has stopped and there's a rumor that a troop of English soldiers are headed this way and they've been asking after us!"

Gareth glanced up at Elena who looked disoriented and dazed as she propped herself up on her elbows, her hair a glorious riot of chestnut curls. "Damn!" he said under his breath as he rolled to the side of the bed and sat up. He leaned over, resting his elbows on his knees, his head cradled in his hands as he tried to slow his breathing. Finally lifting his head, he turned to Elena. "I'm sorry, but we're going to have to leave right away. I know you've not recovered fully and I'd leave you here if I could, but if the English find you, they may wonder why you're here alone." Standing, Gareth arranged his crumpled clothing, being careful to keep his back turned until the evidence of his passion subsided. When he felt collected enough to turn back, he wished he hadn't.

Elena was struggling into her chemise, pulling the bunched yards of ivory material over her head, her slender body creamy in the morning light. Gareth struggled and lifted his hands to help her. He stopped himself inches from touching her, his hands shaking, wondering if she would be insulted by his help. Of course, he thought to himself, considering what they had been doing--what they would have done had they not been interrupted--surely it would not be too forward to simply help her dress...

But Gareth had debated too long. Elena finally got the chemise in place and reached for her kirtle, carefully avoiding his questioning gaze. When she pulled this over her head and began struggling to tie the laces in back, Gareth finally forced his inhibitions down and said, "I will help you with that, my lady." She said nothing as he pulled the laces tight and tied them with shaking fingers. As soon as he was done, she looked around, leaning over to search under the bed.

"Where are my boots?"

Gareth racked his brain. What had they done with her boots when they'd undressed her?

"I--" he began.

"Here they are," Elena said as she carefully edged around him without touching so much as a fold of his clothing and retrieved her worn boots from the hearth where they had dried stiff and misshapen. Gareth tried to speak and had to clear his throat instead.

"They'll soften up after you've worn them a bit. They were sopping wet when we took them off."

Elena finally looked at him, her eyes opening wide with shock. "We?" she squeaked.

Gareth realized she must have been thinking of Cynan and Bryant and hastily said, "Er, rather, the wife of the man who owns this inn. She was very kind and, uh, put you to bed when we brought you here. You were very ill. A fever." Gareth's tongue felt like it was tied in knots. "We weren't sure you were going to live."

Elena frowned. "I've never been ill before." She suddenly remembered Cynan's words. "Gareth! The abbess! She told the English captain that you were on your way to help Richmond. And the soldiers–I think they were the same ones we ran across on the way to your father's house. If they catch you'll they'll surely execute you for betraying King Richard."

"Was that why you were on the road that night? Were you following us? Were you trying to warn us?"

Elena hesitated, clearly flustered. Gareth felt his focus on her intensify. If she cared enough to warn him, perhaps she—his thought was interrupted by the entrance of the innkeeper's wife.

"I thought your wife might want some breakfast before you go tearing off."

Elena looked at Gareth with raised eyebrows. He flushed visibly and turned to the woman. "We haven't time to lose. She can eat at the next town."

The woman smiled at Elena, shaking her head. "A man has yet to surprise me," she confided. "I just knew he'd say something like that. Although, considering how he hovered over you for the past few days, I had hoped he would prove to be more sensible than most." She shrugged eloquently. "Well, no matter. I've packed everything in this sack. You can eat on the way, for no doubt these men will not want to stop until long after nightfall."

Gareth stared at the woman, baffled.

Cynan suddenly stuck his head in the door and said impatiently, "Gareth we really must be leaving."

"We're coming right now," he said, gesturing for Elena to precede him.

"Now you stay dry and make sure they stop and let you rest whenever you feel tired. You've barely recovered from your illness and you've yet to recover your strength," the woman said kindly.

Elena nodded and taking the heavy sack of food, moved out the door and down the hall. Once outside, Bryant helped her onto Isrid's back.

As Gareth came out of the small inn, he saw Bryant grinning up at Elena. He looks like a lovesick fool, he thought with a twinge of jealousy. Quickly repressing that feeling he looked at Elena. How he wished she did not have to ride with him. It was going to be unbearable torture to ride the next two days with her pressed against him. But there was no way around it. He could not bear the thought of her riding pressed so against Cynan or Bryant. Gritting his teeth, he walked over to his horse and climbed on, trying unsuccessfully not to touch Elena. As he leaned over to adjust his stirrups, he heard Bryant talk from the other side of the horse.

"My lady," he began hesitantly. "I must apologize."

"For what?" Elena asked.

"It was my fault you took a dunk in the river the other night. That was no doubt what caused you to be sick so long."

Elena stared at Bryant. Gareth knew she had no idea what he was talking about.

"When we crossed the Dovey, I didn't have a tight enough rein on my horse and when he bolted, the safety line that was tied around us all pulled you into the river. A dousing like that would kill a healthy man and you have every right to be angry with me for my stupidity."

Reaching over, she surprised Gareth by patted Bryant's hand and saying somewhat awkwardly, "There, there. I'm fine now and that's all that really matters, isn't it?"

Her consolation obviously did not sound as weak to Bryant's ears as it did to Gareth's because the young man looked up at her in wonder and smiled sheepishly.

"We've got to move, we're already a day late reaching the meeting and we've probably got English soldiers behind us," said Gareth crossly. The lovesick look on Bryant's face made him unaccountably angry. As soon as Cynan and Bryant were mounted, he nudged Isrid into a gallop.

Their rapid pace prevented conversation and even when they slowed to let the horses rest, Gareth was unsure how to talk to Elena. Clearly their relationship had taken a dramatic turn from the hostility of their first days on the road and even from their wary peace at Eyri Keep. But where exactly they stood as friends or lovers, he knew not.

He tried to see her face, even leaning sideways on the pretext of checking Isrid's girth strap. She appeared lost in thought, her expression impossible to read.

Whatever path their relationship took, they were clearly stuck together. Gareth could not risk her safety—and theirs—by leaving her at another abbey. His father had been certain the abbess at Dinas Mawddwy supported Henry Tudor. They could not chance another mistaken loyalty.

Suddenly weary of trying to figure out his feelings, much less Elena's he forced his mind to consider the upcoming meeting with Henry Tudor's supporters. Though his path seemed to have been chosen for him, he did not begrudge it. He had decided to throw his lot in with Tudor and his kinsmen. Thoughts of battle plans and weaponry kept his thought off his beautiful companion for the next several hours.

Though his mind was otherwise occupied, his body was finely tuned to her every movement and Gareth looked down as Elena shuddered. Surely, she could not be cold; the day was hot and muggy thanks to the days of rain. Still, she had just recovered from a fever...

"My lady? Are you cold?"

Elena started. "Wh-what?"

"You shivered. Are you cold?"

Elena glanced over her shoulder at him. Her clothes were sticking damply to her and her hair was plastered against her neck. He realized it was a foolish question.

"I'm not cold," she said peevishly.

Gareth frowned. Elena had never been anything but haughty and arrogant. He was a fool to think otherwise, a few kisses notwithstanding. But as the memory of that morning rose unbidden in his mind, he could not help but admit to himself that Elena had changed from their first meeting and that she was no doubt simply tired from their journey and her recent illness. She still had the ability to make him feel awkward and tongue-tied, but she had followed them, on foot apparently, to warn them of the English soldiers. And though she had been feverish at the time, he could not help but remember her whispered plea that he not leave her again. And then there was the matter of waking up with her in his arms and her sweetly passionate kisses. There had been nothing arrogant about the way she had twined her fingers in his hair and gasped when he had kissed her--

Gareth shifted uncomfortably in the saddle. They really were going to have to procure another horse. She simply could not ride in front of him across Wales and back. It was awkward, it was tiring, and...and it was going to prove downright embarrassing if her hips kept pressing against his every time Isrid climbed a hill.

When they stopped to let the horses drink at a stream in the late afternoon, Gareth splashed cold water over his head, trying to rid his mind of the picture of Elena's creamy skinned body against the rough sheets at the inn. When they were ready to continue, he shifted packs on the saddle around and mounted first, hauling Elena up to perch behind him. Now why didn't I think of this earlier? he asked himself as he prodded Isrid ahead of the other two horses, blissfully ignoring the questioning glances of Cynan and Bryant.

Two hours later, Gareth was wondering what could have made him do such a stupid thing. Elena had been forced to hold onto his waist as her new perch was more precarious than sitting in front of him had been. The feel of her arms around his waist was nearly as disturbing as was the feel of her backside pressed against him. What was worse was when she had fallen asleep, nearly an hour ago. With her head resting on his shoulder, he could clearly feel the imprint of her breasts against his back. Her grip around his waist had loosened in sleep and her hands lay loosely on his upper thighs, all but brushing his crotch. This was torture!

When they finally stopped to make camp, Elena was still soundly sleeping.

"Don't wake her," Bryant whispered. "She's still not fully recovered her strength."

"I wasn't going to wake her," Gareth said edgily. He pushed his friend's hands away when Bryant would have taken Elena in his arms, but soon realized that he had no way to get down without dumping her on the ground. He reluctantly handed Elena down to Bryant and scrambled out of the saddle. He turned to take Elena but Bryant was already carrying her to the blankets Cynan had laid on a bed of leaves. Stifling the insane spurt of jealousy at the protective air Bryant had assumed over Elena, Gareth unsaddled, fed, and watered the horses before returning to their makeshift camp in the middle of a thick copse of trees.

"Dare we start a fire?" Bryant asked. "Lady Elena surely needs to stay warm and it would make cooking a good deal easier."

Gareth stared hard at his friend who until a few weeks ago could not say "Good day" to a woman without turning beet red and falling over his feet. Now Bryant was efficiently tucking his own blanket around Elena, brushing the hair off her face before he turned for Gareth's answer.

"We'd better not risk it."

"But Gareth--"

"She'll be in a good deal more danger if the English soldiers come across us than she will eating cold food on a warm summer night."

Bryant started to argue when Elena spoke. "That woman this morning gave me a bag of food to eat for breakfast. Surely there's something in there that would not need a fire."

Bryant stared at Gareth indignantly. "Lady Elena is sick for three days and you did not even give her enough time to break her fast before we left?"

Gareth bristled at his tone. "If I recall, you were more than a little anxious to avoid being hung for a traitor yourself."

Bryant had the grace to look abashed. "It's just that Lady Elena--"

The lady in question interrupted their dispute. "Lady Elena would very much like to eat now and let you children finish your squabble somewhere else. Preferably on the edge of a tall cliff in a strong wind."

Cynan laughed as he brought over the heavy sack of food. "I like that. I'll have to remember it: a tall cliff in a strong wind." Laughing again, he turned the sack over and dumped its contents onto Elena's blanket. "I say, what was the name of that inn? We'll have to stop by there again. Look at this feast!"

Gareth and Bryant stopped glaring at each other long enough to look at the pile of food and quickly forgot their argument. Within minutes the four were happily stuffing themselves on cold chicken, cheese, and thick, crusty bread as the last bit of twilight faded from the sky.

As Elena stretched out on her blanket, Gareth surveyed their surroundings. "I'd have us keep watch tonight. I'd not like to be caught unawares."

"What Englishman could find his way through a Welsh forest during daylight, much less on a moonless night?" Cynan asked.

"The moon will be up later and an Englishman searching for a traitor will find his way through nearly anything."

"I'll take first watch," Bryant volunteered.

Gareth nodded. "Wake me in a few hours. I got plenty of sleep last night and should be fine to watch the rest of the night."

"Is that wise?" Bryant asked.

"I'll be fine."

Cynan laughed softly. "You'll hear no arguments from me, Gareth. Bedding down with Bryant in that tiny room was no treat, I can assure you. He kicks and snores. I haven't slept less since I was a newlywed!"

Gareth shook his head at his friend. "How Enid has stayed married to you will forever be a wonder to me," he said as he stretched out on the ground.

"It's only because he's gone so much that she's able to stand him," Bryant joked.

"Perhaps she's hoping he'll die young and leave her money to find herself a new man." Gareth proposed.

"Ha! You're both wrong." Effecting a poetic tone of voice, Cynan said, "Beneath this craggy face of mine is the heart of a lover and 'tis that alone which keeps her with me." He glanced at his friends a moment to see if they believed him and then added, "Well, that and my virile manhood."

Both Gareth and Bryant laughed, their early antagonism gone.

"You should have left it at 'the heart of a lover,'" gasped Bryant.

"'Twould have been more believable," added Gareth.

"A pox on the both of you!" Cynan said good-naturedly.

Chapter 13

"Gareth," Bryant whispered as he gently shook his friend awake.

"Is there trouble?" Gareth asked, instantly alert.

"Not a sound, but I'm falling asleep on my feet. I hope I haven't woken you too soon."

Gareth looked at the position of the stars. "You were on watch a lot longer than you think. Now get some sleep."

Gareth stood and stretched his arms over his head. Carefully placing his feet with each step, he walked around the perimeter of their small camp, patting the horses reassuringly when he reached them. Circling back to where Elena had been sleeping, he panicked at the sight of her empty blanket. When he realized that she was only heading into a small clump of bushes by the stream, he resisted the urge to call her back. Surely there was nothing to worry about. Cynan had been right. No English soldier would be able to track them through this forest. And yet, some instinctive feeling had made him put the watch on tonight when a few weeks before they had all slept soundly within a few miles of the English border.

Elena returned a few minutes later but instead of moving to her bed-roll, approached him and asked, "Is everything alright?"

"Fine."

"You don't sound terribly convinced."

"It's just that I have this feeling..."

"What sort of feeling?" Elena asked as she sat on the ground at his feet.

Gareth struggled to explain it. "Sometimes I get this feeling in the pit of my stomach. It's like my insides are tied in a knot that grows tighter and tighter. My father used to call it my sense of doom because I was sure it meant something bad was about to happen."

"And did it?"

"Usually, no. But sometimes it was right and it saved my hide each time."

"When was the last time that happened."

"The day Richard's entourage was attacked."

Elena rubbed her arms and she quickly glanced around her, trying to peer into the dark of the forest. "What do you think is going to happen?" she whispered.

Gareth gave a soft, self-deprecating laugh. "Unfortunately, my stomach never tells me that." Sensing that Elena was frightened, he sat on his heels and said reassuringly, "Actually, I'm sure nothing is going to happen. In my whole life I've probably had this feeling a hundred times and it's been correct exactly twice. Since it worked last month, I'm not due for another right pre-monition for at least a couple of years."

Elena nodded her head and was about to speak when a horse whinnied far off in the woods. She jumped when Gareth put his hand over her mouth, but remained still, shaking slightly. He leaned close to her and for a moment, in that crazy way the brain has of conjuring abstract images, Gareth wished he could kiss her. Instead, he pressed his mouth against her ear and whispered faintly, "As quietly as possible, stand up and tie your skirts up so they won't be in the way. Then I want you to wake Bryant. Cynan always grunts and moans when he awakes so have Bryant put his hand over his mouth when you wake him. I'm going to get the horses."

He started to move away but Elena grabbed his arm frantically. In the darkness of the forest, her face was no more than a pale blur, but Gareth sensed her fear. Squeezing her hand reassuringly, he helped her to her feet.

Elena hitched her skirts to her knees and secured them as tightly as possible. Turning, she crept over to the nearest sleeping form. To her relief she saw that it was Bryant and she laid her hand on his chest, gently shaking him. His eyes opened immediately and when he saw her, he sat up. Before he could speak, she put her finger across her lips and whispered Gareth's instructions in his ear. Bryant nodded and quietly rolled to his feet. Elena quickly gathered up the blankets and rolled them into tight bundles. Turning, she discovered that Bryant had been able to awaken Cynan without so much as a peep. They all jumped when the crack of another twig was followed by the sound of bushes being brushed aside. Joining Gareth who had managed to saddle the horses, Cynan gestured behind them where they had heard the last noise. Gareth nodded as he took the blankets from Elena and strapped them to his saddle. He pointed in the direction of the stream and indicated that they should walk rather than ride. Cynan and Bryant took the reins of their horses and disappeared into the blackness of the trees.

Gareth put Isrid's reins in Elena's hands and whispered in her ear, "Follow Bryant and walk as quietly as possible." Elena was about to object but Gareth put his hand to her mouth and said, "I have to see if it is the English. We may be fleeing from a family of rabbits." With a quick kiss to her forehead, he turned and was gone. Elena tugged on Isrid's reins and set off after Bryant's horse, trying desperately to worry about her own safety rather than Gareth's. Low-hanging branches scratched her cheeks and caught at her hair but she simply gritted her teeth and pushed on, wincing at the rustle of leaves underfoot, terrified that whoever was behind them could surely hear her heart thumping in fear. They pushed on for what Elena felt must have been hours but was probably only a couple of minutes when a hand came out of the gloom and clamped itself over her mouth. She was about to struggle when the owner of the hand whispered, "It's me, Gareth." Nearly faint with relief, Elena allowed him to pull her along after him as he caught up to Cynan and Bryant.

"I didn't hear them say anything, but if they're not soldiers, I don't know who they are. There are at least a dozen of them and they're all heavily armed," he whispered.

"Do they know we're here?" Bryant asked, looking worriedly at Elena.

"I think not. They would have attacked right away if they knew we were here."

"How can you be sure they're even after us?" Elena asked.

"Twelve armed men roaming the Welsh forest in the middle of the night are not out for fun. They're looking for someone and I'd rather not take the chance that we're not just who they're looking for," Gareth explained.

"A man who rode into town just before we left said they were looking for a group of traitors," Cynan told Elena.

Elena's eyes widened. "The abbess told the English captain you were going to meet with Henry's supporters. That's why I came after you--to warn you. They must still be trying to catch you."

"Why didn't you mention that earlier?" Gareth asked.

"I did--you never paid attention to what I said," Elena shot back.

"Shh!" hissed Bryant as he cocked his head, trying to hear if they were being followed.

"We'd best split up," said Cynan. "If they have three trails to follow, it may confuse them enough to go home."

Gareth laughed shortly. "I wouldn't count on it."

Cynan's teeth gleamed white in the dark as he smiled broadly. "It's worth a try, isn't it?"

"That's the stupidest idea I've ever heard," said Bryant in a harsh whisper. "And I've heard plenty of stupid ideas from you."

"He's right, Bryant," Gareth said. "If they have any sort of tracker with them, they'll be able to tell that there are four of us and that we're headed in the direction of Aberystwyth."

"In the middle of the night?" Bryant asked skeptically.

Before Gareth could respond, Cynan broke in, "Last I heard, Geraint Vaughan was seen around Dinas Mawddwy. He can track a rabbit through a rainstorm."

When Bryant said nothing, Gareth said, "We're only a day's ride from Aberystwyth. We'll meet there and warn the others the English are aware of our plans."

"I still don't think it's safe," argued Bryant.

"Nothing is safe when men are battling for a crown," Elena murmured to herself.

Cynan who overheard laughed softly and said, "True, but I'd wager it's much safer than if women were battling for it!"

"Nonsense, women would--"

Gareth put a hand over her mouth, his whole body tensed as he listened to twigs breaking and branches rustling. Gesturing to Cynan and Bryant to go in different directions, he took Elena's hand and led her to the south and west. Bryant started to object, but Cynan's hand on his arm stopped him and with one last glance at Elena, Bryant headed due west. Cynan waited one more moment before leading his horse toward the north.

***

Elena was practically asleep on her feet. It was all she could do to keep up with Gareth as she held onto the rope attached to Isrid's saddle that Gareth had given her so she wouldn't lose her way in the dark. It was now pitch black. The dark before the dawn, Elena thought. The moon had long since set and Elena could not even see her hand in front of her face. She had no idea how Gareth was able to lead them without hesitation through the dense forest.

The rope tugged in her hand. She had stopped without even realizing it. She tried to take a step forward, but her tired feet refused to budge and she fell in a heap on the soft padding of many years' accumulation of pine needles and moss. Though her cheek was pressed against the damp musty leaves and a rock was digging into her side, Elena thought she had never been so comfortable. I'll just rest here a few minutes, she thought, and then I'll catch up with Gareth.

"Elena, are you all right?" Gareth whispered urgently as he rolled her over.

Ah, she thought as she lay on her back, this is even more comfortable. Her eyes closed with no further urging.

"Elena!" Gareth said more loudly.

Dragging her eyes open, she tried to see Gareth's face. "I'm so tired, Gareth," she murmured.

"I know sweetheart, but we really have to keep moving. I have no idea if we're being followed or not."

Elena nodded and pushed herself up. She hadn't stood more than a second before her knees buckled and she started to sink to the ground again. Gareth caught her and swinging her up into his arms said, "I'll put you on Isrid. I can't believe I made you walk all this way. What an idiot I am. Cynan would box my ears if he knew how stupid I was..." He continued to mutter to himself, but Elena was too tired to try to understand what he was saying.

Gareth heaved her into the saddle and lay her against Isrid's neck. Gathering up the rope she had held onto, he lashed her to the horse so she would not fall off. Pressing a kiss to her cheek, he took Isrid's reins and continued forging a path through the dark forest.

***

Gareth stopped in a sheltered glade and stretched his arms over his head, grimacing at the tightness in his back from so much walking. The sun had been up for almost an hour and he had neither heard nor seen signs that they were being followed. He prayed that Cynan and Bryant had gotten away safely and that their decision to split up had not been a foolish one. Gareth turned and scratched Isrid's ears. Would that the soldiers he had trained with this year past were as uncomplaining and dependable.

"A double portion of oats for you when we reach Aberystwyth if I have to sell my sword to get them," he promised Isrid who nudged his shoulder softly in return. Gareth's smile faded as he turned his attention to Elena who was still sound asleep, sprawled awkwardly over Isrid's back and neck. Brushing her tangled hair back from her face, he studied her pale features. There was a smudge of dirt on her cheek. He carefully wiped it off, wondering not for the first time in the last few days at the change in her. She had ceased complaining, had not even shown fear when they were being pursued. She had, in fact, risked her life to warn them of Richard's soldiers. Cynically, Gareth tried to determine if she had anything to gain from her actions, but he could think of nothing. Why, then, the change? Baffled, he untied the rope that secured her to Isrid and gently lifted her down, laying her in the thick grass under a tall oak. Taking Isrid's saddle off, he rubbed the tired animal down and gave it what was left in the feed bag. With the sack of food the innkeeper's wife had given them in one hand, he stretched out beside Elena.

Elena stirred and slowly pushed herself up. "I'm starving," she said, her voice husky with sleep. Gareth offered her cheese and the last half loaf of bread. Elena took a large wedge of cheese and ripped the bread in half, handing Gareth his portion. They said nothing as they devoured the humble fare and drained the wine in the flask.

When the food and wine were gone, Elena leaned back against the tree and took a deep breath.

"That feels so much better," she said, patting her stomach and closing her eyes.

Gareth nodded, unsure of what to say. Suddenly, Elena sat up straight.

"What about those men? Are we being followed?"

Gareth shook his head. "I don't think so. We made pretty good time and I didn't hear anything other than an owl or two."

Elena relaxed back against the tree, her eyes on Gareth as he rolled up the empty food sack and stuffed it in the bundles tied to the saddle.

"How long can we rest here?" she asked. He had had but a few hours of sleep and could not possibly have the energy to continue much longer.

"Perhaps half an hour at best."

"How much further do we have to travel to reach Aberystwyth?"

"Four, maybe five hours," he said, his eyes closing drowsily.

Elena nodded. She watched Gareth lose the battle against sleep. He slumped down against the tree, his head cocked at what looked to be an uncomfortable angle, his brow furrowed as if even in sleep he was worrying about their safety. Of its own volition, Elena's hand reached out towards him. She jerked it back, but after staring at him a moment longer, she reached out again and eased him onto his side. Pulling a blanket from the saddle, she propped it under his head and smoothed his unruly hair.

Standing, she stretched her stiff muscles and hearing the faint sound of trickling water, foraged through the edge of the forest until she found a small spring. There was barely enough water to splash in, but Elena managed to wash her face and arms and drank the cool sweet water until her thirst abated.

She sat on the rocky bank and stripped off her shoes and threadbare stockings. Though the chill of the water made her inhale sharply, she soaked her feet in the cold water, relishing the quiet beauty of the forest. How odd, she considered, that she should feel so at peace here, in this glen, in this country. It was as if the fever she had suffered had burned away her earlier life, freeing her from the angst of living in the king's court: the constant scheming and manipulating—and that just for the chance to wait on someone of higher rank, or to gain a more prestigious seat at the next feast. The relief of not trying to live down a disgrace, not worrying what others thought of her, was so great, she wondered if she could ever return to Richard's court.

Elena drew her cold feet out of the water and stared unseeing at them. Had she changed so much in such a short amount of time? she wondered. Well had she played the calculated games of court life. She'd been proud of her knowledge, her ability to read people and manipulate them to better her own position. Would she not miss the stimulation of such daily calculation and risk? She searched her heart and mind. No. She would not.

True, there was the dreaded betrothal to the Earl of Brackley. Elena might have been able to wheedle her way out of it, but it had opened her eyes at just how little control over her own life she had had as a member of the king's court. Here in Wales, she had seized her destiny, chosen her path. She had saved the lives of Gareth and his friends. She was no pawn in a larger game. The feeling was as frightening as it was invigorating.

Then, too, there was Gareth. Her feelings for him had rapidly evolved from scorn and hatred to…to…well something far more unsettling. Waking up in his arms, sharing powerful, drugging kisses with him had set her blood on fire, something she'd never encountered with her other, more "noble" suitors. And the thought of someone like Lord Edgeford risking his life for her was preposterous. Elena knew without a doubt that Gareth would die before allowing harm to come to her. It was a heady, utterly unfamiliar feeling to be so protected.

She had no idea what the future held, where she would end up after they reached Aberystwyth, but she would trust—at least for the time being— in the powerful attraction between her and Gareth.

Standing, Elena debated taking off her travel-stained gown and having a proper bath when a step behind her made her realize Gareth must be awake. Looking over her shoulder, her smile nearly turned to a scream. Behind her stood not Gareth but four men, soldiers no doubt, judging from their leather armor and weapons.

"What is your name?" asked one in English. Elena assumed he must be the leader. He was short and stocky, his iron-grey hair clipped unfashionably close against his head, his face furrowed with lines of wear and as tanned as old leather. Dear God, she thought. This is the man the abbess sent to find Gareth! Elena bowed her head, allowing her hair to fall over her face, pretending to humbly grovel to the captain. She glanced up at him to see if he recognized her.

His eyes were black and glittered sharply under bushy grey brows, but they gave no hints that he'd seen her before. "Where do you live?" he asked more harshly.

Elena said nothing, frantically trying to think of what to do, what explanation she could give for being here. Had they come across Gareth yet? No, they couldn't have. They had obviously approached her from the opposite direction.

The man barked his questions at her again, this time in hesitant Welsh.

Elena's thoughts raced through her mind frantically. If he thought she was Welsh, perhaps she could convince him that she and Gareth were not the people he was looking for. Assuming, of course, they even knew Gareth and his friends had an Englishwoman with them.

"Marared," Elena said improvising quickly. "I live in Gwynedd."

The captain stared at her keenly. Behind him the other two began making suggestive remarks under their breath, chuckling lewdly. Sweet Mary! Elena thought. What if this man is accustomed to turning prisoners over to his men?

That worry was cut short when the captain's head snapped around and he glared at his men for a long moment. The men sobered abruptly and he turned his attention back to her.

"What are you doing so far from Gwynedd alone and in the middle of nowhere?"

His stumbling Welsh gave Elena time to frantically think of a response. While he waited for her answer, he nodded to his men, instructing them to search the area. As soon as Elena saw one head in Gareth's direction, she knew what she must say.

"My husband and I are traveling to visit my family in South Wales."

The captain lifted a thick eyebrow. "Where is your husband?"

"He is napping just over there," she said pointing.

The captain called his men back. "I don't trust a woman and especially not a Welsh woman," he snapped. "Stick together in case they're armed."

Elena led the way back through the trees, making as much noise as possible to hopefully wake Gareth. When she finally reached him, she realized he must be more exhausted than she had thought. He had not moved an inch since she had laid him on the ground. Crossing to him, she gently shook him.

"Gruffydd," she called softly as he awoke with a start. "It's alright, it's only me, your wife Marared," she said, staring hard into his eyes hoping he would understand what she was trying to do. Gareth glanced over her shoulder and pushed himself hurriedly to his feet.

"Gruffydd," she said more loudly as she grabbed his hand and squeezed it meaningfully. "They mean no harm. They found me over at the stream and were worried that I was alone, I am sure. I explained that we were only resting on our way to--"

"Hush woman!" the captain shouted in English.

Elena ignored him long enough to say, "--Cardiff."

Gareth stared at Elena in confusion but snapped to attention when the captain said, "I suppose it's too much to hope you speak English."

"I--I speak a little, my lord."

"How nice," the captain said snidely. "Now suppose you tell me where you came from."

Elena stared at Gareth, willing him to give the answers she had already given, but he resisted the urge to look at her for confirmation.

"We live in Gwynedd."

"Yes, I know that. Your charming wife managed to babble that much to me," he said in a tone whose politeness was belied by the razor sharpness below it.

Elena could feel the relief course through Gareth. "We live in Bjaeneau Ffestiniog. We are traveling to--" Gareth paused and Elena prayed he would remember. "Cardiff in South Glamorgan."

"You wouldn't happen to be going by way of Aberystwyth, would you?"

"Aberystwyth? That's nowhere near Cardiff."

"I realize that. But--"

"Aberystwyth?" Elena asked, tugging on Gareth's arm. In rapid Welsh she continued, "Is there a fair on at Aberystwyth? You promised we would go, husband. Remember? When you made me miss the last one?"

Behind him, one of the soldiers laughed until the captain glared at him sharply. The soldier sobered instantly. The captain did not laugh or even smile. He merely scowled harder.

"There are a pack of traitors on the loose in these woods. Have you seen anyone in the last few days?"

"No, my lord. Although we did hear something in the brush last night. Weren't sure if it was man or beast, but it didn't bother us so we let it be."

"And where were you last night?"

"About two miles due north," Gareth lied.

The captain studied Gareth and Elena for several moments before turning away. He took a step and then turned back. "Gruffydd, was it?"

"Yes, my lord," Gareth said hesitantly.

"And your wife's name was...?"

Elena tugged impatiently on his sleeve and said in Welsh, "Are we going to stop and see Bryant's betrothed on our way, husband?"

"Another word from you and I'll have you bound and gagged," the captain shouted at Elena.

"My wife's name is Marared. I believe in English it is Margaret."

"Of course," said the captain. "Gruffydd, you and Marared had best watch yourselves. Traitors are at work in your country and they care not who they kill or maim. Why in Machynlleth, they murdered an honest innkeeper and his wife who had given them food and shelter during the rains." The captain turned away and Elena felt her stomach clench. Beneath her fingertips, she felt Gareth's arm muscles tighten in rage as the soldiers mounted their horses and rode west.

When they were out of sight, Elena spoke. "They," she began. "They killed those people, didn't they? Those people who helped us."

Gareth nodded and because he didn't know what else to do, took her in his arms and held her tightly.

"But how could they have found out?"

"One of the villagers probably told them."

"But...I thought the Welsh always stood with each other against the English."

"Not always. As in any country, there are those who seek to gain the most from whoever is in power." And then, trying to distract her from the deaths of the innkeeper and his wife, "That was fast thinking, telling them we were wed and traveling to Cardiff. I doubt I could have done so well on such short notice."

"I was sure we wouldn't live to see another sunset," Elena said suddenly shaking uncontrollably from a belated case of nerves.

Remorse and guilt swamped Gareth. "I'm sorry my lady. Ever since you've been under my care, you've been in more danger than if you had tried to walk alone back to Middleham. I have needlessly risked your lifetime and again. You must think Wales the most bloodthirsty country on God's planet."

Elena lifted her head from his chest and stared at him perplexedly, her fear forgotten. With a small shake of her head she said, "On the contrary, I have never felt such a sense of home and belonging. I would not trade the last six weeks for the rest of my life."

"But sleeping on the road...you nearly died trying to warn us about the soldiers--"

"Do you jest? Compared to waiting on Lady Elizabeth hand and foot, I've had it easy."

Gareth smiled and peered closely at her face, "I say, what have you done with Lady de Vignon? Surely you are not the woman who said 'I cannot be expected to sleep rolled up in a blanket with three servants'."

The smile faded from Elena's face and she pulled out of Gareth's warm embrace.

"We had better continue to Aberystwyth."

Gareth stared at her back pensively before turning to gather up their belongings.

Chapter 14

They approached Aberystwyth in late afternoon, after having detoured to make sure they were not being followed by the English soldiers. The sky was a brilliant azure, and as they crested a hill just outside of the city, they could see the waters of Cardigan bay, a deeper, tempestuous blue. The breeze coming off the water was fresh and clean and cooled Gareth and Elena as they rode into the city. Elena bent to shake her skirts. As she tried to smooth her hair, Gareth chuckled behind her, amused that she should be worried about her appearance when he was just glad they were alive.

"Worry not, Elena. Though large for Wales, Aberystwyth is too small to scorn you for your appearance. Besides, you look fine," he said reassuringly. He meant it: her windblown chestnut hair glinted like fire in the sunlight and spread about her shoulders enticingly. From over her shoulder he could see her left cheek and it was smooth, like velvet, and rosy from her days in the sun. Glancing a little farther down, he could just make out the soft swell of her creamy breasts.

Elena craned her neck to see the expression on his face and determine if he were joking. He realized she could tell where he'd been looking and smiled guiltily, but she merely shook her head and turned back around. "I did not realize my illness was catching. Surely you must be suffering from a fever if you think I look 'fine.' I have never worn a dress as much as I've had to wear this one," she said, nodding at her travel-stained skirts. "I doubt I could even recognize a fashionable gown if one landed in my lap."

Gareth grinned at Elena's lighthearted tone. Never had he heard her speak with the least bit of self-deprecation. He could not believe this was the same woman who had imperiously ordered him to make her breakfast all those weeks ago. Hoping that her good mood would last, he risked asking her about her change of heart.

"Lady Elena?"

She turned again, her eyebrows lifted at the solicitous note in his voice. "You've never called me that before."

Gareth was momentarily throne off balance. "What? Of course I have."

"No, you haven't," she insisted. "You've called me 'Elena' and 'my lady,' and a few less complimentary phrases, but never 'Lady Elena.'"

Gareth didn't see what her point was and the confused look on his face made Elena laugh. "I wasn't criticizing you, merely commenting on the discovery that you do actually have manners." Gareth scowled at her remark, but she quickly distracted him. "Now what were you going to ask me?"

Gareth considered saying something about her <u>not</u> actually having manners but decided that might cause her to turn into the woman of stone she had been so often in the past. Carefully phrasing his question, he said, "I was just wondering."

"Yes?"

"When we first met, weeks ago, you detested me—all of us for that matter—but now you seem different."

"How so?" Elena asked quietly.

"You seem more at ease. More, well, like one of us."

"But I told you, I have a Welsh grandmother."

"That's not what I mean. I mean, before you were so haughty, treating everyone around you—us--like they were servants. You seemed to think that anyone who was not important in the king's court was simply not import-ant." When Elena remained quiet, he hastily continued. "But since we left Eyri Keep, you escaped the relative comfort of an abbey to reach us, risked your life to warn us of danger, shared your food uncomplainingly, and lied through your teeth to protect me from those English soldiers. Would you care to en-lighten me as to why, or how, you have changed so much?"

Clearly stalling for time, Elena said, "If you think that abbey at Dinas Mawddwy was comfortable, you must have been raised in a barn. I doubt they had a down pillow in the whole musty building."

Gareth stared at her patiently. He knew she would find it difficult to answer for such a change of character. He knew he would be hard pressed to explain why he had treated her so poorly when she first travelled with them. Even now, he could hear the disdain in her voice when he had asked her to dance that long-ago night in Middleham. But the bitterness of that encounter was overlaid with the sweetness of her kisses, the softness of her skin as he had caressed it...

"At court," she began hesitantly, interrupting his thoughts, "nothing ever happens. I mean *really* happens." She paused clearly searching for words. "We change clothes a lot. We whisper about newcomers, we gossip about those we don't like, we try to become the king or queen's favorite and we--everyone, men and women--try to marry to better our position at court. There is no substance to what we do or how we live. We do not build anything, we only tear down. We do not help the king run the country. He has a small group of advisors who do that and the rest of us simply exist. I think 'tis why, when you take us out of that world, we treat you like you are nothing--to make ourselves seem important, seem necessary.

"And then, the more I was away from that world, the more time I spent in your world, the more I realized that what you were doing really counted. Whether Henry Tudor be wrong or right for England and Wales is beside the point. At least you are doing something to affect your world. Even those people we first stayed with--Gruffydd and Catrin--they make things, they pro-duce wool, food--"

"And many, many children," Gareth cut in, trying to lighten her expression.

Elena smiled, but the flow of words did not lessen. "They don't live off the work of other people, they support themselves. And Enid. No one has ever been nice to me like she was. I know your father told her to wait on me, but she went beyond that. I felt like she was my friend."

"I'm sure she thinks the same of you."

"And finally, at the abbey, when I heard that old crow telling the English soldiers to go after you, and I decided to ride and warn you, I felt alive! I felt that I was finally doing something that would mean something!" Elena looked at her hands as if embarrassed at what she had just said. "I--I mean, I knew it wasn't much, but it felt important. Really important, not pretend important." Her words exhausted, Elena fidgeted with the cuff of her sleeve, refusing to meet his eyes.

For himself, Gareth was overwhelmed. Elena had never spoken in such depth about her feelings. Neither had she ever spoken critically of her life at court. But what affected him most was her glowing commendation that he was working for a better country. Realizing that the silence between them had continued, and that she might be feeling awkward at having revealed so much, he quickly said, "In the first place, what you did was more than 'not much.' You saved three lives and since mine was one of those three, I think what you did was very important." He paused and smoothed the hair off her cheek, tucking it behind her ear. "I also apologize for not being more understanding in those first few days. I should have realized that it would take a while for you to get used to sleeping on the ground and bathing in a stream."

"Mistake me not!" Elena said, some of her old spunk returning, "I'm still not used to waking up with bugs in my chemise, and I would take having my luncheon served to me in bed any day over that disgusting stuff you call dried beef."

Gareth smiled and succumbed to the temptation he had been feeling since she started talking. Turning her head gently with his thumb and forefinger, he leaned forward and placed a warm, soft kiss on her lips. When she did not pull away, he intensified the kiss, slanting his lips across hers as her mouth opened. Slowly, Elena began responding to the kiss, matching his firm pressure with sweet movements of her own. With a groan, Gareth pulled away, conscious that they were only moments away from the city walls.

"My lady," Gareth began and then cleared his throat. "I vow that before we leave Aberystwyth you will have a new gown."

Elena laughed shakily and responded, "And with what shall you buy this new gown, Sir Gareth, your good looks?"

Gareth wondered if she was serious about his looks but refused to be sidetracked. Before he could answer, she offered another possibility.

"Perhaps you mean to add thievery to your crime of abduction!"

Gareth frowned and said sharply, "Though I may not have coin to throw away as your suitors in court do, I am not without means. What I wonder is if you'll even have the decency to thank me." Had the woman no common courtesy? Surely if she ever made it to heaven, she would snub St. Peter when he opened the gates for her. As they entered the city, however, he was ashamed at how easily she riled him—both to passion and to anger. He was a fool to take every comment from her as a slight.

He realized he owed her an apology but told himself it was more important he search for the shop he was supposed to meet his father in front of. He would apologize as soon as they arrived, he promised himself. Lord, but the town had grown since the last time he had been here as a child. As they wandered up one street and down the next, Gareth realized that, late as they may be, his father might have no one waiting for him once he did locate the meeting place. Gareth figured the days in his head. They were two days late. His father may have assumed that they had been captured or met with some other accident. He wondered if the planning meetings had already been held or if Henry's representatives were still awaiting the arrival of Welsh lords from the furthest corners of Wales.

"Do you know where you're going?" Elena's question roused him from his reverie.

"I'm trying to locate the shop of Samuel the Weaver."

"Why do you not stop and ask someone?" she said innocently.

"I don't need to ask where it is, I'll find it. 'Tis just that this town has changed a lot since the last time I was here."

"That seems like all the more reason to ask for directions."

"I don't need directions. I told you, I'll find it!"

Knowing Gareth couldn't see the expression on her face, she rolled her eyes and stuck out her tongue. She was going to have a good laugh at Sir Know-it-all's expense when he did finally have to stop and ask. As they wound back and forth along the smooth stone streets, Elena's anticipation and making Gareth eat his words grew.

Elena was forced to swallow her carefully planned comments about Gareth's stubbornness when he yelled in her ear, "There it is!"

Blind luck, she thought. Carefully storing away the subtle insults she had composed--she had no doubt he would provide her a reason to use them later--she concentrated on hanging on to Isrid's mane as Gareth sent the powerful horse galloping down the narrow and crowded street, heedless of the pedestrians and carts full of produce and grain. Elena grabbed the edge of the saddle as they nearly collided with an old man crossing the street. A moldering onion thrown, no doubt, by an aggrieved merchant narrowly missed Elena's shoulder and broke apart against the back of a cart as Gareth abruptly reined in Isrid in front of a small, slate-roofed shop. There was a meticulously carved wooden sign over the door indicating cloth supplies inside.

Gareth had just dismounted and was helping Elena down when the door to the shop opened and Bryant burst out.

"Gareth! Thank God you're alive! We had all but given up hope of your ever arriving."

"We met up with some English soldiers we had to outwit," Gareth explained. "It wasn't hard," he said with a laugh. "Just time consuming. How much have I missed?"

"About a day's worth of plans. And you'll never believe who arrived just this morning," Bryant said as he escorted them into the dimly lit shop. Bolts of wool lined two of the three walls, from thick nubby plaits to buttery soft weaves in a muted rainbow of colors. A third wall held a few bolts of fine cotton and several shelves of precious trims.

"Who, King Richard?" Gareth teased.

Bryant shrugged and shook his head dramatically as he led them down a small hall. "No, you oaf. Lord Stanley, Henry's stepfather."

Gareth paused and in the dark hall, Elena ran into his back. He ignored her jab to his ribs as he asked, "Does Richard not hold his son as a hostage to Stanley's loyalty?"

"Yes, which is why it is so amazing that he's here. He is risking many lives to help Henry plan."

Ignoring Elena, who kept running into him and poking him in the ribs, Gareth marveled at the news. So, Lord Stanley had finally chosen a side. For the past three reigns, Stanley had vacillated between Lancaster and York, showing support for whichever party sat on the throne. The last his father had heard, the influential Stanleys were remaining carefully aloof from the upcoming confrontation between Henry and Richard. Perhaps Stanley's wife, Henry's mother, had finally forced him to take a stand. Gareth felt much more confident in their success with Bryant's news.

The dim hall emptied into a small, tidy living area. Turning, Bryant gestured to the chairs at the table. "Lady Elena, if you will sit here, I will return shortly and try to find something for you to eat." Motioning to Gareth, he led the way to a door in the corner of the room. Opening the door, Bryant started up a narrow staircase, Gareth following quickly behind.

"Wait!" Elena said imperiously. "Where are you going? What about me?"

Gareth turned around and Bryant bent down on the steps so he could see into the room. "Elena," Gareth began. This meeting is between Henry's closest advisors and those of us who are willing to die to put him on the throne. There is no way we can bring a woman to the meeting, much less an English woman from Richard's court."

Elena frowned and stomped her foot. "But I'm Welsh, too. And besides, I almost died for this cause, remember?"

Gareth crossed the room and took Elena's face between his hands, his thumbs caressing her soft cheeks. Elena grasped his wrists but did not try to pull his hands away. Gareth's voice was quiet as he tried to explain.

"As it is, my father and I are very honored to be allowed at this meeting. Were it not for Eyri Keep's strategic location to a marching army and our ability to provide supplies for that army, we would be waiting with every other Welsh farmer for the call to follow instead of preparing to lead. What you did for this cause was very important and you can be sure I will credit you for saving our lives. But I cannot impose on Lord Stanley by bringing you unannounced into this meeting." Kissing her gently on the forehead, he said, "Please, Elena."

Elena shook her head. "But I can contribute! I know Richard's court! I may know something you don't, although I'm sure you will find it hard to believe," she finished sarcastically.

Gareth refused to take offense and said, "I'm sorry Elena." Turning, he rejoined Bryant and closed the door to the staircase.

Ahead of him on the stairs, Bryant said, "I don't think you should be so familiar with Lady Elena."

Gareth, his mind on the meeting upstairs frowned in the dark. "Familiar? What are you talking about?"

Bryant was silent for a moment and then said tightly, "Kissing her, touching her, calling her by her given name alone."

"So?"

"She's betrothed! And even were she not, she wouldn't be able to tell that you were not serious, that you don't care for her in *that* way."

Gareth felt like he had walked into the middle of a stranger's conversation. "In *what* way? What are you talking about, Bryant? I was just trying to comfort her."

They had reached the top of the steps and Bryant paused, his hand on the door handle. He turned around but Gareth could not make out the expression on his face in the dark stairwell. "If Henry Tudor should be successful, Lady Elena will not have to marry that fat earl. Just how do you think a gently bred noble lady will feel when she turns to you only to discover your intentions were not honorable? She's not a serving wench you can romp in the hay with and then forget about. And though she's part Welsh, she lives in England and they are not so tolerant of love affairs and bastard children as we are. Furthermore, Gareth, I will not let you break Lady Elena's heart."

Gareth's head spun. "Bastard children? Have you lost your mind Bryant? I'm not interested in a 'love affair,' a 'romp in the hay,' or anything else with Elena. I'm just grateful to her for her help and trying to keep her from being more frightened than she already is." His words were true, and yet not the whole truth, but he refused to confess things to Bryant he hadn't even had time to admit to himself. A new thought struck Gareth. "Have you more 'honorable' intentions than that?"

Before Bryant could respond, the door swung open, blinding the two men in the stairwell with bright sunlight as Gareth's father's voice said, "Come in boys and thank the Blessed Virgin Mary you're alive, son."

Bryant and Gareth entered the brightly lit room and Morgan hugged his son tightly. As his eyes adjusted, Gareth saw that the room was full of men of all ages. Some were sitting, others were standing against the wooden walls, but all had a look of strained impatience at the interruption and a reckless excitement in their faces, no doubt from the meeting's topic. Gareth and Bryant quickly found an empty spot of wall and leaned against it.

"Shall we continue?" said a well-dressed man with an English accent. His face was thin and bearded; Gareth guessed him to be Lord Stanley. "Fair weather providing, His Majesty will arrive sometime in August. You understand we cannot risk telling any of you where he will land. We can not risk him meeting Richard's men before he has had a chance to meet up with my forces and those you all will be able to muster. Again, for safety's sake, we will not give you any direction as to our plan of attack through England until absolutely necessary.

"What I would like to know is this: How much support does the Earl of Richmond, true heir to the English throne, have in Wales?" His steely blue eyes surveyed the room, carefully examining each man's face. A few of the men standing shifted their weight from foot to foot. Others dropped their eyes to the floor. Gareth knew that much of Wales, like much of England, was indifferent to the latest battle in this "War of the Roses." Common men and women had been affected very little by the fighting between the Lancasters and the Yorks. To most, the battles among the two houses only affected them when it happened in their rye fields or over their vegetable patches. Otherwise, it was nothing more than a skirmish among wealthy gentlemen.

Scanning the room himself, Gareth knew that these men were thinking the same thing. Not many Welshmen would choose to die for a man who claimed the English throne when the next year a new contender may appear with a better claim. Someone cleared his throat and Lord Stanley's eyes narrowed. Before Stanley could say anything, Gareth's father spoke.

"The Welsh will fight for Wales. Should Henry Tudor swear to grant us more rights and freedoms than we've enjoyed under previous English kings, he will find his supporters here innumerable."

Lord Stanley's face flushed and he angrily asked, "Must he bribe you as mercenaries then? Will the Welsh not fight simply for the rightful ruler of all Britain?

Morgan smiled. "There are many men who would claim Richard is the rightful heir. Or the Princess Elizabeth herself. You will have a hard time convincing Welshmen to risk their lives for just another Englishman."

"But he is the grandson of Owain Tudor--a Welsh statesman. You all know that," Stanley argued.

"Yes," Morgan replied calmly. "But will he act like Owain Tudor's grandson? Will a Welsh king of Britain mean a Welshman will be equal to an Englishman? Will it mean the concerns of Wales be given equal consideration to those of England? Will a Welsh grandson mean Welshmen in English government positions?"

Stanley sat back, his elbows on the arms of the chair, his fingers steepled in front of his mouth as he studied Morgan.

"What I am saying, Lord Stanley, is that his name could be Llywelyn and the men of Wales would not die for him without some assurances that Wales will benefit."

Lord Stanley nodded slowly and seemed to be considering something weighty. Finally, he dropped his hands from his mouth as he sat forward. "You may rest assured that Wales will benefit should it support the true king."

When he seemed to have nothing else to say, Morgan looked at the men around the room and then said, "My Lord Stanley, surely you must realize that we cannot convince the farmers and shepherds with such a simple answer. Nay, even I in my conviction that Henry Tudor is the rightful king remember all too clearly how assurances can lose their priority once a goal such as the throne has been reached."

Lord Stanley clenched his teeth tightly. "Are you implying that I will not keep my word or that my stepson will so quickly forget the very people who helped him gain his birthright?"

In a calm, even voice that Gareth remembered so clearly from evening stories in front of the fire, Morgan replied, "Lord Stanley, if you will reflect on my words, I'm sure you will see I meant no disrespect. No one in all of Britain dare doubt your sincerity and no one here dare doubt your stepson's appreciation. Rather, we all know that running a kingdom is a terrific responsibility that requires a king's constant vigilance. In light of that, it would be perfectly understandable for King Henry to be overwhelmed by his responsibilities and be forced to relegate the task of appointing Welsh officers to the future, rather than trying to do everything at once." Gareth had been the subject of his father's rational logic too many times while growing up not to see that Lord Stanley was doomed. "All I ask you to understand is that the Welsh people are not as patient as their rightful sovereign is and they may misinterpret advance planning as forgetfulness. If His Majesty could see fit to perhaps deliver his assurances of change personally, he will be amazed at the number of men who will pour from the mountains of Wales to carry him to England."

Lord Stanley was visibly torn. "Perhaps he could send letters to you local lords and inform you of his plans for Wales."

Morgan smiled warmly. "That would be excellent. In the same missive with his instructions for our troops, of course."

Lord Stanley paused. "Of course."

Gareth breathed a sigh of relief, glad that he was not in Lord Stanley's shoes. Morgan always had a way of making you agree to things as if they had been your idea in the first place. With that the meeting was quickly concluded and the men stood to leave, some pausing to speak to Lord Stanley, others milling about uncertainly. Gareth wondered if they were still unconvinced of Stanley's promises, but he had no idea what had occurred before his arrival. His thoughts were interrupted by Morgan. "We thought you were dead or taken, son. 'Tis good to see you here and unharmed. Did you run into trouble?"

"Almost. We were accosted by a troop of English soldiers who were asking about Aberystwyth. We had to detour to make it look like we were heading to Cardiff."

"Why Cardiff?" Bryant asked.

Gareth smiled, remembering Elena's performance. "Elena told the soldiers we were traveling to Cardiff to visit her family."

"Quick thinking," Morgan mused.

"Did Bryant tell you how she escaped the convent to warn us of that Godless abbess?"

Morgan nodded. "A brave lass," he said with a knowing smile.

Suddenly looking around, Gareth asked, "Where's Cynan?"

"He's on watch--Richard's men have been thick as flies around town trying to find out our meeting spot," Bryant answered.

Gareth looked at the fifteen or twenty men in the small room. "Isn't it going to look a little suspicious if these men leave a weaver's shop all at once?"

"Some of the men will exit out the back," Morgan explained as Bryant was called away by one of the other men. "When the men leave here, they'll go in ones and twos, many with packages of cloth to make it appear as if it is business as usual." Morgan laughed. "I think Samuel was anxious to have the meeting here so he could force us to buy fabric!"

"That reminds me. Do you have any money with you I could borrow?"

"Borrow? You needn't borrow money from me. You've never taken a dime for your work at Eyri Keep. You'll take what I have as little enough payment. But how does Samuel's textiles remind you of money?"

Gareth paused, embarrassed. He glanced over his shoulder, relieved to see Bryant leaving the meeting room. "I...I promised Elena I would buy her a new gown."

"A what?" Morgan's eyes suddenly narrowed. "Cynan told me that you attended Lady Elena when she was ill in her room for several days. Did you take advantage of her? Damn it, Gareth, she's not a simple country girl you can seduce and then forget about! Have I taught you no better than that?"

Gareth was stung. "Da, how many times have I seduced any innocent girl and abandoned her? Of course, I didn't take advantage of Elena." Well he didn't, he thought, she kissed him first and nothing actually happened! "'Tis just that she's been through so much and she's used to having more than one dress. So, I thought it was the least I could do," Gareth argued defensively. "May I have the money or not?"

"Of course, lad, of course." Morgan pulled a leather pouch out of his shirt. "You'd better take it all. It will cost a fortune to have a dress made in a day or two."

"Why a day or two?" Gareth asked. He thought they could spend at least a week in Aberystwyth before returning to Eyri Keep.

"Wait until we're alone with Lord Stanley for me to explain."

Gareth looked from his father to Stanley who was just saying goodbye to the last two men in the room other than Gareth and his father.

"Morgan, I assume this is your son?"

"Yes, Lord Stanley. This is Sir Gareth. He has of late served in Richard's court and could prove valuable if your lordship wishes to go ahead with our earlier idea."

"Is he in agreement?"

"I'm quite sure there will be no problem," said Morgan.

Gareth, increasingly confused and irritated that he was being spoken of as if he were not present, broke in. "Excuse me Lord Stanley, father, what am I agreeing to?"

"Why don't you sit down," said Lord Stanley, "and we will answer all your questions." When Gareth and his father had made themselves comfortable, Lord Stanley turned to Morgan. "Shall I explain or would you care to?"

Morgan sat forward and said abruptly, "Gareth, we would like you to return to Richard's court and try to discover any plans he may have regarding Henry's attack. See if you can discover how much he knows of our plans."

Gareth stared at his father with disbelief. "You want me to *spy* on him?" Morgan looked distinctly uneasy, but Gareth pressed on. "I am a knight of Britain. Is it not enough that I have forsworn to protect the king's life with my own? Should I now have to spy on the very man I am sworn to protect?"

Morgan gazed at Gareth understandingly, but Lord Stanley slammed his hands on the table and stood up, addressing Morgan.

"What is this man doing here, Morgan? Why are you wasting my time with someone who is still committed to that murdering--"

Gareth's fury rapidly matched Stanley's and he broke in, "I do not stand for Richard! But I do stand for Wales and England and by my knightly vows must defend their king."

"Enough!" Lord Stanley bellowed. "You are either for Richard or against him. If you are for him, you would not be here. If you are against him, you will do anything in your power to bring about the end to his treacherous reign!"

"But it's not that simple!" Gareth argued.

Lord Stanley clenched his teeth and threw himself back in his chair. Before he could say anything else, Morgan spoke up. "Why did you not tell me about these reservations in the privacy of our own home, Gareth?"

Gareth could tell his father was upset, but he could not shake the feeling that serving as a spy was the ultimate disgrace. Since allowing Cynan and Bryant to talk him into coming to Wales, he had been struggling with his mixed emotions. He did not think Richard was the king he should be, and what little he knew of Henry Tudor led him to believe he would make a better leader. But having only been a knight for little more than a year, the solemn promises he had made in his knighting ceremony were still fresh in his mind. He had promised not to forsake the trust of his sovereign, nor to bear arms against him. Now he was decided to do both of those acts. That he should also have to spy...

"It is not that I have reservations about the rightness of Henry Tudor on the throne. I do not have reservations about fighting Richard and his men face to face on the battlefield. I do not have reservations about dying for this cause. But spying? That just doesn't seem right."

"Sweet Jesu!" Stanley exploded. "You will die for this cause, but you will not do something to gain information that could prevent your death?" Stanley looked from Gareth to Morgan.

Morgan turned to Gareth and said. "I understand your feelings, son. There is great honor in deciding when something is wrong and then being able to battle for what is right." Gareth felt a moment of relief that he would not have to do as they had asked. "But honor is not always so black and white. Ofttimes, the most honorable path is the one that is the least tasteful to you. Without gaining some knowledge of how much Richard knows and his plans for us, we have little chance of succeeding."

Gareth stared miserably at his father before nodding his head in acceptance. "Very well. I will do as you ask."

"Thank you, Gareth," Morgan said, squeezing his shoulder reassuringly.

Lord Stanley spent the next ten minutes giving details and instructions to Gareth. When Gareth left, he said, "I hope we can trust your son."

Morgan looked sharply at Stanley, but when he spoke, his voice was as ever, calm, and even. "Gareth has a very strong sense of honor and propriety. Once he has agreed to a course of action, nothing will deter him from it. He will come through." Standing, Morgan followed his son downstairs.

Alone in the room, Stanley leaned back in his chair, the lines in his face seeming to deepen with worry and fatigue. "God help us if he doesn't."

Chapter 15

In the small living area downstairs, Elena watched groups of men come through the door in the corner. They invariably started when they spotted her and she nodded as regally as she could to each of them, trying to act like she belonged here. None of the men spoke to her as they scurried down the hall to the front room or ducked out the back door into a narrow alley. Finally, Bryant was among the men coming downstairs and he hurried over to her, a delighted grin on his face.

"Now that is over with, shall we get you something to eat?"

Elena nodded, but looked at the small kitchen across the room apprehensively. Although it was as spotless as the living area, she could see no evidence of prepared food. She knew absolutely nothing about cooking, and having eaten Bryant's cooking on the road, she decided she would rather listen to her stomach growl all night than eat anything they could concoct. She turned back to Bryant with such a resigned look on her face that he burst out laughing.

"I promise, no more dried beef. There is a marketplace just around the corner and there is sure to be food as this town has festivals and fairs constantly during the summer."

"Thank God and every one of his saints," said Elena gratefully. "Lead the way."

They waited out in the cloth shop until the men preceding them had disappeared inconspicuously down the street. While she waited, Elena fingered the rich textures of the cloth stacked on shelves along the walls. She came across one at the bottom of a stack she couldn't resist pulling out. It was a finely woven wool, soft as any Italian cotton, and it was a warm cranberry color, slightly faded, but a rich color, rich as a young girl's lips after her first kiss. Elena shook out the folds of the cloth and held it up against her, admiring the drape as she flared it at her feet.

"Lady Elena?" Bryant interrupted her play. "We can go now."

Elena nodded and folded the cloth as neatly as she could. For some reason, it was nowhere near as small a package as it had been when she pulled it out. Bryant waited patiently as Elena shoved the untidy roll of fabric on top of the neat stack. Half of the piece hung off the shelf, loose threads from the end dangling, but it seemed in no danger of falling to the floor so Elena turned to Bryant with an over-bright smile, took his arm, and steered him away from the heap of fabric.

"Now, what are we going to eat? I'm starving," she said.

Bryant's chest swelled as he covered her hand on his arm with his other hand. "Whatever my lady desires, so shall she eat," he said with a flourish as they left the shop.

The market was indeed just around the corner and it was as boisterous and crowded as any Elena had seen in her travels with Richard's court. As they pushed their way through the crowds, Elena was bombarded with scents and sites. Old men sold fresh-caught fish from blue wooden carts, the unmistakably fishy smell wrinkling Elena's nose. A young boy of eleven or twelve walked on his hands for the amusement of a group of young girls. Everywhere women of all ages, bargained with merchants for this bolt of cloth or those rounds of cheese. As Bryant led her past a row of open-front shops, Elena heard a young pregnant woman convince the baker to give her a dozen rolls for free since she was buying two large loaves of bread anyway. "'Tis just so hard for me to bake. This babe," she said pointing to her protruding belly, "is causing me no end of misery." Elena laughed as the man looked nervously at her roundness before agreeing to her plea.

As they made their way to the center of the large square where the food merchants were set up, a tall man brushed past her, his long hair streaked by the sun, his well-muscled shoulders rippling under his thin linen shirt, his forearms tanned below rolled up shirt sleeves. Elena turned to watch as the man paused to talk to one of the merchants. From the side, she watched him as he burst into laughter, his teeth startlingly white against the tanned skin of his weather-grooved face. Someone stepped in front of Elena, blocking her view and she pushed him aside. As if feeling her gaze on him, the tall man turned his head. When he saw Elena, he smiled broadly and cocked his right eyebrow in a movement that could only be described as suggestive. Elena's eyes widened and she spun around, nearly colliding with Bryant.

"There you are! I though you were following me, but when I turned around, you were gone. It wouldn't be wise to become separated here," he said, firmly clasping her hand in his own. As he pulled her towards another vendor, Elena craned her head around and discovered the well-built stranger staring at a point somewhere below her face. When he raised his eyes and grinned wickedly, Elena realized he must have been watching her hips as she walked away. She gasped and quickly turned around.

There were no men that rudely bold in Richard's court! No nobleman would dare look at a lady like that while she was cognizant of his attention. Elena paused in mid-thought. Of course, no men in Richard's court seemed so...virile, either. There was a confident power in that tanned face that did not stem from a title. Elena could remember no man who held himself so in Richard's court. No man except maybe...Gareth.

"How about some grilled lamb, my lady?" Bryant's voice pulled her from her thoughts, but she did not hear his question. When she looked at him uncomprehendingly, he explained. "They skewer pieces of lamb and roast it over a fire. It's quite tasty."

Suddenly Elena's hunger replaced all thoughts of virile soldiers and

Gareth's appeal. "That sounds wonderful. Buy me two."

Bryant smiled and turned to the old man behind the table. "How much for each stick?"

"Two pence," the toothless mouth replied.

Bryant stared open mouthed at the old man. "Two pence? But the cart just over there is only charging a penny!"

The old man broke into a wheezing laugh. "That is because he serves mutton so dry and tough it takes you a week to digest it! Besides, I flavor mine with a very expensive spice my son has just brought me from the land of the barbarians. Try it," he said, handing a stick to Elena. "It's very spicy."

Elena bit into the tender meat, its juices running down her chin. The strange spice tickled her nose and burned the tip of her tongue but it was wonderfully pungent and she loved it.

"What is this spice called?" she asked, wiping her chin with her hand as delicately as she could.

"'Tis some strange foreign name, but I believe my son said it sounded like cory. Or was it curry? My son has sailed the seas for twelve years and each time he returns, he brings me something unusual."

Bryant turned to Elena. "Is it acceptable, my lady?"

Elena nodded her head, her mouth full. When Bryant paid for only two, she prodded him with her elbow. "I'm absolutely famished," she said as soon as she swallowed. Bryant ordered a third.

With their meals in hand, Bryant led her to a rickety bench on the edge of a small clearing in the market. As they sat, Elena noticed two small, short tree stumps protruding from the ground. "What are those for?" she asked.

Bryant turned to look and said, "Those are Viking stumps. Actually, no one knows what they're really called, but the Vikings introduced this game to the Welsh hundreds of years ago when they were constantly raiding our coast."

"How kind of them. How is it played?"

"A person will stand on each stump, a long rope held between them. When the game is begun, they both pull on the rope. The object is to force your opponent off his stump or pull the rope out of his hands. I imagine someone will begin playing soon enough and we can watch."

"But how simple--doesn't the biggest person always win?"

"Actually, no. There is a great deal of strategy and dexterity in the more skilled players."

As Elena ate, she wondered if women were allowed to play.

***

"Samuel, I would speak business with you a moment," Gareth said nervously.

The middle-aged weaver turned away from the small group of men talking in one corner of his shop. "Business, eh? I'm always willing to talk business, especially if it concerns you giving me money!" He laughed heartily and slapped Gareth on the shoulder. Seeing that Gareth was not laughing, he quickly sobered and asked, "What can I do for you?"

Gareth cleared his throat and began, "I need to purchase some cloth."

"Cloth, eh? I'm not sure if I can help you there." Again bursting into laughter--laughter that reminded Gareth of a braying mule--he turned to the wall of stacked bolts. Spying a mangled piece of crimson fabric, his laughter turned to sputters of outrage. "Look at this! People have no respect for a man's merchandise!" Pulling out the fabric, he shook it vigorously, smoothing out the wrinkles. "Now what type of fabric do you want and how much are you willing to spend?"

As he continued to shake the cranberry-colored fabric, Gareth had a sudden vision of Elena in the rich color, full skirts swirling around her feet, the soft fabric clinging to her hips.

"Is there enough of that fabric to make a lady's gown?"

"Oh, ho! A gown is it? Let me see." Carefully measuring the fabric from the end of one outstretched hand to the middle of his chest, he said, "There are eight lengths here, plus a little I won't charge you for."

"How much does it cost?" asked Gareth, pulling out the leather money pouch Morgan had given him.

Samuel gave his price, but before Gareth could naively hand over the money, Cynan bellowed, "That's highway robbery, old man! Don't pay it, Gareth, I'll take you to a much cheaper shop a couple of streets over."

Confused, Gareth looked back and forth between the two men, Samuel looking worried despite his smooth merchant's mask, and Cynan looking smug and slightly challenging. Suddenly distracted, Gareth asked his friend, "Where did you come from?"

"I just got off watch and came to find out the news."

Quietly, Gareth asked, "Is that really too much for the cloth?"

"I've no idea," Cynan responded in a whisper. "But one thing I've learned from Enid is that you never agree to a merchant's first price."

Gareth nodded, beginning to understand. In a louder voice, he said, "Perhaps I should look at this other shop. I need money for a chemise as well and this fabric would take all I have."

"Now, now," Samuel said as he rushed to block their exit. "You didn't let me finish. When I told you the price, I didn't get a chance to let you know that includes an equal length of this fine linen that would make a beautiful chemise.

"Linen?" Gareth asked, thinking quickly and getting into the negotiations. "Aren't chemises usually made of Italian cotton?" He remembered Elena bragging about that at some point in their journey.

Samuel laughed. "Only very expensive chemises for very grand ladies."

"Precisely," said Gareth and moved to leave.

"Alright, alright. You are stealing more from me than your father did this morning. Here," he said, pulling down a bolt of creamy cotton. "I'll give you five lengths--that's more than enough to make a chemise."

As Samuel measured out the cotton, Gareth fingered the soft wool. "Cynan? Do you think this color will look good on Elena?"

Cynan's eyebrows shot up. A smirk crossed his face and he looked like he was about to say something, but paused with his mouth open, studying Gareth's face. He must have seen something in his friend that made his own face soften as he gently said, "I think that is an excellent choice. Lady Elena will look beautiful in it."

Relieved, Gareth turned back to Samuel and counted out the money. Cynan looked down the hall. "Speaking of your lady, where is she?"

Gareth did not remember seeing Elena in the back room or the kitchen. Just a little worried, he said, "I'm not sure." His purchase in hand, he turned to go back to Samuel's living quarters, thinking she may have been cleaning up.

"Are you talking about that bonny redhead?" Gareth turned to see a short wiry man who'd been in the meeting upstairs.

"Yes, have you seen her?"

His arms full of bolts of cloth, the man gestured with his chin towards the door. "She left with some young man to the market."

"What young man? To the market? Why?"

"I think they were going to get something to eat. The man was upstairs. Your friend, I think."

"Bryant?" Gareth asked.

"I didn't catch his name."

"Food sounds like a wonderful idea to me," Cynan interrupted. "Let's join them."

Gareth nodded, suddenly aware of his own hunger. Turning, he tucked his package behind Samuel's counter. "Don't you dare sell that."

"What kind of merchant do you think I am?" Samuel asked indignantly. Gareth laughed and followed Cynan towards the door. As they left the small shop, they heard the wiry man say, "I'll take ten lengths of that brown if I get the same amount of linen for free, too."

Gareth and Cynan's laughter prevented them from hearing Samuel's sputtered response as they headed down the street.

Coming into the crowded marketplace, Cynan said, "I want three sticks of lamb and a huge tankard of ale!"

Gareth laughed. "Control your hunger for a moment. Let's find Elena and Bryant first."

"Find them in this crowd? We'll never eat!" Cynan wailed.

"Some mighty warrior you are!"

"I'm no warrior. I'm a simple shepherd who's used to eating regularly."

"Of course you are," Gareth said.

As they made their way through the crowds of people, Gareth wondered how Elena would react to his gift. Truly, clothing was a rather personal gift, but after all they had been through together, Gareth couldn't see how Elena would think him too forward. Then again, she could fling his gift back in his face. Perhaps, an insidious voice in his head said, what he feared was that she would reject him, not his gift. Gareth shook his head. Reject him? As if he was even offering himself!

"Gareth, what are we going to do with Elena?"

Glad to have something to get his mind off his feelings for Elena, Gareth looked over his shoulder and said, "What do you mean?"

"I mean, when you return to England, is she going with you?"

"Well, of course. That is her home."

"I know, but what will she tell Richard?"

"Tell him? Why should she tell him anything?"

"Come on, Gareth," Cynan paused as he ducked under a low-hanging sign offering repairs to saddles and bridles. "She's part of his court. You don't think he's going to have worried about her and wonder what she's been through?"

"She can tell him we were simply lost in the forest and made our way back with difficulty," Gareth said.

"Why should she?"

Cynan's question made Gareth stop and look at his friend, forcing people to walk around them. "Why should she? Why shouldn't she?"

Cynan looked uncomfortable. "Look, Gareth, I like Elena as much as you and Bryant do. But our lives are on the line here. Elena still considers herself one of Richard's ladies-in-waiting. She hasn't asked to remain here. We can only assume that she still considers Richard the true king of England."

"But she nearly died trying to warn us of the English soldiers!" Gareth protested.

"I know, I know."

"Then why are you doubting that she will continue to protect us?"

Cynan ran his hand through his hair and then let it drop by his side. Taking a deep breath, he said, "Gareth, Enid is pregnant."

Gareth grinned broadly and said, "Cynan, that's great! Congratulations!"

"No, listen to me. I must be around to be a father to this child. I can't be running off to each new adventure like I've been doing since we were kids. Enid has put up with it these three years we've been married, but I won't put her through it anymore--not with a babe on the way. This next battle I will fight because I have to and Enid agrees with me. But I will be more cautious than I ever have been. And if wondering about Elena's true loyalties makes me suspicious, then I'm sorry."

Gareth stared in open-mouthed surprise at Cynan. Never had he heard his usually buoyant friend so serious or so earnest. And though he thought Cynan was wrong about Elena, he could understand the motive behind his worry.

"I think Da said I was not to leave for three days. I promise you I will discover whether Elena's rose be white or red and we will deal with her accordingly, alright?"

Cynan nodded. "Thank you."

Trying to lighten the mood, Gareth said, "Now let's find those two--I could eat an entire flock!"

***

Elena looked around furtively and when she saw no one was looking, she licked her fingers, leaned over, and wiped her mouth on the hem of her dress. Turning to Bryant, she took the second skewer of meat and went to work on it.

"Look, my lady," Bryant said. "The game is going to start." Elena looked up from her meal to see a young brawny man step up onto one of the stumps, a stout rope in hand.

"Who's foolish enough to think they can pull me off the Viking stump?" he called out.

The crowd, which had quickly gathered, looked around at each other. Within seconds, a wiry man with an unruly shock of black hair pushed his way through.

"You know your boasting always gets you in trouble, Aldred," the wiry man said.

"I doubt there's any trouble you could give me, Owain," the brawny man shot back with a laugh.

Owain bent to pick up the other end of the rope before climbing on the opposite stump. A third man stepped out of the crowd and appointed himself the marshal.

"Are you good men ready?" he asked.

Both men nodded, looks of anticipation on their faces. "Very well, then. On the count of three. One, two, three!"

Hand over hand, the opponents pulled the slack of the rope in quickly until it was taut between them. Then the tug of war began. Aldred pulled so hard his opponent was forced to give up some slack or be pulled off his stump. He gave up several feet of rope so quickly that Owain, still pulling, nearly fell off the back of the stump. The crowd shouted encouragement to both contestants as Owain struggled to maintain his balance and then laughed as he tottered and fell off.

"See?" Bryant whispered in Elena's ear. "That is strategy."

Elena nodded understandingly. She was intrigued by this simple game. Again, she wondered if women ever played it, if they would play it this evening.

Aldred defeated two more opponents, one by pulling the rope clean out of his opponent's hands, the other by simply jerking the rope, and the man on the other end, forward.

"Now if he had given up some rope," Bryant explained. "He could have stayed on the stump longer. Some men just hate to give an inch, though."

Aldred flexed and bent his fingers while he waited for another challenger.

Finally, a man stepped out. Elena's eyes widened and she fervently hoped he would not notice her sitting on the edge of the crowd.

The tall blonde sailor grabbed up his end of the rope and leapt onto the stump. As soon as the count was called, he snatched up most of the slack and began giving short, sharp tugs to the rope. Within seconds, he toppled his brawny opponent and was calling for another.

Elena forgot to eat as she watched the muscles in his arms and back flex and release as he pulled man after man off his stump. Sweat made his thin shirt cling to his ribs and Elena could not tear her eyes away.

"There you are!" Gareth shouted. Elena jumped and dropped the stick of lamb in her lap. With a disgusted sigh, she quickly snatched up the stick and rubbed at the grease spot on her skirt. Wonderful, she thought. Each day away from court and courtly manners was taking its toll on her. Soon she would look and act like a common scullery maid. Before too long she'd have snarled hair and a toothless grin. Turning to glare at Gareth, she was further surprised by his exuberant grin and sparkling eyes. She could not remember seeing him so relaxed or happy before.

"You're certainly in high spirits this evening," she said.

"It's the market. Fairs, crowds of people, food, the atmosphere is contagious. I can't help but enjoy myself." Reaching down, he plucked the stick of meat right out of her hand and began devouring it. Although she was outraged, Elena couldn't bring herself to dress him down for his impertinence. She was still too fascinated at seeing him in such a good mood. It made his entire countenance change; the lines of worry disappeared and his infections grin made his face look boyish and innocent. The shock of hair, which was constantly in his eyes now seemed appropriate, giving him a reckless air that was further enhanced by his next words.

"Ho ho! Viking stumps!" Looking down at Elena, he said, "Did I ever tell you I was an expert at this game?" Elena shook her head as Gareth bolted up to the recently vacated stump opposite the blond sailor. Surely for all his strength he could not defeat the much larger man. Her eyes darted back and forth from the tall, well-muscled man to Gareth, compact and sinewy. Although the sailor was even more appealing now that his face, neck and V of his chest were glistening with exertion, for some reason, Elena found herself watching Gareth. His knees bent, he was crouched down, his feet planted firmly on the stump, the ornery shock of hair temporarily pushed off his forehead. His eyes narrowed in concentration as the count was called and a wicked grin touched his lips.

The smile never left his face as he tugged on the rope. He was not strong enough to gain rope from his adversary, but neither did he give any up. After several minutes of gaining not an inch, the sailor grew impatient and gave a tremendous heave. At the same time, Gareth let his excess rope slide easily through his hands. The sailor tottered on the edge of the stump before losing his balance and hopping to the ground. The crowd went wild, hooting and clapping and Elena joined in. She felt a strange sense of pride that Gareth had won but did not stop to wonder why.

The crowd grew even rowdier as man after man stepped forward to challenge Gareth only to be forced off his stump. Gareth grew sweaty and began breathing hard, but the devilish grin never left his mouth. Finally, he straightened and tossed down the rope. The crowd roared and clapped as he executed a mock bow. Returning to his friends, he threw himself down on the bench.

"I would give my horse for a mug of ale," he said, wiping the sweat off his face with the sleeve of his shirt.

"Then consider Isrid mine," Cynan said. Elena turned and saw him approaching with two heavy pewter mugs in one hand and an enormous roasted goose leg in the other.

"You are a saint, Cynan," Gareth said, relieving his friend of one of the mugs.

"Flattery won't get you out of giving me your horse."

Gareth gestured to the stumps with his chin. "You pull me off an he's yours."

Cynan looked apprehensively at the Viking stumps. " It would be too cruel for me to battle a winded man."

Gareth took a large swallow of ale and leaned close to Elena. "Cynan's never been able to best me on Viking stumps." Looking past her, he said, "Ho, Bryant! Be you ill?"

Elena turned to her forgotten dinner companion who was staring moodily out into the crowd. When Gareth called him, he glanced up and shrugged. "I was only marveling at some people's rudeness." Elena looked out into the crowd to see whom he was referring to, but she saw nothing unusual. Turning back to Gareth, she saw him exchange confused glances with Cynan.

Bryant suddenly stood and said, "I am retiring. Shall I walk you back to the house, Lady Elena?"

"So soon? It isn't even dark yet."

"No, but it will be in minutes."

Elena looked to Gareth who said, "Cynan and I are staying to see the sights. You can remain with us if you like." Elena turned back to Bryant in time to see his mouth tighten. Glancing at Elena, he gave her a weak smile and bent to kiss her hand. "Very well, my lady, I bid you good night." Elena nodded graciously and gave him one of her best smiles. Bryant was the only one who had ever shown respect to her rank. As he disappeared into the throng of people, Elena noticed two young children--a boy and a girl--playing on the Viking stumps.

"Gareth," she said, smoothing her voice to make it appear as if the question she was about to ask was completely ladylike and appropriate. "Do women ever play this game?"

"Do you jest?" Elena experienced a moment of mortification. "This is

Wales. Women do as they please and that includes this game." His eyebrows raised. "Would you like to try?"

"Oh, no," Elena protested weakly.

"Come on, you'll enjoy it. You enjoy knocking people off their pedestals enough, you ought to be great at this!"

Elena was torn between being indignant and grabbing up the rope. Gareth seemed to sense how she felt because he leaned closer and touched her elbow.

"This is Wales, Elena. You can do whatever you want and not worry about what people will think."

Elena wavered a mere second. "I would like to try it."

Gareth grinned and pulled her up. "Well, come on then. Here Cynan," he said, handing over his mug. "Elena's going to see if she has any Viking blood in her."

"No, I'm going to test my balance. There are no Norse in my family."

Cynan laughed. "With as much raiding, looting and ra--er, uh, pillaging as they did, everyone has a little Viking blood!"

Elena's eyes widened at his reference, but Gareth quickly distracted her by pulling her towards one of the stumps and putting the rope end in her hand. He shooed off the children who were clambering on the stumps. Lifting her skirts, Elena climbed up on the nearest stump.

"Be there any lass who'd like to try her hand at the rope?" he called out.

Aldred, the first man Elena had watched was leaning against a nearby booth. "Are you so tired you can't best a man? You must now take on the women?" he yelled mockingly.

"More like he's found no worthy challenger amongst you men and he knows a woman will give him more fight!" said a sassy young woman of fifteen or sixteen as she climbed up on the opposite stump. The nearby crowd laughed at her remark and Aldred flushed but laughed as well.

"No, no," Gareth jokingly admonished. "We've a newcomer who'd like to learn," he said as he handed the girl her end of the rope. "Are you ready, Elena?"

"I guess so."

"Crouch down. There you go. Now remember to use your arms, not your whole body. Are you ready?" he asked the girl who nodded and smiled encouragingly at Elena. "Very well. One, two, three, pull!"

Elena felt the rope being pulled out of her hands and when she grabbed it tightly, she found herself being pulled neatly off the stump. The crowd laughed good-naturedly, but Elena was embarrassed nonetheless.

"Don't worry," Gareth reassured. "That was only your first time. Here, try it again," he said as he retrieved her end of the rope. "Do you mind?" he asked the girl.

"Of course not." Calling to Elena, she said, "Don't think about your rope, miss. Just think on sticking like pitch to the log."

Elena nodded and stepped back up on her stump. Crouching down, she stared at a point on the ground and thought, Stay on the stump! Stay on the stump! When Gareth called out the count, she grabbed up as much of the excess rope as she could and began tugging, all the while staring at the point on the ground and concentrating on keeping her feet on the stump. Within a minute, she had pulled down her opponent and the gained the cheers of the crowd. The girl skipped over to Elena and said, "Well met! You're a natural!"

"Thank you," Elena said awkwardly as she started to step down.

"Not so fast," said Gareth. "You've got another challenger." Surprised, Elena looked up to see a young woman a year or two older than herself climb on the stump.

She easily defeated her second and third challengers, but by then her arms, unaccustomed to such vigorous play, were shaking with exhaustion and the fourth opponent bested her.

"Excellent job!" said Gareth as she sat down. He handed her his mug of ale and when she had caught her breath, she took several ladylike sips of the sharp-tasting but cold brew. "Well, what do you think of our game?" he asked when she handed his mug back to him.

"I think the girls back at court would love it!" Seeing Cynan look sharply at Gareth and misunderstanding its meaning, she hastened to explain. "We are not always proper and stuffy, you know. We play games and have fun, too. Why, even Lady Elizabeth plays tag with us."

"Of course," said Gareth, shaking his head at Cynan.

The trio sat in silence for several minutes just watching the crush of people who were milling about the square. The sun had set and torches were being lit at each merchant booth. Their flickering light gave everything a dreamlike quality. The smoke from the pitch torches mingled with the scent of food cooking, the smell of hard-earned sweat, and the salty tang of the nearby sea. Somewhere in one of the enclosed taverns, a lute and recorder played a lively tune to the accompanying beat of an Irish bodhran.

Elena inhaled deeply and sighed with contentment. She felt utterly comfortable and happy. Happy? she thought with a start. What was there here to make her happy? There certainly were no grand feasts of state with adoring men to flatter and cajole her. She had none of her beautiful gowns or precious jewelry give to her by her mother. There were no waiting maids to brush out her long hair or help her bathe. In fact, Elena could not remember the last time she had really bathed. Splashing around in a stream could not replace a barrel full of hot water and scented soap. Why she should be happy at this odd moment was a mystery to her, but as Elena sat on the hard-wooden bench with the narrow slats of the back pressing against her ribs and Gareth's arm lightly brushing her, she decided that she was truly happy at this moment. As a matter of fact, she didn't even remember the grease stain on her skirt.

Chapter 16

"Well, that does it for me," said Cynan with a yawn. "I am about to fall asleep on this miserable bench. I've had one too many nights of the late watch." Standing, he gave Elena a sleepy bow and said, "Don't let him keep you out all night." He turned and stumbled through the milling people.

"So much for my friend who never slept and was always up for a new adventure," Gareth said wryly.

Elena smiled and leaned forward. Gareth imagined she was weary herself and would like to retire, but he had promised Cynan that he would try to discover where her loyalties lay and they might not have much time alone again before they returned to England. While he racked his brain to think of a way to approach the subject, a breeze brought the fresh scent of the sea and he was seized with an inspiration. "Would you like to see the docks before we retire?"

Elena looked at him dubiously. "Are they safe?"

Gareth smiled. "Don't worry, they're not at all like those near London. Aberystwyth is still for the most part a large fishing village. The most excitement you're like to see is a late fisherman unloading his catch. Besides, what have you to fear? You are accompanied by Sir Gareth, knight of the realm. You think anyone with evil intent dare approach us?"

Elena laughed and said teasingly, "Nay, not with your hair sticking up all over your head like an ogre's!"

Gareth's hand flew to his unruly hair, but he could feel nothing unusually messy. When he saw the teasing look in his companion's face, he joined her laughter. "Well, what do you say?"

"That sounds lovely."

Gareth was surprised by her polite answer. Although she had been astoundingly cooperative of late, her early rudeness and haughtiness had so influenced him that he was constantly surprised by any other attitude from her.

They stood and she followed him through the crowds of people. As soon as they reached the edge of the marketplace, the throng rapidly diminished until they were walking alone down moonlit streets, the faint rush of the sea audible.

"This seems bigger than a large fishing village," Elena said as they made their way toward the ocean. The further they walked from the marketplace, the louder the sound of the water grew.

"Well, in size, yes, it is large, but not in attitude. The folk here consider themselves all family of sorts and they're not very tolerant of people disturbing their home with mischief and mayhem." Gareth glanced sideways at Elena. She was nodding her head slightly.

They came around a bend in the street that opened onto a rocky beach and the weathered docks.

"I've never seen such a sight," Elena whispered, coming to a stop on the edge of the sand.

"I'd have thought you'd seen everything in Britain, traveling with King Richard."

"All I ever get to see traveling with Richard is the inside of musty hunting castles and the filthy streets of London."

"Likes to hunt, does he?" Gareth asked, struggling to direct the conversation towards the current politics as they walked along the beach.

"I think he just uses hunting as a way to make himself look strong and powerful in front of his nobles. You'd think his success at achieving the throne would have made him confident enough in his power, but he seems to be constantly trying to prove himself."

"Maybe that's because he knows he doesn't belong there." Gareth said.

"His claim is a strong as any others. I think he's just nervous by nature. He's always fiddling with his dagger or his cuffs. Always smoothing his hair. It's too bad his wife died. She always had a calming influence on him." Elena bent to pick up a shell. "If it hadn't been for Anne, I don't think Richard would have ever succeeded in his bid for the throne."

"Perhaps that would have been for the best." Gareth felt as if he were walking on the rocky beach barefooted, so carefully was he trying to tread.

"Why? One man on the throne is as good as another. There is really very little difference between kings."

"How can you say that?" Gareth burst out.

Elena laughed at the outraged look on his face. "Come now, Gareth. How is Richard really any different from all of the previous kings?"

"Well, he ignores the rest of England while he lavishes attention and money on the northern part of the country where his cronies live."

"And that is worse than Henry VI's lunacy or his father's outrageous justifications for laying siege on France?"

Gareth paused, all thought of his original purpose forgotten for the moment. "Elena, how old are you?"

"What? That is not a very chivalrous question to ask, Sir Knight."

"Twenty?" he guessed.

"I think not," Elena answered indignantly. "I am barely nineteen."

"All in all, that's not very old."

"Why thank you," Elena said drolly.

"No, what I mean is, that is awfully young to be so cynical about the world and it's leaders."

In the pale moonlight, Gareth could see Elena frown, the creases in her forehead the only flaw in her otherwise perfect face. "I don't think of myself as cynical," she responded slowly.

"'One man on the throne or another, there really is no difference between them' isn't cynical?"

"I'm not a cynic. I'm a pragmatist. I merely like to look at situations realistically so I can benefit the most from them. Now before you give me your holier-than-thou lecture, let me remind you that women do not carry a tremendous amount of clout in this world. The most we can hope for out of life is to marry a husband of means who will keep us from starving and provide shelter and clothing. If he does not beat us, we are considered most fortunate. Can you honestly disagree with me?"

"Yes. In Wales--" Gareth began.

"I don't live in Wales, I live in England. Now answer me. Is there a better life for women in England than what I just mentioned?"

Gareth frowned and shook his head. "No, I suppose not."

"Very well. Now, given those circumstances, I don't think you can accuse me of being cynical merely because I try to better my life as I can. King Richard has provided me with many luxuries for very little work in return. My mother had already given birth to two stillborn children and was locked away in my father's manor, completely cut off from the social life she loved by the time she was my age. Can you blame me for wanting something different and doing what I can to get it?"

Gareth felt deflated. "Of course not." Although everything she had said was true, he was disappointed. Disappointed because when they returned to England, they would see no more of each other. They would not meet to exchange information, they would not await Henry Tudor's landing and word of the location of the battle, they would not be able to walk along the beaches of southern England. He would not be able to admire the creamy perfection of her skin by moonlight.

Once they returned to Richard's court, she would return to her life as a lady-in-waiting and he would be nothing more than a spy trying to sneak information about his sovereign to the enemy. There was no way he could expect her to help him and Henry Tudor, not when it would mean she would lose her position in court, not when it would mean she would lose everything she had worked for, even if he, Gareth, could not understand the appeal of formal feasts and overdressed courtiers. Once Henry took the throne, everyone in Richard's court would be dispensed with. Ladies-in-waiting would be sent back to their parents or the convent they had come from, for surely Henry Tudor would install new ones once he wed. Elena, like her mother, would be cut off from the social life she loved.

"We'd best head back. It's getting late," he said, his voice flat.

Turning, he began walking quickly up the beach to the cobbled street. Elena tried to match his rapid strides but could not in the gravelly sand. Running lightly to catch up to him, she linked her hand through his arm to slow him down. "Where are we sleeping tonight?" she asked.

Gareth did not hear Elena's question until she squeezed his arm and asked him again. He realized then that she was clinging to his arm and slowed his pace accordingly. "Samuel, the man whose shop we were in earlier will put us up tonight."

"You mean we get to sleep inside? And perhaps have warm water to wash in and clean linen to sleep on?"

Despite his disappointment, Gareth smiled at her tone and her questions. "Yes, my lady, you will have all the finest luxury Aberystwyth has to offer." Trying not to think of how much he would miss their bantering once they reached Richard's court, he guided them back to the center of town.

***

As they walked the moonlit streets back to Samuel's shop and home, Elena couldn't help but wonder if she had said something to anger Gareth. Although he answered any question she asked about this street or that shop, he seemed to forget her existence once he responded. For a woman who was used to being the center of a man's attention--especially if he was lucky enough to be taking a moonlit stroll with her--Gareth's distraction bothered her.

Of course, she reminded herself, this is Gareth, the man who could kiss her like she'd never been kissed one night and then throw himself at a coarse serving wench the next. This was the man who had nearly...well, nearly made love to her, and then treated her as nothing more than one of his rough traveling companions. Her life in Richard's court had taught her much about men and their moods, but Gareth belied all she knew. None of her carefully devised "wiles" had worked on him, yet when she least expected it, and was least prepared for it, he would kiss her, with tenderness, or with soul-scorching passion that left her gasping for breath. Gareth seemed most responsive to her when she was completely unconscious of what she was doing or saying. On the other hand, when she acted like a proper lady of the court, he always seemed to grow distant.

So why should he be sullen now? she asked herself. Hadn't she just tossed over every dignity by climbing onto that stump and playing tug-of-war until she was as sweaty as a horse? Elena gazed up at the stars, wishing she could read their supposed messages. Would she never understand this man?

Gareth tugged on her arm, startling her. She hadn't realized she had stopped when she was studying the stars.

"We're almost there," he said politely as she ran lightly to match his quickening pace.

When they reached the shop, it, like every other shop on the street, was dark.

"Have they forgotten us?" Elena asked worriedly. She did *not* want to sleep outside one more night, especially when their blankets, which offered meager comfort, were inside!

"No, I'm sure someone is awake in the back rooms," Gareth assured as he knocked on the door, although Elena didn't think he sounded very convinced.

Gareth tried the handle, but it was locked. He knocked again more loudly, but there was still no answer. He was just about to pound on the door when it swung open.

The sleepy countenance of Samuel greeted them, with voluminous white night shirt billowing, and nightcap askew. He was holding a candle up to inspect their faces. "Saints preserve us, young man, have you no consideration for the hours of an honest working man?" he asked as he opened the door wider for them to enter.

"I'm sorry, Samuel. We were in the market and we lost all track of time," Gareth apologized.

"Humph," Samuel replied as he led them through the shop and down the hall. He stopped in the middle of the hall and opened a door Elena had not even noticed earlier. "The lady may sleep in here. It's not large, but it is clean and comfortable. You, impertinent boy, are upstairs with all of the other men, on the floor." He placed the candle down and disappeared down the hall. Gareth stepped forward and gestured Elena into the room.

As she walked through the doorway, Elena judged that Samuel had been generous when he said the room was not large. It was more of a closet, with a low bed pushed into one corner and just enough room left for a small table. He was accurate on the clean and comfortable part, however, Elena thought. There was not a speck of dust to be seen and the bed was made up with a bright quilt and a small pillow. There was even an ewer of water on the table.

"Do you need aught else?"

For some reason, his question made Elena think of Gareth's passionate kisses. Hastily dismissing that thought from her mind, she said, "No. This should do." She felt like she should say something else, something to make the lighthearted Gareth of earlier this evening return, but she could think of nothing.

Gareth bade her good night and gently closed the door.

The door swayed open slightly after Gareth left and Elena tried to pull it closed again, but there was no latch to keep it tight. Elena shook her head. At least everyone was already asleep. Turning, she began struggling out of her worn and travel-stained gown. She pulled the faded cotehardie over her head, laying it on the foot of the bed and then leaned over to pull off her boots. Pulling off her chemise, she glanced in the pitcher of water. Thank heavens it was full. There was nothing she wanted more than to wash the sweat and dust of travel off her skin. The water was cool and refreshing. She had just put her chemise back on when she heard a light knock on the door.

Elena whirled around at the noise, clutching her gown to her breast, as the door swung open. A red-faced Gareth met her gaze.

"I--I'm sorry, Elena, I knocked, but the door..."

"Yes, I couldn't get it to latch."

Gareth glanced at her thin covering before focusing on a point somewhere around her forehead. I just wanted to, uh, give you this," he said as he thrust a large bundle at her. "Da thinks we'll have enough time to have it made up before we leave."

"Have what made up?" Elena asked as she tucked her gown under her arms and began untying the cloth wrapper. A folded length of the wool she had been looking at earlier fell onto the bed. She sucked in her breath.

"I thought you would like a new dress to return to England in."

Elena looked from the cloth to Gareth who stood uncertainly just inside the doorway. How many men realized the importance of a new gown or took the time to see to its creation? Heedless of her state of undress and the impropriety of her action, Elena threw her arms around his neck. "It's wonderful! I don't know what to say."

She felt Gareth's hands slide around her waist. "How about 'thank you'?"

Though she was not used to saying the words, she laughed and said, "Thank you, thank you, thank you, Gareth." She sobered slightly when she realized that her arms were still around his neck and his hands were now caressing her through her thin chemise. Without quite realizing what she was doing, she leaned up and pressed her lips to his. He responded slowly, tentatively, only opening his lips when she pressed hers against them more insistently. An abstract part of Elena's brain bellowed that this was not included in the conduct befitting a noble lady, but she quickly silenced it as she concentrated on the rush of sensations that were coursing through her body.

Gareth's gentle grip on her waist was now crushing her against him. One of his hands slid up her back to tangle in her hair and cradle her head. Elena moaned softly as she gave herself over completely to his kiss, opening her mouth and allowing his tongue to explore its soft recesses. Elena felt his muscles shudder through his worn shirt as she ran her fingertips over his shoulders and up into his unruly hair. Unable to control herself, she grabbed fistfuls of his thick hair and pulled his head closer to hers so she could return his kiss.

Finally, the kiss ended and Elena buried her face weakly in Gareth's neck where she could feel his pulse race underneath her lips. His grip on her had relaxed and his hands had resumed their gentle caress up and down her back. Despite the excitement of their kiss, Elena could not help but wish she could just go to sleep, here in his arms, so comfortable was she. As she relaxed still further against him, her mind wandered to the cloth he had bought her and his promise of a new dress. Suddenly, she remembered the rest of his words and she straightened.

"Did you say we were returning to England?"

Gareth's face was still flushed, but his eyes were now wary as he slowly nodded. "Aye, in a few days."

"What about the meeting today? Did you get everything worked out?"

Gareth paused before he answered. "Not quite. You see, I," he paused to clear his throat. "I'm not convinced that this whole thing is going to work."

"What? What do you mean?" Elena was thoroughly confused. Had they chased over half of Britain for naught?

"I don't think Henry Tudor will be successful. Actually, I don't think he's even going to try to land in Wales."

"Then this whole trip was a waste?"

Gareth looked decidedly uncomfortable. "No, of course not. I learned some valuable information that helped me decide that the best thing for me to do it return to Richard's court and act like nothing untoward occurred here in Wales."

Elena stared at Gareth, amazed. "What kind of information?"

Dropping his hands from her waist, he pushed past her and sat on the bed. "I'm much too tired to go into now. Besides, I thought you'd be happy to be returning to court. Especially in a new dress."

Elena looked at Gareth skeptically. She was no henwit who did not understand politics. True, she had little interest in them, but she knew that for Gareth to suddenly change his mind--and his allegiance--must mean that something serious had occurred. Studying his face, she forbore from questioning him further. He did look tired, weary even, as he slouched against the wall.

Unmindful of her scant attire, Elena sat next to him on the bed, deciding to drop the subject for the time being. "What made you choose this color of fabric?" she asked, smoothing the pile of wool.

"I thought it would flatter your complexion and hair coloring. Is it all right? Do you like it?"

"Truthfully?" she asked with a smile.

Gareth frowned. "You hate it?"

Elena laughed. "Truthfully, I was admiring this exact color only this morning, wishing I could make a new dress out of it." She laughed again as relief crossed his face and without thought, she leaned over and kissed him lightly on the lips. "Thank you, Gareth." Her gaze trapped by his, she remained in her bent over position. Slowly, he raised his hand and caressed her cheek with his calloused fingertips.

"No, Elena, thank you."

"For what?" she whispered, confused.

Gareth shook his head and drew her down on top of him, kissing her slowly, endlessly. When he pulled back, he brushed the hair off her face and smoothed it down her back. "I have a favor to ask of you," he said.

Elena raised her eyebrows in question.

"Once we return to England, I would rather Richard not know I ever had thoughts of joining Henry Tudor's fight. I feel guilty enough knowing I have broken my knightly vows these past weeks. If I had to face Richard, I would lose his trust, not to mention my life."

Elena nodded, the thought of Gareth dying over a simple misunderstanding creasing her brow with worry and fear. "Of course. Richard need not know anything that has gone on these weeks since we were separated from his ranks."

"Thank you," Gareth said softly, seemingly relieved. And yet, Elena could tell he was still greatly bothered by something.

"Are you sure this is the right decision, Gareth?"

He stared at the flame of the candle on the small table, studying its flicker before answering. "It's what I must do."

It's what he must do, Elena thought as she followed his gaze to the hypnotic flame. How cryptic he could be. She thought of returning to England and court life. How she had longed for the luxury and beauty, how--Elena paused in mid-thought. Returning to England meant returning to her fiancé, the Earl of Brackley. Sweet Jesu, she had near forgotten about the horrid man these past few weeks. How would she face him and their forthcoming marriage? Well, she told herself firmly, she would simply have to convince King Richard to call off the marriage. She was one of his favorite ladies-in-waiting and she had served him diligently. Still, a nagging doubt whispered.

Suppose the earl has offered him something Richard needs. Monarchs were forever searching for more money, more troops, more promises of support. What if she could not convince the king? What if he forced her to marry that corpulent ogre? Elena shivered and turned back to Gareth. His face was hidden in half-shadows, the meager light sculpting his face, masking all hints of the boyishness she had seen earlier this evening in harsh lines. And yet, she still found him incredibly appealing. There was an intensity about him that radiated strength and ability. He was even more handsome than she had thought. The bald pate and bushy brows of her intended flashed before her eyes. Was she doomed to living her life with an ugly old man, not knowing the joys of love in a young man's strong arms, the sweetness of passion she so often heard of in minstrel's songs?

Without a thought to the consequences, she made her decision. She would know love, she would know it this very night, and be damned with her fiancée!

Her decision made, Elena was suddenly overcome with an unfamiliar sensation: shyness. How should she approach Gareth? What should she say? What if he were to refuse? Deciding to simply follow her instincts, she gently grasped Gareth's chin in her hand and turned it toward her.

"I should go," he began. "You must be exhausted."

Her heart pounding, Elena leaned slowly toward Gareth. She stared at the light bristling of stubble that covered his chin and upper lip. Unlike his dark hair, his beard had gold and copper highlights that glistened in the glow of the candle. As she drew nearer, she caught his faint scent and inhaled deeply. Sweat, leather, the outdoors, and something deliciously musky and spicy that she sensed was just him: these were the smells that she had grown to associate with all that was masculine and attractive in the past weeks.

Gareth shivered when she moved her hand from his chin to brush his stubborn lock of hair from his face. Elena could not bring herself to meet his grey eyes, so she ran her fingers through his thick wavy hair, caressing her way down his neck to his shoulders. She could feel the warmth of his skin through his rough shirt as she took a shaky breath. Leaning forward even more, she closed her eyes lazily as she pressed her lips to his warm mouth. She felt a moment's panic when Gareth did not immediately respond, but all thought quickly left her mind when, in a rush, Gareth dragged her body flush against his. Once again, she had only to initiate the kiss to have him meet her more than halfway. Without even realizing she had done so, Elena moaned as Gareth ran his hands up and down her back, the thin chemise heightening the friction rather than diminishing it. He devoured her mouth hungrily, stealing the very breath from her body, before sliding his lips over her smooth cheek to explore the delicate folds of her ear.

Elena dug her nails into his shoulders as she let her head drop back, her neck suddenly too weak to hold the weight of it, although the rest of her body felt light as a feather. Her skin glowed with warmth as if the candle on the table were instead a bonfire, threatening to consume her. Gareth took advantage of her exposed neck to leave a new trail of burning kisses. Elena brought her head up sharply when Gareth's hands swept around her waist and up her midriff to cup her breasts. The sensations his touch sent through her body caused her breathing to come in quick, shallow pants. The rapidly diminishing logical part of her brain realized that Gareth's breathing was just as labored.

Gareth's kisses returned to her mouth as their bodies sank lower on the bed. Without consciously planning to, Elena ran her hands down to Gareth's waist and tugged on his shirt, pulling it out of his breeches and up over his torso and shoulders. Their lips parted for a mere second as Gareth impatiently tugged the shirt over his head and tossed it to the floor. The pressure of his renewed kisses pushed her fully back on the bed and as he followed her down, he pulled off his chausses.

He kissed the silkiness of her eyebrows, the smoothness of her skin, the fullness of her lips.

The rest of their clothing quickly followed, though later Elena could never remember how the sleeve of her chemise came to be ripped nearly off, or how Gareth's breeches had come to land on the candle where they had smoldered for a few seconds before plunging the room in darkness.

The moon sent pale beams through the tiny window, bathing the lovers in its silvery light, hiding the flush of Elena's cheek when Gareth kissed the peak of her breast. His face was lost in shadow as he rolled atop her, but she saw the rugged contours of his visage with first her fingertips and then her mouth. She learned the sculpting of his muscled back, the firm roundness of his buttocks. She drank in his scent as if it were life-giving air and she a drowning woman. She was nearly overcome with so many sensations. One moment, she reveled in the silkiness of his hair, the next, in the saltiness of his skin, the rasp of his whiskers against her neck, the grip of his callused hand on her hip, her breast. Elena barely recognized the delight of one part of him before she discovered a new one. I could spend a lifetime learning his body, she thought, and in the slumberous heat of passion, the thought did not scare her. It enticed her.

Without fear or hesitation, she gave herself to him and he worshiped her for it, kissing and caressing her with a gentleness that touched her soul. His hands roamed her body, memorizing the soft curves that so perfectly fit his hard hollows. Her skin was sweet to the taste, the scent of her hair intoxicating. He buried his face in it before he was distracted by a velvet ear lobe. He was acutely aware of her womanly softness, the vulnerability of her body —strong though it may be with long, lean muscles and taut abdomen. He wanted to cradle her in his arms protectively at the same time he wanted to crush her to him and sink into her body. It was a disturbing and overwhelming feeling, how completely he was in her thrall. He felt his blood pounding, his breath coming faster.

Gareth forced himself to slow down, to make this experience good for Elena. He knew not why she had initiated their lovemaking, nor what the future held for them, but for this one night, he would show her just what she meant to him.

Focused now, he spent endless moments savoring the soft skin of each breast before dragging his lips across her stomach. He heard her breath hitch as his lips brushed soft curls and he grinned wickedly up at her before parting her legs and dropping his mouth to her core.

Elena's back arched off the bed and she grasped a handful of his hair in her hand, mumbling incoherently, "What...you can't...that's..." before falling back and succumbing to the pleasure he wrought. Gareth focused his long-building desire for Elena into that one intimate kiss, wringing sobs of pleasure from her, branding her with his tongue and lips, marking her as his own. He felt the tension in her body build, and while one part of him wanted to bring her to completion, another part—the more primal and ruthless side—needed to posses her. Now.

He dragged his lips back up along her ribcage, not with soft kisses as before, but with nips of his teeth and scratching of his night beard. Elena opened her eyes and in the cold glitter of the moonlight, they were dark and smoldering. She dug her hands into his hair and pulled his mouth to her own, biting gently at his lips, licking his teeth, tangling his tongue with hers. She dug her nails into his buttocks, urging him closer and he complied, sliding his shaft along her tender wetness. He heard her suck in a shaky breath and he repeated the motion again and again until she hissed, "Now!"

He smiled at her imperious tone, but for once was more than happy to comply with her demands. He positioned himself at her entrance and slowly slid home, gritting his teeth with the effort it took to take his time and make it right for her. He heard Elena take a sharp breath and he searched her face, seeing a slight frown mar her forehead.

"Is it…does it hurt? Should I—"

"No!" she interrupted. "For God's sake, keep going!"

Gareth grinned and pressed a hard kiss to her lips as he sank the final crucial bit. His carefully slow pace drove him to the brink of his self-control, but he held back, adjusting his angle, tilting her hips, and caressing her at that delicate juncture. He was rewarded with murmured words of endearment and encouragement; little sighs and moans that stoked his desire to an inferno. His lovemaking took on an urgency that must have translated to Elena for she responded by lifting her hips, tossing her head until finally, the storm racked her body, convulsions of pleasure involuntarily pulling his own release from his body. She cried out and Gareth kissed her hard, swallowing her cry as he smothered his own.

When at last they lay back, exhausted, they snuggled together on the narrow bed as comfortably as if they had been doing so their whole lives.

Chapter 17

Gareth awoke early the next morning as the sun's first rays made their way into a tiny window, high on the wall. He was disoriented for several seconds as he stared at the clean wooden walls of the room. Of late, he had become used to sleeping outdoors, on the ground. As he tried to stretch and found his arm pinned beneath Elena's head, his mind quickly cleared and he turned to survey his bedfellow.

Her hair was a soft tangle of reddish-brown waves and curls spread about the pillow like a silk veil, its sweet scent filling his nostrils and reminding him of the night before when he had grabbed double handfuls of the silken strands and buried his face in their fragrance. Her face nestled against his shoulder was beautiful, peaceful, and, he thought, content.

The last time he had watched her sleep, she had been deathly ill, her face flushed with fever, her hair dampened with sweat. Even when the fever had broken, her eyes had remained slightly glazed with weakness for days afterwards. Then they had almost made love, stopped only by Cynan pounding on the door that English soldiers were after them. There had been no soldiers last night. No Cynan pounding on the door. No illness to befuddle Elena's mind as to what they were doing.

Gareth brushed a feather-light kiss against Elena's brow. No, there had been nothing to stand in their way last night. There had been only love. Gareth swallowed but did not try to deny himself the emotion. Yes, last night he had succumbed to the feeling that had been steadily growing since he had seen her standing at the top of the stairs in Richard's great hall those many weeks ago; the feeling that had grown despite her haughtiness, despite her complaining, nagging, and bickering as they rode through Wales; the feeling that grew tenfold that horrible night he found her huddled in the middle of the road; the feeling that would have to cease once they returned to England, returned to Richard's court.

Gareth took a deep breath and exhaled slowly, forcing himself to forget that last thought. They would have almost another week before he had to hand her back to Richard and to her fiancée, perhaps a few days more if they were lucky and the roads were bad.

Elena squirmed in his arms and opened her eyes, smiling lazily at him. He grinned back at her, immensely relieved at her response. Dipping his head, he kissed her gently, her lips like warm velvet under his mouth. Of its own will, his free hand slid up the smooth skin of her torso to caress her breast. His heart began hammering against his ribs as Elena's hands began their own exploration over his body.

Staring down at her, he was entranced by the fiery colors ignited in her hair as a shaft of sunlight struck it. Her eyes also were illuminated, their cinnamon depths pulling him towards her for another kiss. An inch before his lips were to touch hers, Gareth's lovestruck mind finally recognized the significance of the light on Elena's face. Pulling back abruptly, he saw her scowl.

"'Tis morning, love, and I had best duck out before the others awaken. There are at least three men in this house who would sever my head from my body if they were to discover me in your room."

Elena laughed shakily, and Gareth wondered if she was just now aware of the implications of their stolen night together. Tossing her hair over her shoulder, she sat up as Gareth climbed from the bed. As he retrieved his discarded clothing, she studied his supple body without embarrassment, though her scrutiny made him nervous. Suppose she didn't like what she saw? Glancing nervously over his shoulder, he saw admiration and raw desire on her face. He almost returned to her then and there, consequences be damned, but forced himself to stay focused.

Once dressed, Gareth turned and bent to drop a quick kiss on her lips. "I've no plans today. What say we travel about town and find a seamstress? We've been through enough to have earned at least one day's play."

Elena's eyes sparkled at his mention of a seamstress. Grabbing his face before he could straighten, she kissed him soundly on the mouth before flopping back down on the bed.

"If we have a day to do what we want, then I want to sleep another hour. I've been up with the sun for so many days, I feel like a chicken!"

Gareth laughed and said, "Sleep away, my lady. The day is yours." Carefully opening the door, he peeked outside before quickly leaving. Once in the hall, he stayed where he was a moment to let his eyes adjust to the darkness.

"Gareth!" his father called out from the other end of the hall. Gareth's heart stopped and his mouth went dry. He felt like a twelve-year-old who had been caught peeping at the bathing milkmaids. Full of dread, he turned and watched his father walk down the hall.

"Is she still asleep?" Morgan asked.

Gareth swallowed to force his heart back down into his chest, then he cleared his throat. "Yes, I thought I'd check on her, but she's asleep."

"Poor dear, she probably needs the rest, especially after last night."

Gareth's eyes widened to the point he was afraid they would tumble out of his head. "Last night?"

"Yes. Cynan said you convinced Elena to play on the Viking stumps last night in the market."

Gareth's heart resumed beating. "Yes. She did very well."

"Well, best not to disturb her then. Let's go sit by the fire and talk about your strategy."

Gareth nodded and allowed himself to be pulled down the hall on legs that were rubbery with reaction to almost being caught, and weak from... other things.

***

After Gareth left, wedging the door as closed as it would go, Elena stretched lazily, curling her toes and yawning. This was heaven, she thought. To simply be able to lay here in relative comfort and cleanliness for as long as she wanted. More sleep was definitely what she wanted, but as she lay on the narrow pallet and gazed out the tiny square pane of the window, she found that she was not the least bit sleepy. In fact, she felt as if she could hike across Wales. Elena laughed at the whimsical thought. Two months ago, she would have thought something like, "I could dance all night," or, "I could help Lady Elizabeth change her clothes twelve time today." Still, sleepy or no, it felt wonderful to lay here and know that the day was hers to do with as she pleased. Hers and Gareth's.

She glanced around the room, her gaze coming to rest on the heap of cranberry-colored wool. A new dress! And the finest cotton! She had not been so excited about having a new outfit since her mother had first helped her prepare for moving to Richard's court. The fact that Gareth had thought enough of her to give her such a gift gave her pause.

Sitting up slowly, Elena leaned over and collected her torn chemise. Her cheeks warmed as she thought of the night spent in Gareth's arms, his compactly built but strong body pressed against hers. What would Margaret and Catherine and all the other girls back at court say if they knew what she had done. Not only done, she corrected herself, but enjoyed! She did not regret for a moment what had happened last night. In the bright light of day, she forced herself to admit that she had long found Gareth attractive. But somewhere along their travels, she had come to desire more than his handsome face or broad shoulders. His focus, his determination, the way he put her safety above all else; she had never had someone make her feel as cherished as he did. And this gift...

No, she was not sorry for what happened last night. In fact, she would do her best to see that it happened again before she must face the possibility of a wedding night with Brackley. The wayward thought of the earl this time did not bring an involuntary shudder. Not because she was resigned to her fate, but because suddenly she saw before her not Brackley as a bridegroom, but Gareth.

She gasped aloud at the thought. Wed? To Gareth? He held no land, no position of honor or prestige. The blood rushed from Elena's face and she had to sit down, because suddenly, she found that she didn't care that he was a simple knight, and a Welsh one at that. The realization left her dizzy, as if she'd held onto her plans and expectations for so long that they'd served as her anchor and she was now adrift in a sea of uncertainty. Could she truly be happy with a man such as Gareth? She laughed aloud at herself for such a foolish question. She knew without a doubt that Gareth could show her a happiness far beyond what she had once hoped to achieve. The question was, could he be happy with a woman such as herself? The thought was disconcerting to say the least, for she'd rarely suffered self-doubt, but she found herself in new territory, stripped bare of her arsenal of feminine wiles. She glanced again at the pile of fabric. Such a gift gave her hope that Gareth did in fact return her feelings.

Vowing she would find a way to discover his feelings for her before they reached Richard's court, Elena stood and pulled on her chemise. As she laced herself into her worn cotehardie, she reveled in her plan to burn it and scatter the ashes at sea as soon as her new dress was made.

***

"What have you discovered about Elena's loyalties?" Morgan asked gently as he and Gareth broke their fast on crusty bread and tangy goat cheese.

Gareth pulled his thoughts from the previous night's activities and swallowed his mouthful of bread. "Elena holds no great love for either Richard or Henry, but maintaining her livelihood is, understandably, utmost in her mind. As a mere lady-in-waiting, she would hold no importance for Henry, hence, she would most likely lose her position in court. Although she did not say she would oppose our efforts, neither did she offer help or support."

"Not even if *you* asked for her help?" Morgan asked, eyeing Gareth speculatively.

Gareth looked sharply at his father, exasperated with himself for his adolescent fear of discovery. Deciding to ignore his father's unspoken questions, he shook his head. "I can't do that, Da. She is here now because of a quirk of fate. Because she rode the wrong way on that blasted road after Richard's party was attacked. If she'd had her way, she would have spent these past weeks in the luxury of court, being pampered and flirting with the courtiers." Gareth felt a twinge of jealousy at the thought of Elena flirting with the wealthy, handsome men of Richard's court, but he continued. "We simply can't ask her to make that sacrifice."

His father gazed steadily at him for a long moment and Gareth focused his attention on his meal, willing his expression not to reveal his feelings for Elena.

"You and see seem to get along well."

Gareth nearly choked on a crust of bread. Reaching for a tankard, he washed it down and scowled at his father. "Well enough."

"Perhaps more than well enough, I'm inclined to say."

"More than well enough for what?" Gareth asked sharply, but God help him, he knew.

"What if you married Lady Elena. Your loyalties would be hers and we need not worry about—"

"No!" Though the idea had sprouted in the back of his mind since awakening with Elena in his arms, he could not abide the idea of manipulating her into marriage simply to aid Lord Stanley's plans. Not when his own feelings were engaged. Elena would never willingly marry a man of his station. She had made clear many times what she sought out of life and that was position, wealth, and security. Security he could give her—with his life, if need be. Wealth he had enough, at least enough to keep her well fed, well clothed, well sheltered, though perhaps not as lavishly as Elena hoped for.

But position was a tenuous thing in Wales, and soon all of England if Henry Tudor's plans came to fruition. He knew how important such a thing was to Elena and he would not risk her compromising her dreams.

Liar, hissed a voice in the back of his head. *What you would not risk is your heart, should you lay it before her and have her rejected. Coward!*

Gareth shook his head and clenched his jaw, ignoring the thought. When he spoke, his voice was low and harsh. "Elena is most enamored of her position at court. She would not give it up for life as mistress of a Welsh keep."

"But if we assured her she would have a place in Henry's court--"

"No!" Gareth said more forcefully than he had planned. "Henry won't lose this war without Elena's help and we both know there's every chance we'll be completely crushed. If that should happen, I would not have Elena then be termed a traitor and put to death."

"Alright son, alright. We need not ask her assistance." Morgan watched his son tear almost savagely into his bread. "Gareth?"

Much calmer now that his anger was spent, Gareth smiled apologetically at his father and said, "Yes?"

"I'm not questioning your loyalty to me and this cause, for I know you would lay down your very life once you have committed yourself to something."

"But?" Gareth prodded.

"No buts, I just want to know your feelings."

Gareth was confused and he frowned as he asked, "About what?"

Morgan lifted his hand in an encompassing gesture. "About this whole venture. I believe in Henry Tudor's claim, as do your friends, and I know that *you* are fighting for Wales. But I've yet to hear you say you think we will be victorious. Do you think Richard will crush us?"

Gareth saw the concern on Morgan's face and sighed, tossing the bit of bread he was about to eat back onto the table. "I don't know, Da. Richard has many enemies in England, but he has managed to purchase or cajole or win over many powerful allies as well. And Henry has to get here, gather his troops, and get them to England. I don't know," he repeated as he leaned back on the rickety wooden chair, lifting its front legs off the floor and balancing precariously on the back two. Three men of his own age came down from the upstairs room where they had spent the night. They nodded good morning to Gareth and his father and made their way down the hall to the shop.

Gareth dropped his chair back onto all four legs and turned to face his father, noting the worried look on his father's face. He immediately felt remorseful for his doom saying. "You can't place much faith in my ramblings. In fact, don't listen to me--I'm a green knight with little war experience. I guess I'm still uncomfortable with this whole spying idea."

Morgan waved his hand dismissively. "You're right, of course. For all our self-righteousness, there is every chance we will be slaughtered. We would be fools if we went into battle expecting the angels to help us defeat our enemies and escape unscathed, though I know that's what many men will expect." He paused and took a breath. "I don't want to upset you further, Gareth, but have you thought about what you're going to say to Elena if she's to be kept out of our plans?"

Gareth nodded and glanced down the hall to make sure Elena had not come out of her room. "I've already told her that I have changed my mind about joining Henry's fight and that we will be returning to England in a few days."

"Will she say anything about this meeting?"

Gareth paused. She had promised not to mention his involvement, but if she thought he was standing for Richard, would she not hesitate to tell the king what she knew of this meeting? He chewed his upper lip, feeling the stubble of several day's growth. Gambling on their night together, he said, "No, she will say naught." His father looked at him searchingly and Gareth struggled to keep his face smooth and innocent-looking.

After a seemingly endless few seconds, Morgan nodded and said, "Very well. When will you return to England?"

"In a few days. I would have Elena well rested before we begin yet another journey, and it will take time to have her dress made."

"Ah, yes, her new dress. Was she pleased with your purchase?"

Gareth couldn't suppress his smile. "She was delighted, I think."

"Yes, well what young lady wouldn't be delighted to have a handsome young lad present her with such a generous gift."

"Da," Gareth said. Why was it that his father could one moment treat him like a worldly important man and then the very next, make him feel like a boy of seven?

"Well, it's true. You are handsome. You take after me. Although your mother was quite a beauty as well--had all the boys after her for miles around..."

Gareth stared in amazement as his father continued to reminisce about the past. Was this the same man who had discussed political tactics last night so cunningly with Lord Stanley?

Both men's thoughts were interrupted by Elena's entrance.

"Good morning, Lady Elena," Morgan boomed.

Elena bestowed her sweetest kindly-older-man smile on him before turning expectantly to Gareth, who was standing.

"Good morning, Elena," he said in a husky voice. Her smile deepened seductively and her eyes sparkled intimately at him, making the blood rush to his face and his throat constrict. "Would you--" he cleared his throat. "Would you like some fresh bread or cheese?"

"Yes, come have some, dear girl. Samuel's wife left his pantry well-stocked before she left to visit her kin." As Elena sat in Gareth's vacated seat, Morgan continued, "How did you pass your night?"

Gareth choked on a slice of cheese and looked quickly to Elena who seemed as composed as ever. "Wonderfully," she said with a smile. "It was the most pleasurable night I've spent." Despite his fear that Morgan would decipher just what she meant, he couldn't ignore the tingling warmth that spread over his body at her words. He was glad she had found their encounter equally pleasing.

As soon as Elena was finished eating, he said, "Shall we spend today finding a seamstress for your gown?"

Elena quickly stood and ran down the hall to her room, calling over her shoulder, "Yes! I'll get the cloth now!"

"I understand there are several reputable seamstresses on the third street to the west. Here," Morgan said, reaching into his tunic and pulling out a small leather bag. "Make sure you eat well. Perhaps you should buy another horse, as well, for Lady Elena to ride. It cannot be too comfortable to cross mountains pressed together on one horse."

Gareth refrained from telling him just what was uncomfortable about that situation, and instead pushed the bag of coins away. "You've given me more than enough, Da. I still have more than half of what you gave me yesterday, thanks to Cynan."

"This is not from me, though I'd give it to you if I had it. Lord Stanley asked me to give it to you before he left at sunrise. He said he understood how difficult your task would be and how it was hard to know what was right all the time."

Gareth stared at the small bag for a moment before slowly reaching out to take it. "That was kind of him. He seemed such an ogre yesterday."

"He's in a difficult spot. Richard holds his son as ransom to Stanley's loyalty, yet Henry is his kin as well."

Gareth felt his unease about returning as a spy to England settle on his shoulders like a familiar weight. Was there nothing about this entire war he would not feel guilty for? Before he had time to heap more recriminations on his head, Elena returned, positively beaming as she handed him the heavy mass of cloth and took his arm.

"Do you know where we are going?" she asked sweetly, and if Gareth had not been so preoccupied, he would have marveled at her tone.

"Yes," Morgan answered for him. "I've told him of several places you can try, not a ten minute's walk from here."

"Excellent," she replied. Tugging on Gareth's arm, she said, "Shall we go?"

***

"What a glorious day!" said Elena as they walked down the narrow street. Lifting her face to the warm sun, she inhaled deeply of the salty air.

Gareth glanced over the pile of wool in his arms and smiled. "That is truly something I never thought to hear cross your lips."

Elena frowned. "Why not?" she asked, although she knew the answer. Studying her escort, she saw him look quickly away and knew to what he referred.

"You just seem like you prefer the comforts of a castle and servants."

Elena studied the large formation of clouds that was moving in from the west. She considered responding with a flippant answer but stopped herself. She was determined to test her feelings for him and, perhaps, discover his for her. Deciding to be as honest as he himself always was, she said, "Perhaps I've just grown to appreciate the beauty of other surroundings."

"I can understand how it has been difficult."

"What do you mean," Elena asked, her hackles bristling.

The corner of Gareth's mouth twitched and he said, "What with your own beauty eclipsing everything around you, I can see how it would be difficult for you to notice anything else."

Elena stared at him for a few seconds as an embarrassed flush crept up his neck and suffused his face. "Why Gareth, I do believe you're actually flirting with me!" Before he could stammer an excuse, she said, "You really should have tried it before."

This caught Gareth off guard, she could tell, and with more curiosity than embarrassment, he asked why.

Elena schooled herself not to laugh with delight as she responded, "Well, it's a much more effective method for getting into a lady's good graces than is telling her how rude, demanding, and self-centered she is."

Gareth tried to look abashed, but when Elena herself burst out laughing, he quickly joined her. They continued laughing and teasing one another until they came to the first of the seamstress shops. Gareth hadn't even begun to explain their business when the seamstress curtly informed them that she was entirely too busy to take on any new work. She quickly ushered them out of her shop without so much as a "Good day." Rather than being put off by the woman's rudeness, Gareth and Elena mimicked the dour old woman as they made their way to the next shop, halfway down the street, only to discover it closed.

"We will be successful, Elena, fear not," Gareth said grandly as he shifted the bulk of fabric in his arms.

"Of course we will," she responded, studying his clear grey eyes beneath the mop of dark hair. He really is handsome, she thought. Not in the same way that Lord Edgeford was, for Gareth's features were not as fine, his hair not as perfectly groomed, his hands not as soft, but there was no denying that Gareth was attractive. His squarely cut jaw and sculptured face bespoke a strength that Edgeford utterly lacked. And his hands, while rough and deeply tanned, made her feel things she'd never experienced as they had roamed her body. Though he was not as tall as Edgeford, nor as burly as, say, the blond sailor from the market, he had a confidence about him, a way of carrying himself that made him completely fill her vision, eclipsing all others. As Elena remembered how he rescued her from the band of ruffians, how he carried her across the swollen river, and nursed her back to health, her thoughts returned to their earlier ruminations.

How could she get him to confess how he felt about her? Certainly not with the shallow games she used to entice suitors in court. She was at a loss as to how to proceed.

"I'm sure it's around here somewhere." Elena's thoughts were interrupted and she realized the street had curved and narrowed. "Da said there were three shops right on this street."

"Maybe it has closed down."

"I think not. He asked Samuel just this morning." They had slowed to a stop and Gareth looked up and down the row of shops. The buildings rose to several stories on the left, the shop owner no doubt living above their stores. There were a variety of crudely made signs indicating cobblers, bakers, and even a scribner. But not a hint to indicate a seamstress. To their right, Gareth and Elena were hemmed in by a tall stone wall, the original town wall which had in most parts, been removed to allow Aberstwyth to grow. There were no people on the street and despite the fact there could be no chance of it, Gareth decided this was one place he would not like to meet up with an enemy.

"Why don't you ask in here," Elena suggested, gesturing to the bakery they had stopped in front of. "Then you can buy me a sweet bun."

"You just ate."

"A bit of dry bread and a lump of cheese is not enough to break my fast."

"Would you have preferred some dried beef?"

Elena leveled her sourest glare at him to no effect. "Are you going to ask where it is or not?"

"Why? We'll find it. Maybe it's down a little farther."

"Gareth! Here, give me some money and I'll go ask."

"You're going to pay someone for directions?"

"No, I'm going to ask for directions and then buy something to eat."

Gareth rolled his eyes but pulled out the small pouch of coins. "Here. Gorge yourself."

"Hmph."

Elena disappeared into the dim recess of the bakery and Gareth leaned against the shadowed wall. He looked up and down the narrow street, unable to quell the feeling that this was a dangerous spot. Shifting the heavy bulk of fabric to his other arm, he decided that a little dust would not harm the heavy wool and he carefully set the load down on the baker's stoop, shaking his arms to return circulation to them. Wishing Elena would hurry, he looked down the street once again and froze. Coming up the cobbled lane were three of the rough soldiers he and Elena had stumbled upon in the forest mists. What were they doing here? His sword hand automatically grasped at his hip, but there was no hilt to meet it. Damn! What on earth possessed him to leave this morning without his weapon? Hoping they hadn't seen him, he reached for the handle to the bakery door, hoping to duck inside unnoticed, but his hopes were dashed as he heard, "Ho there! Yes you! Wait a moment."

Perhaps they won't recognize me, he prayed. They had been deeply in their cups that night. He turned to face them but kept his head ducked.

"We're looking for a weaver's shop, but we don't know the name. Be there one around here?" asked the leader in English. Gareth shrugged his shoulders and shook his head to indicate he didn't understand and then turned to leave, planning to make an escape around the next corner and come back for Elena. He hadn't taken but a step when a thick hand clamped down on his shoulder. Gareth twisted quickly, dislodging the hand with ease and landing a solid blow the man's chin, but giving the rest a clear view of his face.

"Say!" said one of the men to the leader, "Isn't he--"

"Yes!" shouted the leader and lunged to grab Gareth who was already running up the street. As he searched for an alley to duck down or a shop to hide in, he cursed his lack of forethought in not bringing his weapon. Had he his wits about him, and therefore his sword, he could have dispatched the three men to their maker and had the corpses moved away before Elena left the bakery with her directions. As he was about to round a corner in the cobbled street, he cast a glance down the lane. The ruffians were, thank God, clumsy and slow in their pursuit. The man he had punched was still clutching his jaw. Gareth's derisive grin faded as he thought of Elena coming out of the bakery while the men were still on the street. So as not to discourage his pursuers until they were out of this vicinity, he pretended to trip on a cobble stone and rolled to the ground easily. As he had hoped, the men yelled triumphantly and redoubled their efforts.

He led them through a twisted maze of streets, praying he would be able to find his way back to the bakery. Every few steps he had to slow his pace so that he would not completely outdistance the rough soldiers behind him. Ahead he saw a small square full of people crowded around a table. Gareth had seen his father dole out justice and punishment often enough to recognize the well-dressed man seated at the table as a magistrate. Pushing his way through the throng of people, Gareth interrupted the proceedings, which seemed to involve the owner of a chicken and a young boy.

"Your honor!" Gareth panted in Welsh. "I am but a poor, honest *Cymraes* being pursued most unjustly by a group of English mercenaries who wish to do me harm because I will not call myself Englishman. They claim there is no such thing as a Welshman because we are all ruled by an English king!" Gareth glanced over his shoulder and saw the soldiers at the outer edge of people, trying to find him over the heads of the crowd. The crowd itself was humming with outrage over Gareth's words and Gareth had to suppress a grin. To deny a Welshman his heritage was nothing short of blasphemy.

The magistrate stood and smoothed his coat over his round belly. "Who are these Englishmen?" he asked, pronouncing "Englishmen" with the same emotion a priest infuses into "spawn of Satan."

Pointing to the rough men, Gareth said, "There they are!"

The magistrate ordered his guards to seize the men, but the crowd descended upon them first, rounding them up with no lack of roughness and dragging them forward. As the magistrate bellowed a sermon on the antiquity of the Welsh culture to the cheers of the crowd, Gareth casually made his way to the edge of the square and then down the street he had just run up.

He reached the bakery just as Elena was coming out, a sweet roll in hand.

"It's just two doors down. Elena said after Gareth pulled back.

A confused look crossed his face as he tried to catch his breath. "What is?"

"The seamstress, of course," she said and took a large bite of roll.

"Of course." He stooped to pick up the pile of cloth and then glanced over his shoulder."

"What are you looking for?" she asked

"I just didn't want to get run down in this busy thoroughfare," he said, deciding not to worry her with his recent exploit.

Elena laughed. "A grave danger indeed," she joked. "We are probably the only people to travel down this street in a month!" She shifted the remnants of the roll to one hand and rested her other in the crook of his arm as they made their way down the narrow street. They stopped in front of the only door that did not display a sign overhead. As the entered the unmarked and dimly lit shop, Elena blinked, trying to force her eyes to adjust after the brightness of the morning sunlight.

Gareth leaned down and whispered in her ear. "Are you sure this is the place?"

Elena looked around as her eyes finally grew accustomed to the dimness. The shop was tiny, with scarce enough room for the rough-hewn wooden table and empty shelves that were pushed against opposite walls. A narrow doorway was covered with a thin piece of cloth. There was nothing to indicate that this was a seamstress's shop. Elena looked at Gareth and shrugged. "Why don't you call out and see if anyone comes to answer."

"Hello?" Gareth yelled. Almost instantly, a thin young woman threw back the curtain and scurried out to meet them. "Are you a seamstress?" Gareth asked her.

The scrawny woman bobbed her head. "Would you like me to sew something for you?" she asked in uncertain Welsh.

"That depends on how good and how fast you are," Elena said. "Do you have any samples of your work we might investigate?"

The woman looked worried. "Only what I am working on now. 'Tis a dress for my niece who's getting married soon."

When the woman simply stood there, Elena prodded her. "Will you show it to us?"

"Of course," the flustered woman said. "Please follow me." She led them through the narrow doorway and up an increasingly bright staircase. Once they reached the top, Elena realized that the cause of the illumination was a high row of windows that let light pour in on the spotlessly clean, if cluttered room. A child of about four or five sat on the floor surrounded by wooden toys. He was entertaining the inhabitant of a beautifully carved cradle. A large table against the far wall was buried under a heap of dark blue cloth. To their right was a small but tidy kitchen, a pot on the stove exuding delicious smells along with copious amounts of steam. Overall, the rooms had a cheery warmth about them that Elena had never experienced in any of the immense and richly furnished, but cold and dark chambers of the stone castles in which she had spent the last year.

"You really should hang a sign out. We weren't sure this was the right place," Elena said.

The woman nodded and, not meeting their eyes, said, "They've taken the last two I put out."

"Who did?"

"The other seamstresses. I don't think they want me on this street."

Elena was just about to tell the woman that was ridiculous, that it was probably only prankster boys, when she finally realized what was odd about the woman's speech. "You're not Welsh, are you?"

The woman lifted frightened eyes. "I'm sorry," she peeped.

"Why should you be? I'm not either. Are you Scottish?"

The seamstress nodded. "My husband was born here and he always wanted to move back, but I don't seem to fit in too well."

"The thing I've learned about these Welsh is that you must simply force them to accept you. They can be exceedingly bullheaded sometimes but they'll back down and consider you one of their own if you're persistent enough." Elena pointedly avoided looking at Gareth for his reaction. Besides, she didn't care what he thought, what she'd said had proven true enough with him, hadn't it? "Now tell us your name and then show us your work. You may speak in English if that is easier."

The young seamstress appeared a bit overwhelmed by Elena, but quickly stated that her name was Annie. Shaking out the blue cloth, she said, "Here is the dress I am making for my niece. I've only the hem left to finish."

Elena handed what was left of the honeyed roll to the young boy and inspected the sleeves, the seams, and the lacings up the back. "You do excellent work. How fast could you make my dress?" Elena quickly explained the style of dress she wanted, completely forgetting Gareth's presence as she discussed the cut, the position of the waistline, and the fullness of the sleeves.

Annie swallowed nervously. "How quickly do you need it?"

Elena turned to Gareth. "When are we leaving?"

Startled out of his daze, Gareth stared uncomprehendingly at Elena. She repeated her question and he said, "Three days."

Annie's eyes bulged but she nodded. "I can do it." She quoted a price and Elena accepted, not even checking with Gareth to see if he had that much money. "Shall I measure you right now?"

"Yes, that will be fine."

Annie gathered her measuring string and looked uncertainly from Gareth to Elena. "And your..."

Elena immediately understood. "My brother can occupy your son downstairs and head off your husband should he come back."

"He won't--he's a carpenter and he's working on a ship that's preparing to sail. Here Oengus," she said, picking up one of the wooden toys and handing it to her son. "Show this gentleman how this toy works downstairs." Little Oengus grabbed the wooden horse in one sticky hand and headed for the door, shouting "Come on!" over his shoulder.

Gareth dumped the pile of cloth in Elena's outstretched arms and whispered, "Brother?"

"It just popped into my head," she responded with a wicked smile. Gareth rolled his eyes and followed the young boy out of the room.

Nearly an hour later, Elena left Annie who was already at work, measuring out the wool and planning to cut the many pieces. She entered the small downstairs room to discover Gareth rolling about the floor, wrestling with Oengus. The little boy squealed with delight as Gareth allowed himself to be pushed over and pinned as Oengus sat on his chest. "I won! I won!" he shouted.

Seeing Elena, Gareth plucked the child off his chest and quickly scrambled to his feet, his face flushed with exertion, his hair tumbled about his brow, the young boy clinging to his neck and shoulders like a vine.

"Are you finished?"

Elena nodded, surveying his rumpled appearance with amusement. "Are you?"

"I was just," Gareth cleared his throat. "I was just keeping young Oengus here occupied so he wouldn't disturb you."

Elena smiled wryly. "Thank you."

Tilting his head back so he could see Oengus's face, Gareth said, "Come, you young scalawag. Give Lady Elena a kiss goodbye."

Elena shook her head and frowned apprehensively. "No, no. That's alright," she began, but it was too late, for Gareth was holding out the little boy who leaned forward obediently and placed a wet and sticky kiss on her cheek. Elena rubbed at her cheek with the back of her hand as the youngster wriggled to be put down and then scampered up the stairs. Gareth straightened and looked sheepishly at Elena. "I guess I'm still a boy at heart."

Never comfortable with children of any age--even when she was one, Elena didn't know how to respond. She had spent her entire life trying to act as mature and regal as possible and the thought of wanting to be a child and romp around was foreign to her. On one hand, she thought it very silly of Gareth to roll around on the floor acting like a fool, and yet some part of her wondered what it would be like to abandon all pretensions and cares of adulthood and simply laugh until her stomach hurt, or tumble in a sweet grassy meadow, or run barefoot along the surf.

"What would you like to do today?" Gareth asked.

Run on the beach, play in a meadow. "It doesn't matter," she said.

"Why don't we explore the city? Da tells me there's a book seller's shop around here somewhere."

"That would be fine." All sense of adventure aside, however, Elena was interested in the bookseller. Her father had indulged her literacy with stacks of expensive books, but in Richard's court, books were not at all the thing for ladies-in-waiting. Another urge stifled, she thought, remembering those long, incredibly tedious winter nights that would have passed so pleasantly had she only had a book or two to read.

As Gareth held the door open for her, he said, "You don't care much for children, do you?"

"Hmm?" Elena said, still thinking of the last book she had read with its glorious illumination. That had been the most expensive book her father had ever purchased, costing more than three new court dresses. At the time, Elena hadn't been sure the book had been worth giving up the gowns, but she had managed to convince her doting father that she needed the book and the clothes, so she had been happy.

Gareth repeated his question and she turned her attention to him. She shrugged and said, "I don't see much point in them."

Gareth laughed. "No point except to populate the world."

"Well, besides that, of course. I know I must have them some day, but I haven't been around them. I was an only child, you see, and children are not kept at court."

Gareth was silent for several seconds as they walked down the narrow street. "Elena, you know we may have created a child last night." She did not respond and continued looking in the shop windows they passed on the widening street, trying to think of herself with a child. Gareth's child.

"Elena?"

She stopped in front of a window in which their figures were clearly reflected in the many thick panes of glass. Elena stared at her reflection for a moment and then turned to face Gareth.

"I'm sure we didn't."

"How can you know." Gareth's eyes widened with embarrassment and he stammered, " I mean…"

Turning to Gareth, she saw the concern on his face and she forced a smile. "Don't worry."

"I'm not worried. I--" Gareth pushed his hair out of his eyes impatiently. "I just want you to know that if you were…with child, I would marry you and, well, take care of you both."

Elena felt her heart lurch. That he would mention marriage not three hours after she envisioned him as her husband was startling. But she did not want a marriage based on obligation. She wanted him to want to marry her. Or, at least, she thought she did. She was still so confused over what exactly she did feel for this frustrating man.

Needing to not think for a while, she dismissed his concern with a breezy, "Let's not fill this beautiful day with worries of any sort. I want to see all the sights this quaint city has to offer." Taking his hand, she squeezed it and pulled him after her as she turned a corner and headed for the center of town, acting as if she had firmly put all thoughts of their lovemaking and subsequent conversation about it out of her head.

***

For Gareth, he could not stop thinking about the subject. Now that the subject had come up, there were so many things he wanted to ask her: did she regret that it had happened? Did she feel anything at all for him, because he was fairly certain now that he loved her. Gareth wished he had Cynan's brashness when it came to blurting out whatever came to mind, but fear of what she might think of him for asking those questions, and fear of what she might answer kept him quiet. Fear! An emotion he had scorned to indulge in since he was in leading strings.

As if they truly were brother and sister, he held her hand as she climbed up steps, answered her endless questions about Aberstwyth, and bought her food when she was hungry.

They spent the entire day traipsing through the shops of Aberstwyth, even talking about their childhood and families, but Gareth never got over the feeling that they were avoiding the most important topic and that was their feeling toward one another. Finally, as their feet were sore and their legs weary from so much walking, they discovered the book seller's shop, only to find it had closed for the night.

"Is that not just my luck," Elena said dejectedly as they sat on a carved log strategically placed in front of the shop.

"We have all of tomorrow free. We'll come back and you can browse to your heart's content."

"Really? Don't you have business to attend to? I mean, some sort of plan to work out or something."

Gareth valiantly ignored the twinge of guilt at lying to Elena as he said, "I told you, I've decided not to join their cause, after all. I'm just returning to England, the same as you."

"Well, I know, but don't you have to convince everyone here that you won't betray their intents?"

"No," Gareth said, more sharply than he had intended. "They know that whatever my feelings, I won't betray their lives. With or without a few Welshmen, Henry and Richard will come to battle. All I can do is return to my king and offer what service I can."

They sat quietly for minutes, each absorbed in his thoughts, Gareth suffering under the burden of deceit; deceiving Elena now and deceiving Richard's entire court upon returning to England. With a humorless grimace, Gareth reflected on his perpetual guilt. Just a few weeks ago, he was suffering at the thought of abandoning his knightly vows to his king, despite his awareness that Richard was not the sovereign he should be. Then when Elena nearly died trying to reach them, he suffered overwhelming guilt that he had dragged her into their messy plans. And don't forget, Gareth reminded himself, how guilty you felt when you first turned Lord Stanley down for this distasteful task. Gareth sighed and adjusted the chip on his shoulder. Elena thankfully distracted him from further gruesome thoughts.

"Are you certain there will be a war?"

Gareth shrugged. "There will at least be a battle."

Elena nodded, watching Gareth closely. "Will you fight in it?"

Her question made Gareth's stomach clench. Of course he would fight in it, but how would he fight for his side? Go along with Richard's troops and then start massacring them from behind? It may be effective for a moment or two, but he would quickly be hacked to pieces. Not that he was afraid of dying, simply that he did not relish the idea of rushing to death's cold embrace without first kicking and screaming.

"Will you?" Elena's strained voice finally registered on Gareth and he realized that she was worried. For him? Did she not want him to die?"

"Undoubtedly. Does that bother you?"

Elena frowned and hesitated before answering. "Well of course it bothers me. I...I don't have any black clothes to wear for your funeral and I won't dye my new houppeland just so I can pay my respects."

"Hoope--land? What in the living world is that?"

"Not hoopey, houppe. A houppeland. That's what my new dress will be."

"What is it?"

Elena laughed at his apparently stupid question. "It's just a style--high waist, full skirt, big sleeves. Started in Germany, I believe. Surely you've seen them on ladies at court. Men too, actually."

Gareth looked at her in horror, hoping this was not a style knights would be required to wear. "Men are wearing houppelands?"

"Of course. Although not as full, and sometimes quite short."

Gareth longed for his childhood in Wales where a rough tunic and comfortably worn leggings got him through year after year. "Who invents these ridiculous fashions?" Gareth asked peevishly, imagining himself trussed up in velvet, scarcely able to breath for a tight collar, sitting through an interminably long court.

"I don't know. The loomsmen, I suppose. It seems each new fashion requires more cloth than the last. There no doubt will be a day when it will require fifteen lengths to make a decent gown."

Gareth thought of the money he had spent on eight lengths of wool and fervently prayed that he never had daughters.

Elena stood and stretched. "Well, Sir Gareth, either we return to our temporary abode or you will be forced to buy me one of those lamb sticks from the square."

Gareth stood also, realizing that the sun was hovering just above the horizon. "Da said he was arranging for the evening meal tonight, so we'd best be heading back."

"Your father cooks?" Elena asked, incredulous.

"He cooks about as much as I do."

Elena wrinkled her nose. "That doesn't mean we're having that horrid dried beef, does it?"

Gareth laughed. "I think Da meant he was arranging for someone to cook food for us. I'm sure he's sparing us from dried beef since that's what all we'll be eating in a few days."

Elena moaned as Gareth took her hand and led her up the street. "Isn't there anything else you can take on a journey to eat besides dried beef? That stuff has no taste and is the consistency of worn boot leather."

"So you've told me every time we've eaten it. I'll see if Samuel has anything else we can take when we leave, but don't get your hopes up. Whatever we take has to last a good week without spoiling."

"Let's hurry home then," Elena said, picking up her pace. "I intend to gorge myself on edible food just in case dried beef is all we have for the next week."

Gareth laughed and allowed her to pull him along, content for the moment to concentrate solely on the feel of her hand in his, her smile as she turned her head to urge him along, and her wind-tousled hair.

They reached Samuel's shop as the sun was slipping into the ocean, just visible in the distance from his doorstep. Gareth paused to watch it flatten and slowly sink, feeling the last rays warm his face with a golden glow possible only at this time of night. As soon as the uppermost edge had slipped away, the evening took on a cool blue light that was somehow suddenly quiet and peaceful. Closing his eyes, Gareth inhaled deeply, forgetting his burdens and absorbing all the peace of the moment. Elena was going to miss real food for a week, but he was afraid he was going to miss this feeling of utter peace for a great deal longer. He opened his eyes and looked up to see the first star of the evening twinkle above him. "Please be a good omen," he whispered before following Elena into the warm house.

Chapter 18

Elena lay awake for several hours, waiting for Gareth to join her. She had no doubt he would, after the previous night and the whole day spent pleasurably in each other's company. To pass the time until he came, Elena thought of her new dress, wishing she had her mother's garnet necklace to wear with it once it was finished. When she had exhausted every seam and hem on that topic, she went over all the sights she and Gareth had seen today, noting their differences from the shops she had seen in London, or one of the smaller towns and villages throughout England she had visited as a lady-in-waiting. She wondered what kind of books the bookseller would have and if Gareth possibly had enough money to purchase one for her. Probably not, she thought, only slightly disappointed. What with fabric, and hiring the seamstress, that alone was probably enough to wipe out a new knight's means.

Elena yawned. Did knights earn any money? She suspected very little. They, like ladies-in-waiting basically lived at the expense of the king in exchange for their services. I wonder how Gareth is expected to attract a wife if he has no means of supporting her, she wondered as she snuggled deeper under the covers. Of course, there was that cozy little keep, nestled in those harshly beautiful mountains. She wouldn't mind living there...she refused to examine that rampant thought and instead allowed her mind to replay the events of the previous night. Once she had decided what she was going to do, she had suffered no apprehension, no qualms. And in his embrace, she had found no discomfort or embarrassment. Gareth's warm hands and drugging kisses had made her feel worshipped. She had never felt so vitally alive as she had during their lovemaking. And Gareth had lost any boyish awkwardness and had expertly wrung from her such pleasures as she had never anticipated. And was there a more deliciously comfortable way to sleep than nestled in his arms, her back pressed to his chest, their legs tangling, his arms cushioning her head and wrapping snugly around her waist? She seriously doubted it. Turning on her side, Elena imagined Gareth was pressed up against her. With a deep sigh, she felt her body relaxing languorously, preparing itself for Gareth's attentions.

Elena awoke to bright sunlight pouring in the small window. Disoriented she pushed herself up to her elbows and looked around. She had only just been thinking that any moment Gareth would be entering her room and now it was daylight. Looking at the candle, she saw only a puddle of wax melted onto the small table. Oh dear. Not even in Richard's well-furnished castles were candles a thing to be wasted. But the candle occupied her mind for just a moment before the larger reality sank in. Gareth had not joined her!

Elena sat fully up and pounded the bed with her fist. What in the world was he thinking? Had she not smiled meaningfully at him last night as she left the dining table, bidding everyone good night? Had she not left her door cracked invitingly so that the candlelight would guide him to her? Had she said aught to lead him to believe that she had not found their night of passion enjoyable? Certainly not!

"You dolt!" she cursed as she threw back the covers and rapidly dressed. She would certainly give him a piece of her mind, she thought as she ran a borrowed comb through her thick hair. Elena paused in mid-stroke. How, exactly, would she go about bringing up the subject? "Where were you last night, Gareth? I waited for you for hours." No. "Why didn't we continue our lessons last night? Aren't I an apt pupil?" Absolutely not. Well, she decided, something will come to me. She'd never before been at a loss for words. Marching down the narrow hall, she came into the main living area where Gareth, his friends, Morgan, and Samuel were talking. The discussion stopped the instant Elena entered the room and she had the distinct impression that she was the topic.

"Good morning," the men chimed, Bryant quickly standing to give her his chair.

"Good morning," she responded, glancing at each man's guilty face before settling her gaze on Gareth. Bryant handed her a bowl of freshly picked berries and a wedge of cheese. Elena slowly ate as she watched the men try to cover their discomfiture by talking about the weather. What exactly had they been talking about? she wondered. She was given no opportunity to decipher that puzzle as Gareth, Morgan, and Samuel stood and moved to leave.

"Where are you going," Elena asked Gareth.

"I must spend today with my father," he said once the two men had left. "Bryant and Cynan will take you to the book shop this morning and then wherever you would like to go. I understand the beach is beautiful at this time of year. Why don't you three have a picnic?"

"But--" Elena began, confusion, disappointment and, yes, hurt feelings swirling within her.

"You'll be well taken care of, Lady. Enjoy!" Turning, Gareth quickly followed his father and Samuel out.

"Well if that isn't ill-mannered," she said.

"Yes, but that's Gareth for you," Cynan said, trying to affect a disappointed face. "Bryant and I have tried and tried to teach him how to behave, but you see, he's just a heathen mountain boy at heart. Bryant and I, however," he continued with a bow, "are experts at courtly manners and gentle entertainments."

"Are you now?" Elena said, trying to infuse her tone with a light-heartedness she did not feel.

"Shut up,Cynan." Bryant was clearly disgusted.

"What? Why? Was I or was I not acting in a manner befitting a duke, Lady Elena?"

Elena laughed in genuine amusement. "Indeed."

Cynan turned to Bryant. "You see?"

"You need not humor him, my lady," Bryant said. "It only makes him worse."

"You mean it makes me better."

Bryant shook his head and looked at Elena as if to say, "I told you so."

Sobering slightly, Cynan stole a handful of Elena's berries and said, "Gareth said you were interested in the bookseller across town. Shall we go there first?"

Elena nodded and finished her bit of cheese as she stood. "I'd also like to stop by my seamstress's shop and see how she's coming on my dress."

"Wonderful! Bryant's never been inducted into the joys of waiting for a woman as she talks dresses with another woman."

Elena couldn't contain her laughter at the worried look on Bryant's face.

Outside it was nearly as beautiful as the day before, but to Elena, something was missing. She refused to allow herself to think that she missed Gareth's presence, but somewhere in her heart, she knew that's what the problem was.

The walk to the bookseller's shop seemed farther than it had the day before, but once they arrived, Elena forgot the walk, her escorts, and Gareth's absence in her bed. The tiny, cluttered shop was stacked from floor to ceiling, wall to wall with books. Elena was amazed at the quantity, especially considering they were in the far reaches of Wales.

"I've more books than most of the shops in London," a stooped elderly man said from a wooden chair in the corner. He laid down the book he was reading and pushed himself to his feet, his hair a wild tangle of thin white curls.

"Yes, you do." Elena agreed. "How did you come by them all, especially here."

"Think the Welsh are nothing but illiterate shepherds, eh?" Elena was slightly taken aback and embarrassed, but the old man laughed.

"For the most part, we are!" He paused in his laughter to cough and wipe his mouth with a handkerchief. "But having ships in and out of the harbor allows me to gather books from all over the world. Look here," he said, gesturing for Elena to follow him as he wove through stacks of books to the back corner. "This one is from the land of sand and heathens. Look at those letters! I'll never in a thousand years figure out what they say, but they are fascinating to look at, aren't they? Old Magnus in the square has a son who sails the seas. Every few years he returns home loaded with strange gifts from far off lands. He brought this to me. Said for all their godlessness, the heathens are very educated and write volumes."

Elena took the book from the old man and gingerly leafed through the pages. She had heard stories of the exotic east, passed around from the time of the Crusades. Looking at the text, she thought, Even the script is exotic. Each page was intricately illuminated with vivid colors and gold leaf. Strange birds and animals shared the border space with dark-skinned men wrapped in voluminous robes, riding powerful steeds and bearing curved swords.

"Where are their ladies?" she asked the old man.

"Eh? Ladies? They don't allow them to be seen."

"Don't allow them to be seen? What do you mean?"

"Just that. Mostly the ladies stay indoor where only their male folk can see them. If they ever do go out, they are covered from head to toe in a black cloak, sometimes not even their eyes showing." The old man opened his eyes wide for emphasis and Elena noticed they were clear with vitality--there was no hazy blurring of age in them.

Her mind going back to the heathen women, she was amazed. How could you possibly flirt without your eyes? Surely such a rule was for common women alone. "What about the royal women?"

The old bookseller scrunched up his wrinkled face in concentration. "Seems to me Magnus's son said the women who are important are kept even more hidden away. They live in the palace and no men but the--now what did he call them?" He turned and rifled through some papers strewn across the table. "Ah, I knew I'd written down. My memory isn't what it used to be, so I make notes to myself. The sultan, that's what their kings are called. These sultans are the only men who are allowed to see these women."

Fascinated, Elena continued turning the pages of the book, wishing she could read the intricate script. None of the books she had ever read had told her about such exotic lands. She had read accounts of Italy and even Greece and they had proven fascinating enough, but the people in them had behaved similarly enough to those in England that they had not seemed so alien.

"What else did he tell you?" she asked, unable to contain her curiosity.

Obviously delighted that he had an avid listener, he pushed a stack of books off of a low bench and wiped the dust off with his sleeve. Gesturing for Elena to sit, he turned to Cynan and Bryant who were standing by the door, looking decidedly uncomfortable. "You need not wait for this young lady, she and I will be occupied for a good while. You may leave and we will send for you when she is ready."

Cynan bowed briefly and told Elena, "I would like to take something back to Enid. If you are comfortable, I will leave you to this good man and return in a while."

"Of course," Elena said graciously.

Cynan looked to Bryant expectantly. "Do you care to join me?"

Bryant shook his head and scowled disapprovingly. "I will wait with Lady Elena."

"There's no need, Bryant," Elena said.

"I will stay," he said implacably.

Cynan looked to Elena and shrugged his shoulders. "Enjoy your books, then."

The bookseller sat in his worn chair with a creak of old bones and old wood. "By the way, I have not introduced myself. I am Llywelyn, named for that great Welsh prince, but, much to my father's disappointment, bore absolutely none of the warrior's characteristics of that strong man save his name. I gather you are called Lady Elena. Despite your Welsh name, I detect an English accent. Am I correct?"

Elena gave Llywelyn an indulging smile and nodded. "I am rarely wrong on such things," he said as he gestured with his chin toward Bryant. "And who might your rude friend here be?"

Elena turned around and realized Bryant was still standing stiffly by the door, his hands clasped in front of him as he maintained his sentry-like pose. "That is Bryant."

"Why don't you come sit, boy. Your legs will go numb with you standing like that. Besides, you might learn something."

Bryant shook his head.

Elena, anxious to hear more of the far-off land of heathens, impatiently gestured to the bench on which she was seated. "Bryant, do sit. Now please."

Hesitating only a moment, Bryant hurried across the small room and seated himself next to Elena, glancing shyly at her from the corner of his eye. More interested in Llywelyn's stories than Bryant's silly behavior, Elena turned back to the bookseller and promptly forgot Bryant's presence.

For the next four hours, Elena forgot not only Bryant's presence, but the hardness of her bench, the cramped tininess of the shop, and even the fact that Llywelyn was a mere merchant and under normal circumstances would not be considered appropriate company for a lady-in-waiting of the court. Elena lost all track of time as she listened to Llywelyn's stories. From time to time, the small man would push himself out of his chair and fetch a book off of this shelf or that. He piled dusty manuscript after dusty manuscript on Elena's lap and asked her what she thought of a particular passage or a bit of illumination.

Elena had considered herself more educated than the other ladies at court simply because of the fact that she could and did read. But her studies had never prepared her for immersion into the world of academia. She found herself at times overwhelmed by Llywelyn's questions and at other times, surprisingly comfortable thumbing through a thick volume while she told him what she thought.

They paused at midday and Elena sent Bryant out to purchase some fresh bread while Llywelyn heated a pot of mutton stew over his hearth. After lunch, they pulled still more books off the shelf, looking for accounts of the furthest reaches of globe. Cynan stopped in to see if she was ready to leave but Elena shooed him off. He turned to Bryant who replied that if Lady Elena was staying, so would he. Cynan shook his head in amazement and told them he would see them back at Samuel's that evening.

So intrigued with her rediscovered passion for books, Elena scarcely noticed when Bryant began to doze, his head nodding forward to rest on his chest. She did not hear his muffled snore as he slipped deeper into sleep. She did finally notice him the very moment he listed to the right and tumbled off the bench.

Setting her book down, Elena rushed to his side. "Bryant! Are you alright? What happened?"

Rubbing his elbow and blushing hotly with embarrassment, Bryant pushed himself to his feet. "I'm fine," he mumbled. "I just dozed off."

"Dozed off?" She looked out the thick window at the front of the shop. "Good heavens, what time is it?"

Old Llywelyn laughed, coughed, and laughed some more. "You don't know how many times I've asked that very question. You know you are a true book lover when you ask it, though."

"I had no idea we had spent so much time here. I--I can't buy any of your books." Elena cleared her throat. Never in her life had she been without money or some means to purchase something. With not a little discomfort, she apologized, "I'm very sorry."

"Nonsense, dear girl, nonsense. I haven't enjoyed myself in years and as you can see, I don't get many customers. Here," he said, pulling the Arabic book from the bottom of the stack. "I wish you to have this. To remember me by."

Elena's eyes widened. Though accustomed to receiving gifts from men, rarely had she been given such an expensive and extraordinary gift. Never had she been given a gift from a man, other than her father, who had not hoped to gain her favor or even her hand. To be offered a gift such as this from an old man who would never see her again overwhelmed her.

"I couldn't possibly." Were these words coming from her mouth? Of course she could accept it! "That book is much too precious and no doubt worth a great deal of money. You must keep it or sell it."

Llywelyn smiled and shook his head, thin white hair flopping about his head. "A book is worth nothing if it is not read and treasured. You may not be able to read the words, but you can read the illustrations and you will certainly treasure it."

"I don't know what to say." Wouldn't Gareth tease her about that if he were here? Remembering Gareth, she knew just what he would expect her to say, and while she still wasn't completely used to saying it, she took the book in one hand, Llywelyn's spotted hand in her other and said as sincerely as she could, "Thank you very much. I will indeed treasure it always." Ha, she thought, Gareth could not complain about that! Thinking about Gareth, she did not even realize it had happened until she was suddenly wrapped in Llywelyn's warm hug. Unsure of what to do, she patted his back. When he released her, she quickly stepped back, but not before noticing his eyes were damp, though he was smiling brightly.

Once outside, Elena clasped the book tightly to her breast. "I want to stop by the seamstress shop and see how my new dress is coming along."

"What new dress?"

"Gareth bought me fabric for a new dress and chemise. We took it to a seamstress yesterday morning and she said she would have it done by the time we returned to England."

"Gareth bought you fabric?" Elena had never heard Bryant speak so sharply or bitterly, and she looked at him quickly to determine what had upset him. All she saw was a moody frown.

"Is there something wrong with that?"

"No, of course not," he said abruptly. Seemingly forcing himself out of his foul mood, he smiled tautly and said, "Do you remember where the shop is?"

Elena blinked. "I have no idea. Don't you know where they are? There are three of them on the same street. Once we reach the street, I'll remember which one it is."

"This is my first time in Aberstwyth. Let me ask the bookseller." Bryant ran back to the small shop. While she waited for him, Elena rubbed her neck, which was stiff from crouching over books all day. Looking up at the late afternoon sky, she felt a sense of peace come over her and she wished unselfconsciously that Gareth were here with her. There was a silence over the town that only occurs on such perfect late summer evenings. The sky was a rich lapis blue, the low-hung clouds impossibly white. Inhaling deeply, she smelled the wetness of the nearby sea as a cooling breeze kissed her face. Truly, Gareth should be here, she thought. He is the one who helped me appreciate such simple pleasures.

Alone with her thoughts since she first awoke, Elena wondered again why Gareth had not come to her room last night. Surely after the previous night and all of yesterday spent together, he did not think she loathed his company. Elena's feminine pride rebelled at the thought that he might have simply not wanted to come to her. A delicious tingle ran down her spine as she remembered their night spent together. No, he had been well pleased. He must have been unable to join her without arousing suspicion. There could be no other answer. Or, rather, she would allow no other answer.

Within minutes, Bryant had returned to her and they quickly found their way through the maze of narrow alleys to the correct street.

"Let me think," Elena said as she gazed at the identical shops that lined the street. "I know it was on this side. There was a baker's shop nearby...Ah, there it is."

"Are you sure?" Bryant asked as they approached it. "There isn't a sign and the inside looks empty."

"That's how I know this is the right place." Elena pushed opened the door and called out for Annie. The five-year-old boy came tumbling down the staircase to answer their call.

"Mama says you is to come dupstairs," he said importantly.

They followed the young messenger to the spotless room upstairs. Nothing had changed except that the mound of cloth burying the large table was now cranberry colored instead of blue, as it had been the day before. Annie was sitting at the table, crouched over a seam.

"If you'll just give me a moment, ma'am, I'll have it ready for you to try on."

"Ready to try on? How have you managed to get so much done?" Elena asked, amazed at the woman's speed.

Breaking the thread with her teeth, Annie stood and shook out the dress. "You said you needed it ready by day after tomorrow. I worked on it all yesterday and today. I still have to put the collar on and hem it, but otherwise 'tis done."

Elena took the gown from Annie, her eyes glowing with pleasure. "It is beautiful." Holding it up to herself, Elena flared the skirt out. "Where can I try it on?"

"Oengus, take this gentleman downstairs until I call for you."

The child, obviously remembering the game from yesterday, immediately took Bryant's hand in his own and pulled him down the stairs. As soon as Annie closed the door, Elena began working herself out of her dusty cotehardie. "I will be glad when I can see the end of this gown."

"Tis beautifully made, my lady," Annie said.

"That may be, but I cannot stand the sight of it after wearing it for the last month straight!" Elena pulled the new dress over her head and held her hair out of the way while Annie quickly laced it up the back. "It fits wonderfully!" Elena exclaimed. She craned her neck to see the dress from every angle. "Leave the hem long in the back." Spinning around crazily like a child, she laughed in delight. "I can't believe I'm so excited over such a simple dress!"

Annie's smile disappeared. "Should I change it, milady?"

Elena stared at Annie, perplexed. Why in the world should Annie want to change the dress? Belatedly, she realized that Annie may have taken her exclamation over the simple dress in the wrong light. "No, of course not, it's perfect. What I meant was, I'm so used to having beautiful dresses..." That wasn't helping, Elena thought. Curse Gareth for making her worry what miserable servants thought! "What I meant was," Elena began again, "I'm used to wearing beautiful dresses and this one is the most beautiful I've ever worn."

Annie's eyes widened. "Do you mean it, my lady?" She clasped Elena's hands in her own work-roughened ones.

"Well of course I do. You have done an admirable job on this gown. I can't wait until it's finished."

"It will be finished tomorrow, my lady. Even if I have to stay up all night working on it!" Annie vowed.

Elena smiled and disengaged herself from Annie's grip. "I'm sure you will." Turning so the seamstress could unlace her, Elena said, "Sir Gareth and I will be by in the afternoon to pick it up. Will that be late enough."

"Oh yes, my lady."

Downstairs, Elena found a distressed-looking Bryant holding a sleeping Oengus. With obvious relief, he relinquished his armload to its mother and took Elena's arm. Once outside, Elena had to figure out which direction they needed to travel. After a false start down a dead end, she remembered where they needed to go in order to reach Samuel's shop. Consumed in her thoughts of her new dress and new book, not to mention Gareth, Elena did not hear Bryant when he first spoke to her.

"My lady?" he repeated.

"Yes?"

Bryant cleared his throat and tugged on the neck of his brown tunic. "About Gareth..."

"Yes? What about him?"

"Please do not misunderstand. Gareth is one of my best friends, along with Cynan. We grew up together and I think of him as a brother."

Elena waited for him to continue, but when he merely looked uncomfortable, she prodded him. "And?"

"Well, for all that I care for him and admire him, sometimes he forgets himself."

"Forgets himself? What do you mean, Bryant?" Elena was quickly growing weary of Bryant's meanderings, but since he always treated her with the utmost respect, she tried to be patient.

Bryant must have sensed her impatience, however, because he said in one quick rush, "Sometimes he forgets who he is and where he comes from. Sometimes he forgets what his father taught him and what he should know as a knight about treating ladies with respect."

"I agree completely," Elena said, ruefully thinking of Gareth's mockery of her position in court. "Wait until we return to England and he tries to call me 'Elena' or speak to me like I'm his horse. Richard will have his head!" She finished with a laugh.

"That wasn't exactly what I meant."

Elena looked at Bryant, surprised to see him flushing furiously.

"What I meant was that he seems to forget sometimes that there are... women...with whom a man may be more—uh--forward. But a lady such as yourself should never be treated in the same manner."

Elena quickly looked back to their path, wondering uncomfortably how much Bryant knew of Gareth's and her new relationship.

"You certainly deserve to have a beautiful new dress, my lady, don't misunderstand me. But I would caution you that Gareth may have forgotten himself when he purchased the fabric and he may forget himself even more when it is finished and you are thankful to him for his generosity."

"What exactly are you saying, Bryant?"

From the corner of her eye, Elena could see Bryant flush more brilliantly red than he had been moments before.

Bryant came to a stop and Elena turned to face him. "I'm afraid he may put undue pressure on you to share your favors with him in an unseemly fashion."

Elena wanted to shriek with laughter. If Bryant only knew that it had been she who had forgotten herself and forced her favors on him in a most unseemly fashion!

"Please know, my lady, that you owe nothing to Gareth, or any of us for that matter. If you should ever feel that anyone is acting the least bit unchivalrously towards you, you have only to call and I will come at once to defend you and your honor."

Elena had heard many a flowery speech from a lovesick man, but Bryant's struck her as being truly sincere and heartfelt. Making a point not to smile, lest he think she was making fun of him, she said as sincerely as she could, "I thank you, Bryant. I will rest assured that you will do everything in your power to see to my well being."

Bryant took her hand and kissed it lightly. "I have only the most honorable intentions toward you, Lady Elena."

"I'm sure you do, Bryant."

To her great relief, Bryant seemed content to drop the subject for the rest of the short journey back to Samuel's shop. Once inside the back living quarters, Elena forgot Bryant's declaration in the noisy cheerfulness of the roomful of men preparing to eat a hearty feast. The kitchen table had been dragged into the main room so everyone could fit around it. Thick wooden plates lined both sides of the table and a huge basket of bread crowned the center. Morgan entered the room with a thick crockery flagon.

"Ah, Lady Elena, Bryant! You're back just in time. Tell me, Lady Elena, have you ever tasted Welsh mead?"

"Never."

"Then you are in for a treat tonight! Sit right here," he said, indicating the cushioned seat at the head of the table. "As our only lady at dinner tonight, you hold the seat of honor. Now sit and relax while we bring in a feast sure to rival any you've had at court."

Oddly at ease with the rough group of men, Elena sat as instructed and watched as they scrambled about bringing stew, roasted meat, and cooked vegetables to the table. Within minutes, the large table was lined with all of the men who had stayed with Samuel for the meeting two days before. A quick blessing on the meal was followed by sheer chaos as hungry men passed around food. Despite their hunger and perhaps uncourtly manners, they made sure Elena was always served first and always received the best of each portion. And true to Morgan's word, the Welsh mead was a treat, just sweet and smooth enough that Elena was on her second mugful before she realized that she was very warm and seemed to find everything highly amusing.

Though she allowed herself only one more mug of the tasty mead, the pleasant mood remained with her all evening as the laughter and conversation grew louder.

"Be honest now, good lady," called out one of the men. "Who are more handsome: Welsh men or English."

Elena pretended to think hard on the subject which made the men laugh, but her response stunned them. "I'd say, English men have the more beautiful faces." Elena smothered a laugh, struggling valiantly not to smile as she said, "But what woman wants a face more beautiful than her own staring back at her over the covers? I'll take a manly Welshman any day!" A small sober part of her brain shrieked when she blatantly looked to Gareth, but she was having too much fun to pay any attention to it.

Much hooting and slamming of mugs against the table followed and the man sitting to her left pounded her encouragingly on the shoulder, nearly sending her out of her chair. This brought on more laughter, which continued over the next hour. When the mead was dispensed and nothing but crumbs remained of the feast, the men slowly and drunkenly made their way to their respective beds. Gareth disappeared outdoors and Elena wished her legs did not feel so wobbly so that she could follow him. She found walking was not as difficult as she had imagined and in fact, she felt better once she had made her way to the cool quiet of her room. A large drink of cool water further helped her regain some of her composure before she struggled out of her gown. She braided her hair and climbed into bed, forgetting to extinguish the candle once again before slipping into slumber.

***

Gareth breathed the cool, ocean-scented night air that smelled so differently from the mountain air of Eyri Keep. He had missed Elena sorely this day, finding it difficult to keep his mind on his father's words, so consumed was he with wondering where Elena was and what she must be doing. He smiled as he thought of her quip earlier about taking a Welshman but that smile faded with wonder as he thought of how she had looked straight at him. What had she meant by that look? Surely she would not have made such a bold statement had she not intended for him to derive some meaning from it. Surely it could not have been merely the mead speaking. Gareth allowed his mind to wander to their passionate night together. Never had he known such pleasure with a woman. And that pleasure had continued out of bed, he realized.

Adjusting his breeches, Gareth took another deep breath and entered the warm room. All the candles had been extinguished and he realized he must have been outside longer than he thought--everyone else seemed to have gone to bed. He forced himself to head for the stairs leading to the big room above but paused with his foot on the first step. Perhaps he should check on Elena and make sure the mead had not made her ill. As he quietly made his way down the narrow hall to her room, his conscience hollered that he was fooling himself if he thought he was just going to be able to say goodnight and leave her.

He knocked softly on her closed door and waited. When there was no answer, he knocked more loudly, hoping no one else would hear and come investigate the pounding. After an agonizing several moments, the door opened. Elena was standing in the doorway, her hair coming out of her braid, spilling over her shoulder. The candlelight behind her shone through her thin chemise, clearly outlining her ripe curves beneath.

"I just came to see if you were alright," Gareth whispered. Elena said nothing, her face hidden in shadows. He was feeling singularly embarrassed when she took a step closer to him, her breasts grazing his chest. Despite the several layers of cloth separating their skins, Gareth felt as if a hot brand had touched his chest. With aching slowness, he bent his head. Elena raised hers and their lips came together in a slow, sensuous kiss unlike any of their past kisses. The spark, which was constantly present between them, steadily grew as their kiss deepened and Gareth slid his hands around her waist to clasp her tightly to him. Her hands tangled in his hair and she kept his mouth on hers when he would have ended the kiss.

Gareth groaned with disappointment when Elena pulled back and stepped away from him. Without a word, she took his hand and pulled him into the room, closing the door behind him. Turning, she gazed at him steadily and Gareth caught his breath at her beauty in the soft glow of the candle. With shaking hands, he cupped her face, tracing the silkiness of her eyebrows, the smoothness of her skin, the fullness of her lips. Without warning, the words "I love you" sprang to his lips, but instead of uttering them, he pressed them onto her mouth, rubbed them into her neck, nibbled them into her earlobe. His heart pounded at the confession he had nearly made and he forced himself to focus on each inch of smooth skin before him rather than wonder at his thoughts.

In contrast to their first night together, their lovemaking that night was achingly slow and hypnotic in its tenderness. When they were sated, their limbs lay tangled together, Elena's face nestled under Gareth's chin, his arms holding her pressed tightly to his chest.

Though drowsy from mead and their lovemaking, Gareth stayed awake long after Elena fell asleep. He had felt responsible for their first night together and had worried that he had coerced her into doing something she otherwise would not have done. But there was no denying that she had initiated tonight's passions. Gareth smiled and pressed a kiss to Elena's forehead as a thought occurred to him. Why had he worried so about their first night together? When had he ever been able to convince--much less coerce--Elena into doing something she did not want to do? That led to a greater question: Why had Elena given herself to him?

For his part, he was not complaining. He would drink in her scent, the feel of her skin, the curve of her body. He would absorb every nuance of her expression and memorize every feature of her face as well as every word she uttered because he was dreadfully sure that he loved her. He loved her in spite of, and perhaps because of, her stubborn willfulness and her blatant self-centeredness. He loved her because she had risked her life to warn him of the abbess; because she had refused to grant him quarter in any of their arguments; because he had never felt so comfortable in another person's company than he had yesterday while roaming the streets of Aberystwyth.

He loved her even though once they returned to England she would disappear into the untouchable realm of the ladies-in-waiting; even though he would be forced to watch her marry the despicable earl; even though he would then participate in the destruction of her comfortable world. Another stone settled on Gareth's shoulders and he pulled Elena even closer to him, wishing there was a way he could take her back to Eyri Keep. He would marry her in an instant if he thought she would be content to be the wife of a mere knight, but while she had made expressly clear that she wanted him in her bed tonight, she had never even intimated that she wanted him to wed.

Gareth swallowed his disappointment as best he could and bent his head to kiss Elena's parted lips. Within seconds, she stirred and sleepily returned his kiss. Gareth's body, unburdened by the weight on his soul, immediately leapt into a state of arousal. As he moved on top of her, the covers they would not need to stay warm slipped to the floor.

Chapter 19

Elena opened her eyes to the late morning sun pouring in the small, high window. She stretched lazily, feeling like a cat full of cream and napping in the sunlight, so content was she. Gareth's warm back was pressed against her side and she rolled over, sliding her arm around his waist and pressing her breasts to his warm skin as images of the past night flashed through her mind. A smile warmed her lips as she thought of the heretofore unguessed-at pleasures Gareth had treated her body to. Never again would she be able to hear a young bride warned against the unpleasantness of the wedding night without laughing. Unpleasantness indeed!

The thought of a wedding night dimmed Elena's smile. Once again she worried she would not be able to convince Richard to break her betrothal to Brackley. She had thought to beg him to betroth her to Lord Edgeford, but the thought of marriage to the pasty young lord was suddenly as distasteful as that to Brackley had been.

Elena's hand eased itself down along Gareth's hip, her nails absently scratching the muscled thigh. She inhaled sharply, a vision of herself as the lady of Eyri Keep filling her mind, and this time she did not fight it. Unbidden, a series of images paraded through her head: the keys of Eyri Keep at her belt as she instructed servants on the renovations of the stone lodging; Enid and she laughing at the antics of Gareth and Cynan as they played with children (Children? a disbelieving voice in her head asked); Gareth coaxing the peasants at her parent's estate into producing more than her father had ever been able to wheedle; endless nights spent just like the previous one.

Elena sighed. She had never in her life experienced uncertainty. Fear, yes--had not the last month taught her that emotion well?--but never uncertainty. She had no idea how she would even go about making those visions reality. From his derision of her engagement, she was most certain Gareth would insist on loving his wife and she really had no idea if he cared for her in that way at all. She had been making men fall in love with her since she was barely a woman with a smile here, a look there, but Gareth was different from all those men. Had she not had that very thought a hundred times before? He was different and she wasn't sure she could make him love her as she had all those others. She was beginning to realize that what she had heretofore thought of as love was in fact nothing more than empty infatuation.

Elena pressed her lips to Gareth's warm, smooth back. The wild thought that she should simply admit her feelings to him and propose marriage made her heart pound so that she feared he would feel it beating against his back. No, she could do that! Perhaps if she implied that since he had taken her virginity, he was not obligated to marry her.

With a newfound maturity, Elena realized that she would not coax Gareth into marriage simply based on their two nights spent together. She had given herself to him freely and to backtrack and say that he now owed her something was not honorable. Besides, she wanted a man who felt obligated to wed her even less than one who saw her as a witless prize to be won.

Wishing her problems would simply solve themselves and determined not to spoil the present by worrying over them, Elena pushed herself to her elbow and began nibbling on Gareth's ear. He swatted lazily in the general vicinity of his ear before slipping back into a deep slumber. Elena giggled as she wiggled up further on the bed to gain a better position. Taking a strand of her long hair, she tickled his nose with the end of it, straining not to laugh as he wiggled and rubbed it. Finally unable to stand it any longer, Elena rolled Gareth onto his back and climbed on top of him, tickling him and poking him playfully.

Gareth squinted at the bright light and groggily raised his head.

"Wake up, you slug-a-bed, wake up! Or I shall tickle you until you do!"

"You think so, do you?" he grumbled, his voice deliciously deep and raspy with sleep.

"Aye, that I do!" she said with a laugh.

So quickly that she did not even realize what was happening, Gareth bucked her off of him and rolled over to smother her with his weight, his fingers tickling her ribs, her ears, and the tender skin behind her knees. Elena's short scream of laughter was swallowed by Gareth's mouth. Immediately, Elena's mirth subsided as she gave herself over to the languorous pleasure of his kiss.

A knock on the door caused them both to jump guiltily and move to opposite sides of the bed, clutching the covers between them. "Yes?" Elena called out. The door, which never quite latched all the way, was open a crack.

"Pardon, good lady," came Samuel's voice through the door. "I was wondering if you were alright. We heard you yelp."

Elena's experience at fabricating excuses for Lady Elizabeth quickly rose to the surface. "I'm quite alright. I stubbed my toe as I was getting back into bed, that's all."

"Of course, my lady. We have some fresh milk and early berries if you will be arising soon."

"Thank you but I'm not feeling well this morning. I think it must have been the mead last night. I believe I will remain abed this morning if not all day." Elena smiled mischievously in response to Gareth's raised eyebrows.

"Ah, um, very good." The voice paused hesitantly. "My lady?"

"Yes?"

"You wouldn't have happened to know where Gareth disappeared to, do you?"

"As a matter of fact, I do," Elena said, enjoying the look of horror in

Gareth's widened eyes. "He knocked on my door earlier this morning to check on me and he told me he was going down to the dock today to see if he could sail out with one of the fishermen."

"Fishermen, my lady?"

"Yes, I believe he is thinking of becoming a fisherman, should his career as a knight not prove lucrative."

Gareth bit his lip to keep from laughing out loud.

"Oh," said Samuel. "Well, uh, I'm sorry to have disturbed you. Thank you." They could hear Samuel shuffling from foot to foot outside the door. "Sleep well, Lady Elena."

"Thank you, Samuel."

"If you need anything, just holler, er, call."

"I will do that. Goodbye Samuel."

"Er... goodbye."

Elena pushed the door closed again, wedging her boots against it to keep it from opening again, and flopped back down onto the bed, her arms cradling her head as she looked at Gareth with a cocky grin.

"Remind me not to believe a word you say through a closed door," Gareth said before he bent down and kissed her on the nose.

"You don't know how many times I had to tell King Richard that Lady Elizabeth was ill, when really all she wanted was to avoid his continuing attempts to convince her to marry him."

"Was he that persistent?"

"Yes." Elena said, preoccupied. She wondered if Elizabeth had viewed wedding Richard with the same distaste she viewed wedding Brackley. Against her will, Elena thought of the other complaints against King Richard. There were the missing nephews, of course. She had always avoided thinking of them because if Richard had caused them to be done away with, what might he do to a mere lady-in-waiting should she displease him?

"Why do you think he was so adamant that she marry him? Did he love her?" Gareth asked.

"I don't see how. They rarely spent any time together and she was always exceedingly cold to him."

"Then what made him continue his pursuit?" Gareth asked as he lay down beside her and ran his hands over her smooth stomach.

"I imagine he thought marrying her would quiet any speculation that he didn't belong on the throne."

"Don't you think that was wrong of him?"

"I suppose." The subject of Richard on her mind, Elena asked, "I still don't understand why you have decided to return to him? I thought you disagreed with everything he stands for."

Gareth was obviously uncomfortable and toyed absently with her breast, apparently unaware that her breathing was growing more ragged.

"He's the king. That's all there is to it." Gareth bent and took Elena's mouth in a thorough kiss that erased all thought of kings or princesses from her mind.

Some time later, Elena brought up a related topic. "What will we tell the king when we return? How will we explain why we've been gone so long?"

Gareth chewed his upper lip for several seconds before answering. "I think we should stick as close to the truth as possible." He paused in thought before continuing. "We'll tell them we became separated from Richard's party in the ambush and thinking we were still being followed, we led the bandits away from Richard's route, west into Wales. We'll say Cynan was wounded--"

"Why Cynan?"

"Or Bryant. It doesn't matter. We'll simply use that as an excuse for going to Eyri Keep. We'll say we stayed there until we were able to return to England."

Elena shook her head. "No, that won't work. Richard will ask why we didn't just drop off the wounded man and then return. Why don't you tell him I was injured and my horse killed? That will explain why I no longer have it and why we weren't able to leave sooner."

She was pleased by the impressed look on his face. "Very good." Gareth's countenance dimmed as he sat in thought. "If Richard would be sharp enough to determine that we could return without Cynan or Bryant, wouldn't he ask why we didn't simply stop at the manor of one of the border lords?"

"Do you know where any of their keeps are?"

"Not really. I usually travel as the crow flies and miss all the towns and manors."

"There you go," Elena said, delighted that Gareth was not only letting her help plan their story, but applauding her sharpness.

"That, my sweet lady, deserves a kiss."

"Just a kiss?" she asked coyly.

***

By noon the lovers were famished, though both were loath to leave the sanctuary of the small room. A gentle knock on the door stopped their whispered plans to get food.

"My lady? 'Tis I, Bryant. Are you alright?"

"Of course I am."

"Of course," Bryant repeated and then paused. "I grew worried because you haven't left you room all morning."

"Well, I've been sleeping and attending private matters."

Gareth mouthed the words "private matters," and grinned wickedly. Elena slapped him playfully on the shoulder.

"Is there anything I can do for you?" Bryant's solicitous voice interrupted their play.

Stifling a laugh, Elena responded, "Actually, I am rather hungry--starving, actually. I feel like I could eat enough for two."

"Shall I bring you something to eat or would you like to come out. I could set up a cozy table for you."

"I believe I would prefer to dine in here."

Disappointment evident in his voice, Bryant acquiesced.

"Oh, and Bryant?"

"Yes, my lady?" Hope sprang eternal.

"Please bring big portions. I'm very hungry."

"Of course, my lady."

Elena and Gareth listened to Bryant's footsteps recede. "You know he fancies himself in love with you, don't you."

Elena shrugged. "I had long suspected as much."

"You're not surprised?"

"'Tis not the first time a man has been in love with me and 'twill not be the last, I am sure," Elena put a sardonic emphasis on the word "love."

Gareth shook his head and grinned. "You don't believe in the word 'modesty,' do you Elena?"

"Modesty? Of course I believe in it. I'm very modest."

"Then how about humility?"

"What good does humility do a woman? It merely gets her wedded to a man of her parents' choosing long before she's ready to suffer the chores of marriage. Or," she continued, heedless of Gareth's prodding smile. "Or it gets her sent to a convent where she spends her days on her knees praying and scrubbing floors."

"Scrubbing floors?" Gareth asked, clicking his tongue against his teeth. "Do you realize the heresy you speak? It would do you no good should the wrong people hear you speak such."

Elena laughed. "What 'wrong people'?"

"Let me think. Parents, husbands, brothers, noblemen, clergymen."

"Worry no longer that I will be locked away for my insanity. Besides Catherine and Margaret, the only person I've quoted such blasphemy to is you."

"Who are Catherine and Margaret?"

"Two of the other ladies-in-waiting."

"And how do they respond to your opinions?"

Elena rolled her eyes. "Well, Catherine thinks I am incredibly brave and destined for greatness. Margaret simply disdains me."

Gareth frowned. "Why should she disdain you?"

"Since she is one whose 'humility' is leading her to a convent, she regards me as nothing more than a self-centered, money-hungry schemer who has no interest in love and little thought for the hearts of others."

"And do you?"

"Do I what?"

"Do you have no interest in love?"

Elena paused, suddenly wary. "Well of course I do."

"It's just that, well, there are other things to consider," he finished. "Like money and power."

Elena did not know how to confess that such things no longer seemed to have the sway over her decisions they once did. The realization was still rather new to her. "They do help make life more secure," she prevaricated, refusing to meet his eyes.

"But if you were faced with a choice: to marry for power and wealth or to marry someone who loved you more than life itself, which would you choose?"

Feeling as if she were trapped, and not at all ready to admit her budding feeling when she knew not if they were returned, she said, "I detest hypothetical questions. The king has already made his decision regarding whom I shall marry."

Gareth persisted. "But what if you are successful in convincing Richard to break your engagement? What if you do face that question in the future? What would you choose? Love or money?"

Elena's heart was pounding in her chest. The trap was beginning to close. Panic and fear replaced her carefully honed poise and confidence. She gazed into his eyes. The emotion she saw in them was intense, focused solely on her. She fancied she saw his deepest emotions in them. Deciding to take the biggest risk of her life, Elena drew a breath to speak—

A knock at the door interrupted her.

"Who is it?" she asked instead, unsure if she were relieved or disappointed by the interruption.

"Bryant, my lady. I have your dinner."

Elena scrambled to her feet and tugged on her chemise. "Just a moment," she called. In a whisper, she asked Gareth, "Where are you going to hide?"

He pointed to the door and gestured that he would hide behind it while she opened it. Nodding, Elena smoothed her hair and slowly opened the door, careful not to open it too wide and bang Gareth in the face. Smiling at Bryant who was staring in embarrassed shock at her chemise she took the heavy tray from him. "You are an angel, Bryant. This looks delicious," she said as she sniffed the thick stew. She turned and set the tray on the small table, noticing with chagrin Gareth's breeches lying on the floor. Whirling around, she started to close the door, only to have Bryant stop it with his hand. Sure that he was going to ask who else was in the room with her, she scowled at him, hoping to intimidate him into leaving.

Bryant flushed and stammered, "I--I'm sorry, Lady Elena. I just wanted to make sure there was nothing else you required."

"No, nothing. I'm am well supplied now. I believe I will continue to rest this day as Gareth mentioned we would be leaving tomorrow. 'Twill not be long before I'm missing the comforts of a soft bed and watertight roof."

Bryant nodded, but kept the door propped open, despite Elena's gentle pushing. "Have you seen Gareth today?"

Trying to remember what she had told Samuel earlier that morning, Elena shook her head. "Nay, I haven't seen him, though he did knock on my door this morning to see if I needed anything."

Bryant seemed relieved by her news and said, "I hope you enjoy your meal. Rest well, my lady and simply call out if you need anything at all."

Elena smiled sweetly. "Thank you. Be assured I will do so." She tried to close the door but Bryant held it open again. Elena quickly switched from a smile to a questioning glance, her left eyebrow raised imperiously in an expression she had long perfected. As always, it worked immediately.

"Excuse me," Bryant said, quickly removing his hand from the door and stepping back. "Good day."

Elena nodded and firmly closed the door. Turning to Gareth, who was holding his shirt clutched to his waist, she suddenly felt uncomfortable, her unspoken confession hanging heavily in the air. Whirling around, she threw herself onto the bed, hoping to regain the seductive playfulness in which they had been swathed for the past twelve hours. As if sensing her plan, Gareth pulled on his shirt and moved to bring the tray to the bed. Setting it on the soft mattress, he carefully sat on the end of the bed opposite Elena.

"What have we here?" he asked, as casually as if they did this all the time: dining half naked in bed after having just made love. Gareth sniffed the stew appreciatively and pulled back a linen cloth to reveal a large chunk of cheese, a half a loaf of bread, fresh fruit, and some sort of desert tart.

Elena picked up the spoon. "I should have asked for two utensils."

Gareth laughed. "No, that would not have looked suspicious. What would you have given for an excuse?" In a falsetto voice, he joked, "Dear, angelic Bryant, I am so hungry I need two spoons so that I may shovel in my food with both hands."

The awkwardness of a few moments before quickly dissipated. Affecting mock offense at Gareth's impersonation, Elena broke off a bit of bread and pelted him in the face with it. Surprised at the attack, he hesitated only a moment before snatching up the missile and launching it back at her. The ensuing bread fight was accompanied by whispered threats and laughter smothered into pillows. It ended abruptly when Elena took a handful of juicy berries and crammed them into Gareth's laughing mouth. His eyes widened as he tried to swallow the mouthful, sweet juices running down his chin. Transfixed, Elena grabbed his shirt and pulled him closer, leaning over the tray which separated them, to kiss the juice from his mouth and chin.

When the kiss finally broke, the food was nearly forgotten but for an indignant rumbling from the depths of Gareth's stomach. They both laughed and Gareth said, "Pray forgive me, sweet lady. I would gladly satisfy your appetite--" he raised his eyebrows suggestively-- "but I fear I will faint with hunger if I do not first satisfy this hunger," he finished, patting his stomach.

Elena rolled her eyes. "Heaven forbid the ever strong and valiant Sir Gareth should do something so weak and detestable as faint! Hey there! You need not devour everything before I get a bite! I have been without food as long as you, now hand over that spoon."

A good while later, their several appetites satiated, they lay in comfortable companionship on the narrow pallet comparing stories of their childhood.

"You mean to tell me," Elena asked incredulously. "That you did not learn to read until you became a squire?"

Gareth frowned defensively. "'Tis not that uncommon for a lad to wait until his training to learn his letters. When did you learn to read?"

Elena squinted her eyes in concentration. "I must have been six or seven."

"Six or seven? You are pulling my leg."

"No, no. Truly, I learned to read and write when I was but a young child."

"Well that is more unusual than me not learning until I was a young man. Besides," he argued, a thought occurring to him. "There are many a churchman who would say it was wrong of your parents to teach you to read at all, you being a girl and all."

"And what would be their reasoning for such a claim?" Elena asked, baiting him.

Gareth shrugged. "Ask a churchman. I just listen to what they preach and most of them say women should not read."

"Then perhaps 'tis time for a new church."

Gareth laughed aloud before catching himself and pressing his hand to his mouth. "Now I know you are pulling my leg. A new church indeed."

"It could happen--"

"Now, now, you would claim it is God's will that women are granted the same intelligence as men? What an unwomanly notion!"

Elena was torn between screeching at him or hitting him over the head when she caught the glimmer in his eye and a twitching muscle near his mouth that belied his antagonistic remarks.

"I believe I enjoy baiting you almost as much as Cynan loves to rile me," he said with a wicked grin.

Elena's eyes narrowed and her lips pursed. She concentrated on giving Gareth her most thorough look of supreme displeasure, waiting for him to squirm and apologize for taunting her. To her utter chagrin, Gareth's smile only broadened. Afraid her facial muscles could not hold the grimace one more minute, she allowed Gareth to kiss her back into a good mood.

"Just a warning, Gareth ap Morgan: I detest merely arguing for the sake of arguing. Don't play the devil's advocate with me."

"You have my word. I shall only provoke you when I truly disagree with you."

Elena shook her head as she snuggled against the curve of Gareth's chest. "For some reason, that does not comfort me."

$$Chapter\ 20$$

Late that afternoon, their lungs crying out for fresh air, their muscles longing for a position other than supine, Gareth and Elena dressed and snuck out of the house, Elena going first to determine if anyone would be about to see Gareth leaving her room. Like a couple of children, they ducked out the shop's front door and ran down the street towards the rocky beach they had briefly visited their first night in Aberystwyth. Once there, they continued their child-like behavior, chasing seagulls down the shore, skipping stones across the water, and dispelling the slumberous clouds that had filled their heads during their lazy day in bed.

The day was bright and sunny with high white clouds dotting an otherwise flawless blue sky. Despite the vigor of the sun, a stiff breeze off the ocean gave the air a tangible briskness that tingled in Elena's cheeks and occasionally brought the sting of tears to her eyes. The beach was deserted and Elena gave no thought to hiking her skirts to her knees as she ran the length of the shallow cove in which the ships docked at Aberystwyth. The coarse sand and smooth rocks went unnoticed beneath her thin-soled boots as she ran. Her blood sang in her veins and she inhaled the crisp air in great, heaving breaths, feeling totally and completely alive.

Glancing over her shoulder, Elena was delighted to see Gareth giving chase behind her, his own cheeks ruddy, his unruly hair for once completely off his forehead as the wind caught it and tugged it behind him. Though he could have easily caught her, he remained at her heels, playfully grabbing at her skirts and her hair, which had come, unbound and now streamed out behind her. Long before she reached the end of the cove, she slowed to a stop and flung herself down on a patch of coarse grass, winded and warm, despite the cool breeze. Gareth joined her on the earthen bed, stretching out beside her, his hands behind his head, his breathing only slightly labored.

Elena cushioned her head on his shoulder and stared up at the brilliant sky. More clouds had gathered, though they were innocently white, devoid of any threat of rain as they sailed across the blue expanse behind them.

"Do you see that cloud over there?" Gareth asked, pointing to a large formation on the northern horizon.

"Yes."

"Don't you think it looks like a running horse?"

"A what? It just looks white." Elena squinted, trying to decipher a horse in the huge blob of cloud.

"No, look carefully. See? Right there is his head with a mane flowing out behind it. You can't really see his forelegs, but his hindquarters and tail are easy to see."

Slowly the image took shape for Elena and she gasped in amazement. "You're right."

Gareth turned his head and looked at her. "Haven't you ever watched the clouds before?"

"Never."

"Truly?" he asked, amazed.

"When would I have lain on the ground staring at the sky? Perchance while Lady Elizabeth was sleeping?"

"What about as a child? I used to have to tend my father's flock and every afternoon I would spend hours imagining stories around the things I saw in the clouds."

Feeling defensive, Elena said, "I was learning to read real stories as a child, remember?"

"Ah yes. Well, it's never too late to learn. Let's look for something else. There," he said, pointing at a cloud directly over them. "That one looks like a huge tree. If I were a child back in Gwynedd, I would imagine that was a magical tree inhabited by fairies."

"Fairies?" Elena asked. "There's no such thing as fairies."

"How do you know?" Gareth asked incredulously.

"There just aren't. I would have read about them if there were."

"You can't learn everything from books, Elena."

She was about to retort when she thought of the past month spent in Gareth's company. Truly she could never have learned what she did from him in a book! Deciding to hold her tongue and watch the clouds, she felt a relaxing sense of peace. The pulse of the surf on the beach, the sun warming her face, the wind caressing her hair lulled her into a state in which she began to pick out shapes and patterns. Amazing how I never understood until now the pastime of cloud watching, she thought. Her inexperienced imagination took a while to actually see the vivid images Gareth had described, but she enjoyed it nonetheless.

After their bodies had cooled from their run, Elena began to grow chilly in the constant breeze and she moved closer to Gareth, plastering herself to his warm side. He brought his left arm out from behind his head to caress her shoulders and back. When she continued to shiver, he sat up. "Let's move around some more. That will warm you."

Elena nodded and allowed him to help her to her feet. She stood patiently, enjoying his attentions, while he brushed the sand and grass off her back and plucked it out of her hair. When she was properly groomed, Gareth took her hand and led her further south along the coast, stopping now and again to show her a shell polished by the pounding surf or point out a sand crab as it made its way across the rough beach. They explored for the remainder of the afternoon, finally making their way back to Samuel's shop when the sun began to dip into the fathomless blue of the ocean.

The instant they stepped into the back room, Bryant accosted them.

"Where have you been?" he asked Gareth in a voice uncharacteristic in its sharpness. Morgan and Cynan glanced up from their conversation, clearly surprised.

"I went down to the docks. I thought I might spend the day sailing. It's been years since I've been on the water. But those fishermen who were going out didn't have room for stowaways so I just roamed the beach. It was a beautiful day. You should have been there."

"I would have had I or anyone else here known you were leaving. You must have arisen quite early," Bryant said skeptically.

"I thought I'd better. Those fishermen usually leave before dawn."

To Elena, it was clear that Bryant was extremely jealous. Though she was well aware he was taken with her, she had given him no intimation that she favored him above friendship. As he turned to her, his hostility was quickly smothered and he asked her, "Where did you disappear to, Lady Elena? I knocked at your door several times this afternoon to see if you were feeling all right but there was no answer. Had I known you desired fresh air, I would have been more than happy to provide an escort."

"I didn't want to trouble anyone. I remembered my way to the beach from the other night. It's not that far so I just walked by myself. I met Gareth down there and he escorted me home."

Before Bryant could say anything else, Elena pointedly turned away and joined Morgan and Cynan at the fireplace. Bryant made sure to fill the empty seat next to her before Gareth had a chance to. He repeated the performance again at dinner, much to Gareth's annoyance. The meal was more subdued than the previous night's, partly due to the absence of the mead, partly due to their reduced numbers. Many of the men from the night before had returned home.

The mood lightened a bit after dinner as they sat round the fire. Samuel and Morgan took turns telling the old stories of Wales. Like the great bards who visited the king's castles, each man wove intricate stories, each trying to outdo the other.

"Well spoken, Samuel," Morgan said when the other man finished an intricate tale of Welsh history. "That is a different version than I have heard before."

"My grandfather taught it me and he was always meticulous about details," Samuel said, a bit defensively.

Elena yawned widely and loudly. Then men in the room laughed aloud but their good-natured laughter did not prevent her from being mortified at her unladylike behavior. Deciding that she need not be so concerned--this was, after all, Wales, far from court life--she stood and excused herself from the men's company. "Thank you for the enjoyable entertainment."

Gareth quickly stood before Bryant could and took her arm to escort her to her room.

At the door to her small room, Elena turned expectantly to Gareth. She knew he could not join her now, with the other men still awake, but she was determined to have a kiss--something she had been denied all evening. Lifting her head, she pressed her lips against Gareth's, waiting for him to return the kiss. When he did not, she pulled back abruptly.

"I do not wish us to be caught, Elena. My father and the others would assume I was forcing myself upon you and we would be unable to return to England until a 'suitable' escort could join us."

Elena nodded, understanding his concern though still disappointed, and went into her room. She slowly undressed and got into bed, laying on her back and staring at the ceiling. After so much time spent napping in bed today, she was not really tired, just pleasantly drowsy from the fresh air and exercise at the beach. No, she did not wish a "suitable escort" to accompany them to England. She was reveling in the pleasures she and Gareth were sharing.

Should she be forced to spend the rest of her life with the Earl of Brackley, she would only have these delicious memories to sustain her. That thought dimmed some of her pleasure and she shoved it from her mind. She must concentrate on the present now, savor every moment. She stretched her arms over her head, curling her toes and flexing every muscle in her legs. When she released her stretch, she felt deliciously relaxed. I'll just close my eyes until Gareth comes, she told herself. Within minutes she was asleep.

***

It proved impossible for Gareth to get away from the other men. His father, realizing that this was the last night he would have his son before sending him into a dangerous assignment was loathe to give up his company, wanting to discuss yet again the plan for Gareth to meet up with the Welsh forces once the battle was imminent. Bryant also seemed determined not to let him out of his sight, even going so far as to follow him outside when Gareth stepped out to relieve himself.

When the four men finally made their way to the weaving room upstairs, Gareth thought he would be able to wait for his father and friends to fall asleep and then sneak downstairs, but Bryant, as if knowing what he had planned, positioned himself right in front of the closed door so there was no way Gareth could open it without waking him. Frustrated, Gareth stretched out on a floor that was not near as comfortable as Elena's bed and wrapped himself in blankets that were not near as soft or warm as her velvety skin. In the utter darkness, he allowed the memories of the day and the previous night fill his head. As a result, though the hour was late, Gareth did not fall asleep for a long time.

***

Early the next morning, Elena awoke, disappointed to find herself alone. Propped up on her elbows, she wondered if Gareth had stepped outside to attend to personal business. Slowly she remembered that Gareth had not joined her at all last night, that they had not made love before sleeping comfortably entwined in the narrow bed.

With a disappointed sigh, Elena lay back down. No wonder she felt groggy. She hadn't slept well at all. As she considered it, she was amazed that she could have grown so accustomed to sleeping with someone else in just two short nights. Back home, she couldn't stand having to share her pallet with two and sometimes three other ladies-in-waiting. She reveled in the emptiness of the bed on those few nights when she had had it all to herself. Now, here she was with not only her own bed, but her own room and what did she long for? A roommate! Well, she corrected herself, not just any roommate. What she truly longed for was Gareth's company. Slowly pushing herself from bed, she began dressing, sending up a brief but heartfelt prayer of thanks that this was the last time she would have to put on her worn blue cotehardie.

She struggled to get it laced up the back, contorting her arms this way and that, and then fastened the tiny buttons up each sleeve from wrist to elbow and tried to smooth some of the wrinkles out of the skirt.

"Hopeless," she mumbled, and turned her attention to her hair which she combed out and wound in a braid. A knock at the door made her drop her comb and rush to answer it.

Cynan's craggy face and lopsided grin greeted her as his rumbling voice said, "Good morning."

"Good morning," she returned, refusing to even consider that the sinking sensation in her stomach was disappointment. She could, after all, live without the man.

"Gareth asked me to take you to your seamstress's shop to pick up your dress."

"Where is he?"

"He and his father went to gather another horse and buy supplies for your trip. Worry not," he said with a grin, "I reminded him, 'No dried beef!'"

Elena smiled and rolled her eyes. "As if I'll be so lucky." Stepping into the hall, she led the way through the shop and out the front door.

"Would you like to eat before we go?" Cynan said, walking quickly to catch up to her.

"Do you jest? I've a new gown awaiting me!"

"I should have known that would be a woman's response. You wouldn't, by any chance, know where we are going, would you?"

"You don't?" Elena paused in the narrow street.

"Do you jest?" he asked, imitating her tone.

"Is it a national trait that the Welsh are completely lost when it comes to directions?"

Cynan laughed and held his hands up in denial. "I could find my way across every mountain range in Wales and let you know exactly when and where the sun was going to set. It's just when you put a poor mountain boy in a town, he has no way to judge his surroundings. For example, look at this row of houses." Elena obliged. "They all look exactly alike. But each tree is different, each rock has its own shape, each stream has its own path. No," he finished, shaking his head. "I can not be held accountable for finding my way in the city."

Elena laughed. "Luckily for us, I know where we are going. And, no, I don't think those houses all look exactly alike. That one there has blue trim while the one next to it has rough wood. The third one down only has one window on the street."

Cynan acceded with a gallant bow. "Very well, you are the true trailblazer, I am merely a stupid shepherd who belongs in the field with his flock."

In good conscience, Elena forced herself to admit, "No, no. To me, every tree looks just like the one before it, every rock is simply a rock and every stream is just wet. It's all just a matter of perspective, I suppose."

"You are too kind, my lady. In that case, lead on!"

Elena found the seamstress's shop much easier this time and she called out for Annie as soon as she entered the empty downstairs room. Once again, Oengus came tumbling down the stairs to ask them to please, "Come dupstairs."

The previously tidy room was considerably messier on this visit. Dirty pots were stacked haphazardly on the rough table in the kitchen and a pile of mending or laundry was heaped on a chair. Oengus's few wooden toys were strewn about the floor. Surprised, Elena glanced around for Annie and found her seated at her worktable, breaking a thread with her teeth on what looked to be the cream-colored chemise.

When Annie realized she had visitors, she stood abruptly, her face reddening as she smiled feebly. "Good morning, my lady. Please forgive my house," she pleaded. "I'm afraid I tend to let things go when I have a project."

Never fond of cleaning herself, Elena shrugged with a complete lack of concern. "It does not bother me." Pointing at the fabric in Annie's hands, she asked, "Is that mine?"

"Yes. I was just finishing the hem. I've finished the over gown as well."

"You had enough time then?" Elena shook her head and laughed. "Obviously you had enough time. What I meant to say was I hope you didn't have to rush unduly."

"No, my lady. It was just the right amount of time."

"Very good. I would like to try it on, then."

"Of course, my lady. Oengus," she called. When the young boy came running from the corner in which he'd been playing, she gestured to Cynan. "Take, er--"

Elena smiled. She had been here three times with as many men. Poor Annie must be wondering exactly what kind of woman she was! "Another brother," she said in order to rest the young woman's mind, though for the life of her, she didn't know what possessed her to bother.

Annie's countenance immediately cleared, but before she could instruct her son, the little boy, used to the routine by now, took Cynan's hand

and led him out. "C'mon. We can't be here while lady changes."

Cynan paused at the doorway and took a leather pouch out of his shirt. Tossing it to Elena he said, "Gareth gave me the money for the dress."

Elena caught the heavy pouch and nodded. As soon as the door closed, she began struggling out of her cotehardie. When she had finally pulled it and her tattered chemise over her head, she threw them in a heap on the floor. When Annie rushed to pick up the discarded garments, Elena said, "You can burn those for all I care."

"No, my lady, this is a beautiful gown."

Elena began pulling on the new chemise. "The gown is filthy and the chemise near threadbare."

"But my lady, 'tis still in good condition. I could get these spots out, for you'll need it on your journey, won't you?"

"If you can salvage it, you keep it. I am so heartily sick of the sight of it that I will not wear it ever again. We seem of a like size. I'm sure it will fit you. Now, where is my houppeland?"

"Here, my lady," Annie said, unhooking the wool dress from where it hung on a peg on the wall. Annie handed it to Elena for inspection.

"Very well done, Annie," Elena said approvingly. The work was truly that of an expert seamstress and Elena had not seen better quality in the finest shops in London or from the handiest of maids in court. Heedless of Annie's flush of pleasure and sheepish smile, Elena handed her the gown and dove under the hem. Annie lowered the dress over her head, tugging the full skirt into place. She deftly closed the laces up the back while Elena folded back the broad cuffs of the bagpipe sleeves to show the ruffled edge of the chemise.

Elena ran her hands over the soft wool, smoothing the collar of the dress and fluffing out the skirt. "I wish you had a mirror that I might see how this looked from afar."

"I do have one, my lady. 'Tis not large, but I think if I hold it at different angles for you, you should be able to see everything." Annie rushed to a large chest of drawers and pulled out a mirror set in an intricately carved wooden frame. "This was my mother's. She gave it to me before we left Scotland." She pointed to a small crack in the corner of the mirror. "This happened as we journeyed here, but otherwise it survived." She climbed up onto a small stool and tilted the mirror until Elena was able to see every angle of her new gown.

"It's wonderful, Annie. You have done an exceptional job." Picking up the leather pouch of money, she asked, "Now, what was the price we had decided upon?"

Annie shyly told her but hastily added, "Unless that is too much since you are giving me this gown as well."

Had Annie been a wily London merchant, Elena would have pounced on the idea and talked the price of the gown down considerably. But for some reason, Elena found herself saying, "No, Annie. You slaved over this gown for the past three days. What you should be telling me is that you are charging me more for the inconvenience."

"No, my lady."

"Yes, Annie. This is why you've let those old hens up the street steal your sign and run off your customers--you're too nice of a person. Now look me in the eye and tell me that you are simply going to have to charge me more."

"But--"

"Annie," Elena said in her best important-lady-speaking-to-a-mere-servant voice.

The young seamstress's eyes widened but she obeyed. "I'm sorry, my lady, but I'll have to ask two-pence more for the gown."

"You'll never make any money only asking for a two-pence. Now give me a real price."

Annie lowered her eyes and quoted a price.

"Very well, if that is what I must pay, that is what I must pay," said Elena, opening the leather pouch. "Now, here is your price, plus some extra because I am well pleased with your work. I would suggest you take some of that money and use it to fix up the downstairs room and put a sign inside your window so it won't be stolen and people will be able to find you. As it is now, from the street this looks like an abandoned building."

Elena picked up her skirts daintily and moved to leave. "Make those improvements soon, Annie. I will be recommending to Samuel the weaver that he should send his customers to you."

"You are the very soul of kindness, my lady," Annie said sincerely, tears filling her eyes.

Elena paused in the doorway. She had certainly never been called that. In fact, the other ladies of the court had often called her unkind. She found she preferred being the soul of kindness, especially when it took very little effort to achieve it. With a regal nod to the seamstress, she swept down the stairs.

"Ooh, pretty, lady," young Oengus said, stopping his roughhousing with Cynan.

Cynan hopped to his feet. "You are indeed a vision, Lady Elena."

"Thank you. Goodbye, Oengus."

"Goobye," he said.

Once outside, Elena led the way back towards Samuel's shop. "You and Bryant will return with Morgan to Eyri Keep, then?"

"Aye, my lady. I'm missing Enid fiercely. It seems harder to be away from her knowing she's carrying our babe."

With a sincerity she truly felt, Elena said, "I will miss traveling with you and Bryant. You both have treated me with the utmost courtesy."

Cynan laughed. "'Unlike our surly friend Gareth, eh? You must pay him no mind, Elena. Gareth must be sorely taken with you to act so rudely these past weeks."

Elena sensed Cynan could be a wealth of information regarding Gareth's feelings if she could lead him in the right direction. Slowing her pace so they would not reach Samuel's before she found out what she wanted to know, she said innocently, "Gareth taken with me?"

"Of course, we all are!" Cynan said good-naturedly. "Why Bryant is so lovesick, he forgets to eat unless I prod him. The only thing that has saved me is the fact that I am a devoted husband. Were it not for my dear Enid, I would no doubt be as melancholy as Bryant or as surly as Gareth."

Elena knew Bryant's feelings. They were evident is his puppy eyes every time he looked at her. Cynan might as well be her brother for her feelings toward him. What she wanted was details of Gareth's feelings. "I don't agree with you about Gareth." It was one of her best strategies, arguing just the opposite. Usually, she used the technique when men said they loved her. If she protested, they would spend their very breath proving to her that it was true. "I fear he can't stand to be in the same room with me."

"No, no. That is not the case at all. You see, Gareth usually treats all ladies with the utmost respect. He takes his vows of chivalry very seriously."

Elena frowned. She did not want to hear how well Gareth treated other women.

Cynan saw her frown and smiled as he continued. "But Gareth cared not a whit about any of the women. In fact, they interested him not the least. Then you come along and he is outright rude to you. He claimed at first that it was because you were a self-centered, uncaring little brat."

Elena's frown deepened. This was not what she wanted to hear.

"Which of course you aren't," Cynan quickly added. "But I interpreted that to mean that you had snubbed his overture to you and it had cut him to the quick. That it would hurt him could only mean he truly fancied you and rudeness was his only defense."

That was a little more like it, Elena thought. "But has he said aught of his true feelings to you?" she asked and immediately cringed. That question was anything but subtle.

"Nary a word. But give me more credit than Gareth, good lady. Though I may seem rough and crass, I can read my friends well and I know what I have said is true." They walked in silence for several seconds before Cynan spoke again. "Perhaps this is not an appropriate subject for me to be discussing, especially since you will be traveling alone with him for the next week. But you need not fear him, Lady Elena. Gareth is, above all things, honorable. No matter what his feelings toward you, he would never force himself upon you."

Elena considered their last bout of lovemaking. No, if anything, she had forced herself on him. It was comical that she should be pretending to Cynan that she was the demure and worried lady when she was looking forward to being alone with Gareth for the very reason that she wanted him to make love to her!

Searching for something to keep the conversation going, she said, "Bryant believes otherwise."

"I know. But he is very jealous. He is jealous that Gareth will get to spend time with you this next week while he must return to Eyri Keep. Perhaps he also sees that Gareth is taken with you and fears he will use this time with you to win your heart." Cynan paused. "I'm sure you must find this entire conversation highly unusual. I'm not even sure how it started." Elena looked at him blandly. "But I guess what I am trying to say is this: should things not go as you might hope once you return to Richard's court, you can rest assured that Gareth will do all he can to protect you and help you. Should you wish, he will even bring you back to Wales where you would have your choice of husbands."

They rounded the corner and walked the last few paces to Samuel's shop.

"I thank you for your confidence, Cynan. It does much to relieve my mind," she said as they entered the building. Inside, Samuel was helping a pair of matrons select fabric. He seemed to scarcely notice Elena and Cynan as they waved and made their way to the back room where Gareth, Morgan, and Bryant awaited them. Elena swept into the room, fully conscious of how flattering her new dress was to her many attributes.

"Huzzah, sweet lady," said Morgan. "You are as lovely as a newborn foal!"

Elena started to frown but laughed instead. Morgan undoubtedly thought newborn foals were, in fact, lovely, and she decided to take his comment as a compliment. Bryant told her she looked beautiful, but Elena scarcely nodded in his direction. She wanted to see Gareth's reaction. Trying to appear casually indifferent, she slowly turned, allowing him to judge her appearance from every angle. When she finally raised her eyes to his but he was not inspecting her dress, he was gazing at her face with a hot passion that made her completely forget the gown.

At a nudge from his father Gareth was suddenly in motion. Walking towards the open back door, he called to Bryant. "Help me bring the horses around front, will you Bryant? Da, if you'll grab the bag of food and meet us outside...Elena, gather your things. We must try to cross as much distance as possible before nightfall."

Elena turned to go to her small room when she realized that she had no things to gather. Since she had left her old dress with Annie, she had not even a change of clothing to pack, and since she had been sleeping in the relative comfort of the low straw pallet, she had not given one thought to the bedroll she had spent so many nights in. Turning to Cynan, she shrugged. "I suppose I am gathered."

Cynan laughed and said, "I suppose you are."

Elena followed him back down the short hallway to the front shop. There, Samuel had managed to sell a stack of fabric to the two middle-aged women who were preparing to leave. Elena suddenly remembered Annie and recollecting her "soul of kindness," paused in front of the women.

"Might I recommend a seamstress?"

The two women looked up, one with a plain but wholesome face, the other with a sustained beauty that Elena hoped she would have in fifteen years.

"We already have seamstresses--ourselves," said the plain-faced one.

"Why? Whom do you recommend?" the beauty asked. "We may need one someday," she added and Elena wondered if she was simply trying to be kind.

"There is a young woman by the name of Annie not ten minute's walk from here who does beautiful work. See?" she said, holding out her skirts for their inspection. "She made this gown in less time than it takes most people to cut the fabric!"

As is the case with most women, the three were instantly friends, discussing clothing. Cynan and Samuel looked on in amazed wonderment as the women chatted for several minutes. When Elena finally turned to leave, she had both women's promises to visit Annie with work.

Feeling positively saintlike, Elena paused in the doorway and turned back to Samuel. "Thank you, Samuel, for your kind hospitality." She nodded graciously and left the shop, her skirts swishing behind her.

Once outside, she joined Gareth, his father, and Bryant who were packing the last bag onto one of the horses. Elena recognized one of the beasts as Isrid, Gareth's own, but the other, a shaggy, stocky beast, she deduced must be the new acquisition. She sincerely hoped she would not be forced to ride the smelly thing. What good would it do to have a beautiful new gown and then ride through the town on a broken-down pony? A thought struck her as she waited for Gareth to finish bidding his father goodbye. Perhaps the pony was to serve as a pack animal and she would ride in front of Gareth as they had so often before. The thought of being nestled against his chest well pleased her and she decided she would accept no other plan.

Gareth finally turned to her after giving his father a short but hard hug and said, "Are you ready to leave?" She nodded and gave him her hand, which he grasped firmly in his own warm one. He indicated the shaggy horse and said, "I'm afraid he's not much to look at, but he is sturdy and will not bolt on you." Elena pulled back abruptly. "Is something wrong?" he asked.

"I am a little fearful of horses," she lied. "Especially when they look like that."

Gareth frowned, no doubt surprised to hear this claim after her weeks in the saddle. "I would give you my horse to ride, but I fear he may be difficult for you to handle. Besides, this one here is as tame as a lamb. He'll not hurt you."

Elena looked beseechingly into his eyes and said, "Please, Gareth. Can't I just ride with you for a little while? Then maybe I'll feel more confident about riding alone."

Gareth searched her eyes for several seconds and Elena sensed that he knew she was lying, but for some reason--perhaps the same reason she had asked to ride with him--he nodded his head and said, "Of course, Elena. Whatever will make you feel more comfortable." He led her to his horse and helped her into the saddle. She curled her leg around the front lip of the saddle so that she was not exactly sitting side saddle, but neither was she astride. Gareth returned to his father and two friends and said, "She is feeling a little nervous about riding alone so we'll just double up until she feels better about the horses." Cynan and Morgan, both obviously used to such feminine logic, nodded their heads understandingly, but Elena could see Bryant's eyes narrow suspiciously on Gareth before he came forward to say goodbye to her.

"Lady Elena, I hope you will remember my words. Know now and always that you only have to call upon me and I will travel the country to assist you in any way I can. I--" he paused and cleared his throat nervously. "I, uh, I wish--" he stopped again and Elena suddenly knew what he was going to say. "I wish you would think of me, umm, as a," he struggled for the words, "as a friend other than the brotherly kind. And if you would like to come back to Wales, well," he inhaled deeply and then said in a rush, "I would be waiting for you and you could come back to me." His speech exhausted, he stood, studying the stirrups that were peaking out from under her hem.

Elena reflected that Bryant's was certainly the most unusual proposal she had ever received. Suddenly finding she had not the heart to turn him down outright, she quickly thought of how the other girls back at court had refused suitors. She could not remember much, but she improvised and said, "You do me great honor, Bryant, by your words. I thank you for them and hope all goes well for you." Well, it was not exactly a refusal, but neither was it encouragement. She hoped it would do. She doubted--even if she didn't end up married to Brackley--that she would ever see Bryant again. Unless Gareth... well, that was a thought for another time.

Bryant, his cheeks red, suddenly stepped back as Morgan and Cynan came forward to bid her goodbye. Elena smiled warmly at Cynan and warned him to hurry home to Enid. Morgan took her hand and she squeezed it while he looked searchingly into her eyes and said, "God be with you, Elena. Go with my son and be well." Before Elena could say anything in response, Gareth swung up in the saddle behind her and she found herself pleasantly pressed against him. Morgan handed his son the reins to the other horse and Gareth deftly tied them to the saddle. Cynan and Bryant backed away as Gareth gathered his own horse's reins and prepared to urge the well-rested horse on. His father's voice stayed him. "Godspeed, Gareth. I hope it will be in this life that we meet again." Elena craned her neck and saw that Gareth was exchanging a look with his father that spoke volumes beyond the few departing words they had uttered. With a gentle nudge to Isrid, Gareth set them off on the beginning of their journey.

Chapter 21

Gareth studied the shops and the tidy homes of Aberstwyth on the way out of town as he had been unable to three days before when they had first entered its limits. He watched small children run along the street next to Isrid, laughing and yelling to one another. He studied the huge white clouds in the sky for unusual shapes. He concentrated on the brisk clip-clop of Isrid's hooves on the cobbled stones of the road that would lead them out of Aberstwyth, out of Wales. He kept his mind on anything that would prevent its wandering to Elena's soft body pressed against his chest, her hips rocking gently against his in time to the sway of the horse. It was entirely too soon in their journey for him to be thinking of making a rest stop. Besides, now that he was alone with her--really and truly alone, with no chance of his father or Samuel or Cynan or Bryant bursting in--he was suddenly unsure of how to act. He wondered if she wished to continue their highly enjoyable lovemaking now that they were on their way back to England and her fiancée. He wondered if she considered him as a careless affaire that was now over and done with.

Gareth squirmed in the saddle. Isrid was climbing the gradual hill that led out of Aberstwyth and Elena's weight shifted, sliding back just enough that she was pressed even more tantalizingly against him. This was going to be a long ride, he thought.

As he tried to inch further back in the saddle, another thought occurred to him. Elena had made it quite clear that she wished to ride with him. He could picture her face just minutes ago when she had told him she was afraid to ride alone. Gareth knew for a fact that she was afraid of nothing-- not even of suffering the consequences of going to her bridal bed without a maidenhead. Furthermore, she had ridden enough in the last month to make her adept at handling any kind of horse, much less one as docile as the one he had chosen for her. Therefore, her claim that she was too frightened to ride alone was simply for the benefit of his father and friends.

Gareth paused a moment, pleased with his deduction and its results. He allowed himself to tilt his head slightly and inhale the sweet perfume of her shimmering hair. In the bright sunlight, it glimmered with fire, changing from chestnut to brilliant red to brown as she moved her head. Several tendrils had come loose from the intricate twists and were caught in a light breeze, dancing about her head like a halo. Gareth smiled at that whimsical thought but his smile slowly faded. All right. So she enjoyed being close to him, feeling his chest and other parts pressed against her back. Perhaps she even intended that they would keep each other warm at night during their journey. That was well and good. What bothered Gareth now, though he was loathe to admit it, was this: What in the name of sweet merciful Mary did this woman feel for him?

The dilemma of two nights before came back to haunt him. Despite her many character flaws, and there were many of them, he loved her. It had been creeping up on him since he had first seen her enter the great hall at Middleham and though he had stifled it when she had snubbed him that night and throughout the next two weeks when she had complained about everything, it had budded in the days they had spent together at Eyri Keep, and bloomed that horrible night he had found her huddled in the middle of the road.

Now that they had shared such passion as they had, she was even more deeply ingrained in his body and soul. He thought of her constantly, even when he was supposed to be devoting his full attention to Henry Tudor's plans.

Though he had told himself two nights before that he would be able to watch her wed Brackley despite his feelings for her, now that they were on the way to that destiny, he questioned his resolve. If Elena were to go ahead with her betrothal, it would mean she felt nothing for him: nothing but desire. The raised another question for Gareth: Would she, if she did care for him, would she tell him? Pride was only one of her character flaws and Gareth was dreadfully worried that pride would prevent her from declaring feelings for a mere Welsh knight who might have been, and still might yet end up, a humble shepherd.

There was only one thing to be done, he decided, his mind returning to the feel of her shoulders leaning comfortably on his chest. He would have to come right out and ask her what she felt for him. He would have to declare his love for her and suffer the consequences of her rejection if it came. Better that than to forever wonder if they might not have made a life together. That decided, there was only one thing left to plan: When would he tell her?

Gareth knew himself well enough to know that once he set his mind on something, he would follow through with that course of action, no matter how difficult, but when? One thing was certain. Now was not the time. He considered his decision for a moment. No, now was not the right time at all.

***

Three hours later when they stopped to eat lunch was not the right time either. It was too soon into their trip, Gareth decided. In fact, the whole first day was too soon into their trip. He figured they would be traveling anywhere from a week to ten days depending on where Richard was. Though Richard's party had been on its way to Nottingham when it had been attacked on that seemingly long-ago day, the king could be at any one of his castles by this time. It would be their first stop, nonetheless. Regardless of how long they would be on the road, it was clear he had plenty of time to tell Elena that he--Gareth swallowed his bite of sausage and bread before he was quite done chewing--loved her. Therefore, he did not need to worry about it today. Or tomorrow either, for that matter.

After lunch, they mounted up, Elena resuming her seat in front of Gareth on Isrid. Gareth neither asked Elena if she wanted to ride her own horse, nor did she offer. As soon as they were comfortably pressed together, they were off.

By midafternoon, the huge white clouds Gareth had noticed that morning in Aberystwyth had turned an ugly grey and now hung considerably lower in the sky, blocking any glimpse of blue heavens or late summer's sun. The first big drops hit them as they were entering a small grove of trees.

"Oh!" Elena exclaimed as a cold wet drop hit her in the face. "It would have to rain as I'm wearing my new dress. I will look like a shapeless sack of grain once this wool is wet."

Gareth studied the gown. "It will hold a good deal of water and keep you cold through the night as well."

"Wonderful," Elena said, her tone belying her exclamation.

"Perhaps you'd best change into your old gown. That way if we do get wet, your new one will still be dry and unharmed."

"I can't."

"Come, Elena. You look beautiful no matter what you're wearing." Had he really said that? It was true of course, but...

Elena twisted her body so she could see his face. "Thank you," she said softly, a strange look crossing her face.

Gareth reined Isrid to a stop and dismounted. With both horses' reins in hand, he pulled them off the narrow road into the trees. Once under the protection of the leaves, few raindrops hit them, but the storm appeared to be increasing. Thunder rang out every few minutes and Gareth had the bad feeling that they were going to be drenched no matter what they were wearing. He helped Elena down and began unlacing the satchel on the pack horse. "In which bag did you pack your other gown."

"I didn't," she said meekly.

Gareth grinned at her. So, she was finally embarrassed over making everyone wait on her hand and foot, eh? Well, perhaps there was hope for her yet.

"Alright, where did Cynan pack your dress?"

Elena's manicure called her attention and she refused to meet Gareth's eyes.

"Elena? Where is your other dress, love?" The endearment had slipped out, but it had obviously grabbed her attention, for Elena looked up at him, her eyes searching his before she said, "I gave it to Annie."

Gareth was stumped. "Who's Annie? Never mind, where did Annie pack it?"

"Probably in her trunk."

Gareth felt like he had awoken in the middle of a conversation of which he was not a part. "Elena, we have no trunks."

"Annie is the seamstress who made this gown. I gave her that old blue rag because she liked it and I couldn't stand the sight of it. So I gave it to her."

Gareth stared at Elena without comprehension. It finally dawned on him what she meant. "So, in other words, you have nothing else to wear?"

"Well of course not. If you will remember, my luggage was separated from me a sennight ago when we were first attacked. I've been wearing that blue gown since. Surely you are not surprised I got rid of it?"

Gareth shook his head as another raindrop penetrated their meager shelter and landed on his head. "What were you planning to do should that gown become wet?" he asked.

Elena shrugged her shoulders. "I guess I didn't think about it raining."

The realization that they were wasting precious daylight in this inane conversation finally penetrated Gareth's baffled brain and he made a rapid decision. Opening the satchel that held his few articles of clothing, Gareth pulled out a thick pair of blue wool hose and his one clean shirt. "Here," he said. "Wear these. At least you'll be able to ride astride and then when we're drenched, you can change into your dry gown."

"But what about you?"

Gareth was suddenly weary of the delay and the reason for it. "Just put these on. I've traveled in wet clothing more times than I can remember. One more time won't kill me."

Elena looked like she was about to say something and then closed her mouth and took the clothes from his outstretched hand. The rain began to come down heavier now and the overhead leaves, drenched themselves, began to drip water down as fast as it fell from the sky. Elena set the shirt and hose on Isrid's saddle and turned so Gareth could unlace her gown. Then, as the wool grew damp, she quickly pulled both it and chemise over her head, rolling them into a compact, if untidy, ball that she stuffed in the protective satchel.

"I've never been good at putting clothes away neatly," she confessed, apparently unconcerned that she was wearing only her boots in front of Gareth. He wondered if she was too concerned about her new dress to worry that she was allowing him to enjoy a full vantage of her body, or if she were simply so comfortable with him seeing her body that she gave it no thought. He incorrectly chose the latter.

As she picked up the shirt, she clearly became aware that Gareth was staring at her nudity. She glanced at him from the corner of her eyes before turning slightly so that her back faced him. Gareth did not complain, enjoying her from this angle as well. When she had the concealing shirt over her head, she pulled her boots off and began to pull on the thick hose. Gareth steadied her as she wobbled on one foot, wondering if he should offer a hand but she soon had the leggings on and was tying the drawstring about her narrow waist.

Judging from her actions and the flustered way she smoothed her hair and tied the cuffs of the rough shirt, Gareth decided that she was, perhaps, a little self-conscious about his being there while she had changed. To make her feel more at ease, he said, "You see? I told you you look beautiful in anything."

As he said it, he discovered it was true.

The blue hose, which he had yet to wear and stretch since Enid had given them to him back at Eyri Keep, fit her legs and hips snugly, showing curves women's full skirts never allowed. His rough linen shirt was too large on her, but it made her appear all the more fragile and appealing for it. Unable to stop himself, Gareth grasped her shoulders gently and kissed her full on the mouth. Elena responded instantly, her arms snaking up around his neck, her lips parting willingly for his mouth.

With a groan, Gareth broke the kiss, though he still held her pressed tightly against him. "We must move on."

"Can't we wait here until the rain lets up?" Elena asked, her gaze firmly on his mouth.

Gareth considered the idea longer than he should have. It was tempting...

Shaking his head, he said, "There will be light for a few more hours despite the rain and I would have us make up for our late start this morning." Seeing her lower lip pout out, he laughed and said, "Elena, don't make this harder for me than it already is. Had I my way, we would never return to England but would spend the rest of our lives here in this grove."

Elena's pout disappeared. "Truly?" she asked, her voice a whisper.

The voice in his head told Gareth that this was the perfect opportunity for him to declare himself. Judging from the look on her face, the voice said, she may very well welcome your proposal. But Gareth hesitated and, in the end, said, "With lips as soft as yours, of course. But we must move on. Come now, climb back up." Elena stared at him a moment before swinging up into Isrid's saddle, sitting astride this time.

"Very well, let's go," she said.

Before climbing up behind her, Gareth pulled out one of their blankets, a thick, scratchy wool affair that smelled faintly musty from having been put away all summer. Once on Isrid, he wrapped the blanket around himself and Elena.

"Phew," she said. "It's too hot to have a cloak on--especially one that smells like a sheep."

"It's not for warmth, it's to keep us dry. Besides, after a while, you may be glad for the warmth. The rain has already cooled the air."

Elena grumbled to herself a while longer and then fell silent. As they made their way east, each remained locked in his thoughts. Gareth's inner voice was chiding him for not speaking his heart when given the perfect opportunity. He argued back that it did not matter when he told her as there was nothing she could do about it until she broke her engagement to Brackley.

The inner voice remarked that they could very well change their course and head straight for Eyri Keep where they could enjoy an extended honeymoon until Henry Tudor landed in Britain. And just what would Richard think for never seeing Elena again? he wondered. Come now, the voice replied. She's been gone so long already, he has probably already written her off for dead. Besides, he continued to argue silently, despite what she thinks, ladies-in-waiting are not crucial members of the court. Richard no doubt has three other women filling in for whatever small tasks Elena accomplished.

Gareth grew sorely tired of his inner discussion and ended it by telling himself, I've a job to do in Nottingham and that's all there is to it. I'll tell Elena how I feel about her when I'm good and ready and not a minute before. Forcing his mind to consider where they would camp for the evening, he resolutely ignored any other arguments the voice may have offered.

Elena, not troubled by such a persistent inner voice, was content to study the landscape they were crossing. Even in the rain, she thought, Wales is a beautiful place. The dark grey sky, rather than draining the landscape of color, seemed to merely enhance the rich tapestry of silver-green grasses, bright yellow flowers, and lush green trees. The narrow road they traveled had been so worn by years of feet and hooves traipsing over it that it was hard as rock and the rain simply puddled in the low spots rather than turning the path to mud and muck. On either side of the road, brilliant yellow flowers with black centers competed for attention with tall strands of grass that bowed gracefully under the weight of the raindrops. Just ahead, a tall willow tree, its base thicker than a man could stretch his arms, dangled its branches over the road. As they rode beneath it, Elena reached out from under the heavy blanket to pluck a long silvery leaf. Feeling decidedly childish and a bit wicked in her manly garb, she twisted around and tickled Gareth's nose with the end of the leaf.

Gareth welcomed the distraction of Elena's teasing and lowered his eyes from the gloomy horizon to her warm cinnamon-brown eyes, which were alight with mischievous sparkle. He shook his head and grinned. "If someone had told me, two months ago, that the right noble Lady Elena, handmaiden to the King of England, would be sitting astride a horse in hose and a tunic, tickling my nose with a leaf, I would have though they were mad."

"Why? Don't you think ladies-in-waiting have fun?"

"Perhaps. But not with men they consider beneath them. And I would certainly doubt they would do it dressed as you are now."

"You will simply not forget that I apparently snubbed you when first we met, will you?"

Gareth's bark of laughter startled a bird that had taken shelter in the roadside grass. The bird squeaked as it arced up and out into the rain. "I can handle being snubbed. But outright rudeness is a bit uncommon, especially when it comes from one the king has set forth as an example for womanly gentleness."

Looking back to that long-ago night, Elena could scarce remember what she had said to Gareth. Something about him being a farmer or going back to his sheep. Whatever it was, it was no doubt derogatory and Elena wondered, were she in a similar situation now, if she would behave the same. For some reason, she thought that she wouldn't, though she was at a loss to determine why. "I had many other things on my mind that night," she said, feeling awkward.

Gareth stared at the back of her head for a moment and then said, "I accept."

Startled, Elena looked over her shoulder. "You accept what?"

"Your apology."

"Apology? I wasn't making an apology. I was simply explaining that there was a great deal going on that night and if my actions were not what they normally are, then that was the reason."

"Uh huh," Gareth hummed, not the least bit convinced.

"What do you mean, 'Uh huh'?" Elena worked her right leg over Isrid's head until she was sitting sideways in the saddle and could better scowl at Gareth.

"I mean how you treated me that night at Middleham was your usual temperament showing through. I was not a prospective suitor, I didn't dress in the latest mode, and I certainly was not in King Richard's circle of important people. Therefore, you decided that I wasn't worth the time or effort it would take to be polite."

Elena frowned and studied her left thumbnail. Though her initial expression seemed to be anger, his words apparently struck a chord for she looked as if she were ashamed at her behavior.

Gareth watched the play of emotions on her face, thankful that she was not throwing his own rudeness back in his face, amazed that she seemed to be taking to heart his words. Not wishing to hurt her feelings, he said, "It's alright, though."

She raised her head and stared at him. "Why do you say that?"

"Because you're different now."

"Different? How?"

Gareth pushed the hair out of his eyes. Luckily, it was just damp enough that it stayed put and did not fall right back into his face. "Well, you just are. You seem--I don't know--kinder somehow. You seem to notice other people's feelings more and people in return like you."

"They liked me before," she said indignantly.

Gareth quickly backtracked. "What I meant to say was they are better able to see your kind side. As a result, they like you more."

Elena was silent for a moment. Then, "Do you like me more?"

Now! the voice in his head shouted. Tell her now!

No! he shouted back silently. Not 'till I'm ready!

"I like you much more," he said with feeling.

"Perhaps I have changed a little bit. Nobody is perfect, you know."

"Certainly not," he agreed.

"It's very difficult to be close to the king. People are forever trying to use you to gain information or favor with the king. In return, they offer you nothing, so maybe I tended to concentrate on my own needs first. And perhaps," Gareth could tell how difficult all this was for her to admit. "Perhaps I have always been a bit," she cleared her throat, "spoiled. Though that really isn't my fault," she rushed to add. "I was an only child and my parents doted on my many accomplishments and I received nearly everything I wanted, so it's understandable if I may have grown accustomed to that."

"Of course it is," Gareth agreed, trying to contain his smile. He wanted to make this easier for her and was amazed that he was hearing those words come out of her mouth. "And you deserve to have everything you want."

Elena suddenly shook off her maudlin feelings and gave him a cocky smile. "I quite agree."

Amazed at her quicksilver change of emotions, Gareth stared open-mouthed at her for a moment. Then he laughed, a loud and hearty laugh. "Nonetheless, you're still not perfect," he said.

"Perhaps not, but you must admit I am pretty good."

"You are very good," he agreed, dropping his gaze to her lips. He grinned when he was rewarded with an honest blush.

The rain had lessened by the time they stopped to set up camp, though a fine mist still blurred the woods with a faerie-like quality, making even ordinary looking trees seem ethereal and enchanted. Gareth led the horses deep into the woods where the drizzle barely reached the ground. He helped Elena down from Isrid and began unsaddling both horses.

"Well, it's not completely dry in here, but we should be warm enough," he said as he scooped away the top layer of wet leaves from the well-mulched ground. Finding the leaves underneath relatively dry, he spread out their bedrolls next to each other. Elena stood watching, thinking that she should probably help in some way. Unfortunately, never having worried herself with such details, she knew not the first thing to do. Hesitant about asking Gareth for direction, she remained by the horses, petting Isrid's velvety nose. When Gareth had arranged the small camp to his liking, he stood and said, "I doubt I'll find any, but I think I'll look around a bit for some dry wood. A campfire would definitely take the chill off our evening."

"I'll go with you," Elena volunteered.

Gareth looked at her in surprise but wisely made not one joking remark. Instead he said, "Thank you," and moved to tie the horses to a nearby tree.

Elena scrambled through the underbrush with Gareth, trying to move as quietly as he did, but it was proved to be very difficult when branches were forever catching in her hair and snagging at her hose. Although, she reflected as Gareth helped her climb over a moss-encrusted log, these clothes make traveling, and firewood hunting, much easier than they would be in a gown, no matter how pretty or new that gown was. Elena felt so unrestrained in her borrowed garb. Her hands were free from holding hems off the ground, her legs were able to take long bounding strides unencumbered by yards of fabric, and, though these were no doubt Gareth's good clothes, she did not have to constantly worry about grinding dirt into the knees or tearing the sleeve on a tree branch. Yes, Elena decided, this mode of dress certainly had its advantages.

Elena followed Gareth's lead in looking for dry wood, burrowing under bushes and pulling apart rotten logs. Though she could not keep her lip from curling in disgust, she managed to keep quiet as Gareth loaded her arms with crumbling logs off of which ants and spiders scurried. When they finally made their way back to camp, the light was nearly gone from the overcast sky. Elena quickly dumped her armload of sticks and began vigorously brushing the dirt and twigs off her shirt. She could not suppress an, "Ugh," when her hand came away from her shirt covered with a slimy moss. With a distinctly queasy feeling in her stomach, she quickly knelt and wiped her hand in the damp grass that carpeted the forest floor. Still kneeling, she glanced up to see if Gareth had noticed her discomfiture.

Though he had what looked like a suppressed grin on his face, his focus was fixed intently on building a fire from the smoldering logs. Relieved, Elena stood and made her way to the bedrolls. They offered little cushioning from the ground but they were dry and still warm from the body heat of the horses on which they'd been carried. She lay back on the ground and stretched, glad to send blood to the muscles that were weary of riding all day. Especially her inner thighs, she thought, flexing the muscles in her legs. She was not accustomed to riding astride and it seemed to require the use of a whole separate set of muscles.

Settling into a comfortable position on her side, she was content to watch Gareth stoke the now burning logs and open the satchel containing their food.

Gareth worked steadily, breaking off a chunk of the heavy bread and taking his knife to the slabs of hard sausage and cheese. Standing, he fetched the boiled leather wine flask and uncorked it. Though he worked diligently preparing their dinner, feeding the horses, and keeping the fire going, his mind was on other things; specifically, his beautiful traveling companion.

He wondered what had possessed her to offer to help and marveled at her uncomplaining attitude when he had handed her the damp and dirty branches. Of course, she had not offered to lift a finger to help prepare the food, but, he rationalized, how much work was there in tearing bread and slicing cheese? She was, he thought charitably, acting less and less overindulged every day. As he sat down next to her, he again wondered if she would ever consider marriage to a poor Welsh knight.

"Are you hungry?" he asked, handing a hunk of bread to her.

"Yes," she said without enthusiasm and took a small nibble.

Gareth laughed. "Well don't gorge yourself all at once on this feast."

Elena smiled. "It's good enough, I just wish traveling didn't mean cold food."

Gareth thought a moment and then scrambled to his feet, pushing his hair out of his eyes. He searched around in the underbrush for several seconds before he said, "Aha!"

Elena sat up from her reclining position. "What are you doing?"

"You want hot food, Sir Gareth will deliver hot food." He held up a long stick proudly.

"I don't mean to offend you, good Sir Gareth, but that does not look like roasted venison to me."

"Patience, sweet, patience." He retrieved his knife and began whittling the end of the stick to a point. When he was finished, the stick was bare of bark and sharply pointed. He then skewered Elena's piece of bread, her cheese, and her slab of hard sausage. "There we go," he said as he thrust the stick out over the fire.

Elena watched, fascinated, as the cheese began to bubble and turn a delicious golden color. The smell of the roasting sausage made her mouth water as drops of grease sizzled into the fire. Gareth carefully turned the stick, wary that the cheese did not melt off, and when he deemed it finished, he carefully removed all three items, stacking the meat and cheese artfully on top of the toasted bread.

"Fit for a queen," he declared as he handed it to her.

Elena shifted her meal from hand to hand until the bread had cooled enough not to burn her skin. She then took a huge bite, scalding the roof of her mouth on the sizzling meat, but enjoying the taste of the gooey cheese and spicy sausage, nonetheless. When she had managed to chew and swallow her unladylike mouthful, she looked to Gareth who was expectantly awaiting her response.

"It's delicious," she said. "I think I will recommend you to King Richard for the position of Chef Extraordinaire when we return."

Gareth's grin of pleasure at her initial response faded when she mentioned Richard. It only reminded him that she would be out of his reach once they arrived at the king's court, and that he was lying to her even now about his plans.

"What's wrong?" Elena asked, worry evident in her voice.

Gareth shook his head. "Nothing."

"Something is bothering you. Is it what I said about making you a chef? I promise I won't tell anyone about your cooking talents if it would make you seem less of a knight." When her teasing evinced no response, she took another approach. "Are you having doubts about returning to Richard?"

Startled, Gareth shook his head. "No, I was just thinking that if Cynan and Bryant found out I could actually make something edible, they'd make me cook every night instead of the three of us taking turns when we're out in the woods. As it is, I have to struggle to make my meals taste bad so they'll offer to cook for me!"

Elena smiled at his response, but Gareth sensed she did not entirely believe him. To his great relief, however, she did not press him further and he vowed to himself to make her forget his temporary lapse into melancholy.

With as much animation as he could muster, he told her of his first night spent in the woods when he was a boy. "Cynan and Bryant and I were finally allowed to go out alone all night. I think we were about eleven years old. As we were preparing to leave the keep, Cynan's father told us to watch out for the bog ghoul who might come steal us away to the underworld. We all laughed, of course, because we were much too grown up to believe in such silly monsters that used to frighten us as children.

"As we made our way into the forest for our grand adventure, I came up with the brilliant idea of sneaking away in the middle of the night and pretending to be this ghoul to scare the wits out of Cynan and Bryant."

"You Gareth? No!" Elena exclaimed, teasing.

Gareth grinned and continued his story. "The start of the plan worked perfectly: I snuck away as soon as they fell asleep, I ran to the stream we were camped near and smeared my entire head with mud. I then stuck leaves and twigs in my hair and practiced my most ferocious growling. As I made my way back to camp, I made sure to crash about, raising all sorts of noise sure to wake the sleeping innocents." Gareth paused and took a swallow of wine.

"You said the start of the plan worked. When did things go awry? Did they realize right away that it was you?"

"No. In fact, they were just coming awake as I crashed through the bushes circling our camp. In the dying light of the fire, I must have appeared quite ghoulish indeed. Cynan and Bryant began screaming most pitifully." Gareth started laughing and Elena poked him in the ribs.

"And?" she asked imperiously. "What happened next?"

Still chuckling, Gareth continued. "I was growling and waving my arms about while they tried to free themselves of their blankets when I noticed something entering camp from the opposite direction."

"What?"

"Coming into the ring of firelight was a creature which made my pitiful attempt at a ghoul seem like child's play. It hobbled into camp and I could see it had a huge hump on it's back, its hair stood straight on end and foamy slobber dribbled down its chin. It was growling horribly and reaching for Cynan who was nearest it. I swear my eyes felt like they were going to pop right out of my head. I forgot all about snarling and sounding demonic and instead began to scream myself. Cynan and Bryant stopped screaming only long enough to turn around and then they joined my chorus. We all took off in different directions into the forest, though we somehow all managed to arrive back at the keep about the same time. We were all blubbering like babes as we told my father our story and I remember wondering why he didn't send out a contingent of armed men."

Gareth leaned back on the bedroll, propping his head up on his hands. Elena curled up next to him. "And? Why didn't he send one out?"

"As we were to discover later, the creature who tried to attack us was actually Cynan's father."

"No!" Elena exclaimed, disbelieving. "Was he mad?"

Gareth laughed. "No. He was simply an incurable prankster. He was forever dressing up and fooling—well, scaring, actually--the children at Eyri Keep. As soon as we discovered that he had tricked us, we vowed to get even."

"What did you do?" she asked, expecting a tale of humorous revenge.

Gareth sobered. "Actually nothing. A few weeks later, Cynan's father fell from the parapets where he had been working. He died within minutes."

"Oh," Elena said, feeling sorry for the absent Cynan.

Gareth looked at her and smiled. "'Tis no matter. It happened near twelve years ago and I'm sure he went to his grave content that he got the last laugh on us."

Unable to stop herself, Elena yawned.

Gareth stood and banked the fire. "Are you tired? Perhaps we should go to sleep. We have many a mile to travel tomorrow."

"I'm not so very tired," Elena said.

Gareth paused in the act of putting another log on the fire and looked at her. Though she seemed to be intently concentrating on braiding her hair, he was certain her words meant something.

"No? Well, what should we do? Shall I tell you of another of my childhood escapades?"

Elena flicked her braid behind her back and looked boldly up at Gareth. "No."

Though no more words left her lips, her eyes spoke volumes and Gareth obediently joined her in the warm bedding.

Chapter 22

They were up early the next morning and on the road by the time the sun cut its lazy path over the horizon. The air held the brisk, pungent fragrance of the last days of summer when every flower is in bloom, every leaf has unfurled, and the grass is at its tallest. Without a second thought, Gareth packed all of their luggage onto the shaggy horse he had purchased in Aberstwyth and settled them both onto Isrid's broad back. Elena again wore Gareth's clothes, content to relinquish her new gown for apparel infinitely more practical for traveling by horseback.

They chatted amiably throughout that day, and throughout the week following as they made their way across England. They were blessed with near-perfect weather, only suffering two days of rain as league after league disappeared beneath Isrid's hooves.

To fill the hours, they told stories of their youth, shared dreams and hopes of their youth, and even admitted first loves and first broken hearts. In the evenings, Elena helped Gareth unload the horses and gather firewood. She even learned to boil water to soften their dried meat into a more palatable stew, their hard sausage having run out on day two. At night, they curled close to each other when the fire burned down to smoldering embers. If the nights grew cold, the lovers did not notice, so intent were they on the other's body, their own pleasure, and the heat they created.

Gareth would have been content to spend the rest of his days traveling. Not once did he notice the food he ate, the hardness of the ground on which he slept, or the discomfort of the slow, penetrating drizzle that doused them for two days.

Later, all he could remember of that trip was Elena pressed against him in the saddle with his arm curled comfortably around her waist; her soft form in his arms night after night; their hours of laughter and shared confidences; and his marvel that she could have changed so much in two short months, going from spoiled shrew to pleasing companion. The only thing that marred the journey for him was the nagging voice in his head telling him he was a fool for remaining silent, reminding him that he was wasting precious time by not telling her he loved her, time that could be spent racing to Eyri Keep should her feelings mirror his. But never in their enjoyable days or passionate nights had she uttered one word of love, one word of encouragement that she desired any more than they already had.

Elena was reveling in the novel experience of saying and doing whatever she pleased with no worry as to how decorous she looked or how ladylike she sounded. It was a remarkably liberating feeling, she reflected, to be able to discuss with Gareth any topic that came to mind and know that he would answer all her questions and ask her some in return. Never once did he tell her that any of her comments were not befitting a lady of the court, or that she should not concern herself with things more suited to a man's brain. Elena had once thought the way she had coerced the men of Richard's court to her will through flattery and flirtation was power. She was now learning the power of using her own thoughts and ideas to change Gareth's mind.

Though she was eager to return to Richard's retinue, she was torn. She loved the richness and the beauty of court with everyone on their best behavior: jewels glittering, velvets rustling, musicians playing, incense-filled braziers smoking. She loved dressing in a new gown to attend a sumptuous feast where men toasted her beauty and laughter filled the hall. On the other hand, she was dimly aware that she would not be able to act in court as she was able to here, in Gareth's company. She would have to return to being a nodding henwit when the king addressed her, smiling sweetly to his rich but dusty old nobles who doddered around thinking they were ever so much more attractive to the young ladies-in-waiting than their sons and grandsons who were young and handsome and had all their teeth.

And then there was her fiancée. Of all the strictures and ladylike rules she would have to obey again once she stepped foot in Richard's court, meekly accepting the king's choice of her future husband was the one she dreaded the most. She was growing miserably certain that she would be unable to convince Richard to break off the engagement at this late date. By now Richard must have already received arms and the men to bear them from the earl's holdings. The king would be indebted to Brackley for his support and his advice and he would not risk them in the upcoming confrontation with Henry Tudor for the whim of a mere lady-in-waiting, be she favorite or no.

All that considered, she continued to fantasize about life at Eyri Keep. She thought of the evenings at Gareth's home spent embroidering by the fire with Enid while Morgan and Gareth discussed moving the flocks of sheep to a new pasture. She remembered the spontaneous festivals that were held for things as common as the birth of a new child or the successful harvest of a field of barley. On days when such an event had occurred, the good news spread like wildfire throughout the small keep, culminating in the kitchen where the three women who cooked for Morgan's household tried to outdo each other with culinary specialties. As they drew nearer to Nottingham and Richard's court, it became easier to imagine herself ensconced there permanently. Cynan had told her that she could have her pick of husbands should she chose to return to Wales, but Elena didn't want her pick; she wanted Gareth. Had he uttered one word of love or one tentative proposal of marriage, they would now be heading away from Nottingham, not toward it. But he remained silent, despite their most intimate exchanges. She felt she had changed and grown much since becoming separated from Richard's entourage all those weeks ago, but her pride would not permit her to fish for avowals of love from him, though she had much experience doing so.

And so they continued, each day drawing nearer to Nottingham. By the time they were on the outskirts of the city, a day's ride from the king's wartime residence, their conversation had become stilted, each submerged in his thoughts and worries for the future, each wishing the other would speak.

Chapter 23

"You shall have a pillow for your head tonight, sweet lady," Gareth said as they rode through the southernmost streets of Nottingham.

Elena roused herself from her thoughts and turned in the saddle. "We're not continuing on?" It was only midafternoon and she had grown accustomed to riding until dusk allowed just enough light to set up camp.

"No," Gareth answered. "We'll have a short day of riding tomorrow as it is. There is no need to exhaust ourselves today especially when I have money enough for a rich meal and a soft bed," he said, jingling the coins in their leather pouch which hung from his belt.

"I want fish for supper," Elena said, sitting up a little straighter in the saddle.

"Fish?" Gareth asked, wrinkling his nose.

"Yes, it's the meal most different from dried beef!"

Gareth laughed. "You've been eating dried mutton."

Elena turned her head and lifted an eyebrow. "Do not even attempt to convince me that there is a difference between the two."

Elena looked around at the small shops and houses they were passing. As they made their way further into the city, the small buildings grew closer and closer together until they were stacked nearly on top of each other. Though she could sense Gareth growing unease with the crowds and the shops, she was familiar with this city. She had spent many hours attending Lady Elizabeth as they shopped for fabrics and furs. Though she had previously been attended by numerous guardsmen and attendants, Elena still felt comfortable as they entered the teeming city.

"I suppose we will have to find an inn soon," Gareth said, more to himself than Elena.

Taking charge, Elena said, "That will be simple. There are several reputable inns very near each other."

Gareth sighed, obviously relieved that he would not have to try to decide on their accommodations. "Very good. Which way do we go?" He had reined in Isrid at a central marketplace into which dumped at least five crooked streets.

"I have no idea."

"Then how do you know there are several reputable inns in the same area?"

"I have spent much time in Nottingham. When I was attending Lady Elizabeth, we would oftentimes rest in the inns in between shopping bouts instead of returning to the castle."

"Well if you spent so much time here doing what you do best, then how is it you have no idea where we should go?"

"I will recognize the street once we are on it," Elena said defensively.

"That doesn't do us much good now, does it?"

Incredulous, Elena turned as much as she could in the saddle. "Well then perhaps you'd like to find us a place to stay, Sir I-don't-need-to-ask-for-directions!" Though it had been a while since Elena had used one of her well-honed imperious looks, she managed to execute it flawlessly and Gareth was squirming uncomfortably within seconds.

"Alright, I'll stop and ask where this mythical street you remember is. Do you at least know the name of the street?"

"Of course I do. Ask for West Dover Street."

Gareth swung off of Isrid and handed Elena the reins to both horses. He entered the shop nearest them, a solicitor's office. As Elena waited, she became aware of the stares of passers-by. Glancing down to see what they were looking at, she realized that she was still wearing Gareth's clothes, which were much wrinkled after a week's wear. Dismayed, she lifted her hand to her hair and found it equally mussed. Elena was mortified. It was enough that she had spent the past weeks looking like a scullery maid. Then she had at least an excuse. She had only her one gown and in it she had been dragged through mountains, streams, and dirt. But now she had a clean new gown sitting in her satchel while she was decked out like a stable boy! Sitting up straight, Elena lifted her chin. No matter, she thought, trying to convince herself. These people are still commoners at heart while I am a lady, regardless of my appearance. Her upraised chin would tell them just that, she decided, besides making it impossible for her to see their critical appraisal of her. Thankfully, Gareth returned within the minute.

"'Tis just a few streets over," he said, taking both reins from her hands and leading the horses up the street.

"Why are you walking?" Somehow, she had thought the people's stares would not seem quite so unbearable if Gareth were sitting behind her.

"My legs have about had it for riding. I thought I would work out the kinks in them by walking. It's not so very far."

Elena glanced surreptitiously from side to side. Although the amount of people out on the street decreased as they left the central market, she still felt as if she were on display sitting so high up on Isrid. Without another thought, she threw her leg over Isrid's rump and shimmied off of the war-horse's high back, landing awkwardly on the uneven cobbled street. Gareth whirled around at her grunt as she landed.

"Elena, are you alright? What's wrong?"

She straightened, trying to ignore her throbbing ankle, which had landed in a pothole. "I believe I will stretch my legs as well."

"You should have told me to stop the horses. You could have hurt yourself."

I did, she thought. "I'm fine," she said. "But let us hurry. I wish to bathe and change clothes as soon as possible."

"Of course. And you will have water as hot as you can stand it, that I promise."

Elena smiled, remembering his promise to buy her a new dress as they were entering Aberstwyth. "And you do keep your promises."

Gareth looked at her, a pleased expression crossing his face. "I do everything in my power to keep them."

"Then promise me a down-filled tick and freshly scented linens."

"I said I do everything in my power, Elena," he said with a laugh. "That, I am afraid, we will have to leave to the grace of God. I think we will be lucky to settle for a straw tick that has relatively few bedbugs!"

"Ugh! If that is the case, then I will hold you to your promise of hot water."

"The hottest!"

They reached West Dover Street within a matter of minutes and Elena immediately recognized where they were.

"Excellent," she said. "If we turn up here, there are at least four inns within two blocks of each other. If we go right, there are two more inns, and several pubs where we might get an excellent meal."

"So which way do we go? Do you have a preference on where you spend you last evening with Sir Gareth?"

Startled, Elena looked at him sharply, a worried frown creasing her brow. This was to be their last night. Why had she not realized it? As she stared at him, Gareth flushed. "I didn't mean...I just meant that this would be the last time you would have to put up with...Which inn do you wish to stay in?"

Torn from her thoughts by his question, she looked up the street, trying to remember which inn had served them best when she had come with Lady Elizabeth and the other ladies-in-waiting.

"I believe the third inn up here has the cleanest rooms. They are also rarely full, if I remember correctly."

"Then let us proceed there immediately. I am glad for your sake if they have clean accommodations, but do you recall if they had good food as well?"

Elena laughed. "Yes, I believe it was most satisfactory." With a devilish grin she added, "I believe their best offering is fish." She was rewarded with a look of horror on Gareth's face.

They walked up the tidy street and paused at a hanging wooden sign that declared it to be the Inn of the Lion's Heart. Gareth peered in the open door. "Shall we?"

Elena hesitated. The last time she had entered this inn, she had been dressed in a gown of blue silk, a necklace of gold inset with sapphires about her neck, her hair intricately braided and wound about her head. As she glanced down at the wrinkled and travel-stained tunic she had thought so practical just a week ago, she knew she could not enter that inn, regardless of whether or not the innkeepers recognized her.

"Let us go to another inn."

"What? Why? This seems like a perfectly acceptable place to stay."

"No, I don't think so. Why don't we go to one of the inns near a pub. That way you can get a real meal."

"I don't understand why we can't stay here and still go eat at one of the pubs." Gareth studied her distraught face. "Elena, what's wrong? Tell me truthfully, now."

Elena paused. How could she possibly make Gareth understand that a lady had her pride? She looked into Gareth's eyes and reminded herself that he had been remarkably tolerant these past weeks. Deciding to put her faith in him she said, "Suppose they recognize me?"

"Recognize you? What do you mean? Why should they recognize you?"

"Because I have been here several times before."

"Good! Perhaps we will get better service." Gareth moved to enter the inn.

"No!" Elena said, grabbing his tunic and pulling him back.

"Elena," he said, exasperation evident in his voice. "What is it? Why should it matter if they recognize you or not?"

"Because," she hissed, "if they recognize me, they will no doubt notice what I am wearing and that I am traveling alone in the company of a man who is obviously not my father! Should word get back to court of such behavior, I would be ruined."

"Oh," Gareth said, comprehension dawning on his face. "Then where should we go?"

Elena gestured down the street. "I never attended either of the two inns down the street."

"Then in one of those inns shall we lodge."

They trudged down the street in the lengthening shadows of the summer sunset until they came to the first of the two inns.

"Will this do?" Gareth asked Elena.

She studied the small inn. The sign hanging over the door declaring it to be The Lamb' Quarters was not painted as brightly or adeptly as the previous inn's, but the inside appeared to be just as neat, and Elena was certain she had never stepped foot in it before.

"This is fine," she said with a nod.

"Let's go, then." Gareth started forward but again Elena stopped him. "Wait!"

"What is it now?"

"I can't go in there looking like this!"

"What do you mean? I thought you said you've never been in here before? Why will they care if you aren't dressed for high court?"

Elena stomped her foot. "It's not that I'm not in a court dress. It's that I'm not in *any* dress. No respectable lady goes around in men's hose and rough tunics!"

Gareth dropped his head back and stared at the darkening sky. When he rolled it forward again, he asked, "What would you have me do, then, Elena? In order for you to change, we need a room. In order to get a room, we have to go inside and pay for one. Since you can't get to the room without going inside the inn, I fear we are at an impasse."

Elena gave her coldest glare. Gareth sighed wearily. "Very well. I will go in and obtain a room. You wait out here with the horses. Try not to be noticed. We wouldn't want anyone from court hearing that you had sunk so low as to wear a practical riding outfit. After I obtain the room, we will go around back and stable the horses. You can then sneak up the back stairs if they have back stairs. Will that suit you?" She nodded meekly. "Good!" was Gareth's response.

He returned in a few minutes and led the horses down a narrow alley to the small stable behind the inn. Fortunately, there was a rickety back staircase and by the time they had attended the horses and made it upstairs, there was a small wooden tub of hot water awaiting them in the room. Elena quickly stripped and stepped into the shallow tub, glad for the tingling of the hot water on her feet and calves. Why was it, she wondered, that bathing in hot water had become the exception the past two months? So absorbed was she in her bath that she did not notice Gareth who, after depositing their scant luggage, sat on the edge of the bed, his right elbow on his knee, his chin cupped in that hand. It was only when she stood, her hair dripping, her body cooling from the hot water that she realized that Gareth was studying her intently.

Since the first night they made love, Elena had not experienced embarrassment or awkwardness in Gareth's presence. Now, for some reason, she felt shy and at a distinct disadvantage as she stood knee-deep in water while Gareth watched her, his eyes dark with something deeper than passion. She reached for the thin piece of linen that was to serve as a towel. Rather, she thought about covering herself. Her arms refused to move. In fact, her whole body seemed to have turned to marble. It was as if she had just laid eyes on Gareth, and he her.

Slowly, Gareth rose and time seemed to slow as he crossed the few steps that lay between them. The pale blue light of encroaching dusk from the small dirty window was the room's only illumination. It made everything in the room, including Gareth, seem ethereal and not of this world. As he grew closer, all Elena could see of him were his eyes, their grey depths nearly black in the dim light. When they grew too close to focus on, she closed her eyes and awaited his kiss. When it came, it was feather light as it skimmed her lips, her damp cheeks, her warm neck. With each meeting between his lips and her skin, his kisses grew bolder and when they returned to her own mouth, they nearly seared her.

Without a word spoken between them, Gareth scooped Elena up into his arms and crossed to the low bed that was the room's only furnishing. As if his reminder that this was their last evening together was foremost in his mind, he made love to her with an intensity and boldness that left Elena senseless. In their previous bouts of lovemaking, they had given and taken equally. But tonight, Elena felt as if Gareth were another man. He was clearly in charge of her passion and her body. Gone tonight were any of his endearing boyish qualities like when he had asked her approval of this kiss or that caress. Tonight, he was a man confident in his abilities, confident that he would wring out of her passions and emotions she would feel with no one else.

They still had not spoken near an hour later when they finally arose in the near total darkness of a summer's eve. Gareth quickly bathed while Elena struggled into her gown unaided. She combed her hair with her fingers, wishing she at least had the hairpins necessary for the simplest of fashion's coiffures. She would have to settle for a plain braid down her back. As she began plaiting her still-damp tresses, Gareth's voice stopped her. "Don't. Leave it loose."

Elena turned to him, surprised. "But I don't even have a veil to cover it."

"I don't want it covered." When she still hesitated, he continued, "Please, Elena. Let me enjoy your beauty one last evening. Surely word will not reach Richard's court that you went to supper with unbound hair."

Elena shook her hair loose and raised her eyebrows at Gareth. "Better?"

He pulled his shirt over his head and smiled. "Perfect," he said softly.

As they made their way down the narrow front staircase, Gareth took Elena's hand in his own and tucked it into the crook of his arm.

***

Supper in the Henry Billingsley pub was more than adequate to make up for their week's worth of eating camp food. Glad that in the noisy and crowded pub no one seemed to notice her, for women generally did not eat in public rooms. She ordered a second portion of the savory stew and helped herself to a large slice of Gareth's meat pie. The thick mug of ale placed in front of her was delicious and she drained it not once, but twice that evening. And when Henry Billingsley himself placed a plate of hot and crusty currant tarts in front of her, she felt it would be churlish in the least to turn them down. By the time they left the boisterous crowd in the pub, Elena felt as though she would burst from food and her head was pleasantly fuzzy from the strong ale. In fact, so pleasantly fuzzy was her mind that she did not notice that Gareth remained glumly silent as they made their way up the darkened street to their inn. Once in the small upstairs room, Elena giggled helplessly as she tried unsuccessfully to unlace her houppeland. Throwing her hands up in mock despair, she gave up and flopped face down on the bed.

Gareth tossed his shirt onto the small pile of luggage in the corner and said, "Come Elena. You can't sleep in your gown. Stand up and let me help you remove it."

"No," said Elena, her voice muffled by the pillow.

"You will be much more comfortable once you do."

"No."

Gareth sighed. "Why won't you stand up Elena?"

"Because I can't find my arms," she said with a giggle.

"That's probably because you're laying on top of them. Here," he said, grabbing her shoulders and rolling her over. "Now can you find them?"

"Oh yes," she said expansively. Lifting them up, she threw them around Gareth's shoulders and pulled him down on top of her.

"Elena!" Gareth tried to sound severe, but the laughter in his voice won out. He never would have thought to see the regal Lady Elena tipsy. Would she never cease to amaze him? Rolling off of her and standing, he pulled her to her feet and began unlacing her gown.

She wobbled on her feet but seemed content to remain still while he hung her gown on a hook on the wall and then removed her chemise. She held onto his shoulders while he tugged off her boots but when he moved to stand up, she fell over, her torso draped against his back. Gareth paused, uncertain if she were playing or merely passed out. "Elena?" he called. When her only answer was rhythmic deep breathing, he wrapped his arms around her legs and stood, her body limply draped over his shoulder. He carefully deposited her on the low bed and drew the covers up.

Minutes passed as he watched her sleep, memorizing every curve of her face, which was illuminated by a shaft of moonlight. As he looked on her, he was reminded of another night when he had tried to imprint her beauty in his mind: the night she had ridden to warn him of the traitorous abbess. Then, as now, he had feared losing her, though now the fear stemmed from the thought that he would have to watch as she married the repulsive earl, see her grow round with his child, wondering if the child were the earl's or his own.

Gareth wished there were another option to tomorrow's short journey. The voice in his head, which had been silent for days, now awoke to taunt him and remind him that had he spoken his heart a week ago, he might now be wed to her and safely in Wales. Or she would have rejected him and it would be easier to erase her from his mind and his heart. Well, perhaps not easier, but at least his pride would not have allowed him to pine for her the rest of his days. Gareth sat on the edge of the bed as the series of weights tied round his neck and shoulders settled back into their places. For the past week he had shoved them aside, forbidding them to mar his time alone with Elena. Now they were back, heavier than ever and clamoring for his attention. Worry, guilt, and apprehension bowed his shoulders and he rested his head in his hands and prayed for assistance--something he could not remember doing since he was a child.

Some time later, he kicked off his own boots and climbed into bed, pulling Elena to him and holding her tightly as he waited for the dawn.

Chapter 24

Elena awoke late the next morning to a bright shaft of sunlight pouring in the dirty windowpane and a timid knock at the door. Groggy, she sat up and pulled the covers to her chin as she said, "Yes?"

A young girl with a pink-scrubbed face and her hair tied in a kerchief stuck her head in the room and said, "Excuse me, milady. Yer husband asked me to help ye get ready for your travels today.

Elena nodded and studiously ignored the flush of pleasure she felt at hearing Gareth referred to as her husband. It had been the most expedient way to secure their room the night before. "Very well. You may enter."

The young girl quickly entered the room, shutting the door behind her, and bobbed an awkward curtsey. Elena glanced around the room for her clothing. Spotting it hanging on the wall, she said, "You may bring me my chemise and gown."

The girl scurried to fetch them and in a few minutes, Elena was dressed. "I can also fix yer hair, lady. I've two older sisters who allow me to fix theirs all the time."

"Have you a comb and pins?"

"Aye, yer husband gave them to me," she replied, bringing them out of her apron pocket to display. "Bought new they were just this morn."

Elena smiled to herself and sat on the corner of the bed. The young girl, who introduced herself as Mary, went to work, combing the tangles out of Elena's long hair and jabbering about going's on in the city. "Do you know the king is in residence at his castle just outside the city?" she asked.

"Really?" Elena said.

"Yes. He's been there near a sennight and he's not once been to town."

"Is that unusual?" Elena asked, knowing that it was. Richard loved to make a display of his power, especially in the northern parts of England where he was more popular.

"Aye, he's been in his castle this whole time and soldiers from all over have been arriving."

"I wonder why."

"I do too, milady, though whenever I ask my father, he boxes my ears and calls me impertinent."

Elena, whose ears had never been boxed, turned in horror to look at Mary. "How horrid."

"He don't mean it and I'm so fast that he usually never catches me. All the same, he never answers my questions."

The girl rattled on for another ten or fifteen minutes while she braided and twisted Elena's hair into three buns--one over each ear and another at her nape. When each section was secured with the new wooden hairpins, Mary handed her the comb. "There's a mirror downstairs you can look in, yer lady-ship. I hope you like it."

Elena patted her hair, judging the style. "I'm sure I will. Thank you."

Mary grinned broadly. "Yer welcome, lady. Yer husband awaits ye out back when yer ready."

Elena left the small room and went downstairs. There was a smoky mirror hanging in the small dining area and she judged Mary's work to be quite acceptable. She smoothed her collar and shook out her full skirt before exiting the back door into the small stable area. Gareth was securing the last satchel on their packhorse when she approached him.

"Good morning Gareth."

Gareth whirled around and the appreciative look in his gaze warmed her cheeks. "Good morning. I thought we could stop at that pub and break our fast before continuing on to the castle."

Elena nodded, thinking that in a few hours, they would be separated--she to the quarters of the other ladies-in-waiting, he to join the other knights no doubt training for the imminent battle. Looking to the horse he had pur-chased in Aberstwyth, she thought of their entrance into the bailey of Not-tingham castle. Though she had grown accustomed to riding in the saddle with Gareth, she knew they must not arrive pressed together on one horse. It would be difficult enough to convince everyone at court, especially those who envied and despised her, that she was not a fallen woman. Nodding to the horse, she said, "It would probably be best if I rode that horse today."

Gareth frowned and then, as if realizing what she meant, nodded and looked away. "Of course. I'm just used to--"

"I know," she interrupted, wishing she could explain that it would go harder for him if Richard discovered Gareth had taken the virtue of one of his attendants, especially one who'd been bestowed on a supporter; knowing that she could never explain the nuances of court life in a few words.

Gareth quickly rearranged the leather satchels so that Elena would be able to ride her horse. When he was finished, he helped her into her makeshift sidesaddle. Taking the reins of both horses, led them out of the narrow alley and down the cobbled street to Henry Billingsley's pub. As he turned to help her down, he paused. With her hair intricately arranged, her back straight, and her new gown spread over her horse's back, she looked every inch the noblewoman. She looked nothing like the impudent lass he had made love to beneath the star-sprinkled velvet of the summer night's sky in Wales. Intimi-dated against his will, he carefully helped her down and stiffly escorted her into the pub.

Henry Billingsley remembered them from their previous meal and he bid them a hearty welcome, bringing mugs of ale and a plate of cold meats.

Elena ate the meat but avoided the ale. She had felt a definite change in

Gareth's attitude toward her since she had bid him good morning and she was at a loss as to how to bring back the smiling, teasing Gareth of just a few days ago.

They ate in uncomfortable silence and left the pub as soon as the platter was cleared. Gareth lifted her into her saddle and paused, his hand on her knee. "My lady," he began.

"Yes Gareth?"

He looked up into her eyes. "I--you will be back in the comfort of His Majesty's court before dinner." Elena had the distinct impression that was not what Gareth had intended to say, but he quickly turned and mounted Isrid.

They made their way slowly out of the city, content to let the horses choose the easy pace. They exchanged comments about the weather and the scenery they passed as they made their way towards Nottingham castle which loomed on the horizon.

Silently, Gareth chastised himself, hating that he hadn't taken advantage of one of hundreds of appropriate times to tell Elena that he loved her, to beg her to marry him. What was pride now, he thought? What matter if she had rejected his love from that first day? 'Twould have been better to suffer the misery of wounded ego than to forever wonder if they might have made a life together if only he'd had the courage to speak. Sentries on the parapets of the castle wall had spotted them and called out for identification.

"Lady Elena de Vignon handmaiden to King Richard and Sir Gareth ap Morgan, knight of His Majesty's realm," Gareth yelled back to the sentries. "We are only now reunited with the king after becoming separated from His Majesty's entourage near Middleham." One of the soldiers left the parapet and within minutes, the great wooden castle gate was creaking open.

As they passed into the shadow of the castle, Elena shivered, though not from cold. The day was warm, with nary a cloud in the sky to keep the sun's warmth from the earth. Elena shivered because the shadow was like a seal to her fate. Who knew how long it would be until Richard married her to Brackley? Elena had been around castles enough to know that this one was preparing for war.

As they passed through the thick stone walls on either side of the gate into the bailey, she saw knights training for battle: engaging in mock combat, preparing their horses for war, repairing worn armor. The full impact of the inevitable war with Henry Tudor struck Elena. She wondered what would happen to her--friends? Yes, friends back in Wales. Surely they did not have the weapons or the armor or the training that these knights had. She looked to Gareth and was greatly relieved that he had chosen the side that was most likely to win, most likely to keep him alive. As if feeling her gaze upon him, Gareth turned and smiled grimly back at her.

A foot soldier approached and saluted Gareth. "The king has been notified of your arrival, Sir Knight. Please continue on to the main hall," he said, gesturing to the large stone fortress that was the king's residence and meeting rooms.

As they drew nearer, Elena heard her name called from up above. "Elena!" cried Margaret. "You're alive!" Elena glanced up in time to see Margaret turn from the second-story window and call down the hall, "Your Majesty, it's true! Lady Elena is alive and she is here!"

The sense of doom which had settled on Elena as she passed into the castle's shadow grew heavier. Behind them, the knights in war training began a melee of blows and shouts. Elena's heretofore calm horse suddenly grew nervous, jumping and sidling away from the noise as it pressed up against Isrid. "Gareth!" Elena called, frightened.

"Easy," Gareth said to the horse as he grabbed the reins and sawed back on them. The horse calmed somewhat though it continued to jerk at the reins. Elena's apprehension grew and she looked to Gareth for help as she held onto the edge of the saddle with both hands.

"Elena," he said in a low voice. "There is something I must tell you before we are surrounded by people and separated."

Distracted by the huge carved doors which were suddenly thrown back, Elena looked up to see Richard surrounded by people start down the stone steps into the bailey. The urgency in Gareth's voice called her back. "Elena! I must tell you! I have tried to say this for the past week, but I just--"

Richard and his entourage were drawing closer. "What Gareth? What is it?"

"I love you." Another burst of metal upon metal clattered behind them and Elena's horse tossed its head wildly, jerking the reins out of Gareth's hands. Several groomsmen rushed up to grab the horse and in the process, pulled it away from Isrid. Elena stared in amazement at Gareth, unable to respond, especially as they were drawn further and further apart in the crush of people.

"Elena, sweet girl," boomed Richard's voice. She dragged her eyes from her lover's face. "We had all but given up hope that you were alive. What a joy it is to see you well and unharmed." Suddenly fixing Gareth with a suspecting glare, he continued, "You are, I trust, unharmed?"

Still reeling from Gareth's admission, she had to force her mind to concentrate on the king's question. "I--yes, I am in excellent health. Sir Gareth saw to my every need and protected me with utmost chivalry."

"I would expect no less," Richard said, though he had yet to remove his gaze from Gareth's face.

As she looked at her king, Elena noticed that his face had an ashen color to it and deep circles marred the skin beneath his eyes. He fidgeted with the jeweled belt at his waist and her eyes were drawn to his hands which trembled slightly. His nails were ragged, the cuticles torn. The matter of Henry Tudor must be weighing heavily on him, she thought.

"Come," he said, gesturing to the grooms to help her down. "I must hear everything about your adventures."

The groomsmen helped her off of the still-jittery horse but before she turned to follow the king, she gazed at Gareth who was now even further away. He was surrounded by his fellow knights who were plying him with questions, but he ignored them, his gaze locked to hers.

"My lady?" said the soldier who was waiting to escort her after Richard. Tearing her attention from Gareth with an effort that felt physical, she turned and allowed herself to be led away.

***

From across the bailey, Gareth watched Elena being led after the king. When she had disappeared into the great hall, he turned his attention to those knights gathered around him.

"What in God's creation happened to you?" asked one he recognized as Sir Jasper.

"Why did it take you so long to return?" asked another.

Gareth climbed off of Isrid and began leading him to the stables, explaining as he went.

"We were separated after the attack on the road from Middleham," he began. "I was sore injured and knocked unconscious. When I came to, it was dark. I set up camp and there Lady Elena found me. She had been taken by the attackers and then released." Gareth suddenly remembered that the story he and Elena had agreed upon was that <u>she</u> be seriously injured. "The good lady was in quite a bad state."

"Had she been raped?" asked an impudent young knight he did not know.

"No! Only sorely mishandled and dumped from her horse." Gareth wished to God that he and Elena had planned out more carefully what exactly they were going to say. On the trip here they had just seemed to have so many other things to think about...Tearing his thoughts from that path, he continued with his careful fabrication. "She was bleeding and near unconscious herself. I was in fear that she would die were I not to seek help, but since I am not so familiar with that part of England, I knew not where I might find a safe place to take her for treatment so I escorted her to my father's home."

"In Wales?" Sir Jasper asked, disbelieving.

'Tis not so very far," Gareth replied.

"But you could have returned to Middleham or continued on down the road to find us."

Gareth's mouth was going dry. He wasn't sure he was going to be able to carry this off and he wished with all his might that Elena were here. She was so much better at making up believable excuses. "I knew not what had become of His Majesty's party. As I said, I had been knocked unconscious--no doubt left for dead by the brigands who had attacked us--and when I came to, I was surrounded by bodies you had left behind. For all I knew, everyone had been killed or taken hostage."

The men nodded, recalling the frantic flight that day. Encouraged, Gareth continued. "For all I knew, Tudor had landed in England and was attacking. For myself, I would have sought him out and fought to my death, but

I did not want Lady Elena to fall into our enemy's hands. Who knows what that bastard would have done to such a beautiful lady." He glanced around to see if he was going too far. "The safest thing I could figure would be to take her to a place I knew to be safe until she recovered and I found out what had happened."

"You did well," said Sir Jasper with approval. Gareth felt a twinge of guilt at the older knight's praise. He had always looked up to Jasper and felt him to have one of the levelest heads of all of Richard's spurs. That he was deceiving this man turned his stomach sour. He removed Isrid's saddle and rubbed the war horse down. He remembered how as a squire he had dreamed that he would be the most honest, most chivalrous, most trustworthy knight of them all. What a farce his goal had become. He would be so glad when this whole mess was over. Either Henry Tudor would win and Gareth would be given a chance to live up to his youthful ideals under a new king, or he would die on the battlefield, wherever that may be. The thought of dying did nothing to ease his nausea.

He shook his head and took a cleansing breath. If death turned out to be his destiny, he decided philosophically, at least he would die having told Elena that he loved her.

The next day Gareth found himself in front of the king in the middle of a formal court. He had been summoned midmorning and had waited these past two hours at the back of the packed main hall, waiting for the royal high chancellor to call him forward. The messenger who had brought him word of Richard's summons had no explanation for it. Nor had the two-man armed escort who had made sure he arrived in the hall in plenty of time. Though he refused to allow himself to worry over the king's desire to see him, he couldn't help but wonder if he'd been found out. How inglorious, he thought, to be caught and executed without having accomplished one thing for Henry Tudor's cause.

Gareth shook his head to clear it of such dark thoughts. That Richard could have found him out was nonsense. Who here would possibly know of his involvement or his mission? Only Elena knew that he had even attended the meeting in Aberstwyth and--a cold shiver of doubt trickled down his spine. Suppose she had told Richard about Aberstwyth? No! he told himself. Though she had not returned his words of love yesterday, he was certain she would not reveal his meetings with the rebels. The doubt lingered. Gareth craned his neck, trying to spot Elena in the crowd of richly dressed nobles sitting in the first rows of the audience. He knew that if he could but lay eyes on her, all worry would leave his mind and he could focus on what he might say to the king to convince him of his loyalty. Though he stood on tiptoe and held onto the shoulder of the man in front of him for balance, he could not make her out and had to content himself with remembering their shared nights of passion, their companionable conversations along the way to Nottingham, and every other incident in the past weeks that had made him believe she must care for him, at least a bit. At least enough not to wish to see him hung as a traitor.

What then had prompted Richard to call him forth in court, and to send an armed escort to ensure that he arrived? He could only wonder and hope for the best.

The high chancellor called forth one of Richard's influential vassals from the south and announced the marriage of the man's daughter to the son of a northern lord. Gareth wondered if it were simply another attempt to bring the more rebellious regions of southern England in line with the north which favored Richard and from which he drew his greatest political support. The crowd shifted and between people's heads, Gareth could see the prospective bride, a young girl of perhaps no more than fifteen or sixteen, fair and blond and appearing none-too-eager to wed her fiancée. Gareth took a step sideways to better see the young man. He was young and good looking enough with broad shoulders and a noble brow. Gareth could not imagine why the girl should be so reluctant looking. It was not as if she were having to marry an ugly old ogre like Brackley.

Brackley. Gareth searched the hall for him, but the crush of people was too great to pick him out. Gareth ground his teeth. So consumed was he in his own worries since receiving his summons this morning that he had given no thought to the horrible fate Elena was facing. He prayed that Richard would not press for the wedding to be performed before Henry Tudor landed. He swore to himself that he would seek out the repulsive man on the battlefield and seek his death that Elena might be free of the man for good.

As the royal high chancellor called him forth before the king, Gareth prayed that he would live to see the battlefield. He held his back straight, his head high and forced his eyes to remain on the man who wore the crown. When he had entered the king's presence, he presented a low and formal bow. "Your Majesty," he said clearly, bending to one knee where he waited with bowed head for Richard's permission to stand.

It did not come immediately. Instead, he remained on his knee while the hall quieted. Still Richard did not speak. Gareth felt a glimmer of sweat coat his brow. This did not bode well.

"Sir Gareth ap Morgan," the king boomed. "You have been absent my court for some time and in the presence of one of my ladies. I have heard report of your story but I would have you tell me in person, that I might judge the veracity of your tale."

Still in his bent position, Gareth said, "Of course, Your Majesty. I am confident you will judge it to be true as I have always been a true and loyal knight to yourself and to England."

"Do not coddle me, man!" Gareth wished he had not spoken. Richard was obviously in one of his paranoid rages. "You disappeared from my ranks at the same time we were attacked by brigands--brigands who may very well have been supporters of that bastard Tudor. Furthermore, you disappear with one of my ladies-in-waiting who is the fiancée of one of my closest allies, Earl Brackley. You admit to having traveled alone with her, having given no thought to acquiring an appropriate escort, even though you must have passed several manors and not less than three convents! You drag her to Wales and then return her here as you please when you are done with her with no regard for her station or her good name! What do you have to say for yourself?"

"You Majesty--"

"Stand up man. Do not cower before me!"

Gareth flushed as he stood. He held his posture painfully erect and his voice was tight when he answered. "I know not if the brigands who attacked us on the road were supporters of Henry Tudor. I do know that I dispatched two of them to their maker before I myself was injured and lost consciousness. Surely someone amongst the group saw me battling to protect you and yours."

"Aye, my liege," came Sir Jasper's voice across the hall. "He fought well and nobly that day and killed by my count four opponents, not two."

Richard's gaze darted past Gareth's shoulder to the knight striding down the aisle. When Sir Jasper came to stand by Gareth's right side, the king studied him intently for several seconds before returning his glare to the younger knight. Gareth was torn between the feeling of relief that Sir Jasper was defending his case, and the ever-present guilt that was reminding him that he would no doubt be facing his present champion on a battlefield soon. With a strength of will born of the realization that his life depended on Richard believing his partial-truths, Gareth suppressed the guilt and instead concentrated on making his story as believable as possible.

Tilting his head towards Sir Jasper, he continued, "I killed four men that day and was wounded in return. I was knocked unconscious and, I can only presume, left for dead both by the brigands and my fellow knights--an understandable mistake." Gareth thought that a subtle shifting of the guilt might sway Richard in his favor. "When I came to, I had no idea what the outcome of the skirmish had been: whether Your Majesty had escaped or been seized along with the rest of your troops." Gareth's attention was drawn to Richard's hands. His left hand toyed with the royal signet ring on his right, twisting it, removing it, replacing it. Suddenly, as if the king realized his fidgeting had been caught, he quickly placed both hands on either arm of the throne, grasping them tightly until his knuckles whitened. Gareth jerked his attention from their nervous movements and returned to his story. "It was not long after that I discovered Lady Elena who I believe had been taken hostage by the brigands to ensure their escape and then later released. She was as ignorant as I concerning Your Majesty's survival," Gareth suddenly remembered that Elena was supposed to have been injured and he quickly made up an injury that would require at least a fortnight recovery. "Furthermore, she was bleeding profusely from a cut on her scalp and could scarce remember her name or what had happened."

Richard's gaze shifted again and he addressed someone in the crowd.

"And have you recovered sufficiently from your injury, Lady Elena?"

Gareth turned and felt his heart lurch. Seated on a bench in the front row of attendants to the court was Elena, dressed in a gown of deepest blue, heavily embroidered with silver thread. An expensive silver pendant graced her smooth neck and her hair was intricately braided and woven about her head. She looked as foreign to him as if she had only just arrived from the southernmost tip of Italy or the easternmost reaches of the Steppes. But when she turned her gaze to meet his, she was the woman he knew most intimately, the woman he loved. Still looking at him, she answered the king. "Aye, Your Majesty. I am well recovered, thanks to Sir Gareth and his family."

"Ah, yes," Richard boomed, "your family." Gareth turned back to face the king. "Tell me now, why you chose to take the Lady Elena--the wounded Lady Elena--through forests and over mountains to be attended by your family when there were manors and convents at every turn."

This would be his most difficult argument to convince, Gareth knew, and he tried to appear as guileless as possible as he said, "In all truth, Your Majesty, I did not come across a manor or convent. You see, I feared traveling the roads for Lady Elena's sake. I was worried that if we ran into these same brigands, she might not escape with just a wound to the head." Gareth paused, desperately trying to keep the charade up. "I was also worried that she would not survive the wound she had received. She faded in and out of consciousness as we traveled and I thought I might waste days looking for a manor while in that time I could easily get her to my father's keep where I knew she would be well taken care of." He paused and took a shaky breath as Richard stared at him.

The king licked his lips and then chewed on his lower lip while he tapped his finger with the signet ring against the arm of the throne. The sharp clicking sound seemed even louder to Gareth's ears than the low rumble of conversation by those who had lost interest in the business of court.

Finally, the king spoke. "And when Lady Elena had recovered, you and she immediately returned to see if I had arrived at Nottingham."

Gareth thought frantically to determine if there was anything else, he should add. He could think of nothing. "Yes. We traveled to Nottingham and learned in the city that you were in residence and in all health."

"And you swear this story to be true?"

"On my sword and on the good service I have provided you since first I came to your court." Gareth held his breath, waiting to see if he would be believed.

"Very well," Richard murmured. Raising his voice to its court-addressing level, he said, "We are thankful for your service in protecting Our life and for rescuing and protecting Our good Lady Elena. We charge you to remain with Us as We will no doubt require service of this caliber again." The king turned to his high chancellor and began discussing the next issue.

Gareth bowed, backed up several paces, and bowed again before turning and leaving, Sir Jasper at his elbow. When they had exited the main hall into the bright afternoon sunlight which filled the large bailey, Sir Jasper spoke. "Don't take his skepticism to heart, Gareth. The king is greatly occupied with Henry Tudor's threat and he sees a spy in every shadow."

Gareth kept his face an immobile mask. His attempt to thank Sir Jasper was waved away. Instead he asked the senior knight, "Were those brigands who attacked us Henry's men?"

"No. As it turns out, they were men hired by Elizabeth Woodville to capture her daughter out of Richard's grasp. Apparently, the woman has lost all reason and she feared Richard meant to force Elizabeth to marry him simply to cement his claim to the throne, as if he needs that."

Gareth thought that if what little he had gleaned from Elena about Richard's plans for Lady Elizabeth were true, the mother was uncannily shrewd rather than mad. The two men made their way to the far end of the bailey where a group of knights and men-at-arms whose presence was not required in court were practicing swordplay. Gareth and Sir Jasper paused on the edge of the practice field, watching the men.

"We've no idea exactly how many men Tudor will be able to gather once he lands. He has the assistance of several foreign crowns and, so our King's spies tell us, much support from Wales, for Welsh blood runs in his veins."

Gareth thought he should not appear *too* innocent so he said, "I had heard as much--he is French too, am I correct?"

"Yes, he is the grandson of Henry V's widow, Catherine, who was the daughter to the King of France. No doubt the French king is his most generous benefactor." Gareth knew Henry Tudor's lineage, but nodded his head as if learning it anew. "His only claim to King Richard's crown is through the bastard children of John Beaufort."

"I thought they were legitimized."

Sir Jasper scoffed. "Only on the condition that they never lay claim to the throne! Which just goes to show you what the deviousness of the Welsh will push through." He paused, his eyes widening as he looked at Gareth. "Gareth, forgive me. I did not mean to imply--"

Gareth raised his hand to stop the apology. "Please, Sir Jasper, think nothing of it. I'll be the first to admit that the Welsh can be calculating--what other reason could explain why there used to be so much fighting between the lords of Wales." Sir Jasper nodded and the two men turned their attention back to the mock battles being waged.

Though Gareth pretended to be studying the men's form and style, he was reflecting on Sir Jasper's words. Aye, the Welsh could change their loyalty in a heartbeat, but usually they did so only when Wales was being trod upon. Had Richard not allowed English priests to replace the Welsh clergy, or English lords to rule Welsh lands, Wales would even now support him as King of England. But most importantly, had Richard not supported the laws which denied a Welshman the rights of citizenship merely because Welsh blood ran through his veins, he would not now be having to worry that Henry's army would be greatly comprised of Welshmen seeking the same rights every Englishman took for granted.

As Gareth stood there, surrounded by the noise of a productive, war-prepared castle, all of the arguments against Richard brought up at the Aberstwyth meeting came back to him. They coalesced into a solid determination to see a better king on the throne. *Cymru*, which could really only be translated as "Welshness," flowed through his veins and the weight of guilt and indecision which had bowed his shoulders since he had first heard of Henry Tudor suddenly slid off and broke into pieces about his feet, to be kicked away with the slightest shift of the spurs which adorned his worn boots.

He looked to Sir Jasper who was shouting instructions to a new knight on the field. He would no doubt be facing this noble man on the field, for Sir Jasper believed most firmly that Richard was God's choice as King of England. But suddenly, Gareth felt the same passionate response to Henry Tudor's claim.

No doubt if he had been born and raised in northern England, and Sir Jasper had grown up in Wales, their loyalties would be reversed. But fate had decided they would soon fight for different kings and no amount of guilt on Gareth's part would change that. With an invigorating sense of freedom and relief, Gareth strode forward and picked up a wooden sword from the pile of practice weapons and joined the hard-practicing men.

Chapter 25

Elena spent her next few days enjoying the comforts of velvet gowns, down-stuffed pillows, hot meals, sweet deserts, music in the background, and hours spent embroidering with the other ladies-in-waiting. After she had entertained them with a carefully constructed story of her adventures, they had returned to the normal court gossip of flirtatious intrigue and fashion faux pas--or so it seemed. Elena could not help but suspect that the old rumors surrounding her virtue were resurfacing. Though she seemed to have resumed her position as cherished handmaiden, there was something different about the entire court's attitude toward her, especially the other ladies-in-waiting.

As Elena worked on embroidering a tapestry one afternoon, she wondered if perhaps it was her attitude towards them which had changed. Mayhap both. Certainly she tired more rapidly of the inane banter the women often indulged in. The political machinations of court seemed somehow more vulgar and blatant than she remembered them. And lately, when she had been attending Richard, she seemed to feel an odd repugnance. He was constantly in a foul mood, yelling at his advisors, attendants, and serfs alike. At one time or another during his day-long meetings with advisors he accused everyone in his court of conspiring to dethrone him. Whenever Elena brought refreshments into the map-strewn study where he spent hours each day planning his defense against Henry Tudor, Richard regarded her warily, as if he suspected her of eavesdropping or snooping through his papers. No more did he have flattering words for her. Not once did he ask after her family, bidding her send his regards to her mother when next she wrote as he had before they left Middleham castle all those weeks ago.

Elena paused to rethread her needle, judging the effect of the tapestry. Its base was of heavy gold fabric and onto it she was working an intricate design of pomegranates, vines, and lions in rich jewel-colored silk threads. Returning to her work, her reflection of her present life resumed.

More and more she seemed to be spending time alone, sewing or staring out the window at the men practicing for war. During those times, like now, she did not have to decipher the veiled hostility of the other women of the court and she was free to let her mind wander. More often than not, her mind led her willingly to thoughts of Gareth and his last-minute declaration of love. Over and over she replayed that scene in the bailey. She saw the intense look on his face as he realized they were about to be separated. She could hear his voice, low and hoarse as he said, "I love you!" In her mind she stared at his face as her skittish horse was dragged away and she was lifted from its saddle. Sometimes, when she was feeling particularly alienated from the other members of court, she would rearrange that last scene. She would have Gareth proclaim his love right before they reached Nottingham castle. Then, instead of entering the great gates, they would turn and ride as fast as they could across the landscape and not stop until they reached Eyri Keep where they would marry.

Other times--times that made her cheeks flame with embarrassment and excitement--she would imagine the words escaping him in the heat of passion. Or in the tender quiet afterwards when they lay in each other's arms. Regardless of how the scenario began, it always ended the same: with their return to Eyri Keep. Eyri Keep had become an ideal in her mind where she was cherished without having to manipulate others, where she was admired without hostility, where Enid and Elen had proven themselves to be true friends who did not pretend to like her one moment and disdain her the next. And Eyri Keep was the place where she would look forward to her husband's return. As it stood now, she was dreading word of Brackley's return to Nottingham.

Catherine, the previously timid kitten, had somehow grown claws in the intervening weeks and had informed Elena that her fiancée had not been overly dismayed to learn of her disappearance and that he had, in fact, shown her, Catherine, undeniable partiality of late. Catherine had rambled on a great deal about the questions that were arising concerning Elena's good name after having spent so much time alone with a man. She had also made it quite clear that she felt she was infinitely more suited to being the earl's wife than was Elena. Elena had long ago learned the value of keeping her mouth shut on certain topics and she knew that should she say anything regarding her reluctance to wed the earl--especially to Catherine--the words would quickly find their way into Richard's ear.

Elena would have liked nothing better than to see Catherine wed to the repugnant man instead of herself, but considering Richard's mood of late, she knew that she must be very careful about how she broached the subject of her betrothal lest he grow enraged and wed her to Brackley immediately out of spite.

Her hands shaky at the thought of the earl, Elena stabbed her thumb with her needle as she took a stitch.

"Damn!" she exclaimed, dropping the thread and squeezing the offended digit. A bright red drop of blood welled out of the prick and she moved instinctively to put her thumb in her mouth. She paused, hand in mid-air as she remembered her mother telling her that blood from a seamstress's hand rubbed into a seam brought good luck to the wearer of the garment. Elena found a bright red flower on the tapestry and rubbed her thumb on it. The cloth would not be worn, but perhaps if hung in her room, would bring her good luck. At this point, she reflected, she needed all the good luck she could get.

A knock at the door was quickly followed by a page who brought word that the new Countess of Salisbury was in residence and King Richard charged his ladies-in-waiting to attend her on a horseback ride about the castle grounds.

Elena left her needlework and the privacy of the large sewing room to quickly change her clothes and join the small group of women gathered in the great hall. Amongst the women were Richard and another well-dressed man Elena assumed was the Earl of Salisbury. Presently they were joined by a regal looking woman of perhaps thirty who was closely attended by a smug-looking Catherine. Elena wondered again when Catherine had grown so cocky but with a mental shrug of her shoulders, attributed it to life in the court. Thank my stars I have never been so worried about my position in Richard's court, she thought.

Richard presented the small group of ladies to the Countess and Elena suppressed an instinctual feeling of danger when Richard merely mentioned her name to the Countess and moved on to the next lady. Every other time Elena had attended his noble guests, Richard had made a special emphasis when introducing her. He had told this Duchess or that Lord that Elena was his prized attendant, or that as they were his favorite vassal, so must they have his favorite lady attend them. As a result, Elena had been showered with gifts and had been privy to many conversations she would have otherwise been excluded from had Richard not made a point to recognize her value and importance. That he was now ranking her with the group of ladies who were only trusted to prepare trays of edibles and help arrange skirts was unnerving.

As the ladies were helped onto their horses and began riding around the bailey, Elena ignored Catherine's inane chatter about this building or that sight. She instead mulled over the loss of her status as the king's favorite. To her surprise, she found it did not bother her, but she did worry at Richard's reasons for it. Had he merely grown weary of her or were there greater reasons for his recent coldness towards her. Elena was not oblivious to the fact that people disappeared from court, never to be seen again. She was also aware that if Richard thought she had gained any sympathies to Henry Tudor during her stay in Wales, if he had somehow found out that she was in the very house where Tudor plans were being laid, her life would be very short indeed. All her protestations of innocence, all her vows of loyalty would mean nothing, for Richard dealt quickly and harshly with those suspected of betraying him from his highest advisor to the lowest serf.

Elena thought of the court she had attended just a few nights past. She had held her breath while Richard had questioned Gareth for she knew that Richard would have never wasted court time questioning a knight unless he doubted that knight's loyalty. That he had not charged Gareth with any crime did not relieve her of that worry. Should Gareth have any enemies in this court or should anyone discover that they had been to Aberstwyth, his life would be forfeit quicker than hers would.

The small group of women rode around the perimeter walls to the far corner of the bailey where men were training with swords, shields, and pikes. While the other ladies chatted and laughed with the Countess, pointing out the most handsome knight or the most adept with the sword, Elena sat still on her horse, mesmerized by the sight of Gareth, who leaned against a cart on the far side of the training soldiers. Bareheaded, shirt sleeves pushed past his elbows, arms crossed lazily over his chest, he laughed at something an older knight was telling him. One of the practicing knights called out to him and Gareth nodded and bent to pick up his helmet and shield. Elena studied every detail of his appearance, memorizing it for future daydreams.

"Elena!" Catherine called shrilly. "Isn't that the handsome knight you spent a month with alone?"

Elena dragged her gaze from Gareth and turned to Catherine who, with her question, had gained the attention of the Countess and the other three ladies-in-waiting. Though Catherine's face appeared blandly innocent, Elena saw straight through her ploy. "Indeed, that is Sir Gareth who rescued me from the brigands who attacked us and escorted me into the safekeeping and protection of his noble father."

"But how humiliating," Catherine persisted, "to have no privacy while traveling through the dark woods of Wales, spending every night with this man you hardly know."

Elena refused to let Catherine get the best of her. "Surely you are exaggerating, Catherine. You will have the good Countess here fearing for her very life when near one of His Majesty's knights. Sir Gareth was a paragon of chivalry and virtue as he escorted me to safety. I not once encountered an unsavory moment in his company and I would trust my life and the life of my mother into Sir Gareth's hands without hesitation." Ha! Elena thought, you'll have to be in this court a few more years before you can think to make me look bad, Catherine.

"What adventure!" the Countess of Salisbury said, obviously intrigued by Elena's experience. Deciding to show Catherine exactly what she was up against, Elena turned on her favorite-lady-in-waiting charm and set out winning over the visiting noblewoman.

"Indeed it was. And as for the Welsh forests being dark and ugly places, I must tell you I have never seen such lush beauty. They are quite peaceful and I would vouch that they are less plagued by villains and robbers than are our own English woods. I am sure your ladyship would find them most pleasing."

"I would love to visit them," the Countess avowed. "But tell me, weren't you afraid? From what Lady Catherine has told me, I had feared for your virtue and soundness of mind after such an excursion."

Elena smiled smugly at the furious Catherine. "I've no doubt you did. But as usual, Lady Catherine worries herself far too much about my virtue. Why, I would not have felt more comfortable in the presence of a priest and a host of nuns. Not once did Sir Gareth initiate an unwanted advance. It would do Lady Catherine a world of good to go through such an adventure as I had so that she might realize not everyone is as wicked as she seems to fear they are."

The Countess nodded and urged her horse closer to Elena's. "But tell me, what of sleeping in the forest at night? Weren't you frightened of goblins and evil spirits?"

Elena described the Welsh landscape to the intrigued Countess, being careful not to vary from the story she and Gareth had so far told. She answered question after question, delighting in watching Catherine fume.

"My lady, perhaps you would like to see the flower gardens now?" Catherine finally interrupted.

"What's that?" the Countess asked. "Yes, of course. I suppose we are making these poor lads nervous with our continued observance, aren't we?" The Countess laughed and the ladies-in-waiting followed suit, tittering behind their hands. Elena smiled, but her eyes were drawn to practice field where Gareth was battling another man in armor with mock swords. Though his opponent stood a head taller than him, Gareth bested the man's strength and knocked him to the ground, holding the mock sword to his throat a second before leaning down to help his opponent up. When both men were standing, they took off their helmets, laughing and comparing battle techniques. Gareth slapped the man companionably on the shoulder before turning to leave the battlefield. Elena's breath caught as he glanced up and saw her watching. The grin left his face and he stared at her, his eyes burning hotly as his gaze scanned her face, her figure. The other ladies were leaving and Elena knew she must follow but she could not escape his gaze.

Finally, Margaret turned her horse and rode back to Elena, "Elena! Are you coming? We're off to view the flower gardens."

"Yes, I'm coming," Elena murmured. She urged her horse to slowly follow the others, but kept her gaze locked onto Gareth. Twisting in the saddle, she watched as Gareth lifted his hand to his lips. She returned the action, wishing with all her heart she could stop and speak to him. But with what excuse? She could not risk stopping with Catherine--and who knew how many others?--watching, hoping for a reason to cast suspicion on their relationship. Turning back around, she urged her horse to a faster pace and caught up with the group of women as Catherine was describing how instrumental she was in helping Richard have the most beautiful castle gardens. Elena rolled her eyes and allowed her mind to wander back to Gareth.

Chapter 26

"My liege," said the burly man who knelt before Richard in the main hall. The man was covered with dirt from the road, his hair sweaty, his armor a strange combination of leather and metal, with French and German styling. The three men who knelt behind them with heads bowed were garbed in equally motley armor. "My liege," the leader said once again, finally gaining the king's attention.

"What is it?" he asked shortly.

"My liege, we report to you upon orders of the Earl of Brackley."

Richard surveyed the men briefly, visibly disbelieving their claim of service. "We have no need of mercenaries. We have twelve thousand loyal troops to attend me should We need them. Be on your way."

"My liege?"

Richard turned back to the man. "What is it? Do you not understand God's English? I've no need of mercenaries."

"We are not mercenaries, my liege. We have spent these last weeks in Wales."

Richard's brows raised in understanding. "Did you learn aught?"

"We learned the rebels held a meeting in Aberstwyth. A host of Welsh malcontents met to plan their attack on your grace. Rumor has it that Lord Stanley attended."

Richard choked on his bile. He had long suspected Stanley would betray him, had demanded his son as hostage to prevent such an action.

"Who else attended?"

"Welsh rebels–"

"Names, you fool. I know they were Welsh!"

The man wiped a dirty hand across his sweaty brow, leaving a muddy streak. "We didn't–we could not find the meeting's location. We thought we came across one man, but he–that is, the Welsh helped him to escape."

"Did you see Lord Stanley there?"

"We spoke to a barmaid who swore she had waited upon the man, your grace."

"But you did not see him, did not speak to him."

The man shifted his weight. The floor was no doubt hard on his knees. "No, your grace."

Richard sighed heavily and leaned his head on the high back of his chair.

"See Sir Jasper. He will assign you duties." The men stood and bowed before backing away. "And do not dare to present yourself to me filthy from travel again."

The four men hurried out of the hall in search of Sir Jasper.

Chapter 27

A thousand candles lit the great hall of Nottingham castle as servants stumbled over each other in their haste to bring heavy trays of food to the thick wood tables. The wine flowed ceaselessly and the rich aroma of fresh-baked bread and thick stews competed with the smoke from the great fireplace and the sweat of men who had ridden hard hours to break bread with their sovereign. As Gareth surveyed the bustling scene, he felt a strange sense of deja vu. This could have easily been the last great feast at Middleham castle. The night he had first laid eyes on Elena. The rowdy men around him laughed as they recalled the foibles of the squires they were training. A comely serving girl leaned over his shoulder, setting a platter of roasted venison in the middle of the table. She pressed her breasts against his shoulder and lifted her eyebrows in invitation at him when he looked up. He smiled politely and turned back to his mug of ale, hoping the girl would not be flirting with him all night. Two of the king's dogs broke into a fight over a bone tossed on the ground and a page ran forward to separate them. At the head table, the king was in conversation with the Earl of Salisbury and several other nobles.

It is as if nothing has changed, he thought. Nothing except that now I am a traitor and a spy intent on bringing down Richard. Refusing to succumb to feelings of guilt he had resolutely put behind him that morning, he pushed that thought away. Nothing has changed, he reflected, except that I am in love with a woman who will no doubt be wed to another before the leaves fall from the trees. I am in love with her, he thought, and I will have to watch her pledge her life to another, will have to watch her exit the hall on his arm for her wedding night, knowing her more intimately than her husband ever could. Gareth set his mug on the table and rested his head in his hands. Somehow that was a worse feeling than any of the guilt he had felt over his appointed mission.

"Be you ill Gareth?" asked Henry, the taller man he had bested on the practice field earlier. Placid of countenance and disposition, his broad face was full of concern as Gareth lifted his head from his hands.

"No," Gareth said, forcing a smile, "too much ale, that's all."

Henry's face cleared and he grinned broadly. "Aye, that's an illness I'm well familiar with!" The man returned his attention to the wealth of food in front of him and Gareth relapsed into his thoughts of Elena. Instead of the subtle torture of thinking of her upcoming wedding night, he recalled every detail of her face when he had seen her on horseback earlier today. She had been wearing the dress he had purchased for her, though the accessories she had added had changed it into the gown of a lady of rank. A jeweled belt worked in gold adorned the high waist and the collar had been closed with an intricately-wrought gold brooch. Her hair had been encased in gold wire baskets on either side of her head and a fine veil had covered the glory of its chestnut color. As he had watched her, he was sure he could have never touched that satiny skin. This was not the woman who had lain so passionately in his arms. She was an aloof stranger, she must be. But the look in her eyes and the way she had watched him had reassured him. Reassured him that he was an ass for having kept silent so long about his feelings for her.

He raked his fingers through his tangled hair. It could not now be undone. They must each answer their own destinies. Looking up for something to distract him, his eyes locked onto the sight of Elena entering the hall. As on that night when he had first seen her, she was alone, standing at the top of the three steps which led into the main hall. She was surveying the colorful scene before her and she was even wearing the same green velvet gown that she had that night. Gareth remembered thinking that night that any lady wealthy enough to wear such a gown would never see anything in a man such as himself. She made her way slowly to the ladies' table and sat at the end farthest from the head table. As he watched, she smiled at the lady sitting next to her and did not look up again as she ate. Gareth frowned, worried. This was so unlike her, he thought. She should be sitting at the head of that table as Richard's favorite.

Scarcely touching the food on his own plate, Gareth watched as she picked at her food and then stood to leave. He rose also and moved to intercept her behind the huge central fireplace. There they would be out of sight of Richard and the other important guests. Gareth waited close to the fire which was necessary even in the heat of summer to warm the cold stone of the castle. As Elena walked past him, he said as casually as possible, "Good evening, Lady Elena."

Startled, she turned towards him and when she saw who had spoken to her, her eyes widened. "Gareth!" she whispered. Glancing furtively around, she quickly joined him behind the fireplace. She extended her hands to him and he took them in his own, rubbing them briskly to bring warmth to them. For moments they stood, staring at each other, unable to speak.

Finally, Gareth said, "How are you?"

Elena lifted her shoulders in a delicate shrug that seemed to belie her response, "I'm alright. How are you? Have you received any trouble for your absence?"

"No, everyone seems to be accepting our story."

Elena nodded. "I'm glad." As if striving to find something safe to discuss she said, "And how is Isrid?"

"He is well, although I think he misses our constant traveling. He was unusually jumpy when last I rode him." Though he hated himself for asking, he could not stop his next question. "Has Richard informed you of when you will be wed?"

A shadow immediately crossed her eyes and she pulled her hands from his, clasping them in front of her. "The earl has not yet returned from Hastings. I imagine the king will inform me then what his plans are for me. And you? Are your plans going well?"

Gareth's heart skipped a beat. "What plans?"

"Your preparations for war. I saw you practicing today."

"Yes, they are going well."

"Good."

Gareth gnawed his lower lip. This was not what he wanted to be saying. He did not want to be wasting precious seconds babbling about inane topics like his horse and battle practice. Trying to steer the conversation along a different route, he said, "You were wearing the dress I bought you today."

Elena's gaze dropped to her still-clasped hands. "Yes, it's...it's one of my favorites. I wear it quite often."

Hoping he was not wrong to find encouragement in her words, he took a deep breath. "Elena, about what I said the other day."

She raised her eyes to his. "Yes?" she breathed.

"I--"

"Lady Elena! I'm so glad I found you," a young page rushed up to her and bowed awkwardly before continuing. "The Countess of Salisbury is retiring and she requires your attendance. Will you come?"

"Of course."

The young man waited expectantly, no doubt planning to escort her to the countess. Elena turned and took two steps and then paused. "Run along then, I know the way to her chambers." The page looked apprehensive but obeyed. As soon as he was gone, she turned and ran the few steps back to Gareth. Before he could utter a word, she pressed her lips to his, her body molding itself naturally to the curves of his own. His hands moved up to embrace her, but she was already pulling away, turning and running lightly out of the main hall.

Gareth leaned against the stone fireplace and touched his fingers to his lips. They still tingled from the soft pressure of her own and like a drop of wine to a thirsty man, only made him long for more. If only that blasted page had not appeared!

***

"Your Majesty," said Sir Jasper. When the king turned his attention to the knight, the man bowed respectfully.

"What is it Sir Jasper?"

"Your Majesty, these men who have recently joined us have begged for a moment of your time. They claim they have information you will find of the utmost importance."

Richard looked to the rough but slightly cleaner soldiers who waited several paces behind Sir Jasper. Turning back to his meal, he said, "We have already spoken to these men once today and heard all they know. We have accepted them as soldiers. See that they are well-assigned and leave Us be."

Sir Jasper bowed his head in deference. "I am aware Your Majesty has already spoken with them, but they seem to be under the impression that they have discovered news of the rebel's meeting in Wales since this morning."

Richard looked up sharply. "What?" Standing, he strode to one of the smaller rooms that opened off of the main hall. The king stopped in the middle of the room and demanded of the men who had followed, "What news have you of the traitors in Wales?"

The same burly man who had spoken for the foursome earlier stepped forward at Sir Jasper's urging. "My liege, whilst we were in Wales flushing out rebels, we learned from the abbess of Dinas Mawddwy that a certain knight was on his way to Aberystwyth for the meeting of the rebels. This knight was a man who serves you even now in your hall."

Richard's eyes narrowed and his thin lips compressed until his mouth was a narrow line of anger. He gripped the fur edges of his mantle with knuckles that were white. "Who was it?"

"I believe I heard him referred to as Gareth. Gareth ap Morgan."

Sir Jasper gasped and Richard looked at him sharply. "Does this surprise you, Sir Knight?"

The older man cleared his throat. "Indeed it does, Your Majesty. Sir Gareth has proven himself to be nothing other than the most loyal and obedient of your knights. And if he were a rebel, why would he return here, to your service? Why would he not simply remain with the other rebels and await Henry Tudor's landing?"

"Perhaps he hopes to learn our battle plans, how many men we train, what our weaknesses are," the king bit out. "I will have his head for this."

"Your Majesty, I must protest. At least give Sir Gareth the chance to defend himself and his honor."

"Why should I?" In his impatience, Richard slipped out of the use of the royal "We," and his hand had moved to the decorative sword he wore on his belt.

Sir Jasper stepped forward and lowered his voice. "Because, sire, these men are former mercenaries, newly come to your service. What assurance have we that they speak the truth? Perhaps they only hope to gain your favor?"

Richard studied his knight for several seconds before nodding briefly. "Very well, let us return to the feast hall. We will get to the bottom of this now."

"Your Majesty?" Sir Jasper said.

"What is it now, man? You try Our patience with your constant interruptions!"

"I beg your forgiveness, but would it not be better to wait until the feast is over and the people have dispersed? Surely Sir Gareth's service has earned him that much respect before he is accused of treason."

Richard's voice was low and cutting when he answered. "Surely Our service as king has earned Us the respect of knowing immediately if one of Our knights has betrayed Us."

Sir Jasper bowed and said, "Of course, Your Majesty."

The knight and the four soldiers followed Richard back into the feast hall where fruit pies were just being served. Richard strode to the front of the raised dais on which the head table sat. Within seconds, all voices in the hall were silenced. "Where is Sir Gareth ap Morgan?" he boomed.

Behind the fireplace where he was thinking of Elena, Gareth started, recognizing the king's voice though he could not see who called him. Dashing around the great stone pillar, he called out, "Here, Your Majesty."

"Attend Us."

Gareth rushed to the front of the hall. There was no award the king would be bestowing, no honor he had earned. His pulse doubled its pace and he felt all his muscles tighten with tension when he spotted the four mercenaries he had twice before run into, the last time being in the streets of Aberstwyth. There could only be one reason the king was calling him forward now. Bowing low before the king, Gareth said as loudly and as confidently as he could, "Your Majesty?"

"Sir Knight, have you sworn fealty to Us?"

"Yes, my king."

"And will you swear it to Us again? Tonight? Now?"

Gareth paused for the briefest moment. "Of course, Your Majesty."

Richard held out the hand with his signet ring and Gareth knelt and took it in his own damp palms, reciting his vow of fealty to the king and to England. Before he could rise and back away, hoping that was all the king desired of him, Richard stopped him. "And now, Sir Gareth, We would ask another question of you."

Gareth waited, his nerves and muscles tightening in tandem. "Your Majesty?"

Richard looked down his nose at his knight. "Have you betrayed Us and your vows of fealty by attending a meeting of traitors in Wales?"

Gareth clenched his teeth tightly, trying to steady himself, desperately trying to think of something to say that would save his life. "I told Your Majesty that I was only at my father's keep in Northern Wales."

"We remember very clearly what you have told Us, Sir Gareth. But you see, these men here," Richard gestured to the four rough men who stood to the side, "claim they ran into you in Aberstwyth, several days travel from your father's keep, is it not? And, coincidentally, where We have recently discovered a meeting occurred to plan aid to the Tudor dog! What have you to respond?"

"I can only suppose they are mistaken in identifying me as that man."

"Gareth is of a common height and coloring for a Welshman, Your Majesty," interjected Sir Jasper. "It could easily happen."

"Were there only one man who had spotted him there, We might be inclined to believe this claim. But there were four! Four men who saw you in the intimate company of traitors!"

Gareth felt his stomach clench. Before he could speak, Sir Jasper spoke up again.

"Your Majesty, I beg you to consider the source of this story. Four men, yes, but four men who have not given you loyal service. Four men who only just arrived at Nottingham today, who may, in fact be spies themselves! Surely Sir Gareth's previous service must stand him in your favor now."

"Sir Jasper, your protestations of what We must or must not think do not endear you to Us. They do, in fact, lead Us to wonder if you are in league with this man." Sir Jasper opened his mouth to speak, but Richard stopped him. "We will hear no more. Guards! Take this man into custody. He is no longer one of Our knights." Turning, Richard walked around the table and resumed his seat. Gareth felt as if there were no blood, no strength in his limbs for he could not move them. Could not even feel them. When the two guards grabbed him by his arms--two guards he had helped train--he was unaware of their painful grasp or that Richard was stripping him of his knight's chain. These were left on the dais as he was pulled out of court. Though all else was a blur, Gareth saw the pained look on Sir Jasper's face as he left the hall.

The two guards said not a word to him as they led him out of the main hall to a stone tower where the prisoners were normally kept. One of the guards addressed a captain who was just coming out. "Sir, His Majesty has another traitor for the tower."

"Well you'll have to take him to the cellars below the main hall. We've no room for the prisoners we've got. I sent a man to the cellars just this morning with two prisoners. He will still be on duty and can take this one from you." The captain sighed and rubbed his eyes. "I wish we could get these men tried and either hung or released. We've too many men spending time on guard duty instead of preparing for war. The king must be--" The man stopped as if suddenly realizing who he was talking to. "Go about your business now," he said brusquely.

Gareth's guards dragged him back to the main keep and hauled him down a flight of stairs that had not seen much maintenance. The stones were cracked and slippery with dampness. One of the guards cracked his head on a low-hanging beam and cursed abruptly. When they reached the dank-smelling cellars, a feeble torch illuminated the guard's post where a beefy man dozed on a three-legged stool, his head leaning against the damp stone walls. His snores were interrupted when one of the guards kicked the man's stool.

"Wake up you lazy oaf! We've another prisoner. Stand up and open one of the cells."

The groggy man saluted and fumbled with the keys at his waist. "Here," he said, gesturing to the wooden door in front of him. "This one was emptied this morning when the king ordered the man's execution." He opened the door and stood aside while the other two guards pushed Gareth into the cramped cell. Gareth stumbled in the darkness, coming to land on a musty-smelling pallet of straw. The door slammed shut behind him and he heard the bolt slide home.

The two king's guards berated the man for his appearance and demeanor before leaving. Gareth heard the beefy guard grumble about their treatment as he settled himself back on his stool. Within seconds, the snoring had resumed.

Gareth wedged himself in the corner of the small room, sitting on the old straw pallet. He forced himself to think of the one thing that would not drive him insane with worry over his imminent execution. He forced his mind to conjure Elena and the way she had rushed back to kiss him. He allowed no other thoughts to enter his mind but those of their passion-filled trip from Wales, the all too short nights they had spent in that tiny room in Samuel's house. He refused to think of the bugs he was now bedding down with and the way the axe would look as it whistled through the air on a collision course with his neck. He thought only of Elena.

Chapter 28

Elena awoke the next morning wondering if she could convince the Countess of Salisbury to ride through the bailey again so that she might catch another glimpse of Gareth. She had just finished dressing and was waiting for the young servant girl to finish with her hair when there was a knock at the door.

"Enter," Elena called, but Catherine, who was having her hair washed, called out angrily, "No, do not enter! Elena, if you do not mind, I am not prepared to receive anyone."

"For heaven's sake, Catherine, it's not likely to be the pope calling for confession. What matter if a page sees you with wet hair?"

"It is not seemly and I, if no one else in this room, am well aware of the importance of behaving in a seemly manner at all times."

Elena wondered if Catherine was referring to her weeks spent with Gareth. More than once had Catherine implied that Elena could not be a true lady after allowing herself to spend nights on the road alone with no chaperon. Elena had managed to grit her teeth and say nothing, knowing that was the only way to deal with someone like Catherine, but now she had remained silent long enough.

"You only behave in a 'seemly' manner when there is someone of import to impress. Were you to behave all the time, you would not be so catty to the very women who have made you who you are in this court today."

"Don't you dare try to tell me you are the reason His Majesty treasures me so!"

"Ladies, please!" interrupted Margaret. When Elena and Catherine continued to bicker, she yelled a little more loudly. "Will the two of you shut your mouths for one moment? I will answer the damned door myself."

Despite her anger at Catherine, Elena laughed. "Are you sure they allow language like that in the convent, Margaret?"

"They would if they had to deal with you two," Margaret said over her shoulder as she reached the door. She stepped outside and in a moment returned, looking apprehensively at Elena. "The summons is for you, Elena. The Earl of Brackley has returned and King Richard calls you to his meeting chambers."

"The earl is here?" Catherine said, sitting up, heedless of the water dripping from her hair.

"Yes, he is here," Margaret said, answering Catherine, but staring at Elena. "But the summons was for Elena and Elena alone."

"That's ridiculous. I am sure the earl will wish to see me as well." Catherine grabbed the linen towel from the serving maid and began vigorously drying her hair.

"Would you like me to call the messenger back? He was most specific in relaying the king's words. The earl is, after all, betrothed to Elena, not you."

Catherine glared at the other women, but Elena ignored her. "Did he say why?"

Margaret smiled sympathetically and shook her head no. Elena suspected Margaret alone knew of her secret dread of marrying the repugnant man and for the first time, Elena felt a camaraderie with the other woman she had never before experienced. Returning the smile, Elena stood and left the room, forbidding her knees to shake as she walked down the stairs and into the large map-strewn room in which Richard was sitting with the earl.

Richard was the first to notice her presence. "Ah, Edmund, here is Elena now." When she was but a few feet from the men, Elena curtsied gracefully and slowly rose. From beneath her lashes, she watched Brackley, dismayed to find him even crueler looking than she had remembered.

For several seconds, not a word was spoken. Elena could not imagine why the king had called her forth if not to tell her of her impending marriage. When the king finally spoke, however, it was not to her.

"Look on her well, Edmund and decide if you will have her though she be a fallen woman."

Elena looked up, stunned. "Your Majesty?"

"Do not play the naive chit with Us, lady. Lady Catherine has kept Us well enough informed and she is convinced, as are We, that you did not hold yourself as befits a member of Our entourage. Now it is up to the earl to decide if he will have you anyway. We have offered him wife of any of my other ladies, ladies whose virtue We can be certain of. Edmund?"

The earl leaned back in his seat, surveying Elena from head to toe. "I care not if she is pure. In fact, I rather think I will prefer bedding a new wife who is not a virgin. Perhaps your experiences," he put an ugly emphasis on the word 'experiences,' "in Wales will make my wedding night all the more enjoyable." Turning to the king, Brackley said, "I will still have her if her dowry is the same."

"Aye, I've padded it well enough. As for you, lady, be very thankful that the earl is as understanding and tolerant as he is. Were he not, and your indiscretions had cost Us his valuable friendship, We would not like to think of what might have happened to you."

Elena's breaths were short and shallow. She had to fight the overwhelming urge to flee. Simply turn and flee and stop only long enough to grab Gareth and beg him take her from this place. Why had she returned? Gareth had been right, Richard cared nothing for her, only how she could serve him! He cared for nothing except holding onto his crown.

Richard had turned back to Edmund and was discussing the transfer of her dowry. He had completely dismissed her from his thoughts, so it seemed, and he would never think of her again, now that she had served her purpose.

"Your Majesty," she said with a quavering voice. Taking herself firmly in hand she said louder and steadfastly, "Your Majesty!"

Richard looked at her sharply. "You should be attending your trousseau, lady. What is it?"

"I cannot marry the earl."

Richard's complexion became mottled with anger as he said, "You most certainly can. It has already been arranged. You will be wed come Sunday."

"No, Your Majesty, I cannot marry him."

"And why not?" the king bit out, digging his nails into the wooden arms of his chair.

She straightened her shoulders. "Because I love another and may carry his child." Elena braced herself to be physically beaten, or at least screamed at. Instead, the king laughed coldly.

"In love with who? The puny Welshman whom I've stripped of rank and thrown in the dungeon where he awaits his well-deserved execution for being a traitor? Tudor has landed twelve days ago and I vow he will not live to hear word of the usurper's journey." Elena felt as if she were about to faint. "'Twould be best if you forgot him. You will wed the gracious earl and We will hear no more argument from you. Furthermore, if you prove to be a reluctant wife in *any* aspect, We will charge you with treason and condemn you to death."

Elena closed her eyes and summoned every ounce of strength she had not to cry out at Gareth's imprisonment. Steeling herself to sound as innocent as possible, she said, "Nay, my king, I know nothing of this Welshman of whom you speak except that he escorted me to and from his father's keep in Wales. I am in love with the man whom my parents hoped I might marry since I was a child. When last he visited your court, I was overcome with such love that I forgot myself and gave him my virtue. Even now, his babe grows in my womb. Please, Your Majesty," Elena fell to her knees, hating Richard, but knowing she must play her part well if she were to escape with her life. "I beg you to release me from my engagement to this good earl who deserves a more suitable wife."

"Pregnant or no, you'll do as I say."

"Aye, but I won't marry her," Brackley broke in. "I'll not see my possessions passed on to another man's bastard."

Desperation evident in his voice, Richard said, "Then, good sir, take your pick of another of my ladies. There are many more beautiful than this fallen angel."

Brackley stood and said in a voice that was barely polite. "I am not certain I should do so--any one of them may already have given birth to a passel of brats. I will wait. In the meantime, I will return to my estate. I have been absent long enough on errands for Your Majesty and I am certain my affairs are lacking because of it." The earl left the room and in a flurry of motion, the king stood and grabbed Elena by the shoulders, pulling her upright and shaking her until her head snapped back.

"If you have cost me a battle for want of that man's soldiers, I will slit your smooth throat myself!"

"Your Majesty, I beg you!"

Richard pushed her from him and threw himself back in his chair. With an act of will that was physically evident, he regained control of his anger. "Pray forgive me, lady. The worries of the crown may push a man to actions he would not otherwise commit. I am even still learning to control my anger when people stand forcibly in my way."

Elena panted raggedly, praying that she would not hear her death sentence come from the king's lips.

After several seconds of silence, Richard turned back to her. "Do not look like a frightened rabbit, caught in a hunter's snare. You will live to see another dawn, though not in my presence."

"What does Your Majesty mean?" Elena whispered.

"You will pack your trunks and be ready to leave at first light. I am returning you to your parents. There you may marry your childhood sweetheart and bear him a passel of children. Frankly I care not what you do, as long as you are not in my sight. Thank your father and mother for your goodly service these past years and send them my wishes for a prosperous harvest time." When Elena remained where she was, shocked, he said, "Leave now, lady, lest I lose my temper again."

Curtsying quickly, she turned and fled. She ran through the main hall and out the large doors. She ran, heedless of those she brushed past or knocked over, and did not stop until she reached the small arbor where she flung herself on a wooden bench, tears streaming from her eyes. What had she done? Surely, she was relieved that she would not have to marry the repugnant earl. In fact, she was even glad to have been relieved as a lady-in-waiting. But what of Gareth? What was to become of him? Her hands shaking, her breath coming in frantic gasps, Elena realized that she was becoming hysterical. Digging her nails into her palms until the pain calmed her, she stood and began pacing beneath the shady trees.

Alright, she thought. I am safe. I will not see the king again, and as soon as Catherine and Margaret leave the room, I will pack my trunk. Now, what of Gareth? Elena's stomach clenched with worry at the thought of him in a dank dungeon, his spurs hacked off, facing death for his moment of indecision as to which man he would support as king. Didn't the fact that Gareth was here, training with Richard's other soldiers prove his loyalty to his king? Had Richard lost all sense?

Gareth must be freed. That was all there was to it. She would free him and together they would escape. They could go to France for a few years, perhaps until Richard died, and then they could return to Eyri Keep. The fact that she was no longer a lady-in-waiting to the king, that she was no one of any great importance suddenly dawned on her, and rather than feeling dismayed, she found tremendous relief in the fact.

No more would she have to worry about acting just so or pretending to like people she detested. Now if that foul Brackley came her way, she could turn her nose up and walk away. The new sense of freedom further resolved her to helping Gareth escape. Together they would begin a new life.

Brushing the now-forgotten tears from her cheeks, Elena began to plan their escape. They would need money, but she had plenty of jewels--surely enough to buy safe passage to France. Since Richard didn't want to see her again before she left, once outside the castle gates it should surely be no problem for her to change her destination. Once she freed Gareth from the dungeon, he could meet up with her down the road and they would head for France. Once there...well, once there Gareth would have to make some plans.

Accustomed to getting her way, Elena saw no reason why things wouldn't go according to her plans. Smoothing her hair and shaking out her skirts, Elena headed back to the main building. Once inside, she raced up a smaller back staircase and entered the room she shared with Catherine and Margaret. She prayed that she would not have to face Catherine again. Though she had found herself relieved to no longer be a lady-in-waiting, she did not think she could stand to see Catherine smirk and preen over the news. Nay, if she had to endure one spiteful statement from the brat, Elena felt sure she would not be able to stop herself from ripping every hair from Catherine's head.

Opening the door to their chamber as quietly as possible, Elena was relieved to discover it empty. She quickly rushed inside and threw open her trunk. Packing as carefully as she could, she crammed her best gowns and half of her jewels into the trunk. The rest of the jewelry, she placed in an embroidered pouch. She fastened the pouch under her full skirts and moved about to see if it was evident.

Satisfied that it was well hidden, she fetched her cloaks from the hooks on which they were hung. One of these she would have to sneak down to Gareth to help disguise him when he made his escape. Elena looked at both of them, trying to decide which would be the least conspicuous for Gareth to wear. With a sigh, she realized that neither of them would work. One was a rich red velvet with ermine lining and the other, though a simple dark blue wool, had gold couching covering every inch of it. With a sigh, Elena looked up. A thin grey cloak with a full hood hung on the farthest hook on the wall. It was the cloak Margaret wore when she visited the convent she soon hoped to join. It would be perfect, but--

The door creaked open and she started. When Margaret entered, she breathed a sigh of relief that it was not Catherine and took it as a sign that she should ask for the cloak. Before she had a chance to voice the question, Margaret spoke.

"Is it true you are to leave immediately? Tonight?"

"Is it tonight now? When last Richard spoke, it was merely before first light," she said dispassionately.

"It is true then?

"Aye, it's true."

"But why? You have long been one of Richard's favorites." Margaret walked closer and surveyed Elena's packed trunk.

"I have not been a favorite since I was in the company of a man not my husband or father for weeks."

"That is ridiculous. It was all well explained! Surely he would not send you away on a mere suspicion!"

"On no, that is only why I am no longer his favorite. I am being sent away because I refused to marry the Earl of Brackley."

"You did? But why?" Margaret's face pinkened. "I mean, I know of his purported cruelty, but I thought you were pleased with the new rank it would give you."

"I told Richard I could not marry Edmund because I was in love with another man. I even said I was going to have his child."

"Are you?"

"No. At least, I don't think so." Elena expected to see condemnation in the pious Margaret's eyes, but instead she saw something which surprised her. She saw compassion and...respect? Before her "adventure," Elena and Margaret had always been at odds, Margaret making no effort to conceal her disapproval of Elena's methods to gain favor and attention, and Elena scorning Margaret's avowals that a life in the church was the only way a woman could gain any sort of freedom. Now, Elena thought, I too see the uselessness of life as a lady-in-waiting, and court life, for that matter, where we walk on eggshells hoping we don't annoy the king and we agree to marry ugly old men just to gain a title or the king's favor.

Deciding to risk at least part of her plan, Elena drew Margaret to sit down in the sunny window seat.

"Margaret, there is another who would leave this castle tonight, but may be detained if he is recognized. May I use your cloak? I'm afraid you may not get it back."

"Of course you may have it."

"Are you certain?"

"It is a small enough affair. I shall scarce miss it."

"Thank you, Margaret! Here," she said, standing and retrieving her own two cloaks. "You must take one of these in return."

"No, no. That's not necessary."

"Well of course it is. It's only fair we trade cloaks. Now which one do you like? I think the red would look divine with your dark hair."

Margaret shook her head.

"The blue then? It would set off your eyes."

"Really Elena, it's alright. They are both beautiful--"

"Take them both, then." Elena held them both out.

"They are a bit too fancy for my taste. Besides you will need warm cloaks at your parent's home. It is near the Scottish border, is it not?"

"I will only need one cloak and so will you come winter. You know how drafty these halls become when that winter wind is blowing."

"I hope to be a novice nun at St. Mary's convent by wintertime this year. Such cloaks as these would be inappropriate to wear over my plain habit."

"Oh," Elena said, disappointed that her noble gesture was defeated. Brightening, she said, "Well imagine the altar vestibules this red velvet would make! And there must be enough fur lining to make warm slippers for all of the nuns. And imagine how virtuous the sisters will think you when you show up with this cloak and begin hacking it to bits."

Margaret laughed. "Elena, the convent is not like court. You don't have to make grand displays to gain attention and favor."

"Maybe not, but surely it will start you off on the right foot, won't it?"

The dark-haired girl laughed again. "Very well, Elena, I will take the cloak. Now, do you need further help?"

Elena paused. "Do you know where the dungeons are?"

"I've never been there, but I believe they are in the tower just north of the main hall. Royal hostages are kept in the upper rooms and common prisoners are kept below. Why do you need to know?" Margaret quickly shook her head. "No, never mind. Tell me not. I don't want to know. Just be careful, Elena. If you were to displease Richard again, especially with anything having to do with a prisoner, you would no doubt be executed. Richard has become easily agitated and very short tempered since the attack outside of Middleham. The king has recently learned that Elizabeth Woodville hired men to rescue her daughter so that Richard would not be able to marry her and gain a further stronghold on the throne."

"I know. Princess Elizabeth told me."

"Do you also know that Richard is convinced Henry Tudor will land before summer's end."

Elena started to ask Margaret what she thought of Henry Tudor, but they were suddenly interrupted by the entrance of Catherine.

"Oh my, you're still here? I would have thought you'd have slunk away by now."

Elena thought of half a dozen cutting responses to Catherine's gibe. The wickedest of them all was about to spill from her lips when she stopped herself. Deciding it would gall the simple Catherine even more to simply ignore her, she turned back to Margaret as if there had been no break in their conversation and said, "When do you hope to join the abbey?"

Margaret answered her before responding to Catherine who was still standing in the middle of the room, looking indignant. "The letter bearing my father's permission should arrive within the month. I hope to become a novice by the end of September. Catherine, dear, did you need something?"

"I need to change to a more appropriate gown. His Majesty has asked me to be one of the few who will join he and Earl Brackley as they hunt. I believe the earl asked for my company specifically. It seems he has broken his previous betrothal."

This last was said as Elena stood to leave. She gathered up the grey woolen cloak and headed for the door. Before she reached it, however, she turned and faced Catherine's malevolence with a cat-who-ate-the-rat-smile. "Actually, it was I who decided I did not wish to marry someone so old and repugnant as the earl. It seems you are once again gathering my leftovers, Catherine." Elena opened the door and swept out the small room as regally as a queen. She marveled again at Catherine's obnoxious personality change, but in truth, Catherine's about-face occupied her mind for a few seconds at the most. She quickly set her thoughts to getting to Gareth and freeing him. She had a tentative plan formed but she wasn't sure it would work if there were more than one guard on duty when she reached the north tower. Well, she would simply have to improvise, she decided. She had always been able to think on her feet; she would simply trust in her instincts to take over.

Rushing quickly down the back stairs normally only used by servants, Elena made her way around the kitchen to the buttery where the vats of wine and ale were kept. The room was dimly lit but, thankfully, empty. Elena scooped up a pewter tankard and moved to the back of the room where the best wines were kept. Although she had long resented some of the lowly tasks of being a lady-in-waiting, such as keeping the inventory of the buttery, she was now glad of the experience because she was able to move confidently through the gloom and open one of the strongest wines Richard had purchased from France, filling the tankard to the brim.

Draping the cloak over the heavy tankard, she quickly exited the buttery and made her way out the back kitchen door. Crossing the dirt bailey between the main hall and the north tower, she peered in the open door. Three men were sitting about a small table.

"Now what do I do?" she muttered. She was trying to figure out a way to get the men--or at least two of the men--out of the tower when she overheard Gareth's name being spoken.

"I can't believe Sir Gareth would betray the king," one of the men said. "He's always seemed like the most upstanding of all the knights."

A second voice spoke up. "The king sees ghosts in every shadow anymore. If Tudor doesn't invade soon, the king will have us all in prison for being traitors." There was a pause before the second man spoke again. "Do you know where they've put Sir Gareth?"

"Down in the old cellars. I wouldn't keep a dog there, but we've so many prisoners in here, he had to be put somewhere."

Elena sent an unformed prayer of thanks heavenward. Perhaps there wouldn't even be a guard! she thought hopefully. Shifting the heavy tankard and cloak to her other hand, she was about to sneak off when the third man spoke.

"Sir Gareth deserves to lose his head and he will by week's end. He's a traitor and a liar and you two will die with him if you don't stop slandering the king. Now get on with your duties. You've had more than enough rest."

Elena heard the scrape of stools against the stone floor and she quickly turned and ran as quickly as she could with her heavy burden. The last thing she needed was to be caught eavesdropping on the prison guards. Making her way back into the main keep, she wound through the labyrinth of back halls trying to find the stairs which led into the cellars. She had only passed by it once before since coming to Nottingham, being content to send servants on any unsavory errands.

With each corner she turned she grew more and more frantic. Suppose the king was angry enough to order Gareth's execution tonight? Suppose the executioner found the cellars before she could? With each step the tankard of wine seemed to grow heavier and her arm muscles trembled with the strain. She was on the verge of panic when she turned a corner and discovered the staircase. Taking a deep breath and trying to compose her face into a pleasant smile, she prepared to put all her skill at flirtation and flattery to work.

She descended the dark stairs, bracing her hand against the cold walls and ducking a low-hanging beam halfway down the steps. She finally emerged into the cramped cellars and wrinkled her nose at the unpleasant aroma which permeated the cold moist air. She glanced in the cell closest her and saw a sickly older man curled on the pallet, shivering and coughing in his sleep. A large grating sound behind her made her jump and she quickly whirled around, sloshing wine over her hand and onto the cloak. As her eyes adjusted to the gloom, she discovered the cause of the noise--a snoring guard propped against the wall.

God is with me this day, she thought. Perhaps I can free Gareth without this man even waking! Quickly setting the cloak and tankard down, she rushed from cell to cell, trying to find Gareth. She found him in the cell right in front of the sleeping guard. He was huddled in the corner of the cell, his legs pulled up against his chest, his arms wound round his knees and his head resting on his forearms.

"Gareth!" Elena hissed. "Gareth! Wake up!" Gareth didn't budge and fear seized Elena's heart. Glancing behind her to make sure the guard was still asleep, she turned back to the narrow window in the door and whispered louder, "Gareth! It's me, Elena!"

Gareth lifted his head suddenly, looking confused. When he realized who she was, he pushed himself to his feet and quickly crossed the few steps to the door. "Elena! What are you doing here? If you're caught--"

"Shh!" she hushed him. "I've come to free you. Gareth I..." she was about to tell him she loved him, but the unfamiliar words stuck in her throat. Swallowing, she chastised herself and drew to mind the picture of him being led to the executioner's block. That thought spurred her on and she said, "I--I love you, Gareth. I can't let you die." Slightly embarrassed, she took a step backwards, but Gareth's hand shot through the narrow window to grasp hers. He pulled her hand through the opening and pressed it to his lips, his gaze locked to hers, silently reaffirming his feelings for her.

The guard's loud snore was followed by several sharp snorts and Elena whirled around, staring at the man fearfully. He was waking up. "Damn!"

she mouthed. She had hoped to free Gareth without even awaking this gross ruffian. The man opened his eyes and then stumbled to his feet when he saw Elena.

"Who--where did--" As he realized that Elena was no common serving wench he bowed awkwardly and said, "My lady, is there something I can do fer you?"

Swallowing her grimace of disgust, Elena drew on her most flattering smile.

"You can tell me your name."

"Osgood, lady," he said with another awkward bow.

Elena forced herself to remember her objective and blinked her eyes coyly. "Osgood is absolutely my favorite name! You must think me terribly forward, but I've noticed you about the castle and--"

"*You've* noticed *me*, my lady?"

"Well of course. What lady wouldn't notice a man as strong and as handsome as yourself? It has taken me days just to discover where you would be on duty alone so that I might approach you."

Osgood stared dumbly at Elena while her words slowly sank in. It was evident when they did because a broad, half-toothless grin split his face. "Well aren't you a clever little thing to chase me down here!"

"Yes, and I've brought some wine that we might enjoy it while we get to know each other."

A frown creased Osgood's thick brow. "I ain't allowed to drink while on duty. Why don't you save it till after I get off? Say, after supper? We could meet in the stables."

Elena pouted prettily, her lower lip pushed out and quivering delicately. "But I shan't be able to get away then. And who knows the next time we might meet? Won't you have just a little? You're so big and strong, surely a few swallows won't impair your watchfulness." At the appeal in Elena's eyes, Osgood melted like a piece of fat over a fire.

"Well, of course a sip won't hurt me. Besides, how can I refuse a pretty little lady like you?"

"You can't, of course." Elena rushed to retrieve the heavy tankard of potent wine.

"You didn't happen to bring some bread or meat with you, did you? I haven't eaten since sunup."

Good, Elena thought. "I'm so sorry, it was all I could do to get my nerve up to bring wine. Next time I'll bring a whole tray of delectables for you."

"I don't want no delectables, just a meat pie or mayhap a fruit tart." Elena held her breath as Osgood took the wine and lifted it to his lips. He paused just before taking a swallow and said, "Next time, lady?" a disgustingly lurid smile on his lips.

Elena forced her nose not to wrinkle and instead smiled coyly. "Of course next time. How else are we going to get to know each other?"

"How else, indeed? And I'm hoping I'll get to know you real well!" He took a large swallow of the dark wine and smacked his lips. "I'll be damned if that ain't the best spirits I've tasted."

"Well take another swallow. I picked out the very best wine just for you."

"Maybe just one more. Then I better stop else I'll not stop and then won't we have fun?" His one more sip took him four swallows to down and when he lowered the pitcher, he blinked several times as if to clear his vision. "That's damn fine drink, lady. But how'd you come by it?"

"I work upstairs," she said vaguely.

Osgood took another swallow and then sat back down on the low stool that had recently served as his napping post. "Why don't ye set yourself down here with me and we'll get more friendly?" he said, patting his knee.

Before Elena could think of what to do, Gareth's voice behind her yelled, "NO!" She whirled around, surprised, but found Gareth was not looking at her. He was glaring at Osgood threateningly, which, she thought, was rather ridiculous considering he was unarmed and trapped behind a locked door. Furthermore, he was impeding her best efforts to free him. Before she could attract his attention and convince him that she knew what she was doing, Osgood stumbled past her and slammed a meaty fist against the door.

"Get back, ye dog. Ye're no knight, so I hear, and you'll not be frightening this lady who's come to see me!" Osgood swung around to face Elena and wavered on his feet. Grasping his head with one hand and the wall with the other, he paused for several moments. "Oh," he moaned, "I moved too quickly."

"Here," Elena said, grabbing his elbow and leading him towards the stool. As she moved the inebriated guard the few steps to his seat, she threw a meaningful glare over her shoulder to Gareth and mouthed the words, Be quiet!

She maneuvered Osgood onto his stool and then picked up the half-empty tankard. "Here, darling, take another sip--it will clear your head."

Osgood obediently gulped the wine and in a move amazingly fast for his increasing condition, scooped Elena onto his lap, his fingers digging firmly into her waist.

"Now, pretty lady, let's get to the 'knowing' part."

Striving to maintain her composure and prevent her revulsion from showing--the man smelled as if he slept in a sty with the hogs and what was left of his teeth were grey--Elena braced her hands against his chest so that he could not pull her closer.

"Why don't you have some more wine? I picked it out especially for you."

"I'm already half-way to drunk. Are ye trying to make me pass out?" His foul breath was hot in her face and Elena felt a draught of queasiness pass through her.

"Of course not, my dear one. It's just that I don't know when next I'll be able to bring you such a fine wine and I want you to enjoy every drop of this one."

"Well then," he said and belched, making no effort to divert the foul fumes from washing over Elena. "'Tis only fitting that you have some of this vintage. Here."

"No really, I--"

"Here," Osgood said more forcefully and Elena took the tankard, fearful what the drunken man would do if she protested further. Tipping the heavy vessel, she allowed the wine to touch her lips and then quickly lowered the tankard.

"You're right. This is delicious."

"Surely that's not all you're going to have," Osgood protested, shoving the tankard back to her. His clumsiness increasing, he sloshed wine over the edge of the pitcher and down the front of her dress.

"Oh!" Elena exclaimed. She longed to slap the man's face and then dump the contents of the tankard in his lap. Instead she said as sweetly as she could through clenched teeth, "I am not nearly as strong or large as you are and wine affects me dreadfully!"

"Good!" he leered. Then, as if suddenly struck by a thought, he leaned back and studied her face. "Ye know, here we are gettin' to know each other and I don't even know yer name."

Elena considered giving him her real name--after all, the man was no doubt too drunk to remember what she looked like, much less her name, but inspiration and caution struck and she said, "Catherine. Catherine is my name."

"And a beauty it is, too," Osgood toasted with another swig of wine. He lowered the tankard, peeked in it, and declared, "There's no point in leaving such a small amount, is there?" Elena shook her head, but she doubted if his question required a response since he was already tipping the tankard to drain the last drops of wine. Setting the pitcher on the floor, he wiped his mouth on the back of his hand and belched again. To Elena's great relief, this belch was mostly concealed behind his hand.

"Now, let's get down to knowin' each other," he said and wrapped his arms around her more tightly.

Elena panicked. He appeared nowhere near the verge of passing out and his behavior was rapidly getting beyond her control. Standing and twisting abruptly, she tried to disentangle herself from his grasp. His reaction, much slower than a few minutes before, was to grasp for her shoulder, but instead of grabbing the fabric of her gown, his fingers became entangled in the delicate necklace she wore. The fine chain snapped and slipped unheeded to the ground as she pulled back abruptly. She whirled around in time to see Osgood waver on his stool before landing on the ground with a grunt. The drunken man seemed surprised to find himself amongst the filthy straw on the cold stone floor, and unable to push himself up. Elena darted around him and snatched up the heavy pewter tankard. Inspired by fear and conscious that at any moment another guard might come to relieve Osgood, she swung around and brought the tankard down with a thud on his head. She gasped when nothing happened. Or rather, when something happened--Osgood slowly turned to look at his assailant. Elena wasn't sure she would have the temerity to bring the tankard down again. She breathed a prayer of relief when his eyes slowly rolled back and he sprawled further on the ground.

Taking a deep steadying breath, she tried to calm herself, only to yelp when a voice said, "Elena!" She was certain that she had been caught but quickly realized that it was Gareth who called her. She moved in a rush to the door of his cell but he stopped her. "The keys, Elena! The keys are on his belt!"

Elena leaned over the unconscious guard and groped for his keys. Her fingers finally felt the cold metal of a skeleton key and she pulled it free. There were three keys tied with a grimy strip of leather. The first key fit the lock in Gareth's cell door but refused to budge. The second opened the rusty bolt with a protesting screech. As soon as the lock clicked back, Gareth swung the door open and Elena ran into his arms. Their lips quickly met in a kiss filled with relief and passion.

Elena tore herself from their embrace to snatch up the grey woolen cloak. "Here. You must wear this so that we can get you out of the castle grounds."

Gareth needed no further prodding to hurry and he swung the cape around his shoulders as he followed Elena up the narrow stairs. When they reached the top, Elena gestured for him to wait while she peeked into the hallway to make sure no one was about. She heard men's voices and she quickly ducked back into the darkness, willing her heart not to pound so loudly. They were guardsmen! There was no doubt about it! She heard them complaining about their vigorous training schedule and, as their voices drew nearer, speculating if they would see any profit from the war with Henry Tudor. Elena turned to Gareth with questioning eyes. What would they do if they were caught here? Surely both their lives would be quickly forfeit.

The men passed by the dark staircase where she and Gareth were hiding and continued on down the hall, their voices growing fainter as they turned a corner. Hot relief flooded Elena's limbs. She felt Gareth push her forward and she quickly moved out into the empty passage. From the corner of her eye she saw him pull the hood up over his head as she led him through the maze of deserted halls until they reached the least used entrance to the main keep.

Once outside in the late afternoon sun, Gareth took the lead, pulling Elena after him as they darted to the stables. They paused behind the large stone and wood building.

"Gareth, what are you doing? You must get out of the castle grounds!"

"Not without Isrid. He's my only chance to reach Wales and Eyri Keep."

"No! You mustn't go there! That's the first place Richard will send men once he realizes you've escaped. This is what you must do." Elena quickly outlined her plan for him to meet up with her once she was outside Nottingham and escape to France. When she was done, she glanced around to make sure they had not been spotted. Turning back to Gareth, she was surprised and suddenly shy at the look on his face. "What?" she asked.

"Why do you want to go with me to France?"

Elena fidgeted. She was exceedingly uncomfortable with saying how she truly felt. Let her convince a man with flirting and coyness that she loved him--not like this, when she felt as if she were laying bare her very soul. Glancing around again only delayed the inevitable. She turned back to Gareth and forced herself to say it. "Because...because." She swallowed. "I love you," she blurted out.

Gareth's answer was to pull her as tightly to him as he could and crush her lips with a kiss that bespoke passion, acceptance, and longing. When the kiss finally ended, Elena was embarrassed and found herself unable to look Gareth squarely in the eye. Even when he tipped her chin up and softly called her name, she kept her eyes downcast. Only when he repeated the words he had first said two days ago did she look at him.

"I love you, Elena, and I would take you to the farthest ends of the known world if circumstances were different. But..." His voice was rough with emotion.

"But what?" Elena demanded. She was still a little unsettled at having spoken her true feelings.

"But I must return to Wales--"

"Why? That course is one of certain death!" she interrupted.

"No. I don't think Richard will waste the men it would take to follow me and I must reach Wales soon."

"Fine, then we will meet up and go together."

Gareth shook his head and traced the line of her cheek with a rough finger. "I can't take you, my love."

"Why not?" Elena demanded. This man made no sense at all. They finally declare their love for one another, she offers to give up a life of comfort and ease for him and he tells her no?

"I go to Wales to join Henry Tudor's troops as they gather."

Elena rolled her eyes and sighed. "Gareth! Not a fortnight ago you decided that the man had no claim to stand on and you wanted us to return to Richard immediately. Now you've changed your mind again?"

Gareth bowed his head and said contritely, "I must apologize to you, Elena."

"Why?" The day's events, combined with Gareth's quixotic responses was making her feel as if she were losing her mind.

"I never intended to fight with Richard. I only returned to learn what I could about his troop strength and his plans. I lied to you because I was afraid that you would betray our cause if you knew the truth."

Elena stared at him, her brow furrowing as what he said sank in. "In other words, you didn't trust me!"

"It wasn't a matter of trust--I just," Gareth pushed his hair out of his eyes and sighed. "You had no reason to care for Henry Tudor and I felt you would be safer if you simply didn't know what was going on, for there is every chance we will be defeated. I had to protect you and that was the only way I knew how."

"But if Richmond is victorious, I will be just another lady-in-waiting to be married off to appease some lord! Did that thought never cross your mind?" Elena's voice betrayed her rising hysteria and Gareth put his hands on her shoulders to calm her. Elena pushed his arms away and demanded a response.

"I did think of that possibility and I was hopeful that if I petitioned Henry, he would grant me your hand. For I do love you, Elena. I think I even loved you back when I hated you."

Elena refused to be appeased and was still furious for having been left out of Gareth's plans. "And what now? I am to travel this very night to my parent's manor, banished from Richard's court because I refused to marry Brackley."

Gareth stared at her, "Why did you do that?"

Elena stamped her foot and glared angrily at the sky. When she lowered her head to look at him, a tear spilled down her cheek, tracing a wet path. "I've already said it--because of you! Because I love you!"

"Ah, sweet." Gareth quickly pressed his warm lips to her. "It is best you return to your parent's home. You will be safest there, I think."

"And what of you? You ride not to safety, but perhaps to your death? And all while I sit in the country and twiddle my thumbs! This is not the first time I've saved your life, Gareth ap Morgan. The least you owe me is the chance to remain with you, perhaps help you again."

"There is nothing I would like better, my love, but I must ride treacherous terrain for I dare not get within a league of any traveled road. Though you have become an excellent horsewoman, I fear you will slow me too much in which case we might both lose our lives."

Elena stamped her foot again. How could she love such a man? Surely her reason had long since left her!

"If I live through this, I promise to come for you, Elena. I promise."

Still angry, she refused to answer him or meet his eyes. She heard him sigh and felt his hands on her upper arms. "Goodbye my love." He kissed her softly and waited for her to say something. When she remained stonily silent, he turned to go.

In an instant, he had disappeared within the hazy darkness of the stables. Suddenly drained, Elena collapsed against the rough wooden wall. She allowed her mind to go pleasantly blank until she realized that it would be very close to the time Richard had ordered her departure. If she were not calmly gathered and ready to go when her escort came for her, it would look suspicious indeed. Curse Gareth! she thought. He would put her in just such a predicament.

Pushing herself away from the stable, she rushed back to the main keep and hurried up the back staircase to her room. To her great relief the room was empty and she quickly smoothed her hair and washed her face. She had only just closed the lid on her trunk when a loud pounding on the door startled her. Taking a deep breath and willing herself to remain calm, she crossed the room and slowly opened the door. "Yes?" she said to the three men standing in the hallway.

The one closest her spoke up. "We have come to escort you to your father's home on order from His Majesty, King Richard."

"Of course, " she said pleasantly and stepped back to allow the men room to enter. "That is my trunk there. Let my gather my cloak and I shall be ready."

"The King did not say we were to take your trunk, lady."

Elena laughed, hoping the men did not detect the nervous hysteria in the sound. "Don't be silly. Of course I shall take my trunk. It contains all my clothes--you wouldn't want me to go without my clothes, now would you?"

The men looked at each other awkwardly and then two of them moved to retrieve the leather case. The third seemed to be suppressing a grin, but Elena paid him no notice as she quickly gathered her blue cloak and a cloth pouch in which she carried her small personal things. Without another glance back, she preceded the guards out of the room and down the main stairway. The few people she passed in the main hall fell silent and watched her as she made her way towards the huge door. Elena willed her warm cheeks to cool. She would not give these gossip-mongers the satisfaction of seeing her depart in disgrace. She would make it appear as if she were all too happy to be leaving Richard's court, which in fact, she was. Smiling and nodding at the gawkers, she walked slowly and gracefully outside where the huge, mangy horse she had ridden from Wales awaited her. The guards carrying her trunk loaded it onto the pack horse and then climbed on their own mounts, paying no heed to Elena who was waiting for assistance. The third guard--the one who had seemed to find the way she had handled the other two men upstairs amusing--hastened to help her onto the sturdy beast. He was tall and lanky and his brown hair, though short, was also lanky. A thin mustache and beard covered his face but did not disguise his friendly smile. His shoulders were narrow and looked bony even through his rough tunic but he swung her up onto her horse with little effort. Though he looked nothing like Gareth, something about the man reminded her of him. When she was settled, she smiled prettily at him and then gathered the reins. The helpful guard quickly mounted his horse and led the way towards the main castle gates. They rode through the opening in the thick stone walls and Elena breathed a sigh of relief. She had not had to see Richard, Brackley, or even Catherine. Within two days, she would be home. Though she had not thought of her parents much in the last few months, she now looked forward to seeing them and spending time in the peaceful quiet of her father's substantial library or the neatly tended gardens where flowers, fruits, and vegetables grew in neat, even rows and beds. Yes, in two days she would be home and she could only be happier were Gareth with her. No, not Gareth. He was an evil cad who constantly toyed with her emotions and reason! Elena pursed her lips and refused to think of him further.

Chapter 29

Gareth looked over his shoulder, fully expecting to see a contingent of armed men hot on his heels. He was pleasantly surprised to see nothing but hazy fields of wheat and flax dotted with an occasional serf or farmer finishing his tasks. The sun was just touching the horizon and when Gareth turned back to his course, its golden beams warmed his face and filled his eyes with their radiance. For all that it was a beautiful sight, he wished he were traveling any direction but west. The light in his eyes made it difficult for him to guide Isrid around obstacles. Shifting in the saddle, trying unsuccessfully to escape the blinding sunset, he trusted in his horse's ability to pick a safe path as they traveled through fields and forest. Luckily the sun would dip beneath the edge of the earth in just a few minutes. Then he would make quicker time-- until darkness forced caution on him again.

Unable to see exactly where he was going and therefore unable to concentrate on his path, Gareth's mind crept back to the image of Elena's face as she admitted her love. When she uttered those words, he could have cheerfully faced the executioner's blade, content that he had won what no man ever had. He lost all awareness of the hardness of the saddle, the discomfort of the sun in his eyes, even the worry that Richard's men where after him, prepared to present his head to their king as proof of Gareth's punishment. All those thoughts were lost as his lips tingled with remembrance of Elena's last kiss. She had offered to escape to France with him, leaving the comforts and wealth she had lived her whole life with. She had offered to travel with him, perhaps to certain death, across the country as he ran for Wales. Surely she had not made those assertions lightly. It had taken every ounce of strength he possessed not to agree to her mad plan. Even now his heart ached with regret that he had not done so.

Gareth pulled his mind from the recent past and looked to the distant future when the inevitable battle between Henry and Richard was over. If Henry won, Gareth meant to wed Elena. Since she had been dismissed from Richard's court and sent home. That meant she would not be around when Henry took possession of all of Richard's castles, and Henry would not have the opportunity to bestow her upon one of his more powerful supporters as a reward or marry her off to one of his adversaries in hopes of gaining an ally.

Gareth was uncertain of what his position would be in Henry's new government, but if he was not granted means which would provide for Elena and himself, he would return to Wales where he could at least offer her the comforts of Eyri Keep which would one day be his. Elena seemed to have grown fond of the rambling manor and he would do everything in his power to make it profitable.

As the sun slid halfway behind the horizon, Gareth's fond daydreams were interrupted by two unsavory thoughts: the first was the memory of Elena's fury when he had told her he had lied to her about his plans in Richard's court. Suppose she talked herself out of love while he was gone? He wished he could have had more time to explain, to diffuse her anger, but he had to make good the escape she had granted him. He only prayed he would be granted the chance to see her again, to right the wrongs that had plagued them since their first meeting.

Next thought was as disturbing as Elena falling out of love for him, if not more so. Suppose they did not win? Suppose Richard's superior troops--and if nothing else, Gareth had discovered that Richard had upwards of 10,000 troops he could rely upon--suppose they won? In their most hopeful estimates, Henry's supporters had only come up with 7,000 troops. There was certainly a very good chance that they would not only be defeated, but decimated to the last man, in which he prayed that Elena' father would find her a husband worthy of her, one who would not try to curb her strong spirit. That last thought made Gareth's stomach clench.

Before Elena had uttered her love for him, Gareth had resigned himself to watching her wed another man. He figured that she had only viewed their affair as a tryst to be forgotten once she married a man of rank. Now that he had her love, however, he could not bear the thought of another man with her.

The last rays of the sun finally sank beneath the horizon and Gareth found himself able to see where he was going. He spurred Isrid to a faster pace, grateful to have something to think of now besides losing Elena.

Chapter 30

Elena had spoken not a word to her escorts and she had no intention of doing so until they reached her father's manor. Though she strove to deny it to herself, her silence was not a result of the men being beneath her. She was too preoccupied with cursing Gareth and wondering just what she was going to say to her parents when she returned home.

The latter was easy enough. She could simply tell them that she had grown weary of court life. That was true enough. She could even go so far as to say she had lost favor with the king by refusing to marry an old codger of Richard's choosing. That was very nearly the complete truth. Either way, she was confident her parents would not question her return. In fact, she suspected her father would actually be relieved that she was no longer a lady--in-waiting. He had been hesitant when her cousin Sarah had offered to help her gain the court position. He had, in fact, tried to bribe her with several new gowns and a new palfrey if she would but stay at home to "keep him company in his old age." At the time, of course, she had longed to escape the gentle pace of manor living and the marriage hopes of a neighboring swain. Now she would revel in the peace of not having to constantly worry that she had been slighted for this favor or that, that her newest gown would be out of fashion before her allowance arrived, and any number of trivial subjects that had occupied her mind for the past two years.

That problem solved, the remaining hours on horseback were devoted to cursing the day she laid eyes on Gareth. Of all the gall! she thought. She saves his life not once, but twice and what does he do? He leaves her! Abandons her to what fate may await her and leaves. Not only leaves but scorns her love!

Her newly developed sense of fairness started to protest that he did not scorn her love, but she refused to have any of it. She offered to leave all luxury and perhaps live her life in danger and poverty (which, in Elena's mind constituted no servants and only two new gowns a year). What did he say in return? "I'm off to join the Tudor army. I lied to you about my original intentions and now that you've freed me, I'm going to leave you to Richard's men and run off to play hero."

Very well, she admitted, perhaps that wasn't exactly what he had said. That annoying sense of fairness gained a foothold and reminded her what Gareth <u>had</u> said: "I love you, Elena, and I would take you to the farthest ends of the known world if circumstances were different."

"Well it doesn't matter what he said, does it?" she muttered. "I'm still here and he'll no doubt end up dead by year's end."

"My lady?" the kinder of the three guardsmen said.

"Nothing," Elena replied abruptly, and then, since he had been polite to her while the other two men had been barely respectful, "I'm just talking to myself. How much longer must we travel tonight?"

"We shall reach a small inn before midnight and rest there until morning. With this full moon, we could travel all night, but the horses will need food and rest as, I'm sure, will you, my lady."

Elena said nothing but thought that she would not be able to sleep no matter how far they rode tonight. Her nerves were still taut from helping Gareth escape and worrying that her role in his escape would be discovered. She didn't think there could be a way of connecting her to him other than the guard, but he had become so drunk, surely he could not remember what she looked like. She did hope, however, that he remembered what name she had given him. She grinned in the darkness as she thought of Catherine being suspected of aiding a traitor. It would be no less than she deserved. Amazing, was it not, what court life could do to some people? Elena shook her head with disappointment. Poor Catherine had become the epitome of the manipulative, calculating and single-minded courtier. And in such a short time, too.

Blissfully ignoring the fact that until a month past, she could have put Catherine's actions to shame, Elena returned to her litany of curses against Gareth.

Chapter 31

"And you've no idea when you were set upon by these two large men?" Sir Jasper asked the bleary-eyed Osgood.

"I told ye, sir, I was on watch since dawn this morning. Since there's no windows down there, I've no idea if it was morning or evening, day or night. All I knows is that these two men came down and knocked me over the head. I only came to when my relief came on duty and that was not more than an hour ago. If ye look here," Osgood said, bending his head and pointing to the top of his head. "I've got the knot on my head to prove my story."

Sir Jasper scrutinized the increasing bump beneath the guard's greasy hair and asked, "Where, then, did this tankard, which smells like it had good wine in it, come from?"

Osgood swallowed visibly and shrugged his beefy shoulders. "I guess one of the men who attacked me brung it with them."

"So you didn't have even a sip?"

"Well, uh--"

Sir Jasper held up a hand and said, "Before you answer, Osgood, you should know that the guard who found you smelled spirits on your breath and spilled wine on your shirt. Are you sure you didn't merely pass out from drink allowing the prisoner to escape on his own?"

"No sir! I was knocked unconscious! See? Here's the bump I got. It still hurts, too."

"Yes, I've already examined it, Osgood. I'm sure it does hurt. But you did drink the wine, did you not?"

Not overly keen even when sober, Osgood's befuddled mind succumbed to Sir Jasper's gentle but insistent questioning. "Yes, sir, I did. I'd been on watch since dawn and I hadn't had a bite or drink all day."

"I understand. Where did you get the wine from?"

Clearly, Osgood had not thought of a response to this question, but one look at Sir Jasper's set face told him the man would accept nothing but the truth. "A lady."

"What lady? A serving maid?"

"No sir. She was a lady. She smelled really good and she didn't talk like a wench."

"Did this belong to her?" Sir Jasper held up the delicate necklace which Osgood had pulled off of Elena with his drunken clumsiness.

"I don't recall." Belatedly seeing a way to shift some of the guilt, he changed his story and embroidered it as well as his feeble imagination would allow. "Actually, I think I broke that when I was fighting her for the keys. Ye see, she gave me this wine and said food was on the way. I thought she was just a wench bringing me my dinner so I started to drink it. There must have been witchcraft in it because it was stronger than any wine I've ever drunk. Anyhow, when she saw it was affecting me, she grabs for my keys, but I tried to fend her off--that's when I must have broke her necklace. Then she pounds me on the head and knocks me out."

"I see," Sir Jasper said with a frown. "And I don't suppose you've seen her before or know who she might be?"

Osgood shook his head gingerly for it still throbbed. "As I said, I thought she was a new servin' wench bringing me my supper."

"I thought you said she was definitely a lady."

Osgood licked his lips. "Well, lady, wench, not much difference, eh?"

Sir Jasper pressed against his temples with the thumb and midfinger of his right hand. Dropping his hand, he returned his weary gaze to Osgood. "Do you remember what she looked like?"

"She was real pretty."

Sir Jasper waited for more information. When none was forthcoming, he prodded, "Her hair? Her eyes? Do you remember their color? How about the color of her gown? Surely you must remember more than that she was pretty."

"It's real dark down there and she did trick me into drinking that wine. But it seems..." Sir Jasper felt he could see Osgood's mind struggling to re-member. "It seems she told me her name. It was Clarice." Osgood shook his head. "No, but something like that."

Sir Jasper's patience clearly shortening, he said, "Very well. She's pretty and her name is something like Clarice."

The strain in the knight's voice was not lost on Osgood and fearing for life and limb--no one allowed a prisoner to escape in King Richard's guard--Osgood kept babbling. "No, it wasn't Clarice, it was...Catherine! That's it! I swear it on the grave of my father, whoever he may be. Her name was Catherine. She told me right before she hit me with the tankard. Her name was Catherine and she was really pretty and she smelled good. I think her dress was red and she had long silky hair," Osgood was obviously making up things now, so worried was he that Sir Jasper would have him flogged. "She was real fair, too."

With a loud sigh, Sir Jasper said, "You are dismissed, Osgood. Return to the barracks and do not leave until I grant you permission. If you remember anything else, send word to me immediately."

Osgood bowed awkwardly and backed out of the room, congratulating himself for having so cleverly gotten out of that mess.

In the small antechamber where he had questioned the simple-minded guard, Sir Jasper wondered what in all of England would have pos-sessed Lady Catherine to assist Gareth in escaping. Had she taken a fancy to the young knight? Sir Jasper didn't see how the two would have even come in contact with each other, but there was no accounting for the fancies of the young. What the king would do to the chit, he knew not. Shaking his head in pity for the no-doubt love struck lass, Sir Jasper rose and left the room to search out the king.

***

"Lady Catherine."

"Your Majesty," Catherine said with a deep curtsey. This was it, she thought. He was now going to tell her that she would become a countess as soon as her wedding trousseau could be prepared. She had been nothing but honeyed sweetness to Earl Brackley and she had no doubt he was well taken with her. She had even thought of a way to convince her new husband to allow her to remain at court for a while so she could lord her exalted position over the other ladies who had thought her a ninny since she first came to court, nine months before.

Smoothing her face into a pleasant expression that could instantly pinken with surprised pleasure at the news the king was sure to impart, she looked up into Richard's narrowed gaze. What she heard made her mouth drop open in an unbecoming gape.

"Lady Catherine, how is it that you came to help Gareth ap Morgan escape from Our prison this day? Do you not know that you have committed an act of most heinous treason?"

"What? Gareth who? Your Majesty, I--"

Richard slammed his hand down on the arm of his chair. "Do not toy with Us, lady. We are well enraged at your betrayal as it is. Where is Gareth ap Morgan? Has he left for France to meet up with the dog Tudor or is he headed for Wales?"

Though her legs were quaking with the effort to remain standing, Catherine cleared her throat and said, "Your Majesty, I humbly beg your forgiveness, for I do not know of what you speak. Who has escaped? What have I done?"

"That is what We would like to know." Richard's voice was hoarse with anger.

Sir Jasper stepped forward and without the king's permission, addressed Catherine. "Good Lady, were you in the lower chambers anytime today?"

"Heaven forbid, no! It's horribly nasty down there. Why on earth should I go there?"

"Would you mind telling us where you spent the day?"

"I was with His Majesty's entourage as he hunted! Remember Your Majesty? I rode with the Earl of Brackley? I was wearing a blue gown."

Sir Jasper turned to Richard for confirmation. Grudgingly, the king answered, "I do not remember seeing you with Us, but I did authorize your presence with Us."

Turning back to the nervous Catherine, Sir Jasper asked, "And what did you do upon returning to the castle?"

"I went upstairs to bathe and dress for the evening meal. Margaret was in the room, you can ask her."

"That won't be necessary." Pulling the broken necklace from his pocket, Sir Jasper asked Catherine, "Is this yours, my lady? A guard found it and thought he had seen it round your neck."

Catherine recognized the expensive piece as Elena's and was tempted to claim it since Elena would never be back for it. Her lingering fear over being barked at by the king stopped her. "No, Sir Knight. That necklace belongs to Ele--Lady Elena."

King Richard stood so abruptly and forcefully that his chair tipped backwards, crashing loudly against the stone floor. "Of course it does," he bellowed. "Why have you wasted Our time, Jasper? By now that conniving bitch could be anywhere. She's probably hooked up with ap Morgan by now and they are on their way to tell Tudor all they can about my troops!"

Catherine's eyes were wide with fear and surprise at seeing Richard nearly mad with rage. Bowing quickly, she backed out of the room as fast as she could. Once outside the room, she leaned against the cold damp wall and tried to stop her trembling. For an instant in there, she had thought to visit the executioner at dawn. Now that she was safely out of Richard's sight, she realized that his rage was directed at Elena and she smiled. Straightening from the wall, she began humming a tuneless song as she walked upstairs. Perhaps it does help to tell the truth, she thought.

<h1 style="text-align:center">Chapter 32</h1>

Elena was going to drop out of the saddle if the rode one more league. Was it but a few hours ago that she had thought she'd never be able to sleep? She now felt as though she could fall asleep in the narrow culvert that ran next to the moonlit road. "How much longer to the inn?" she asked wearily.

The two soldiers who had ignored her thus far looked at each other and then returned their attention to the road. The ever-polite guard--did he have a slight accent? Elena was too tired to decide--urged his horse up next to hers and said, "We should arrive any moment, Lady. Do you think you can last a few more minutes?"

There was a definite lilt to the man's speech, Elena decided. Not bothering to answer his question (after all, she had to go on whether she thought she could hold out or not), she posed one of her own. "Are you Welsh? Your accent reminds me of my recent visit there."

One of the unfriendly soldiers turned in his saddle and stared at Elena and the third man. Disgusted with his ill manners and physically exhausted, she did not suppress the urge to stick her tongue out at him. The rude man turned back around and Elena returned her gaze to her companion just in time to see him hide his look of unease at her question behind a broad grin. "I am from all over England, lady. I've traveled so much that I don't remember where I'm originally from."

"Well, you sound Welsh," she replied. "Though you are a bit taller than most Welshmen."

"There you have it. For I am indeed tall. Perhaps I'm a Viking. I understand they are a tall breed."

"So I've read. But they are also a large people and you are rather scrawny to fit their mold."

"Scrawny? Lady, you wound me to the quick!" He grabbed his chest and pretended to be injured.

Elena laughed and thought that, while he might have reminded her earlier of Gareth, he now seemed very much like Cynan. Suddenly realizing that she did not know his name, she requested it.

"My name is David, good lady, at your service." He executed a little bow and leaned toward her. In a conspiratorial whisper, he added, "And I am a good sight more fun than those two up there, as, I can tell, are you."

"Even though you escort a fallen favorite of the king's into exile?"

"The king's loss is my gain."

Elena laughed again and decide she would make it another league or so. Nonetheless, she was relieved when they came round a bend in the road and found the small inn perched beside the road. The windows were dark, but the brusque guards pounded on the wooden door until the innkeeper answered.

"We've need of rooms."

The old man in his nightshirt and cap rubbed his eyes and surveyed them.

"Now old man."

Elena wondered if Richard was aware that the training of his troops was greatly lacking in chivalry and patience. It occurred to her that lately, Richard himself was greatly lacking in chivalry and patience. The old innkeeper moved back to allow the men to enter and as David passed, he said, "Many thanks, good father. Though my comrades are too exhausted to say it, we are very sorry to wake you from your well-deserved slumber."

Elena, spurred on by David's courtesy, smiled at the surprised old man and added, "Yes, we thank you for your service." Again she was amazed at the response that small phrase seemed to evoke in people. First Annie the seamstress, now this innkeeper.

With white nightshirt billowing, the old man deposited the two surly guards in a dank room at the back of the inn and then showed Elena to a rooms upstairs. David elected to stand watch outside her door.

"We shall need to be on the road shortly after sunrise, so if we could have breakfast waiting for us, you will be well rewarded," David told the man.

"Of course, Sir Knight."

"Sir Knight? Ho I like the sound of that. But not me, cousin."

Elena smiled wearily at the old man as he passed back by her room and then she shut the door and collapsed fully clothed on the bed. She was asleep before she could even think of undressing.

***

Moments later, a pounding on the door woke her. She lifted her head from the lumpy pillow and forced her eyes to part. They were momentarily blinded by the bright sunlight which poured in the small, thick window. The pounding came again and Elena pushed herself up and staggered to the door. David burst in and quickly closed the door behind him.

"Lady, did you help free Gareth ap Morgan."

Still sleep befuddled, Elena said, "What?!"

David shook his head. "It doesn't matter. Either you are innocent and I must help you or you did help him and it will be my honor to help you."

"What are you talking about?" Though she whispered, panic made her voice squeak.

"More of the king's guards have arrived. They are outside waiting for the innkeeper to rouse our fellow travelers. They are here to haul you back to Nottingham to stand trial for helping a traitor escape." Elena began shaking and her eyes opened so wide they hurt. "Don't worry, Lady. Even now the innkeeper's boy is saddling our horses. We will be away before they realize what has happened."

"Why...why are you helping me?"

"Because I am indeed Welsh, my lady, known more often as Dafydd rather than David and I would not see Richard execute another person to satisfy his paranoia over losing the throne. Come now, and step quietly."

Torn between confusion and terror, Elena allowed David--no, Dafydd--to lead her out of the room and down the stairs. At the foot of the staircase, he paused and peeked around the corner. Turning back to her, he said, "They are still outside waiting. We must sneak out that back door where we will find our horses. Are you ready?"

Elena barely managed a nod but gathered up her skirts for the run. When Dafydd said, "Now," she bolted after him, ducking out the partially opened back door. A young boy closed it behind them and then gestured for them to follow him. They ran across the small patch of hard-packed dirt to the stables where their horses were ready and waiting. Dafydd quickly helped Elena into her saddle and then leapt onto his own horse. He swung his horse around, nearly trampling the young boy who was holding a sack.

"Here," he said. "Grampa put some food in here for you."

"Thank you, lad," Dafydd said softly with a grin. He scooped up the sack and led the way into a tall field of wheat behind the inn.

Her heart pounding with fear, Elena kicked her mangy horse to follow Dafydd's. They tore down row after row, sometimes trampling the tall strands of wheat. They were soon out of the field and Dafydd led them up a narrow wagon trail, casting worried glances over his shoulder from time to time. Afraid she would lose her balance and tumble to the ground should she risk a look behind them, Elena clung to her horse and concentrated on following as closely behind Dafydd as she dared.

After what seemed like an eternity, Dafydd led them into a cove of trees which soon turned into an ever-thickening forest. The weak morning sun barely penetrated the dense span of trees overhead and the horse's hooves made only a dull thud on the mossy ground. The palpable silence combined with the hazy light lent a sense of security and Elena slowed her horse. Dafydd also slowed his mount until the two horses were even.

"Is something wrong, Lady Elena?" he asked in a whisper. "No. I just thought we were far enough away to be safe."

"Safe from immediate detection, yes. But there were easily six soldiers sent by Richard. Combined with our two amiable traveling companions, they have enough to spread out over a goodly distance and track our progress. If it would not overburden you, I think it would be advisable to continue as fast as we can until the horses tire."

"Of course," Elena agreed.

He grinned his approval and spurred his horse to a faster pace. Elena followed suit and wondered to herself, Why couldn't Gareth have spoken so gallantly when he was dragging me through the Welsh mountains? Unbidden, his words of the day before popped into her mind. "I loved you even when

I hated you." Why on earth should he have ever hated her? With commendable self-deprecation, she allowed that perhaps she had been a trifle difficult, but that had been before she had, well, grown up. Elena paused in thought to hold onto the lip of the saddle as she urged her horse over an enormous fallen tree. Safely over, she returned to her musing.

Perhaps grown up was too strong a phrase. After all, she had not always been difficult, had she? It was just that living under the strain of serving as a lady-in-waiting may have caused her to be a bit...short-tempered. And in her position, she had to give orders, so if Gareth had taken offense, well, that was his problem.

What mattered was that once away from court, she had realized--er, remembered--that other people had feelings and that a person's lower position in society did not necessarily mean they were lesser beings. Elena shuddered as she thought of the Earl of Brackley. There was a powerful and prestigious man who was about as base and crude as the lowest serf. And then there was Annie, the seamstress from Aberstwyth, who had probably gone days without sleep so Elena would be pleased with her new dress. She was a dear, if a bit timid.

Elena took a deep breath of the dewy morning air and exhaled, feeling cleansed and refreshed, despite the danger surrounding her. It was good to be back to her old self, and it was no surprise that given her sweeter disposition, Dafydd was most chivalrous in return. Elena wondered what would have happened between she and Gareth had they not clashed so much those first weeks. If he truly had loved her then, perhaps he would have confessed it sooner and she might even now be mistress of Eyri Keep.

Well, she decided, there was nothing to be gained from might-have-beens. It was better to look to the future and wonder what it held for Gareth and her. Would he seek her out after the confrontation between Richard and Henry? Would he live to seek her out? No, she would not think of that possibility. Of course he would live--she willed it so and sweeter disposition or no, she was still as determined to have her will. Very well. If he did live, of course he would come for her and she would accept him only after making him grovel for forgiveness for abandoning her. There was only so much a lady could take, after all.

***

They rode through the seemingly endless forest for hours, the only indication of time passing was Elena's rumbling stomach for the forest grew no lighter than it had been in the morning, so dense was the foliage. When she thought she should faint with hunger, Dafydd finally stopped by a small spring and allowed the horses to drink and rest.

"Shall we see what the good innkeeper has provided for us to eat?" he asked as he helped her down from her horse and fetched the bag the young stableboy had given them.

"It could be dried beef and I would eat it, " Elena replied as she sank to the soft ground by the cheery, burbling stream.

Dafydd untied the leather thong that held the bag closed and peeked inside. "Looks like we have bread and cheese." Reaching into the burlap sack, he pulled forth a huge loaf of dark bread and a hunk of cheese protected in its cloth rind.

"I apologize for the lack of table linens--and tables, for that matter," Dafydd said as he presented the loaf to Elena with a flourish.

Elena laughed wearily while she tore off a piece of bread. Taking a bite, she reveled in the softness of the fresh loaf. "After the last month, linens and tables are the exception rather than the rule!"

"Traveled a bit, have you?"

Elena was surprised. Given that he had mentioned Gareth this morning, she had assumed Dafydd was well-aware of their adventures. "Did Gareth not get a chance to tell you all that we accomplished in such a short span of time?"

"Actually, I don't even know Sir Gareth. Well, I know *of* him, but I've never been introduced, and until he was thrown into the dungeon, I didn't know if he was a supporter of Henry Tudor or not. In fact, I'm still not sure if his job there at Nottingham wasn't the same as mine: to learn what we could of Richard's intentions."

"But I thought--"

"That since we were on the same side, we knew of each other's existence? No, that would have put both of us in danger if one were captured and tortured."

"Then you were there to spy on Richard?"

"In a nutshell, yes. But was that not your position?"

"I didn't even know Gareth was spying on the king. He told me he had changed his mind and decided to support the king after all. Even after I had saved his life and offered my help," she said with a frown.

Dafydd cleared his throat and shifted his weight from foot to foot. He paid particular attention to slicing a wedge of cheese and handing it to her before speaking. "I'm sure it was for your own safety. War and spying are not lady's pastimes."

"Perhaps not, but it seems I have been in the middle of it since the Woodvilles attacked Richard's entourage."

"It was the Woodvilles, then?"

"Yes, they wanted to help Elizabeth escape."

"I don't blame them. So, Richard has put you in the middle by hounding you for that information?"

Elena laughed. "If only it were that simple." In between bites of bread and cheese, she gave him a brief version of her travels through Wales, carefully leaving out those parts which had nothing to do with the conflict between the Lancasters and the Yorks.

"Had I a cap, I would take it off to you, Lady Elena. You have done more for Tudor's cause in a few weeks than I have seen since I left Wales last year."

"I've done nothing to help or hinder him. I've merely been dragged from one assignation to another."

"But you don't mean to tell me you support Richard?" he asked incredulously.

"Two days ago, I did not really care who was king. And since I have left Richard's court, I guess I still don't care whether he rules or a Lancaster rules. How much does it really affect the land? A few taxes here, some scant improvements there. I am more relieved that I will not have to fawn over the king and live with the cattiness of the other ladies-in-waiting."

Dafydd shook his head. "I suppose you are right in some respects, but does it not matter to you that--" He stopped himself and stared at a leaf on the ground for a moment. "Do you really see no injustices in England that should be corrected?"

"None that I know of," Elena said unsurely.

"In Wales, there are English priests in our churches, in our cathedrals. English lords dispense justice--their form of justice, not ours--and an Englishman is always given preference over a Welshman in any dispute. We have seen more Englishmen in Wales since Richard became king than I or my father can remember."

Uncomfortable, Elena shrugged and concentrated on eating. Trying to change the subject, she asked what their route would be.

"If we continue along this basic direction," he answered, gesturing with his chin to the barely discernable path they had been following, "we will exit the forest a few miles north of your father's manor. We can then backtrack on the main road and we should be safe from Richard's soldiers. It is my hope that they spent the morning searching for us and then gave up and returned to Nottingham."

Elena thought of the soldiers and then remembered the innkeeper and his wife in Wales. Her stomach clenching around her meager meal, she hoarsely whispered, "Do you think they will harm the innkeeper and his grandson?"

Dafydd was silent for a few seconds. "I--I don't think so. I told the man to act as though we had left in the middle of the night. The worst that will probably happen is that they won't pay their bill for their lodging and will no doubt demand ale and a hot meal for free since they are on 'king's business'."

"Perhaps I should have my father send money to the innkeeper to pay for our rooms."

"I paid him well before I woke you. I fancy he thought we were star-crossed lovers trying to escape your untimely marriage to a more worthy suitor."

Elena thought of Gareth and Brackley and wished that situation was the greatest of her problems. "How long do you think it will take to reach my father's estate?"

"Not more than a day longer than it would had we traveled the road. Through this forest, we travel as the crow flies, while the road tends to wind back and forth, traveling through each village. I expect we will arrive late afternoon tomorrow."

"How nice," Elena said. "More sleeping on the ground."

Dafydd flushed. "I'm sorry, Lady Elena."

Elena was instantly sorry for her sarcasm. Was it truly better to be constantly worried about other people's feelings? A month ago, she would have browbeat this poor man into finding her an inn--and a decent one at that. She sighed and said, "No, you misunderstand. Beds, like supper tables, have become a novelty for me. I shall feel much more at home out here under the stars."

Dafydd gazed at her skeptically and then helped her to her feet. "Well I am very used to straw ticks and pillows. I shall be very much put out tonight!"

Elena laughed and allowed him to lift her onto her horse.

***

They passed the night under the branches of a giant oak tree. As Elena eased herself down onto her thin blanket, she decided that, used to it or not, she still preferred the comforts of a real bed complete with sheets, pillows, and blankets.

The last time she had slept under the stars, she had Gareth to cushion the hardness of the ground. His chest had proved a most comforting pillow and his arms, though hard with muscle, were wonderfully satisfying to sleep in. She propped her head on her folded arm and squirmed about, trying unsuccessfully to find a position in which a twig or pine needle or stone did not poke into some part of her body. Through the last month of hard riding and strenuous exertions, her body had lost much of its soft roundness--roundness which had, a month ago, provided some relief from the hard objects she was now lying on.

Elena finally rolled onto her back and after some minor adjusting, found a fairly comfortable position in which she was neither poked nor jabbed. Her physical ailments temporarily abated, she allowed her mind to return to Gareth. She wondered where he was, if Richard's men were after him as well, and if he was thinking about her as much as she was him. In the drowsy state before sleep, she had no energy for the anger of the day before when she had cursed the day she had lain eyes on him.

Instead, she envisioned a few months into the future, when, the war between the roses settled and over, Gareth would ride to her father's manor. In her dream (was she dreaming now? it was hard to tell), his arm was in a sling and Isrid was coated with battle dust. But that endearing lock of hair was still in his grey eyes which were searching for her amongst the crowd of servants and family members who had gathered outside to welcome this brave warrior. Finally locating her, he swung off his horse and strode through the throng of onlookers (does he seem taller now? she wondered in some abstract part of her dream).

Upon reaching her, he sank to his knees, and Elena decided he was going to beg her forgiveness for abandoning her and plead for her hand in marriage. He opened his mouth to speak, but instead of words of love, blood poured from his mouth. She screamed as Gareth pitched forward and she saw the feathered shaft of an arrow protruding from his back. She glanced up to see Cynan holding a bow. "Traitor!" he yelled. "She's a traitor to the Welsh and she serves Richard! Richard who--"

Elena awoke with a start, her eyes not seeing the predawn light of the horizon, but instead Cynan's angry face screaming at her. Unclenching her hands which were twisted in her skirts, she realized she was drenched in sweat. She wiped her brow with the cuff of her dress and took a shaky breath. She glanced over to Dafydd and saw him sleeping peacefully a few feet away. Willing herself to relax, she stretched out and forced her mind to act rationally. In the first place, Gareth and Cynan were close friends, raised together since they were babies. In the second place, she had never seen Cynan exhibit the least bit of temper, much less anger, so her mind must have conjured someone else's image and Cynan was just the first name she thought of. Was she a traitor to the Welsh? She had only recently begun to acknowledge the fact that Welsh blood ran in her veins, that her mother had been born and raised in Wales.Furthermore, she had only the day before learned the exact details of Richard's unjust treatment of the Welsh from Dafydd. Besides, what could she as a woman do? War was men's business--they were the ones who started them, let them be the ones who ended them. Elena's well-honed skill at rationalizing her way out of responsibility gave her cold comfort that morning. Though she was no longer shaken by her bad dream--and after what she'd been through lately, who could blame her from suffering nightmares?--she was unable to return to sleep and instead watched the horizon through a narrow break in the trees as the sun rose, bringing warmth and dispelling shadows.

Before long, Dafydd stirred and rose groggily to his feet. Not realizing she was awake, he stumbled past her into the trees, his eyes mere slits in his face. By the time he returned, Elena had folded her blanket and retrieved two slightly bruised apples from the bag the innkeeper had given them. She handed one to the still-befuddled Dafydd and he plopped down on the ground to eat it.

"I'm sorry," he said when he had devoured it. "I'm not very good at waking up in the mornings." Pushing himself to his feet, he began to saddle the horses. Elena collected his blanket and the food bag and stuffed them into one of the packs on his saddle. By the time they were ready to travel, the sun had taken the chill off the air and Elena's nightmare was but a scant memory in the back of her mind.

They rode at a brisk pace through the edges of the forest, stopping at midday to water the horses in a shallow pond and then continuing on . By late afternoon, Elena's stomach was loudly reminding her that a mere apple was not sufficient food for the pace they were forced to keep.

"Dafydd, we really must try to find something to eat. I am near faint with hunger. Surely we can venture to the road by now."

Dafydd turned in his saddle and gave her an apologetic smile. "I'm sorry, Lady Elena. I'm afraid I've not proved a good escort in any respect, have I? First, I make you sleep on the ground without so much as a pallet, and now I starve you to death. Unfortunately, we would have not have had what little food we've eaten were it not for that good innkeeper. If you can make it a few more hours, we should be safe to leave the forest. There should be an inn or village where we might beg some food."

"Beg?" Elena asked, aghast. "Why beg?"

Dafydd looked even more sheepish. "I'm afraid I gave the last of my coin to the innkeeper for helping us escape."

Elena felt amongst her skirts and found her pouch which contained her few jewels and what small amount of coin she had left. "Find us food and I will take care of the bill," she said imperatively but with a small quirk of a smile.

Dafydd bowed awkwardly in the saddle. "As you command, so shall it be."

He spurred his horse to a faster pace and led them in a more westerly direction. Within the hour, they had emerged from the trees and made their way across rough fields until they located the road. This far north, the road was but a narrow path of dirt and rocks, but once on it, the horses did not have to pick their way through bramble and fallen logs and they were able to make much better time as they doubled back to the south and the small village just north of her parent's estate.

Chapter 33

They entered the small village of Swansonbury at dusk and Elena quickly led the way to the tiny inn which boasted only two rooms for let and three small tables in its dining room. The smells wafting on the peaceful summer's eve air made Elena's mouth water and her stomach growl in eagerness for a good meal. She dismounted without help and as soon as she felt the circulation return to her legs, she strode to the wooden door and pushed it open. The room was narrow and long. The ceiling was low and the floor, dirt, but the walls were whitewashed clean and the small tables were neatly arranged in the room. A sturdy wooden table was propped against one of the walls and upon it were several large pitchers of what Elena assumed to be ale.

Her reception by the innkeeper and his wife was polite if a bit awestruck. Elena ordered a huge meal and paid them handsomely for it. The innkeeper stammered at the amount in his calloused hand and insisted she must stay the night.

"It will be long dark by the time you arrive home. You are more than welcome to stay here as our honored guest and ride out in the morning."

Elena considered his offer. She was exhausted, more so now that she had a full stomach and to simply lie down and sleep for hours and hours sounded like heaven. But something, some worry niggled at the back of her mind. It spurred her on to continuing home.

"I thank you for your hospitality, but I've been absent too long. I wish to return home as quickly as possible. Besides, it won't be but another hour on horseback."

"Of course, Lady, of course. Safe travels!" he called out as she and Dafydd quickly climbed atop their horses and headed down the single narrow road of the town.

***

Though it had been well over a year since she had last traveled the road from Swansonbury to her father's large wooden manor, there was not much chance or their becoming lost. The road forked about two miles south of the village: the eastern fork leading back to Nottingham and the western fork leading directly to her home. They were also graced with a full moon which rose early to spill its cool, crisp light and allowed them to proceed at a rapid pace down the pocked road.

Though she had long scoffed at superstitions of any type, Elena could not quell the nagging worry that something was wrong. She jumped when an owl hooted to her right, and turned quickly, half-expecting to see Richard's men bearing down upon them. After several minutes, Dafydd seemed to pick up on her skittishness for he asked her quietly, "Lady Elena, is something amiss?"

She studied his face in the pale light. She felt foolish, alright, but the Welsh were a superstitious lot, weren't they? After all, Gareth had told her of his premonitions. Perhaps Dafydd would understand. "I--I don't know. I just have this very odd feeling that something is amiss. I'm sure I'm just being silly, but..." she trailed off and shrugged her shoulders, trying to make it appear as if she weren't really worried.

In response, Dafydd scrutinized their surroundings and nudged his mount closer to hers. "Silly feelings have saved my life more than once."

They continued down the road in silence and Elena was relieved to see the fork in the road up ahead. When Dafydd looked to her for direction, she gestured with her chin to the western road. Elena decided that her "feeling" had indeed been a simple case of overwrought nerves.

"There is a hill in front of us so we won't be able to see the house until we crest it," she explained. Dafydd nodded in response and they urged their horses to a faster pace. The short climb up the hill which normally seemed to pass in a few seconds seemed interminably long tonight and Elena attributed it to her exhaustion and earlier worries.

When they finally did reach the top of the shallow hill, she smiled and prepared to sigh in relief. There just ahead was the manor--or what should have been the manor. Instead lay a pile of rubble, smoke still pouring from recently burnt beams, scorched timbers cracking as they continued to tumble to the ground. The breath she had taken to sigh was caught in her throat and her eyes widened until they ached. "Father!" she screamed, except it came out as a cracked whisper. She kicked her sturdy horse as hard as she could and set off down the hill.

"Lady Elena!" Dafydd called out after her. "No!" He quickly caught up with her and grabbed the reins from his hands. "This was no doubt the work of Richard's men and they may still be about." He glanced quickly around and then urged his mount into the small orchard just off the road, dragging the reins to Elena's horse behind him. He quickly leapt off his horse and reached up to drag Elena down. She fell off her horse and into his arms.

"Father, my parents...I have to find them," she said.

"We will," Dafydd assured her. "But first we must make sure that Richard's men are not still here awaiting your return."

Elena nodded and tried to gain hold of her panic. Dafydd wrapped both sets of reins around a tree branch and said, "Wait here. I will go see if anyone is about."

"No!"

"What?"

"I will go with you."

"But--"

"Dafydd, if Sir Gareth were here right now, he would recognize my tone of voice as one which means I will not be refused." Just mentioning Gareth made Elena feel better and she stared at Dafydd meaningfully.

"Very well, Lady. I imagine Gareth could tell me quite a bit about knowing you."

Under normal circumstances, she would have been mightily offended at his meaning, but now she simply said, "Aye, and I only hope we all live that he may know me further."

Dafydd offered her his hand and she took it as he led the way through the trees. Even in the midst of the orchard, the acrid smell of smoke overpowered the sweetness of the apples which covered each tree in abundance. Elena choked down the bile that rose at the thought of her home destroyed and forced her mind to wonder where her parents were. Surely they were not dead! Surely they had escaped. Finding no relief in thoughts of her parents as they stumbled over tree roots, Elena instead turned to the men responsible for destruction. That they belonged to Richard, she had no doubt. She had oft enough in the last year seen Richard become so enraged as to lose his grasp on logic and order something which he later regretted. He could have easily fined her parent's heavily for her actions; or better yet, stripped the estate and all titles from them. Instead he had no doubt ordered a troop of men to ride their horses into the ground to reach her father's home so quickly.

The more she thought of the whole scenario and the more she choked on the smoke from her family home, the angrier she became.

No, she thought, angry wasn't the ride word. Though she'd had little experience with her present emotion, she knew it to be rage. Rage that grew and tinted her vision red as she and Dafydd continued to push through the thick orchard. Rage that gave strength to her exhausted muscles and pushed her forward until she was leading Dafydd. Rage that did what her newly discovered pride in being Welsh could not: it made her turn firmly and wholeheartedly against Richard of York.

No longer was she ambivalent to whoever wore the crown of England. Though she was but a young woman with, now, little or no wealth, she would do all in her power to drag him from throne. And if she discovered that he had found and killed Gareth, she would not rest until she had--

They had reached the moonlit clearing before the house. Dafydd insisted she remain in the protective cover of the trees and Elena did not argue. She watched as he silently crept across the ground, blending in with the shadows. He climbed over the rubble that had been the sturdy walls and disappeared amongst the blackened ruins of her home.

Elena strained her eyes trying to see what had become of Dafydd, strained her ears trying to hear something other than the cracking of scorched timbers.

She whirled around at a rustling behind her but it was only Dafydd, returning through the woods.

"My parents. They are–"

"Come, my lady. Let us return to the village. I promised you would sleep in a bed tonight, did I not?"

"No! My–"

"They are dead, my lady," Dafydd said as gently as he could.

Elena's knees buckled and Dafydd caught her as she sank to the ground. "I am sorry, Elena," he whispered.

***

Sometime later in the innkeeper's cleanest room, her tears exhausted, Elena longed for Gareth, longed for his arms to comfort her, his shoulder to lean her weary head upon. Where was he tonight? Was he dead too? No! That she would not accept. She rolled onto her back and wiped the tears from her face. She did not know where Gareth was now, but she knew where he would be soon. He would be at the battle between Richard's forces and Henry's. Very well, then. So would she.

Chapter 34

On the outskirts of Lichfield, Elena and Dafydd stopped and made camp. They had traveled at a breakneck pace since hearing of Henry Tudor's landing and subsequent march to the heart of England.

"Wait here until I determine who holds this town."

Elena nodded but said nothing as he turned to leave. She unsaddled her horse and set about gathering firewood. She stared into the small blaze and absently ran her hands through her cropped hair, mourning its loss only briefly. She felt as though she had aged a lifetime in the last week and the fact that she had needed to cut her beautiful hair to pass as a boy was of little consequence.

Nearly an hour passed before the Welshman returned.

"Neither man holds Lichfield. They are gathering near Market Bosworth, halfway between here and Leicester. They will no doubt come to battle on the morrow." Disappointment was evident in Dafydd's voice. "There is no way we can arrive before the battle is over. The day is spent and they will surely fight come dawn's first rays."

"Then let us travel all night."

Dafydd shook his head. "No. You are exhausted. My humble presence will not determine the course of the battle one way or the other. We will leave at first light."

Elena ignored him and rose to saddle her horse. "We leave now."

"My lady," Dafydd said with a chuckle. "Sir Gareth is either the strongest-willed man alive or the most hen-pecked!"

"I'm sure he would say both," Elena said with her first smile in days.

***

The dawn broke brilliant and clear over the horizon. Elena and her escort rode unaccosted into the Tudor camp after one of the Welsh sentries recognized Dafydd. Dafydd left her with the pages and squires who were too young to fight.

"For your own safety, my lady, please stay here. I would not wish to face your Sir Gareth should aught happen to you."

"Go with God," Elena replied, though she had no intention of obeying him. She must find Gareth, must see him before he took the field in case this battle was–no, she would not consider his death.

Elena took off in the direction Dafydd had taken. Surely he sought the Welsh troops. She could just see his head bobbing as his loping gait carried him through the somber men who prepared for battle. Though the morn was clear and sweet, there was a heaviness in the air that prevented the usual morning banter and laughter. Men would die today, Elena thought. Perhaps these very men. Elena crossed herself. So long as it was not Gareth!

A troop of squires leading their knight's warhorses crossed between her and Dafydd. She jumped to keep sight of his head, but all she saw were muscled withers and flanks, streaming manes and tails.

When the horses had passed, Elena ran to catch up with Dafydd, but he was nowhere to be seen. Frustrated, she tugged at her cropped hair. Where could he be?

"You there, boy!" A large hand grabbed her shoulder and swung her around. "Do you not heed your master's call?" A slender blonde man scowled at her. He was long of chin and broad of brow, but handsome, nonetheless. But for his helm he was fully armored.

"You are clearly too young to be fighting. You are not trying to sneak onto the field, are you? Where is your knight?"

"Sire," a man panted as he ran up to the blonde man. "Lord Stanley yet awaits with his troops. He did not heed your summons, but neither does he join Richard's men."

The blonde man's mouth twisted wryly. "He no doubt waits to judge who will emerge victorious before committing himself. Send word to him that we will await his leisure amongst the bodies of Richard's men."

The messenger appeared confused but obeyed. "Yes, Your Grace."

As the blonde man turned back to Elena, she suddenly realized who he was and sank into a curtsey. Belatedly realizing that young boys did not curtsey, she continued down to the ground, affecting a faint.

"Hold, there," Henry Tudor said as he bent to help her up. "Are you ill?"

"Nay, sire. Only...only hungry. 'Tis been a while since I've eaten."

Henry frowned. "You've not eaten and you wander unarmored through the ranks. I will have words for your knight. Who is master of your household, boy?"

Elena thought frantically. She was about to name Gareth's father, but did not want to gain him trouble from the would-be king. "I belong to no household, sire. I only sought to...to help Your Grace in any way possible."

Henry rumpled her hair and smiled indulgently. "'Tis very brave of you." He glanced up as his trumpeters called his men into formation. His squire waited as his elbow to hand him his helm. "You can help me most now by staying alive. Should I emerge victorious this day, I will need such devoted men as you. Join my pages with the baggage. You will be safe there."

"Yes, your grace," Elena said, bowing and backing away as quickly as possible. There was no way she would be able to find Gareth now, with thousands of men moving toward the battlefield. She began to make her way to the back of the lines but was swept forward by the rush of troops.

"Let me through!" she cried, but her plea was lost in the battle cry of thousands of men. She made small headway before being swept forward again. Without knowing how, she found herself at the crest of the hill. She glanced down and gasped.

The battle had begun. The archers were exchanging volley after volley of arrows, the Welsh easily discernible with their longbows which wreaked havoc in the enemy's line. The man beside her was struck in the throat by a stray, lucky shot. Elena screamed and redoubled her efforts to push her way through the line. "Let me through, I say. By order of his grace, Henry Tudor."

That had some effect and Elena was roughly pushed to the back of the lines. Bruised and feeling as though she had fought a battle, she collapsed on the trampled ground to catch her breath.

She returned to the baggage line where the pages were pretending to fight their own battles with tree-branch swords.

Several of the pages tried to get her to join in their games, but Elena refused, curling up on the ground beneath a cart. She prayed with a devotion she had never felt as the minutes slowly crept by.

To her surprise, she awoke sometime later. Terrified that she had missed something, she scrambled out from her hiding place.

"I tell you, the battle is over!" said one of the pages.

"Our orders are to remain here," argued another.

"And miss our share of the bounty? I think not!" the first boy said and left with a small group for the ridge. Elena hurried to keep up with them and thus had her first view of the aftermath of the battle.

In a small field which would have barely held a flock of sheep, ten thousand men had met in fierce combat.

There was not an inch of ground that had not been trampled, turned, or bloodied. The lush grass was flattened and torn to a matted pulp on which the dead and wounded cushioned their heads.

Everywhere she looked, one gruesome sight or another met her eyes. Bodies were hacked beyond recognition, laying haphazardly where they fell, some on their backs where they gazed sightlessly at the bright blue sky overhead, others face down in the trampled dirt which a ceaseless flow of blood had turned to mud. Moans of tortuous pain reached her and she saw trembling hands lifted, voices begging for help.

The battle was definitely over, she thought a bit wildly as she choked down the bile which rose at the sights and smells assailing her. But who had won? She saw men held prisoner in small groups by soldiers with pikes and swords, but whose men were they?

A shout drew her attention across the small valley she saw a man pulling something from a cluster of bushes. Elena squinted and saw the light reflect off the objects shiny surface. The crown of England! she thought. Wide eyed, she watched as the man strode towards a small group of men in the center of the field. The man approached the group and bowed as a tall blond man stepped away from the crowd. The blond man took the crown and held it in the air so that all could see it before he set it firmly on his head. Elena exhaled with relief. That was not Richard, but Henry Tudor, now King of

England. So intrigued was she with what was going on below her that she shrieked in fear when a man on horseback rode up to her.

"Sweet Mary, but you frightened me!"

The man laughed and gestured with his chin to the center of the field. "And you frightened our new king with that scream."

Elena turned and saw Henry shaking his head and laughing with the men around him. He gestured for her to join him.

"Well lad, it seems you did not obey my orders to stay with the baggage."

Elena's eyes widened. Had she truly crossed the king? "Forgive me, your grace, but I seek a friend."

"Am I not your friend?" he joked with the intense joy of one who had gambled everything and won.

"Of–of course sire..." Elena did not know what to say.

"Go on then and seek your friend." Elena turned to leave. "Boy!" Henry called and something in the way he said it made her realize he knew she was not a boy. She turned around, but Henry only winked at her.

She felt her face warm but her embarrassment was quickly forgotten as she resumed her search for Gareth.

Twenty paces behind the king, crouched on the ground were Gareth and Bryant. "Gareth!" she called as she pushed past her father and began running towards him. Gareth lifted his head wearily, but when he saw her, he quickly pushed himself to his feet and lifted her off the ground as she flung herself at him. His arms crushed her body to him and she reveled in their strength. He was alive and unharmed! Her heart sang with the news and as soon as he lowered her to the ground, she grabbed his head and forced it to hers so that she might see his face. What she saw astounded her.

Gone was the boyishness that had been present even in their most intimate and most dangerous times. That unruly lock of hair which was forever getting in his eyes was held off his forehead with clotted blood. Sweat and grime drew harsh lines around his eyes and mouth and his eyes looked weary beyond his years.

Elena's heart constricted with grief and worry for him. As he turned and led her to where Bryant was still crouched on the ground, she realized the cause behind his inexplicable sorrow.

Lying in a pool of blood from the huge gash in his midriff, Cynan lay quietly. His head was cradled in Bryant's lap and his friend's tears had washed clean the craggy face. Bryant and Gareth had closed his eyes and smoothed the hair back from his brow and through her tears.

Elena wondered that Cynan should look so peaceful in death. Choking back a sob, she pressed her knuckles to her lips and looked to Gareth. His own eyes were dry but filled with a grief so terrible it made her weep all the harder.

"Oh Cynan," she said, crossing the few feet between her and his still form. Heedless of the tears which flowed down her cheeks, she knelt beside him and with shaky hand, reached out to caress his forehead. She gasped to feel it was still warm and made her wonder if perhaps he yet lived. She raised hopeful eyes to Bryant's face but he only shook his head. Her voice thick with tears and sorrow, she whispered. "I shall miss you Cynan. Who will tease Gareth about his bad manners the next time he tells me I'm selfish? Who will make me laugh when I've just swallowed a bug from sleeping on the ground?" She inhaled sharply, trying unsuccessfully to stem her flow of tears. "Who will boil that dreadful dried meat for me and serve it as if it were roasted venison? Who will--" her voice broke again, "who will take care of Enid? Oh Cynan!" Unable to control her grief at her first loss of a friend, she hunched over, crying. She felt strong hands grasp her shoulders and lift her to her feet and when she lifted her face, she saw Gareth's moist eyes before he drew her to him in a crushing hug. She returned the embrace just as fiercely and begged God's forgiveness that she was thankful that Gareth had not been the one to die.

By the time Gareth released her, she had gained some control. She wiped the tears from her face and asked Gareth, "What will we do with him?"

"We will have to bury him here," Gareth said.

"No!" Bryant shouted. "We must take him back to Wales, to Enid!"

"How, Bryant? In this heat? And would you have Enid see him dead with a babe on the way?" No! Let her remember him as he was, alive and smiling. Let us remember him that way with her."

"But to bury him here, so far from home with these English!" Bryant cried.

Gareth knelt down and grasped his friend's shoulders and Elena could see the physical effort it took him to prevent the tears from spilling over his lids. "His body only will remain here. His spirit is already with Enid and their unborn babe in Wales. It flies to the top of the Eyri mountains even while we bicker her over his remains."

"He will have a Christian burial befitting a hero of Wales."

Elena started at the voice behind her and turned to see the new king standing behind them.

"I hope this was not the friend you sought," Henry said, gesturing to Cynan.

Elena shook her head no.

Henry looked to Gareth who held her hand. "This man and all the others will be seen to with respect and gratitude for their ultimate gift to England.

"As for you, Sir Knight," he said, gesturing to Gareth, "I understand your spurs were hacked off by my predecessor." Without waiting for a response, the new king continued. "Clearly, you are a noble and chivalrous man, worthy of much more than the title of Knight, but since I have nothing else to offer you, I would at least reinstate you to that position."

"I thank you," Gareth said hoarsely.

His attention clearly moving on to the next subject, Henry Tudor said, "Tend to your comrade," as he turned to leave.

***

Though the evening was not chilly, Elena was glad for the warmth of the campfire around which sat the Welshmen. Watching the yellow flames lick hungrily into the dark night seemed to cleanse her mind of the horrors she had witnessed today. The soft blue of the fire that quickly ate the dry wood seemed to warm the chill of Cynan's death and Elena felt herself relax. Gareth sat beside her on the hard ground, his hip and shoulder touching her own. Heedless of the others or what they might think, Elena laid her head on his shoulder and sighed when he rested his head on top of her. She felt as though she could remain in this position forever, even through the discussion of the day's battle.

"When it looked as though Stanley was not joining us, I thought we were lost," Dafydd said.

"Aye," Gareth's father agreed. "And I thought he had set us up in Aberstwyth with all those instructions."

"Why did he hesitate?" one of the archers asked.

Morgan shrugged but Gareth said, "Richard did hold his eldest son as hostage. Perhaps he only sought to wait until Richard would be unable to send the order for his death."

"I heard that when Richard threatened Stanley's son unless he joined supported him on the field, Stanley sent back word that he had other son's," Morgan said.

About the cozy circle of the fire, men smiled grimly at Stanley's bravado. Elena reflected that they were only smiling at the careless words because the young man had not been executed.

"Well, for all that he was a devious man in his life, I will go so far as to say that Richard at least died well, as a king should," said a Welshman Elena did not know.

The men nodded in agreement as Gareth added, "Many men in Richard's place would have allowed themselves to be taken hostage in the hopes that they would be allowed to live. Richard did at least have the dignity to go down in the fight."

"And took several excellent men with him," the Welshman said.

Elena tilted her head to look at Gareth but his gaze was lost in the fire. She watched the light and shadows play against the strong planes of his face, in the stubble which covered his square jaw, in the gray depths of his eyes. He must be thinking of Cynan, she thought. His father's voice pulled her attention back to the conversation.

"And now it is time to rebuild this country."

"Enid must rebuild her life," Bryant said bitterly.

There were several seconds of silence at his words but Morgan declared an end to the mourning when he said, "But for now we must rebuild this fire so that we may cook this enormous pig King Henry has sent." Three men behind Elena and Gareth came forward carrying great logs and they quickly stood and moved out of the way. Once they were beyond the circle of firelight, Gareth grabbed her hand and pulled her after him as he led the way to the other side of the tethered group of horses. Alone and out of sight, he pulled her tightly to him and buried his face in her hair.

Elena grabbed fistfuls of his hair and turned his face until she could kiss him. He returned her passionate kiss with equal fervor and in the heat of the embrace, the tension and heartache of the day dissolved. When the kiss finally ended, they were both shaky with its effects and neither spoke for several moments. Finally, Gareth started to speak, stopped, cleared his throat, and started again. "Elena, I must make you understand why I left you at Nottingham when you helped me escape. I know you must think that I was thinking only of my own goal of reaching Wales and King Henry's army, but I swear to you that I was only concerned with your safety. I had put you in enough danger since the day I met you that--" Elena stopped his words with her fingertips and then replaced them with her mouth.

"I love you," she whispered against his lips.

She grew worried when he inhaled sharply and said nothing. In the pale light of a half moon, she could not judge what emotions were playing across his face and she wondered if he had only claimed he loved her weeks ago because she had helped him escape Nottingham's dungeon.

"Elena, I--I have nothing to offer you but a small keep that will one day be mine but which will always be hard work. I know there are things you want out of a husband, things that are important to you and--"

"Do you?"

"Of course, you have told me often enough what you desire and the security that wealth and power can provide should be yours."

Elena could tell, even in the dim light, that he was thrown off balance by her next question. "Gareth, are you the same person you were two months ago when Richard's entourage was attacked?"

"What? Of course I--"

"No, no," Elena interrupted, "think. Are you really the same or have you changed in any way?"

Gareth stared at her as he thought of her question and Elena had to suppress a giggle. He really was so easy to maneuver and she loved him for it.

"I suppose I have changed in the way I think and act. Certainly in the way I feel about you. I used to hate you, you know."

"I know," Elena said ruefully. "Now don't you think I have changed in many ways as well?"

"I don't know, you still seem to demand--and get--your way continuously."

When Elena merely glared at him in response, he said, "Yes, you have grown considerably since first we met."

Placated, Elena continued with her strategy. "Yes, I have. And part of that growth has been to realize just what is important in life. I've come to learn that love and happiness mean more than wealth or power. <u>You've</u> taught me those things." Elena began to think that Gareth was going to force her into saying exactly what she meant and she didn't know if she could be <u>that</u> humble. Thinking of how much she loved him, she decided she could, but before she could open her mouth, he spoke.

"Does that mean you could settle for a drafty Welsh keep with a great view of the mountains?"

Elena laughed at his non-proposal but decided it was better than no proposal. "Do you come with it?"

"Of course."

"Then I can settle for a mud shack."

Gareth grabbed her into his arms once again and swung her off her feet. She stifled the urge to squeal in delight for fear that the men at the campfire would come running. When he finally put her back on the ground, he kissed her firmly and Elena felt herself growing warmer with their shared passion.

"How is it that in just a few hours I could go from complete despair over Cynan to ecstatic joy?" she asked when their lips finally parted.

"Because Cynan would have preferred us to be joyful," Gareth replied solemnly. "He found joy in everything and it is only right that we celebrate that joy and remember him for it."

Elena nodded in agreement. As she hugged her fiancée tightly, she looked to the night sky and gasped.

"What is it?" Gareth asked.

"I just saw a shooting star. Do you think it is a bad omen?"

"No. I think it was Cynan."

"Gareth?"

"Yes?"

"I love you."

"I love you too."

Chapter 35

An eagle screamed high above the mountains which sheltered Eyri Keep. The last of the snow covering the shallow valley in which the keep sat had melted and pale green grass shoots and crocus buds were peeking out to inspect the soft spring day. Inside the keep, a woman screamed in pain.

"I hate you Gareth ap Morgan," Elena shouted, twisting the bed linens as another strong contraction swept over her.

"That's what you said when little Meg was born, darling."

Elena panted shallowly. "I mean it this time."

"Of course you do my love."

Enid entered the bedroom with a stack of clean linens. "Really, Elena," she teased, "you're scaring poor Bryant. He can hear you all the way down-stairs. He's beginning to feel guilty about what I'll be going through soon." Enid smoothed her wool gown over her swelling abdomen and smiled.

"Well he should feel guilty," Elena said, gritting her teeth and trying to breathe through the pain. "And you would too, you oaf," she said, addressing her grinning husband, "if you had any feelings whatsoever."

Gareth leaned down and kissed her sweaty brow. "I have more feelings than you know."

The door opened again and a three-year-old boy stuck his head in. "Momma," Cynan's son said, "Papa Bryant just threw up."

Enid rolled her eyes and after ordering her son out of the room, said to Gareth. "You can either stay here and take your wife's abuse, or you can go down there and help my husband get some fresh air."

"What a choice!" Gareth said.

"Make sure," Elena said in between breaths. "Make sure Meg is alright, too."

"As you wish, sweet."

Gareth kissed his wife's forehead again stared at her damp face with worry he refused to voice. Leaving the sunlit room, he went in search of his queasy friend. He found Bryant just outside the front door, sitting outside on an overturned barrel, his head in his hands.

"Don't tell me the man who marched into battle without flinching has been brought to his knees by a woman's labor pains."

Bryant lifted a pale face. "Don't you tell me her pains don't affect you!"

Gareth's grin faded. "Of course they do." Sitting on the stone steps into the keep, Gareth sighed. "I guess I forgot how much pain she went through having Meg. Once the baby is born and all is well, the bad parts just seem to fade."

The two men were silent for several seconds before Bryant spoke. "Gareth, do you think it's alright that I married Enid?"

"What?" Gareth asked. "Of course it's alright. Why would you think otherwise?"

"I sometimes feel guilty about it. As if I had loved Enid even when Cynan was alive and that I just took advantage of his death and her helplessness."

Gareth laughed and then quickly smothered it at his friend's worried expression. "I'm sorry, Bryant, but the thought of Enid helpless is amusing."

"You know what I mean," Bryant said with exasperation.

"I know. But what I also know is that you never thought of Enid as anything more than a friend until last year. And I also know that Cynan would have chosen you above all others to be a father to his son."

"Do you really think so?"

"Yes."

As if embarrassed by the intimacy of their conversation, the two men fell silent for several minutes. Finally, Bryant said, "Thank you."

"You are welcome."

A loud crash behind them was followed by a small child's loud wail. Both men quickly stood and entered the hall. "It's mine," Gareth said when he saw his daughter sitting on the floor in a puddle of honey. The metal pitcher which had held the sticky stuff was overturned at her feet. "Oh Meggy," her father said. Crossing to her, he picked her up under the arms and held her away from him as blobs of honey dripped off of her. "Cleaning you up ought to take all day."

Cynan's young son ran into the main hall to see what all the racket was. Pointing to the sticky mess, he said to his step-father, "Meg made a mess!"

"Yes she did," Bryant agreed, his mood visibly lightening.

✦✦✦

That evening, Gareth knocked lightly on the door to his bedchamber and then entered. A bank of candles gave the room a soft golden glow and bathed his wife in their radiance. As he entered, he decided that is was her radiance that lit the room instead. She was propped up on several pillows, her glorious hair spilling over one shoulder as she held their new baby against the other. "Hello my love," he said.

She looked up and smiled. "Come meet your son."

He carefully eased himself onto the bed beside her and curled his arm around her. Pressing a kiss to her sweet-smelling hair, he looked at the tiny sleeping face that was pressed against her breast. "He is beautiful."

"I rather think so," she agreed, smiling at the man who had given her the richest gifts in her life, starting with his love.

Turning his attention back to her, he traced her satiny cheek with his forefinger, relishing its softness. Losing himself in the cinnamon-warmth of her eyes, he said, "Do you still hate me?"

"I never did."
"Do you still love me?"
"I never stopped."

About The Author

Michelle Morrison

Fresh out of college and ever in search of a knight-in-shining armor (besides being a lover of medieval history and all things British), Michelle found a medieval re-creation group. There she got to see how sword and shield battles occurred first hand, and learned just how hard it was to camp and cook with a train and big drapey sleeves.

Writing has always been a part of Michelle's life and it was love of writing that led her to graduate magna cum laude with a degree in Professional Writing which she then used to write and edit technical manuals and reports for Los Alamos National Labs and Sandia National Labs. Needless to say, such writing left her craving something....jucier. Around this time, she read her first historical romance and she was hooked. Her first book (which hopefully you will never read) was soon followed by other, much better manuscripts (which hopefully you will read).

Medieval times changed and so did Michelle's interests. She moved on to Regency historicals and wrote six more romances set in the proper (and improper!) 19th century England.

Michelle lives in Albuquerque, NM. Visit her at www.michelle-morrisonwrites.com

The King's Rebel

Amidst the turmoil of the battle for the Scottish throne, bonny red-haired Meghan Innes and darkly handsome Black William meet at a Mayday celebration. They delight in the blush of new-found love until Meghan learns that Black William is actually William Bruce, cousin to the self-proclaimed king of Scotland, and enemy to her own clan. But when Meghan's father is captured by the English, she must swallow her pride and appeal to King Robert and his cousin William for help in freeing her father.

Forced into each other's company, can they conquer their differences and rekindle their love?

War disrupts their tenuous bond as they find themselves pawns in the deadly battle between Scotland and England.

The Stolen Crown

A Kingdom at Peace...
Harold Godwineson, Earl of East Anglia and member of King Edward the Confessor's advisory council ignores both tradition and his father to marry a common-born woman to join him in his quest to maintain England's fragile peace.

Adith Svanneshal has survived a Viking attack and the death of her promised husband, neither of which prepare her to become the Countess of East Anglia. But she is determined to prove herself, and discovers a knack for gathering information her husband would never hear..

Together, Harold and Adith survive exile, betrayal, and a visit to Duke William's Normandy. When Harold finds the crown of England on his head, they begin their most treacherous journey yet.